arcadia

ALSO BY JAMES TREADWELL

Advent

Anarchy

arcadia

❧ A NOVEL ❧

James Treadwell

EMILY BESTLER BOOKS

—

ATRIA

NEW YORK LONDON TORONTO SYDNEY NEW DELHI

ATRIA PAPERBACK
An Imprint of Simon & Schuster, Inc.
1230 Avenue of the Americas
New York, NY 10020

First Emily Bestler Books/Atria Paperback edition February 2016

EMILY BESTLER BOOKS / ATRIA PAPERBACK and colophons are trademarks of Simon & Schuster, Inc.

For information about special discounts for bulk purchases, please contact Simon & Schuster Special Sales at 1-866-506-1949 or business@simonandschuster.com.

The Simon & Schuster Speakers Bureau can bring authors to your live event. For more information or to book an event, contact the Simon & Schuster Speakers Bureau at 1-866-248-3049 or visit our website at www.simonspeakers.com.

Manufactured in the United States of America

10 9 8 7 6 5 4 3 2 1

Library of Congress Cataloging-in-Publication Data

Treadwell, James.
  Arcadia : a novel / James Treadwell.
    pages ; cm
  I. Title.
  PR6120.R426A88 2015
  823'.92—dc23

                                    2014017839

ISBN 978-1-4516-6170-5
ISBN 978-1-4516-6172-9 (ebook)

If this be magic, let it be an art
Lawful as eating.

WILLIAM SHAKESPEARE, *The Winter's Tale*

I

Utopia

1

From the top of Briar Hill he can see the whole world.

Once upon a time there was a stone plaque up here. Rory remembers it, mostly. There was a map on it which told you what you were looking at, which island in which direction. Why you'd need a map when you can see all the islands just by turning around—Home lying right next to Briar, blackened Martin peeking over its shoulder, Maries and far-off Aggies across the Gap, and then the two bleak mounds of Sansen where no one but the gulls ever lived, even before—he can't now imagine. Anyway, the plaque's gone. Or it's still there but buried forever under the gorse, so it might as well be gone. Everyone's been telling him how fast he's growing but the gorse is growing faster.

He perches on tiptoes at the highest point of the clearing and surveys the world.

As always, he looks for the Mainland first. On very clear days, if you face the north end of neighboring Home and then stare over it and way way across the sea, there's a smudge on the horizon. That smudge is the Mainland. It's the only sign of anything beyond the world: another world. It's not much even on a clear day. It looks like smoke, or something you could blink out of your eye.

He remembers bits of it, but the memories are also turning into smoke. A year and a half's a long time when you're ten. He remembers the helicopter most vividly, the noise it made and the smell of it, and the grass buffeting underneath. Other things come in flashes. Big square signs beside wide roads, glittering when lights hit them.

The red and green people who told you when it was safe to cross. A paper cup full of stripy straws.

You can't see it this afternoon. There are no clouds at all, but an autumn haze blurs the horizon despite the breeze. Everything there is in the world is arranged in a ring around him, islands and rocks. The rest, in every direction, is just the sea.

He remembers watching boats from up here, in The Old Days. In the Gap separating Briar and Home from Maries and Aggies, where the other people live there used to be boats all the time, little boats, medium-sized boats, sometimes boats as big as islands (which doesn't seem possible but he asked Laurel once and she said yes, there really were).

There isn't a single boat out of harbor.

He's never seen so many birds.

The blackberries are never as good around the top of the hill. He'll have to go back down in a bit and start picking. He's only climbed all the way up because it's such a nice afternoon, and (secretly) for the chance to see what he sometimes sees out amid the foam and spray and rocks on the far side of Briar. A glimpse of a whiteness which stays, instead of dissolving into mist.

Just thinking about it makes him feel guilty. He fingers the plastic bags rolled up in his pocket. He can't go home until he's filled one with blackberries and the other with sloes. He'd better get started. If Laurel and Pink see him standing around on top of the hill not doing anything they'll tell on him, or at least Pink will, though the two of them should be busy at the Farm and it's out of sight from here.

On the other hand, the later he gets back to Home, the less likely it is he'll have to do another job before bedtime.

For some reason this idea makes him remember sitting in the classroom at school staring at the clock.

This memory isn't fuzzy at all, even though it's been summer and winter and now another summer finished since he last set eyes on that clock. He spent a lot of time staring at it, in The Old Days. He remembers, exactly, which configurations of its thin and thick hands meant happiness (end of lesson, time to go home) and which meant despair (less than halfway through the lesson, less than halfway through the day). Something's missing from the memory, though. The key to it. What the clock was *for*, what it was *about*. Whatever it is, it's like the plaque with the map. It must still be there somewhere but it might as well not be.

Once his mother took him to watch Scarlet's class do an assembly at their school, the big school on Maries, where Scarlet and Jake went by boat across the Gap every day. The assembly was about somewhere called Germany. Scarlet had learned lines about sausages and said them aloud; then the whole class stood in a line—Scarlet was between her friends, who were Tilly and Adam—and sang a song which went *O Christmas tree O Christmas tree*. Scarlet was so nervous about doing it she cried and shouted at their mother for days beforehand when she was supposed to be learning her lines about the sausages; that's why Rory still remembers. But what he can't remember anymore is what they meant: *Germany, sausages, Christmas, Tilly, Adam*. They're to do with a different world, when there were things other than what you can see from here, on top of Briar Hill. They're gone. Like Scarlet and Jake.

Someone's coming.

He can hear huffing and rustling up the steep track through the brambles. Laurel or Pink, it must be, though they crossed from Home at the same time he did so they shouldn't nearly be finished getting milk. If they find him standing around not working he'll be in trouble. He pulls one of the bags from his pocket and unrolls it hurriedly. There's nothing to pick up here at the top of the hill but he'll have to pretend he thought there was.

But it's not Laurel or Pink. It's Ol.

This, Rory knows straightaway, is not good at all.

Ol stops as soon as he comes into the clearing. "Whatchya doing here?"

Instinctively, Rory glances across the narrow Channel towards Home. If anyone was looking across to Briar they'd see the two of them. "You're not supposed to be here," he says.

" 'You're not supposed to be here,' " Ol mimics, in a whiny voice.

"How'd you get across?"

"Flew."

Rory stops scanning the shore of Home to look at Ol and immediately wishes he hadn't. Ol is grinning a Got You grin.

"Whatchya think, stupid? Rowed, didn't I?"

"In a boat?" Rory says. That's how bad he's starting to feel.

"No, in a tractor. 'In a boat?' What's wrong with you?"

Rory's never liked Ol much. He's supposed to like Ol because they're the boys so they play together a lot, but Ol arranges the games so he wins every time, and he's always talking like he understands all sorts of things Rory doesn't just because he's three years older. This time, though, Rory doesn't care about Ol being rude. He's much more worried about the fact that he's here at all.

"Who said you could take a boat?"

"No one."

"You just took one?"

"Don't be such a girl. Whatchya doing, anyway? Picking? Better get on with it, I bet your mum's gonna want that whole bag full."

Rory reddens. Ol's mother is Molly and everyone in the world knows that Molly is Nice. She doesn't badger Ol all the time. Rory often sees Ol playing by the pond while he's bicycling past on his way to do whatever boring job his own mother's told him to do. It's always Molly who comes by to ask if Rory can play with Ol for a bit instead of working. His own mother never goes to ask if Ol can play.

"If someone sees—"

"Oh, shut up. I don't care. Anyway they're all over on the far side. Some stuff washed up. They'll be busy with it for ages." Ol advances up the clearing, gazing around like he's daring anyone to look at him. Rory's hands are beginning to feel clammy. Ol not being allowed on the water isn't like Laurel not being allowed to touch anything after she's been in the chicken coop until she's rinsed her hands, or Rory not being allowed to use more than a speck of toothpaste. It's proper not being allowed. It's frightening and serious and to do with the things the women talk about in lowered voices in other rooms. It's to do with Them.

The very moment he has that thought he can't help looking over Ol's shoulder towards the spiky rocks beyond the far side of Briar, and, as if it's his fault for thinking of Them, he sees it: a glimpse of whiteness at rest.

"You're not going to tell, are you?" Ol says. "You better not. You're not a sneak."

It's unmistakable. The sea froths and spits where it meets the rocks, but above the turmoil a still white shape has settled.

"If you sneak on me I'll put your head down the toilet. One of the old toilets. I mean it."

"I won't." Rory can feel his cheeks going stiff and heavy and hot, like his face knows he's trying to hide something. "Let's go down," he says.

"I told you, no one's going to see."

"Come on. Laurel and Pink are at the Farm."

"So what."

"Let's go see what they're doing." This is desperation. He hates it when he's with Laurel and Pink and then Ol shows up. Ol always tries to act older in front of Laurel and the two of them whisper and giggle and he ends up stuck with Pink. But Rory's bad feeling is getting worse. It's really important that Ol not be here. Really, really important. Ol has to go back to where he's supposed to be. Everything's always got to be where it's supposed to be, that's one of the Rules they live by since What Happened.

"I know what they're doing." Ol makes squeezing motions with his hands, grinning. "Sticking their hands under goats. No thanks. I like it up here." He stretches and makes a show of admiring the view.

"Don't!" Rory squeaks.

"Don't what?"

"You're not supposed to look."

"I know I'm not supposed to," Ol says, exaggerating the words and fixing his most contemptuous sneer on Rory, which at least stops him staring around. "You know what? I'm fed up with it. It's stupid. You're allowed on Briar, why shouldn't I be? I'm fed up with everyone acting like I'm a prisoner."

Over his shoulder, across the little rocky scoop of bay between Briar and the Western Rocks, the glistening white shape makes itself upright. Rory knows he has to get Ol back down the hill right now, before something very bad happens. But how can he? You can't make someone do something when they're older, that's not how it works.

"I think They're gone anyway," Ol says. "No one's seen one of Them for ages. If they ever did. It's all a story old women made up to stop me doing what I want, that's what I think."

"Let's go," Rory says. "Please."

Ol sighs. "You're such a pussy."

"I won't tell anyone you were here if we go now."

"I bet you're scared you'll get in trouble."

"I'm not."

"Liar. I know, let's play something. We could have a war for this hill." Ol turns around quickly, inspecting the lie of the land.

"No!" Rory's head is a fog of panic.

"Go on. You start at the bottom and I'll be the defenders." Ol's studying the clumps of gorse, eyes down. "We can use pebbles for ammo. Ten hits and you're dead."

By some miracle Rory spots his one chance through the fog. "You go down," he says. "I want to be defenders."

"You're crap at it." Ol crouches and scratches up a handful of pebbles. "You always give up."

"I won't this time."

"Yes you will."

"I swear I won't."

Ol's not really listening. He's thinking about places for ambushes. "And no saying I missed you when I didn't." It'll be all right as long as he concentrates on the earth and the gorse and the crannies he can hide in, as long as he doesn't look out across the bay. "There's more than one way up here, isn't there?" he says, straightening, shading his eyes against the bright water beyond Briar, looking out across the bay.

"Ol," Rory says, but that's all he says. He's not Molly. He's not an adult. He doesn't know how to tell someone to do something so they have to. He's the youngest person in the world apart from Pink, and he can't even order Pink around because she only listens to Laurel. "Ol," he says again. "Let's go."

Ol's stopped looking around. He's standing there, both hands shading his eyes now, squinting into the distance, where the white shape is.

None of this is actually happening. It's not allowed. It can't be.

"What's that?" Ol says. He sounds funny.

"Nothing," Rory says. "Come on." He tries to tug Ol around.

Ol almost loses his balance before he notices what Rory's doing. "Oi!" He smacks Rory's hand away. "Leave off."

"You mustn't look," Rory says. "You can't."

But Ol's looking. He's looking with his eyes and his mouth and his whole chest. He's sort of swallowing. His mouth's hanging open and the top of his sweater's going up and down, up and down.

"Is that . . ." he says. He sounds a bit confused.

"No," Rory says. "It's just waves."

Ol looks down at him, then back towards the scattered jagged islands in the bay. He spots the place where the other path descends the hill, down its far side. He pushes Rory away and sets off in that direction.

"Ol?" Rory trails after him. Any moment now an adult's going to appear out of the bushes and fix all this. Any moment now. "Ol? Where're you going?"

"There's something over there," Ol says. Fingers of gorse scratch at his heels.

"We've got to go home. It's getting late." Everything Rory says just bounces off Ol's back. Something bad is now actually happening, and all he's doing is following it, watching it skid and slip down the path, telling it to stop though it won't listen. The path's suddenly steep. He tries to grab Ol's coat but he can't, or he doesn't try hard enough. "If you don't go back now everyone'll know you're gone. They'll kill you."

They'll kill you. He's said it aloud. He meant something else, but the words came out. Rory loses his footing, drops to the ground in shock.

"Only be a minute," Ol says, vaguely, going on ahead.

Rory looks at his scuffed and dirtied hands. That's when he realizes he's not holding the plastic bag. He must have let go of it at the top of the hill when he tried to grab Ol. He's got to go back and get it. He can't go home without filling it up, both of them. It might have blown away by now or got caught in the gorse and been torn. He remembers his mother saying: *Whatever you do, don't let the bags get torn. Understand?* His mother's not Nice like Molly.

Ol slips around a spray of bramble ahead and goes out of sight, just like that. The bramble's thick with purple fruit. Rory stares at the space where Ol used to be, breathing hard.

"Stop," he says, not very loudly.

He can hear Ol slipping his way down the hill. Now he's on his own again. No one's in sight. He's got two bags to fill before he rows back across the narrow Channel between Briar and Home, and he might even have lost one of them. You can't lose anything useful, that's another Rule. You just can't. In The Old Days you could buy another one but now if you lose something, that's it, it's gone forever.

He stands up. Below him he can see rooftops of houses where people used to live, mostly covered in ivy. Beyond them, hidden behind trees, is the Farm, where Laurel and Pink are busy doing the things they have to do. Everyone's got to do the jobs they're given, or none of them will survive.

Nothing else is to do with him. It's not his fault.

He scampers back to the top of the hill. The plastic bag's impaled on a fist of gorse. A pair of dunnocks are flitting around it; they dive away as he approaches. It's been punctured below the handle but it's still usable.

Rory doesn't want to look over towards the Western Rocks but he does anyway. The slender white shape has moved. For a moment he thinks it's gone, but then he sees a wave with a white crest coming towards the Briar shore, a white crest which never breaks. Something about the shape of the crest makes his palms tingle and his mouth feel dry.

The gulls on Sansen are screeching by the hundreds.

All the best berries are around the foot of the hill, and sloes are on the shoreline near the church. He hasn't even started picking and the light's already thinking about turning yellow. He sets his face away from the west and concentrates only on where he's putting his feet.

2

e's up in the Drying Room washing blackberries one by one in a tiny basin of fresh water when his mother clatters open the door below and puts her head up the staircase.

"Rory?"

"What?"

"Have you seen Ol?"

Rory carefully places another berry on the perforated tray and wipes his fingers on his trousers.

"No?" he says: like that, like a question.

"Do you know where he's got to?"

"No," he says. "Why?"

The Drying Room is a long open space on the first floor of what used to be a restaurant for the Club. It's used for drying now because the wall on the side facing across towards Briar is all double thick glass, catching the sun. In the summer it's almost too hot to work in even if all you're doing is washing fruit. It's well-sealed too, built not long ago with a tight floor and a good roof like all the Club buildings. In The Old Days Rory never set foot in it. The Club wasn't for people who lived on the island. But he cycled past thousands of times and remembers the glass being clean, even in winter when the restaurant was closed. Now it's salt-smeared and spotty. The sun's gone down behind Briar; it's dull in the room. He's pretty sure his mother can't see his face properly.

"We can't find him. No one knows where he is."

"Really?"

"He didn't tell you he was going off somewhere?"

"No."

"Are you sure?" Her voice has that hurry in it, which means she's stressed. She's not like Kate or Fiona or Viola or even Molly or Missus Anderson. His mother Can't Cope. He heard Laurel say that to Pink once when they didn't know he was listening. "He must have said where he was going to play. Think, Rory!"

He waits for a moment so it seems like he's thinking, then says, "I didn't hear him say anything."

"Somewhere inside. Around the hotel, maybe? Could that be it?"

He can tell she's not really listening to him at all, so he just says "Dunno."

From outside someone shouts, "Connie!"

"I'm in here!" she shouts back. The door clatters again and in comes Missus Shark, whose name isn't actually Shark but the kids call her that because it's close to her name, plus she's very ferocious. Rory could have identified her by the sound of her feet even if she hadn't shouted. It's a small world.

"Anything?"

"Rory hasn't seen him."

Missus Shark's head comes up the staircase too. "Since when?"

Rory really has to think this time. "I saw him by the Pond this morning. Playing in the Hide."

"This morning," Missus Shark says.

"Yes."

She turns to his mother and lowers her voice. "The blue dinghy's missing," she says.

"What?"

"The blue dinghy. It's not on the beach. Someone took it."

There's a nasty silence.

"Which boat did you take?" his mother asks him, though she knows which boat he took since she was waiting on the Beach when he rowed back from Briar. She's getting worked up and can't think straight.

"I took *Rat*. Remember?"

"And the girls took the yellow one."

"Yeah."

"Oh God," his mother says, to no one, unless it's actually to God. She clutches the banister. "Oh God."

Missus Shark says, "We mustn't panic. We don't know what happened yet."

"I want you to go back to Parson's," his mother says. *Parson's* is the house they live in now. Neither of them call it *home*. They had their own house once, where they lived in The Old Days, with Dad and Jake and Scarlet. It's a shell now, full of sand and nettles. "Right away."

"What about doing the berries?"

"Forget the sodding berries!"

Missus Shark puts a hand on his mother's shoulder. "Connie."

"Parson's," says his mother. "Now."

Missus Shark looks at Rory with an expression he can't read. "He'll be all right. Let him finish."

There's another Rule. They learned it the previous winter, when things kept going wrong and Missus Stephenson and Missus Hatchard died. The Rule is that whenever you're doing a job to do with food or fuel you have to do it properly until it's finished, no matter how long it takes or what else you think of. It's only a bag of blackberries; when they're dried they'll just be a few handfuls. But there'll be days in the coming winter when those morsels of sweetness will feel like the difference between giving up and going on.

"I want him inside," his mother says. Her voice is sort of scraping.

Missus Shark gives Rory a sad look. "Tell you what," she says. "You stay here with him. There are enough people looking."

His mother tightens her grip on the banister. In the silence they all hear a terrible sound, a distant scream which makes Rory think of the illustration in one of his books showing people with the wrong religion being burned at the stake, teeth bared and eyes popping out. "Oliver!" It's Molly, somewhere up the lane, howling across the island. "Ol!" Rory turns back to the tray, dips another berry in the basin, gently shakes it out.

*   *   *

His mother sends him to Parson's as soon as everyone else is out of sight. As he's climbing the Lane he looks back across the Channel towards Briar, though she told him not to stop. It's getting dusky, and there are torches bobbing around on the far shore. No one uses torches unless it's an absolute emergency. They'll run out one day, like the toothpaste.

He guesses they've probably found the dinghy by now.

It feels strange sitting up in bed, reading by candlelight, alone in the house. His mother said it was all right to light one of the candles, but it's been burning a long time now: he's finished seven comics already. Usually his mother sits at the end of the bed while he goes to sleep. That's what's supposed to happen after dark. She's always calm then. She talks about how they're going to be all right. *We'll manage,* she says, *you and me.* He doesn't know whether he should try going to sleep on his own. Eventually he snuffs out the light because he's used up half a candle all in one go. He lies down like he normally would. He's not even slightly sleepy. He lies in the dark thinking about the fact that there is no more Ol. After a while he finds himself thinking about his father and brother and sister as well, remembering what it was like when they too stopped being there.

He must have dozed off anyway because he doesn't hear Viola come in. The first he knows of it is her murmur at the door.

"Rory?"

She's got a candle in a glass lantern. It casts weird shadows on her face.

Rory sits up. "Where's Mum?"

Viola doesn't come in. She stands in the doorway like she's embarrassed about something. She's wearing warm clothes, coat and gloves and boots. The smudgy light makes her face a sad mask.

"Everyone's at the Abbey," she says. "I said I'd fetch you. Your mum's with Molly."

Viola is Laurel and Pink's mother. Actually she's their auntie but she acts like their mother. She's not Nice like Molly, exactly, but she can definitely Cope, she doesn't get stressed out the way his mother does. Tonight she's full of mysterious gentleness.

"You'll need to get dressed," she says. "It's too dark to bike. We'll walk over."

Rory changes from pajamas into the clothes he was wearing. While he's pulling on an extra sweater Viola says, "I'm sorry, Rory. We found Ol's clothes. His sweater and his shoes. On Briar, on the far side. Right at the edge of the bay."

"Oh," Rory says.

"He won't come back," says Viola. "You know that, don't you. I'm so sorry."

He bends down and does up his shoes. "Am I going to sleep at the Abbey?"

Viola holds her lantern up higher to look at him. "We decided we all ought to be together tonight."

"All right."

The sky's almost completely dark. Clouds have blown in, which at least stops it from getting cold. By Viola's light they walk down the Lane to the Pub and then along beside the Channel. Briar is just visible, a long lump of deeper black. The road twists around the Club and then skirts the Pond. Rory doesn't have to see these things to know exactly where he is, step by step. It's a small world, and Home's a small part of it. You could walk all the way around the island in a morning.

"I don't know what made him do it," Viola says beside him. He's always liked her voice. Laurel's is the same. Though Ol says they sound posh. (Said.) "He knew why it mattered. Was he angry about something? Do you know?"

If there was anyone in the world he could say something to it would be Viola, but he can't. He knew what was going to happen to Ol and he didn't stop it, and now Ol's dead.

"Don't think so."

"You wouldn't do anything like that, Rory, would you? Something you'd been told you mustn't do?"

"'Course not. Definitely."

"It's so important. You do understand that? How important it is?"

"Yeah."

"I thought maybe They'd finished with us," she says.

Rory's glad of the darkness. They're on the Abbey road now, heading away from the shore. He can smell the big trees above and around them. Things are scuffling around in the leaves.

"I wonder why They hate us so much," Viola says, a quiver in her voice. "He was just a boy."

With a strange sort of delayed shock Rory realizes something which should have occurred to him straightaway. There aren't any other boys now. Not even on Maries or Aggies, so everyone says, but even if there were they'd never risk the crossing, so he'd never see them. He's the last boy in the world.

They've lit the fire and a lot of candles as well, more than he's ever seen before. No one's saying it's a terrible waste. In fact, no one's really saying anything. They're all gathered in the big room, everyone except Ali, who's sick, and Doreen, who's too old to sit up in the night. They're all quiet except for Molly, who's crying in little squeaky snuffles. Rory's mother runs over when he and Viola come in and hugs him without a word. Laurel gives him a bleak red-eyed look and then turns away. There's more light in the room than he's ever seen at night before but it still gives out halfway to the high ceiling, so it's like there's a cloud of brown shadow floating over them all, drizzling unhappiness. The women take it in turns to sit by Molly, curling up around her, holding her hands, but no one seems to know what to say to her for long.

He's seen this scene before. Many times. Probably they're all thinking how many times it's been, except Pink, who's managed to go to sleep in the seat under the tall window, wrapped in a (pink) blanket. After What Happened it was like this over and over again, women crying and holding each other, Rory never knowing where to look or what to say.

For some reason his mother did it differently. She does her crying by herself, at Parson's. He's seen her get the album out and look at pictures of Jake and Scarlet, but it's only when she doesn't know he's there. When they're talking at bedtime she almost never cries. She likes to pretend instead that Dad and Jake and Scarlet are somewhere else, all fine, that they made it to the Mainland. Rory goes along with it. He used to believe it was true because his mother said it so often, but when he told Pink she laughed at him, *how stupid are you,* and she's right, of course. Boats used to come and go all the time in The Old Days (and planes, and the helicopter). Now there's nothing. Nothing survives the sea.

Missus Grouse stands up. She's an old lady and her skin's blotchy. She's always cold, even in summer, so tonight she's wearing so many layers it makes her look as wide as she is tall.

"We ought to catch one of Them."

It's the first loud thing anyone's said since Rory arrived. Everyone looks startled.

"We really ought to. Why do we sit here and let Them do this to us? We ought to get one of Them and hang them from the gibbet where They can see."

Kate stands up and goes over to Missus Grouse.

"I mean it," Missus Grouse says, crossly. "They need to be taught a lesson. We've got to fight back."

Kate's a grown-up but quite young. There's a big picture of her on the wall of this very room, a painting. The Abbey used to be her house, if you can even call it a house when it's more like a mansion. In the painting she's wearing a black dress with sparkles and her hair is long and she looks sort of creamy, like a petal. The real Kate has almost no hair at all and wears trousers and sweaters like everyone else. Ol says she looks like a boy. (Said.) She leans close to Missus Grouse and says something too quietly for Rory to hear.

"It is *exactly* the time to talk about it," Missus Grouse protests. "What's going to happen to us if we don't try to stop Them?"

When she says that, half the people in the room turn to look at Rory. Molly's one of them. In the candlelight her face is dead white and veined like the bowl of an old sink.

* * *

His mother wakes him up with a *shh*. It's first light. Grey misery's seeping in through the big window and spreading around a roomful of sleeping women and their various snores. Everyone must have slept in the big room instead of going upstairs, for company. Missus Grouse is in a chair with her head back and her mouth open, grunting so noisily it's surprising everyone else isn't sneaking out too.

They creep out the side door. The dawn feels damp and heavy but it's good to be outside in clean air, though he's cold and stiff from sleeping on a rug. The chickens are fussing in their room. His mother bangs the door to scare them away from it and goes in, reappearing with two eggs.

At the end of the Abbey road they come out from under the drooping wet branches of the big trees and stop, looking across the Channel. There's Briar Hill, dead ahead, a colorless mound. Gulls loop around it, yelling at each other.

"Do you know what happened to Oliver?" his mother says.

"Viola told me."

"But you understand. What actually happened?"

He's not sure what she means but he says, "Yes."

"That he didn't do what he was told."

"Yes."

"And They took him."

"Yes."

"He might have only looked for a second. That's all it took. Just a second. Because he went where he wasn't allowed to go. A second's enough. Do you understand?"

"Yeah. I understand."

His mother draws in a shivery breath. "It must all have happened while you were there."

"I suppose," he answers, after a pause, and then adds, "Laurel and Pink were there too."

She turns to look at him. From the look in her eyes he can tell he's going to have to be careful what he says. "It's got nothing to do with Laurel and Pink."

He doesn't answer. He sort of leans forward, encouraging her to start walking again, but she doesn't budge.

"Rory," she says.

"What."

"You . . ." She's hesitating over something. "You like Laurel, don't you?"

He wasn't expecting this at all. He has no idea what the right answer is. "Yeah?"

"She's your friend."

"She's all right."

"Look at me, please. Do you ever . . . ?"

He knows from experience that it won't be all right to stop looking at her, so he waits.

"Laurel's pretty, isn't she?" his mother resumes. "Don't you think? Nice-looking. Rory, I said look at me."

"Is she?" It's all Rory can think of.

"It's all right, there's nothing to be ashamed of. It's normal. Do you ever . . ." It's as if she's not looking at him but at something right in front of his face which only she can see. "Do you ever think about her?"

"What?"

A quiver of irritation breaks her stare. It's a danger sign. "Think about her. You know, in a special way. Like . . . Like with a funny feeling."

"No," he says.

"I mean a feeling like you really like her. Like you want to be, you know. Special friends with her."

"No," he says again. This is a nightmare.

"It's all right if you do. It's completely normal."

"I don't."

"I'd never tell anyone. That's not why I'm asking. You can always trust me, I'm your mum. You know you can always trust me? Right?"

"'Course."

"So you'd tell me, wouldn't you? If you ever thought it might be nice to, I don't know, give Laurel a hug, something like that. Just a normal thing. Do you ever feel like that?"

"Dunno."

She presses her lips tight. Disappointment.

"I could say," he adds, in a rush. "If I did."

Better. She doesn't quite smile but a cloud passes.

"Good boy," she says. "I know it feels funny talking about it. You've always got to tell me, though. Tell your old mum."

"I will," he says.

Thank God, she starts walking again. His face is hot despite the dawn chill.

"I knew it would happen," she says, in a more normal voice, a bit further along. "Molly was never strict enough with him. He was out of control even before all this started. He always did just as he pleased, that child."

Rory knows it's best to mumble agreement.

"Not like you." She gives him a quick hug. "Thank goodness. Sensible boy you've always been."

He decides this doesn't need answering.

"Happiest in bed with your comics, aren't you."

"Yeah."

"You don't mind that we don't go and stay with everyone else at the Abbey?"

"'Course not. I like Parson's." This he can say without watching his words. Since the winter everyone else has been living in the Abbey, to save fuel by not having people burning fires in different places, except Esme, who says she's used to her solitary ways and couldn't get on with the change. Molly and Ol also stayed in a separate house, of course, in the woods in the middle of the island so Ol would never be anywhere near seeing the open water, but Molly'll be moving to the Abbey now. Rory can't imagine how they can stand it, all the snuffling and shuffling and snoring and the smell of old women everywhere. Pink's always trying to get him to come and stay there. She says he must like comics better than people. She means it as an insult but it never sounds like one to him.

"Just the two of us," she says, squeezing his hand. Pink also said they're being Selfish, and it's not Eekonomical to use their own candles and light their own fire, though Parson's is very well insulated and has a stove which looks like something out of a spaceship so actually it's incredibly Eekonomical. He's also overheard some of the women whisper about his mother being Selfish, but he doesn't care, as long as he can have a room where he knows no one's going to come and bother him after he's finished with all the day's jobs. Pink would never leave him alone if they lived in the Abbey. She thinks all the comics are stupid, though seeing as she's never read one how would she know.

His mother's still holding his hand, so when she stops again he has to as well.

"Whatever happens," she says, "it'll be all right if it's you and me together, won't it?"

"Yeah," he answers, cautiously.

"You won't tell anyone what I said, will you? About Molly. It's not her fault. I shouldn't have said it. Poor Molly."

"I won't."

"It was always going to happen. Eventually."

"Yeah," he says, and then, "What was?"

"Oliver."

"Oh. Yeah."

"Always going to happen," she repeats. She shakes her head, gazing across towards Briar. "Stupid to think anything else. Just a matter of time. No matter how careful she'd been."

He waits.

She sighs and wipes her eyes. "I'm sorry. We all think about poor Molly and forget it's hard for other people too. You must be feeling sad about it too."

"Yeah," he says, wondering whether he is or not. It's odd thinking about Ol not being there anymore, but he doesn't know if that's the same as sad.

"They're so cruel."

"Who d'you mean?"

This was a stupid thing to say. She turns to him, welling with the beginnings of anger.

"Who do you think? Who's taken away so many people we loved?"

"Sorry, Mum."

"Your own father."

"Dad and Jake and Scarlet might have made it," he says. He and his mother say this to each other quite often, at bedtime. They smile at each other when they say it, to feel better.

"Of course they didn't make it."

Rory feels it like a blow.

"No one made it. No one's ever come back. Don't you understand they'd have come back if they could? People only ever leave. They drowned like everyone else."

He stares at his feet, eyes stinging. After a bit she says, "Rory, Rory," and tries to hug him, but he's too busy fighting off tears. Then she starts talking about what a good sailor Scarlet was, and how Jake and Dad would have hid belowdecks while she steered them safely to the Mainland. She's forgotten that this version of the story was his idea in the first place. He got it from a comic story about a Greek hero who tied himself to a mast to listen to the Sirens while everyone else plugged their ears and rowed past. It's too late for the lie now, there's no comfort in it. As they come past the Club and out by the Beach he looks up the narrowest part of the Channel to the big rock off the shore of Briar, where the gibbet is. He imagines a glistening white body dangling there, turning back and forth in the wind, and feels sick at heart.

Back at Parson's his mother gets the stove lit using the electric clicker and makes scrambled eggs with bits of spring onions and some flakes of fish scraped from yesterday's bones. They eat slowly, chewing for a long time. She watches him carefully, as if she's gone back to checking that he chews each mouthful at least ten times, though he learned to do that ages ago. Normally when they're having breakfast they talk about the things that need doing that day and who's going to end up doing what. This morning she doesn't say a word. Normally when they're finished they stand up and she stretches and then he does the cleaning and tidying up while she gets their clothes ready to go over to the Abbey for the Meeting. This morning the plates stay dirty on the table and she's staring into space.

Finally he asks, "Isn't there going to be the Meeting today?"

"I'll go in a bit," she says, vaguely. She's obviously thinking about something else.

"I could go back to Briar," he says. The Meeting's when they decide (or in fact Kate and Fi decide) who's going to have which job that day. If they're going to miss it he'll have to think of something to do on his own. Everyone has to do something. "There's lots of good berries over there still."

She slams her hand over his wrist so hard it makes him jump.

"What are you talking about?" she says. "I thought you understood."

He bites his lip.

"Listen to me," she says, which is stupid, because it's not like he has any choice. "You're not to go to Briar on your own. Ever. Or over the east side. Not anymore."

"But—"

"Never! Never, ever. Understand?" She shakes his wrist. "Understand?"

He mumbles *yes* because he has to. But he knows she's feeling something he can't feel, her own special anger and despair, and he doesn't think he'll ever understand that. Maybe when he's grown up.

3

For the next couple of days it's as if no one's looking at anyone else properly. He remembers what it was like when he was smaller and What Happened had just started happening, and everywhere you looked there was someone missing and someone else crying or shouting or fighting, and he had the dreadful realization that the adults were no less helpless and bewildered than the children. He remembers creeping in and out of their house, passing his mother sitting like a zombie at the kitchen table, wanting to ask her what was happening but knowing if he did she'd go hysterical. There's a little bit of that feeling now.

He's afraid of running into Molly. Everyone talks about her in hushed voices, as though if they say her name too loud she'll break. Even Laurel's on edge. The two of them (Pink's too little) are set to work wheeling barrows back and forth between the north fields and the Club, carrying loads of cut barley and spelt to the big shed. Rory pushes the sliding door aside one time and finds Laurel sitting on the bare floor with her legs and arms crossed, staring furiously at nothing.

"What's wrong?"

The place smells of dust and straw.

"I hate them," she says.

"Who?"

"All of them."

"What's happened?"

"They think we're lying. Me and Pink."

"About what?"

"Missus Anderson said Ol would never have gone to Briar by himself. I heard her. They think we made him go. Everyone just wants it to be my fault."

Rory feels a flush of uncomfortably hot shame. "It's not your fault."

"'Course it's not. I'm not the one killing people. But they can't do anything about Them so they blame me."

"Sorry," Rory says.

"They're just stupid old women."

Rory tips the barrow out, sending up another dirty cloud of dust. He says: "You know what Missus Grouse said?"

"What?"

"About catching one of Them. Hanging them."

"Stupid cow."

"They couldn't really do that, could they?"

Laurel chokes out a contemptuous laugh. "Can you imagine?"

He's spent the last couple of days trying very hard not to.

It's another whole day before he finds a chance to slip off on his own. His mother's gone to the Abbey for a Meeting, adults only. Everyone will be inside for a while. Pink and Laurel aren't allowed at the Meeting, which means they'll go to the place they found at the back of a laundry cupboard upstairs in the Abbey, where there's a hole in the wall that lets them spy on what the adults are doing. He went with them once or twice but it was so boring he couldn't see the point. He's told his mother he's going to stay at Parson's and read comics.

Once he's sure the coast is clear he goes out up the Lane and takes the path at the top past the north fields. It's a gustier day, grimmer, with spots of thin rain, and grey showers moving around in the distance. They always look like they're hardly moving at all but he knows how different it is if they catch you. He keeps a nervous eye on them. There can't be any wet clothes around when his mother gets back.

It feels like summer's over for good. In The Old Days, every day had its own name and number. Like Thursday the Seventeenth, or the Twenty-Fourth of April. Despite being invisible these labels were terribly important, and told you whether it was summer or not, whether it was the week or the weekend. It's impossible to imagine now. It's like trying to tie words to the wind. Missus Anderson claims to know "what day it is" still—she says she's kept count, though no one believes her—but Rory can't see the point: *this* is the day it is, these stately drifting clouds and pellets of rain. They used to know what the weather would be like before it happened, he remembers that too. It used to organize so much of what he did, which clothes he put on, where and when he could go and play, whether Dad was going to get the boat out after school. When he concentrates on The Old Days that's the impression he gets most strongly: patterns, timetables. At School there was a piece of yellow paper pinned to a board. The paper had a grid on it which parceled up each day into rectangular chunks and told you what you were supposed to do in each chunk. Everything was like that. First it was time for this, then that, then time for something else. Particular things happened in particular places, separately. Their house was different from other people's houses and their stuff was different from other people's stuff, even if it was the same stuff. There were invisible divisions everywhere, like the straight black grid lines on the yellow paper. They've all blown away now. The world's just what it is, without labels.

The north end of Home is high ground like the hilltops on Briar, except that it's not a hill but a whole plateau, a wide flat heath. Once he's past the scrubby trees which protect the north fields from the wind he's in a totally different landscape. Even in The Old Days it was empty and bleak up here, just dead-looking ankle-high heather in every direction. It's brown instead of green, peaty soil and bristly stunted plants. Nobody ever comes this way (which is a good thing since he's completely exposed). You can't grow anything to eat here, there's no wood to cut for burning. Ol can't come up here because it's high enough that you can see the open sea. (Couldn't.) All that's here is the ruins of the Castle, but nobody except Rory's interested in them.

The ruins look particularly tragic this afternoon. Everyone calls it a Castle but it couldn't have looked anything like the ones in the comics even before it was ruined. The doorways are tiny. Viola says people were smaller long ago, when it was built. He usually stops to have a little poke around its roofless stone rooms, but not today. The Meeting's guaranteed to take a pretty long time—he knows how much the women love talking—but still, he's absolutely got to be back at Parson's before his mother. He can't dawdle.

The paths up here are like channels cut in the heather. Nothing grows on them except patches of some moss that's nearly black. There are still a few tiny flowers among the scrub. He strips off a small handful and holds them in his fist.

Past the Castle you suddenly become much more aware of the sea. The top of Briar curves away on one side and the Channel becomes open water. Now there's surf below, the relentless swell driving directly against the islands. Eastwards, on the opposite side to Briar, Martin's a long scar across the horizon still as black as the moss even though the fire was more than a year ago. Between Martin and Home lies a wild smattering of shoals and sandbars and grass-tufted outcrops, all shadowed by the rocky fists of the northern islands where the water's always in a fury. As the promontory of Home narrows around him, the sound he thought was the wind turns step by step into the constant grinding of the sea. The air's full of noise and movement, spinning gulls, the flavor of salt. He might as well be on a different island from his mother and Laurel and Pink and everyone else. It's a sea-place here at the north end of Home, a bird- or seal-place, not a place for people.

The tide's about halfway. He clambers down the last slope over stone and tough grass until he's overlooking a small cove of shelving rocks. He's learnt the best way across them by now, hopping from peak to slab while the sea slithers and hisses through gaps below. Once he's out as far as he can safely go he pulls his clenched fist from his pocket, checks the breeze, and tosses the handful of minuscule flowers into the water.

"I'm here," he shouts. He doesn't know whether it makes any difference but he always does it anyway. He's well hidden down in the cove, and even if someone else was walking around the north end, which no one ever is, they'd never hear a thing over the racket of the gulls and the waves.

For that matter he doesn't know whether the flowers (or it might be an interestingly patterned stone, or an apple core, or, if he's daring, a nail or something else useful) help either. People do this kind of thing a lot anyway. Esme plaited a doll out of straw and hung it from a tree when they were planting in the spring; it was gone the next day. Laurel says Libby has special places where she pees on the ground.

He's never tried peeing in the sea. He's pretty sure that would be wrong. He sits and waits.

He doesn't know how long a minute is, or an hour. Invisible grid lines laid over days and nights: all gone. He waits quite a long time, and then She's there.

He can never catch the exact moment when She comes up from the sea. It always happens too quickly, or when he's not looking. She's pushed up like spray, skimming over and through the tumbled rocks, and by the time he realizes it's Her she's still again, balanced at the edge of solid ground while the water twists and surges and slaps behind. She stands as if her feet barely touch the rock, as if she hardly weighs anything. She always makes him feel shamefully heavy and slow.

"Hello again," she says.

Her eyes are the only bit of her that have any color. Her skin's a flat white like cooked fish, faintly veined with lines too grey to count as blue. Her hair's that nameless shade things go when they're slick and wet. If she stays long enough and it dries enough it'll turn another kind of white, like old straw or shells. Her lips and the nipples on her droopy puddle breasts have no more color than her nails. Where her belly meets the bit between her thighs there's a soft-looking dark patch. Once he and Pink played a game where she'd show him hers if he showed her his; she didn't have anything like that there. He feels safest looking back at her eyes, even though there's something scary about their glassy blue pallor, as if they'd be hard to the touch.

"Hi," he says.

"I think you're taller," she says. "Or your face is changing."

No one else sounds like Her. Sometimes when he's by himself in a small echoey room he tries to imitate her voice. He can't even get close. Whispering's too flat and soft, hissing's too blunt. She sounds like a pool of water humming.

"I'm growing," he says. He can never think of anything clever to say when he's with Her.

"Yes," she says. "And one day you'll be a man." She reaches her right arm out towards him. She does this almost every time but he's never dared touch her. He takes a half step back.

"Not for ages," he says.

Her arm drops. She lies down as smoothly as water flowing and spreads flat on her back over the rock. If he tried it all the sharp points and edges would be torture but she makes it look like she's in bed. "That's all right," she says. "I can wait. I can wait days and days and days, it doesn't matter." She blinks slowly and makes a kind of cold smile. "I'm very patient."

"All right," he says. To be honest, he's often not exactly sure what She's talking about. Especially right after she's just appeared he's usually feeling a sort of dizzy thrill, which makes it hard to pay attention.

"It's a relief," she says, "you know. Being patient. In the sea you don't really feel that there's such a thing as time at all. Everything just flows."

"Yeah. I bet."

"You'd like it. It's easier."

He laughs, slightly awkwardly. She does this sometimes, talking like he could be one of Them, though she obviously knows he isn't.

"I'd get cold. I'd need one of them wetsuits."

Her smile widens very slowly. It's not a proper smile: it uncurls, like a starfish's arm.

"You're funny," she says. "Rory."

The dizzy feeling tingles and buzzes inside him.

"What have you been doing?" she says, letting an arm trail lazily over her head, as though she can see the top of the wave arriving to skim her fingertips. "What sorts of things have been happening to you these days?"

"Nothing much," he says. "Same as usual. Except Ol died."

"People are always dying, aren't they?" She says it the same cold calm way she says everything.

"He was my friend," Rory says, a little stung. He thinks of Molly's wrecked and drained face, and Viola saying *I wonder why They hate us so much.*

"That boy."

"Yeah. Ol. He's got a name, actually."

"Tell me about him."

"What d'you mean?"

"Tell me what he was like. What sort of boy he was." She shifts a little, almost sleepily. She's asking him about Ol the same way she'd ask him about what he'd had for breakfast.

"Why do you care?"

"I don't," she says. "I don't care at all. I just like hearing your stories."

Rory stares at her. One of Them, the enemy. If anyone knew that since the end of winter—since he first came here hiding from Pink, who was chasing him around being annoying, and saw Her (or didn't quite see her) rising from the waves—he'd been coming to talk to her pretty much as often as he could, they'd probably kill him. They'd probably hang him from the gibbet like a Traitor. But he can't stop coming.

"That's mean," he says.

"Is it?"

"You're supposed to care about people. 'Specially if they just died."

"I didn't know that."

"Was it you? Who took him?"

"Of course it was us. Silly."

"I mean you. Actually you. I saw . . ." The tingle turns into a flush of shame. "I thought I saw you."

"Maybe," she says. She's not teasing. She doesn't do things like that. She sounds like she can't remember, or can't be bothered to remember.

"Why d'you do it? Why d'you kill him?"

"I've never killed anyone. Only you do that."

"No I don't. I never."

"You," she says again. "People."

"We don't. What about Ol? You just said it was you."

"We took him," she says. She's not arguing. He can hear himself sounding hot and whiny like he does when he's trying to get Ol to stop teasing him or saying stupid things, but she's talking just like she always does. "He came to us because he wanted to, so we took him."

"Yeah, well, that's the same as killing him, then."

"I don't think it is."

"It's not like he can come back, is it? Can you bring him back?"

"No one goes back," she answers at once.

"So he's dead."

"Of his bones," she says, "are coral made." She laughs, actually laughs even though they're talking about Ol drowning. It's the fizz of beached foam popping in the air. "Though not really."

"What's so funny?"

"Nothing."

"Why are you laughing, then?"

"I was thinking of something from long ago and it felt strange." She rolls on to her side and props her head up on her arm. In the comics women are all smooth and long and sort of tight and flowing at the same time. Though she's naked she's not like that at all, she's a bit knobbly, but there's something about looking at her which is even better than looking at the superheroes in their costumes. "Do you ever have that feeling? When you can hardly believe that what you remember really happened to you?"

"You don't even notice about Ol being dead," he says. "Do you."

"The sea's full of wrecks," she says. "Is that my fault? Most of them are much older than me." She holds her free arm out again. "They're beautiful. Do you want me to show you? I'll hold your hand the whole time, I promise."

He shivers. He shouldn't be talking to her.

"I have to go," he says.

*   *   *

Laurel and Pink are on their bikes. They come whirring down the lane behind him just before he reaches Parson's.

"There he is!"

"Rory!"

"*Shh!*"

They skid to a stop. Pink always brakes by putting her feet down, though she's not supposed to because it wears the soles out faster. They're both red-faced and breathless and they talk at the same time.

"Guess what," Pink begins.

"Where have you been? You said you'd be in Parson's."

"Guess what!"

"I thought your mum said not to go out."

"It's something about you!"

"Shut up, Pink."

"We heard them and they were all talking and we couldn't hear everything but they kept saying *him* and *have you asked him* and—"

"Pink, shut up. We've been riding all over looking for you. You better get inside, they'll be finished by now."

"Yeah and—"

"Pink!" Laurel's six years older. She almost counts as a grown-up. When she tells her sister off she sounds exactly like Viola.

"You shut up!"

"They're definitely planning something. Your mum is. We heard them talking about going to Mary's—"

"I said that!"

"No you didn't."

"I was going to till you interrupted!"

"No one can understand anything you say. Pig."

"Don't call me—" Laurel mimes a slap. "*Ow!*" Pink screeches, even though Laurel's hand didn't go anywhere near her face. "That really hurt!"

"Will you be quiet! Rory, next time there's a Meeting you better come. I think your mum's going somewhere. Missus Shark said *what will we do without you*—"

"What?" Rory says. It's the first word he's managed to get in. The girls stop jabbering and stare at him. Pink's face is all shocked and earnest, like she's just been told someone's best secret.

"I don't know exactly," Laurel says. "We missed the beginning. And you can't hear everything from the cupboard, especially when Pink's squiggling around all the time."

"I wasn't!"

"Shut up. They were definitely talking about you, though."

"I said that," Pink mutters.

"You and me'll go next time. Without Pink."

"What? No you won't!"

"*Shh!*" Rory holds up a hand. They all listen. Somewhere over the crest of the lane, towards the Pub, a very squeaky bicycle is laboring uphill.

Laurel and Pink look at each other and then start pedaling away past Parson's and the church without another word. Rory looks at his shoes and trousers. They're flecked with the coppery mud of the heath. He sniffs his hands: they smell salty. It's the kind of stuff his mother will notice if she's in the mood. He tears up a fistful of long grass and wipes his clothes hurriedly.

4

She wakes him up the next morning. It doesn't feel early; he must have had a long sleep. She's wearing the thick dark blue coat and the waxy trousers.

"Are you going fishing?"

She sits on the end of the bed as if it's bedtime and pats his legs through the blankets. "Not today," she says. "I'm going over to Mary's."

"Why?"

"There's something we might need. I'll be back tonight."

"What do we need?" He sits up. There are lots more houses on Maries, hundreds more, so they have a much bigger Stash, though Kate says they don't look after it as well and they argue about it more. He's never actually met the women who live there but he knows there are more of them too. They sound a bit scary. Missus Anderson used to be one of them before she decided to come to Home, and she says they sometimes even fight with each other.

"I'll tell you about it later."

He remembers what Laurel and Pink were trying to tell him yesterday afternoon and suddenly wonders whether his mother wants them to go and live on Maries instead. His stomach twists and his face falls.

"Don't we have everything we need here?"

His mother stands up. "I said we'll talk about it later. I ought to get going. What's wrong?"

"Nothing."

Sometimes it's like she's not looking at him at all, but other times she can tell when he's upset just by looking. "I'll be fine," she says. "It's not as bad over there as all that."

"I know."

She examines him. "You're still sad about Ol, aren't you?"

His face burns. "A bit."

"Of course. We all are. We'll go over to the church on Briar in a day or two and say good-bye properly. Everyone'll feel better after that."

"OK."

"Now." She leans on her knees. "You work hard today, OK? Be extra helpful. They're going to carry on with the harvest, but with me away and Ali still not feeling well all you children will have to help all day. And poor Molly won't be up for much either. The weather might turn soon, we can't waste any time. Promise you'll do that?" He nods. "And Rory."

"Yes?"

"You stay between the fields and the barn, all right? And here. I don't want you going off on your own. All right?"

"'Kay."

"I mean it. I've asked everyone to keep an eye on you so I'll know if you do."

"I won't."

She gives him a leathery kiss, the collar of the blue coat scratching his neck. "Good boy. OK then. There's a bit of bread downstairs and the stove's still warm, you can heat it up. Viola'll come to fetch you when they're ready to start in the fields. You can stay here till then. Read your blessed comics."

But when she goes he squirms back under the covers and closes his eyes. Before he woke up properly he was lying in the dark imagining that She was holding his hand and they were swimming together deep in a warm green sea, diving for sunken treasure.

The storm comes fast.

Kate's the first to stop. She's far ahead of everyone else, as usual, near the top of the field. She rests her scythe on the ground and leans over it, the only sign that she might be getting a bit tired. She looks up at the sky. A moment later everyone else feels it too: the sudden gather of the wind.

"Here it comes," Missus Shark says.

"All right!" Kate shouts from the top of the field. "Let's get all this in!"

As everyone starts hurrying up the unevenly reaped rows the sky over Briar goes the green of Rory's dream. The trees begin to hiss. A few leaves shake loose. Rory's been pushing barrows again, all morning long; now Laurel joins him and they start running with them. By the time they're back from the next trip to the barn it's as dark as twilight and the wind's blowing so hard they have to tie tarpaulins over the barrows. "Properly," Kate says, kneeling beside him to pull the twine straight. "Take your time. Do it properly." Everyone's shouting instructions at each other. A tarpaulin cracks and whips in Rory's hands as if it's come to life, and then the air seems to turn black. The rain starts, not a few warning drops but a lashing curtain of water like the sea emptying itself. Missus Grouse shrieks. Libby's face is a grim mask. Suddenly Rory can hear exactly what everyone's thinking: *winter*. Darkness, sickness, hunger, dread.

Kate keeps her head, sends Fi to close up the barn and the greenhouses, and steers them to shelter. Soon they're all in the Pub, wet layers dripping over the big racks in the kitchen. There's a thick reek of damp exhaustion mingling with the Pub's moldy carpet smell. Missus Shark goes off to make sure Ali and Molly are OK but otherwise there's nothing much anyone can do but wait. The storm throws itself at the windows like hailstones. There's a brief discussion about lighting a fire but everyone knows it's not cold enough, not yet, not when wood's so precious and the leaves are only just starting to turn. Rory and Pink get the red and yellow balls out and play their version of pool. The pool table's the only furniture left in the Pub. It's mostly made out of plastic and slate and it's too heavy to move, so no one ever tried chopping it up to burn.

"Connie wouldn't have started back until later anyway," he hears Missus Grouse say. She's louder than everyone else even when she's trying to be quiet. He looks up and discovers that everyone's turned his way, except for Kate who's looking daggers at Missus Grouse. Viola gets up from the floor and comes over to the table.

"Did your mum tell you where she was going today?" she asks him.

"Yes. Maries."

"She'll have seen this coming. She won't try and get back till it blows over. She'll be fine."

He lines up a shot, balancing his fingers on top of the red ball. "I know."

Viola rubs his back. "Goodness me. Listen to that wind."

Still leaning over the table, squinting towards the yellow ball, he says, "What's she doing over there?"

Pink makes her wide-eyed face at him and tries to mouth something. It looks a bit like she's choking. Rory rolls the balls. His shot misses.

"I don't know, exactly," Viola says, although not until after a distinct pause, during which her touch disappears from his back. "Just talking to some of them, I expect."

"God," Missus Grouse declares, across the room. "I wish there was still some booze."

"Oh," Missus Anderson says. "Don't."

"A bottle of whiskey. And a bag of pork scratchings. Are we sure we've completely emptied this place?"

"Please don't, Vera. I can't stand it."

"And some bloody men." Even Missus Shark titters. "Good Lord. Things must be getting desperate if I'm missing them."

Viola turns round.

"I don't mind it," she says, "but don't ever say anything like that in front of Molly, all right?"

There's a tricky silence, made sharper by the click of the balls and the drumming rain.

"Oh, do let's not all be so serious," Missus Grouse says. "Anyway, I don't want to forget what it used to be like." Her tone of voice suggests that everyone else does.

"I doubt any of us are likely to," Viola says. "I think about John every single day."

Rory hates it when the adults start doing this. He looks out of the small window. Its panes are weeping raindrops. It's only a short run up the hill to Parson's but he'd get soaked through.

"Well, then, why don't we talk about him, for goodness's sake? No one ever *says* anything."

Libby stands up. "Is there an umbrella in here somewhere?"

Lots of people start talking at once. Usually what happens next is it ends up with little groups of two or three women in different corners, whispering about the people in the other groups, and then Kate has to make a speech about how important it is that We All Stick Together and Everyone Gets On. Kate's the only one everyone else will always listen to. They all know that without Kate none of them would be able to stay on Home, they'd have to troop over to Maries and take their chances there like the survivors on Martin had to. When things were at their absolute worst last winter Kate was the only one who knew what to do. Laurel and Ol make fun of everyone else but when Ol tries to make fun of Kate Laurel tells him to shut up.

(Tried.)

The thing is, Rory hates being in the room for one of Kate's speeches. He always feels like he's being told off. He hates the way everyone looks at each other sneakily and shamefully afterwards. Some of them will cry and say they're sorry. Someone'll break down and start wailing about how terrible it is, and someone else will go and hug them and say it's all right even though it isn't, even though in The Old Days they were warm and dry and had chocolate and TV and everyone's phones worked and there was no Them. He tells Pink he's giving up.

"That means I win."

"Yeah. Good game."

"Where're you going?"

None of the adults are listening. "Anywhere else."

"It's pouring!"

"So what." He heads off to the kitchen to collect his coat.

"Rory?" Kate's the only one to spot what he's doing.

"Yeah?"

She comes into the kitchen, out of the babble. "I don't think you should go out in this." The coat's still dripping wet but he shrugs it on, not looking at her. "Wait a couple of minutes, it never rains this hard for too long."

"I'll be fine."

"Rory."

When he tries to leave the kitchen it turns out she's squatting in front of him, her close-cropped head at his level. She's got very searching eyes.

"You're upset," she says.

"No I'm not."

"I know what you mean. I hate listening to the squabbling too. It's so stupid, when literally all we have is each other. Tell you what, why don't you and me and Pink go for an explore in the upstairs rooms?"

"I'm going back to Parson's to read," he says. "Mum told me to stay there."

"Rory, your mother's—"

"I'm going," he says, and walks around her quickly, because however much Kate talks she's not the kind of person who forces you. Other people call after him when he heads to the door but no one can stop him. It's not like The Old Days. There's no School or home or family, any more than there's Germany or sausages or booze or men. He can do what he wants.

There's something no one's saying to him. It's obvious.

His shoes are so wet he can hear them squelching. His trousers are sticking to his legs. It doesn't matter. Both shoes and trousers are nearly too small for him and he wouldn't be able to pass them on to Pink anyway, she's the wrong shape. The trousers will be cut up for rags or bandages and they'll use the shoelaces to hold bags shut or sew tarpaulins together. They're finished with being clothes because there's no one after him and there never will be. There's no one new in the world. No one comes back.

He said he was going to read, which means when someone comes looking for him to make sure he's OK and tell him everything's going to be all right they'll go to Parson's. So at the crest of the lane he turns off towards the fields instead. He needs a poo and there's a house over there where the toilet still works as long as you fill the top. Muddy water's pouring out of the hedges. He has to keep his chin almost on his chest or he can't see at all, the rain's battering his face too hard. He's soaked through. They're going to be furious with him, they're going to kill him.

They're going to kill him.

No one's saying it to him because they don't need to. He's the only boy left. All the men are dead. That's how things are after What Happened. All the men have had their turn, and all the boys, all the way down to Ol, and next it's going to be him.

He doesn't understand it. Of all the things he doesn't understand, it's the biggest, the most mysterious and important. He knows it's Them who kill the men, but how can it be, when he talks to Her and nothing bad happens? He knows They're a terrible curse on the sea—Missus Stephenson used to say They were God's curse, sent to make everyone suffer for the world's wickedness—but he talks to Her and she's not a curse, she's just someone to talk to. You could almost say she was Nice. The adults talk about Them like they're sharks or devils but she's not. She listens to his stories and talks about feeling happy or sad. She's a person, a girl, he can tell by looking at her. She hasn't got a fish's tail or vampire teeth. If she was going to kill him why hadn't she done it ages ago?

But a few days ago Ol was there, and now he's gone.

He takes an overflowing bucket from outside the open doorway of the house, finds a place to hang his coat inside, and sits down to poo. He doesn't want anyone to find him. He thinks how easily he could hide from everybody. He knows where everything is on Home, all the empty rooms in all the empty houses. He knows all the places where food's kept. He could hide from everyone forever, sneaking around the island, keeping out of everyone's way. He wouldn't have to listen to the women crying and hugging and making speeches anymore, or do boring tiring jobs even though he's only ten. He wouldn't have to stop his mother cracking up.

He cleans himself up with leaves and freezing water. Despite what Kate said it's as wild as ever outside. His feet are encased in their own little skins of wet sock and swampy rain. He thinks of Parson's, the stove, his bed, his stacks of comics.

He's got nowhere else to go. It's a tiny world. A prison.

He slams the bucket back in place with a bang and stares moodily down the track.

There's someone there.

Only for an instant, the blink of an eye. He pushes wet hair away from his eyes, rubs them, and the person's gone.

"Hello?"

He thought he saw a face looking over the hedge at him. He was sure he did. But he can't have, because who'd be in the field now? And he knows everyone in the world, and everyone in the world knows him, so who'd disappear like that, so quickly it's like they weren't there at all?

"Kate?" Why's he thinking of Kate? He thought he saw the shape of a head, just a face. No hair. But it wasn't Kate. He knows exactly what Kate looks like. He knows exactly what everyone looks like. It can't have been anyone. A bird, perhaps, or just a trick of the eye. The driving rain makes everything fuzzy. He rubs his eyes clear again. There's definitely nothing there, just the ivy flapping at the top of the hedge.

He hurries back to Parson's at a clumsy run.

By the time the storm blows itself out it's almost dark. He's at the Abbey with everyone else, dried out and warm enough. Viola came to fetch him since his mother won't be back until tomorrow now. He can smell food cooking slowly downstairs. Kate's gone to see where any blowdown is—she and Fi'll be out with axe and saw as soon as it's light—but otherwise the whole surviving population of Home is there, apart from his mother. She won't risk the Gap in the dark. She'll stay with the Maries people overnight, eating whatever they give her to eat, sleeping wherever they let her sleep.

The mood isn't good. Viola's already yelled at him for *going off like that.* Laurel's cross because she had to ride all over Home in the rain looking for him. They can hear Ali coughing in the warm room above the landing. Molly sits red-eyed and upright in the corner and won't eat anything. People take it in turns to go over and murmur to her, each one looking like they're marching to the gallows as they cross the big room.

It's only a matter of time before someone mentions The Future. Like the weird green light before a storm, there's a particular atmosphere which comes over the big room in the Abbey when a conversation about The Future is about to break. It's the atmosphere of people thinking. When there's not enough chatter, when Missus Grouse isn't forcing someone to play Scrabble and Fi isn't talking about new places they could try growing things and Pink isn't shouting for everyone to watch her doing handstands, Rory can see all the faces go quiet and sort of out of focus, and he knows the thinking is starting. They're thinking about what it's really like being them, here, what it really means to be completely alone in the world, digging and scraping and fetching and carrying and struggling all the hours of every day just so they can keep themselves fed. The atmosphere's heavy in the room this evening.

Esme's the one who starts it. This is a surprise. Esme's the quietest of all of them. She's a dreamy old lady with a dotty smile. Ol says—said—she believes in fairies, which was meant to be a mean comment (you could always tell by the sneer) though Rory never actually understood why.

"The thing is," she says, "it won't be so bad this winter." She's got a nice throaty voice. "We're much better prepared this time."

Molly looks up suddenly. "What about next winter?" she says. "And the winter after that?"

Everyone's so startled to hear her speak aloud that the whole room goes completely still, even Pink.

"Do we just go on?" Molly's voice is crackly with the despair they all spend so much time trying not to feel. "Look at us. Getting older every winter. Until."

There it is. The Future. Molly makes her hands into fists and pushes them into her lap like she's trying to squeeze out her own juice. She crouches over again, flinching away when Doreen tries to comfort her, and stops talking, but it's too late now, the cloud in the room has broken.

"It can't go on forever," Viola says. "It's just not possible. Think of all the people in the world." She doesn't sound like she believes herself. "Someone will find a way to get things going again."

They all become intensely aware of Kate's absence. When they're floundering around like this it's Kate who steps in and cheers them up, mainly (it occurs to Rory) by stopping the thinking. Missus Shark makes an effort, standing up briskly and saying something about getting on with the whelks, but it's not the same.

"No one's out there but Them," Molly says, in the direction of her lap, as if Missus Shark hadn't even spoken.

"Molly dear," Missus Grouse says, with a hint of reproach.

"When They've finished with the men perhaps They'll work on starving us."

Doreen casts a panicked look at Rory. "Molly!"

Rory can't stand it. He hates being in the room when the women get together. It's like they have the same conversation over and over and over again. Someone gives up, someone else tries to jolly them into keeping going, then next time they swap over and the comforter becomes the comforted. He puts down the chess piece he's been fiddling with and gets up from the window seat.

"I'm just going back to Parson's to get some comics," he said. When Viola came to get him he was so put off by being yelled at that he forgot to bring any.

"Now?" Viola says, astonished. "I don't think—"

"I'll be right back."

"It's nearly dark!"

"I know the way."

"I'll come with you, then."

"I want to go by myself."

"Rory, your mother wouldn't—"

"Viola," Esme says. The room's gone quiet again so everyone can hear her.

Viola folds her arms. "I don't think it's a good idea."

"He'll be fine," Esme says, smiling her dotty but oddly magnetic smile. "Off you go, Rory. Don't dawdle, though."

There's one of those wordless grown-up arguments going on. Rory doesn't know exactly what it's about but he takes advantage of Viola's hesitation. "I won't," he says, and hurries away before the mood changes. He grabs a sweater and some gloves in the back hallway and goes out the side door into wet leaves and darkness.

The storm-rinsed air's such a relief. He feels his way across to the shed where the bikes are. It's not full dark yet but the trees that protect the Abbey and its precious gardens from the salt winds are thick overhead here. He has to fumble around to find a bike that's not too big and has a dynamo.

Electric light.

In The Old Days he remembers rooms full of it. It doesn't seem real when he thinks about it. It's like remembering how there used to be people everywhere, spilling out of buildings. The crowded island and the places full of color, without shadows: they feel like they're somewhere else, vivid unlikely fantasies from the panels of a comic. He pedals fast to escape the Abbey in case Viola's sent Laurel to follow him after all, and the faster he pedals the louder the dynamo on the front wheel whirs, and the wobbly yellow gleam in front of him fills and stretches and goes whiter and whiter. There are two buildings on Home with working solar panels, the Abbey and the old Laundry, but the power has to be saved for things like the fans they use for winnowing or the rechargeable clickers that make sparks to light fires, no one wants to waste it for lamplight, at least not until the middle of the winter. So Rory only sees the glare of electricity when he's cycling at night as fast as he can. It's hypnotic. It's like he's got lightning powers and he's blasting through the darkness, making the edges of the road look brilliantly sharp and strange. The twigs blown down by the wind snap satisfyingly under his wheels. Everything smells of soaked earth. He races down the Abbey road and out under the not-quite-invisible sky. The shallow water in the Channel's muttering, fidgeting, still agitated though the storm's passed. He weaves through the Club, smelling the rampant honeysuckle as he brushes around tight corners. He can go as fast as he likes: there's no one else around and he knows every turn like the back of his hand. At the Pub he swings up the Lane. The light fades to dirty yellow as the slope slows him down, pulsing visibly as he turns the pedals over. He's breathing hard.

A huge ghost-pale shape appears with no warning at all at the edge of the light and springs in front of him. Rory gasps. He grips the brakes. Everything goes completely dark. The same instant he's knocked off the bike. He hears it clatter on the road but he doesn't fall on top of it because something's got hold of him. Something's breathing harder than he is. His flailing arms thud against it, right in front of his chest. He goes rigid and cold with shock. There's a little moment of stillness, enough for him to register his pounding terror. Then he's pulled up and he can feel that something's right on top of him, in his face.

"Where do I go?" snaps a voice. It's strange in a hundred different horrifying ways. Almost the strangest of all is that it's the voice of a man. "Where is quiet? Nobody sees?" The grip is hands on his sweater. It shakes him urgently. "Hmm? Where? Tell me this!"

At last Rory grasps that he's being attacked. He lifts his hands to try and pries the grip away. "Get—!"

No sooner has he opened his mouth than it's covered, fiercely. "*Sssss!*" A hand's squeezing his jaw. "*Silenzio!* You shout, I kill you." The hand pushes his head back painfully. "Kill you! You know?"

Rory's eyes are wide as a cat's, but it's too dark to see what's happening. Someone's got hold of him tightly and his neck's beginning to hurt so he can't breathe, that's all he knows. A man. A stranger. There are no strangers and all the men are dead.

"I need place to go." Another strange thing is the man's accent. It's foreign. It's from somewhere else, somewhere not in the world. "You show me. Quiet place. Hot. No person. You know this place? You show me quick."

The hand's very strong and very angry. He's going to choke soon. "I can't breathe!" he tries to say, but it's muffled by the hand. "Get off me!"

The hand relents. He gasps.

"You know, *ragazzo*?" He gets shaken again, not so hard. The looming presence recedes a bit. "House. *Deserta*. I need this place. You show me."

The voice is speaking very fast and very hungrily. It's the urgency that gets through to him.

A house. The man wants to know where there's an empty house. "There's—" He licks his lips. His mouth's like sawdust. "There's lots of empty houses."

"*Va bene*." The man straightens. Rory can sort of see his outline now. He hardly looks tall enough to be a man at all. He can't be one anyway because there aren't any. Fear's making Rory's brain shake as well as his hands and he can't think properly at all. "Now. Show me."

Where is he? He's lost his bearings. "They're all empty. Everyone stays at the Abbey."

"No persons?"

"Anywhere. You can go anywhere." He needs to say what the voice wants him to say or the hands'll hurt him again. It sounds dangerously furious.

"You show me." The grip relaxes further. It's about to let him go. His legs take some of his weight. They're wobbling like leaves. The shadow leans in and he has the impression of a face. He thinks it's bald. "Listen, *ragazzo*. You shout, you run, I kill you." Without sound or warning there's a hand at his neck again, throttling. It happens so fast he can't even gasp. "Like so. You know?"

Absolutely terrified, Rory nods.

"*Va bene*. Good." The hand lets go. He crumples to his knees, gulping. "House here, this ones. No one comes? All *deserti*?"

Something clicks. The man wants a place to hide in. He'd have to if he's a stranger. Rory points ahead, his arm trembling. "That way," he says. "Down the hill. Past the church. After the church no one ever goes there."

"*Chiesa, si*. I know this. No one comes? You know this?"

"Me and Mum use the white house at the corner. The others are all ruined."

"*Ecco*, no one? Is all quiet?"

"Yeah. After the church."

"You lie, I kill you." The man seizes his shoulders.

"I'm not—"

"I see you. I see in the night, like this. Where you go, I find you, I kill you."

Rory's completely certain this is true. "I swear," he says.

"Now. You listen. *Domani*, you bring clothings, food. Next day, *si*? Yes? You say nothing. To no one." The man shakes him hard to emphasize each word. "You. Say. Nothing. You say one thing, I kill you. You bring clothings and food, near here, put here. You know?"

His heart's twisting and untwisting itself in his chest. "You want . . ."

"*Vestiti*. Clothings. Food. You bring, alone. Put near here. Say you do this." An arm curls round his neck and the voice is in his ear. "Say it!"

"'Kay," he croaks.

"Say it! What you do!"

"I . . . I get you some food and clothes. Bring them here."

"*Si si si*. Next day. Morning."

"Tomorrow."

"*Domani, si*. Listen. Attention. You say nothing. You don't say you see a person. You don't say you bring food. All quiet."

"I won't."

"If you lie—"

"I won't! I won't tell anyone!"

There's a pause. The man breathes in his ear, rapidly. He has no smell except an air of violence, the smell of threat. Though everything's dark but the deep indigo sky, Rory has the impression the man's naked like an animal.

"You come with yourself. If I see one other person—"

"I won't."

"You see bird kill *ratto*? Small animal."

"Rat," Rory says.

"Rat. Bird kill a rat. I am like this." Nails dig into the skin of his neck. He whimpers. "*Subito*, you are dead. So. You don't lie."

He's so frightened he's tearing up. He can't speak.

"You know?"

Shoulders hunched, he gives a tiny nod.

The man lets him go. "Next day," he says, withdrawing a little. "Or you are dead." There's a very soft noise, like a bird in a hedge. The shadow passes him, swift and certain, and disappears ahead. The sea shuffles and grumbles in the distance and his breath scrapes in his painful throat. Otherwise it's quiet. There's no one there. He takes a small step backwards. Nothing happens. He's alone.

He finds the bike in the road. It takes him a while to work up the courage to mount it. He wheels shakily down the hill and follows the telltale yellow gleam back to the Abbey.

5

T here he is!"
"I thought you were getting comics!"
"What's wrong?"

He's been trying to think of what to say. All he can come up with
is this:

"Nothing."

"Rory?"

Something soupy and vegetably is cooking. Faint light's trickling
into the back hallway from the big room. Laurel, Pink, and Viola are
carrying buckets of warmed water up from the kitchen.

"Did you fall off your bike?" Laurel asks, with a kind of disappointed sigh.

Yes, that's what happened. His hands and trousers are badly
scuffed. "Yeah."

"Oh, Rory." Viola puts her two buckets down and hurries to
inspect him. "You twit. Are you all right?"

"Didn't you get comics?" says Pink.

"I'm fine."

"What happened to your neck?" Viola's hands gently turn him
towards the best of the weak light.

"I . . ." He puts his hands up. "I fell on something."

"You haven't cut yourself, have you? Come in here." She shep-
herds him towards the big room.

"Pretty stupid to go riding around in the dark."

"Laurel, don't." Laurel's been cross with him all day. Or is it that he's been cross with her? It seems incredibly unimportant all of a sudden. He needs to get away from them all so he can work out what's happening to him.

"I'm fine. Just need to lie down for a bit."

"Take those to Ali, you two," Viola says over her shoulder, ignoring Pink's squeal of complaint. "Come on." She's steering Rory along. "I should never have let you go."

"Just an accident," he says.

"You looked shell-shocked. Was it a bad one? Did you hit your head?"

"Is the bike all right?" Laurel says nastily.

The bike's in the shed where they keep the bikes. Why shouldn't it be? His head's whirling stupidly. He doesn't know what he ought to say and what he can't say. There's a man on Home, a stranger. He ought to tell them. He ought to warn everybody. It's the most astonishing thing that's ever happened, so astonishing that he doesn't really believe it himself. But he can't say anything or the man will kill him.

"It's nothing."

There's a small room farther back in the Abbey with a light that's plugged in, one of those bendy arm ones. Viola frowns everyone else away, takes him in there, and switches it on for a few precious seconds. In the hesitant electric glow he can see how spattered and scratched he is. Viola peers around his collar.

"You've got horrible bruises. What did you do, ride into a branch?"

"Yeah," he says. "I did. A branch."

"Looks like no cuts, thank God." She smiles a little. "Still your mother's going to kill me."

He winces.

Everyone else is asleep. Even the coughing's stopped. The upstairs floors of the Abbey are perfectly dark and full of wheezings and mumblings and snores. Viola's put him in the room with Laurel and Pink, making a bed with cushions from the sofas downstairs. He had to pretend to be asleep when the girls came in so they wouldn't want to chat. Laurel knew he was pretending but he kept his eyes shut anyway and ignored her nasty comments.

That was a long time ago. He's no nearer sleep.

Eventually he slides himself out from under the blankets until he's lying on the carpet, then gets to his hands and knees in the dark. Laurel snuffles and rolls over. It turns out she's inches from his face. He can smell her breath.

He's been thinking about how he can get food and clothes.

Pink sleeps with a hand-wound lantern on her bedside table. It's because she's still afraid of the dark, though no one's allowed to say so. He feels his way to the table and pokes around gently until he's got hold of the lantern.

The handle grinds when you turn it and he can't risk waking anyone up. He'll have to find his way to the door in the dark. He's never slept in this room before (still hasn't, come to think of it). If he bumps into Laurel's bed and she sees what he's doing, what's he going to say?

While he was lying in the dark, waiting as long as he could possibly make himself wait so he could be sure all the women were asleep, he thought a lot about telling Laurel. She wouldn't go telling everyone else and she might know what he's supposed to do.

But he can't. It's not even because he's afraid of the stranger finding out and killing him, though he is. It's more that he can't imagine what he'd say. *There's a stranger on the island. A man.* She'd just laugh at him and say he's been reading too many comics. Perhaps he has been reading too many comics.

He slides his toes across the floor, painfully slowly. He's been planning this while he waited in the dark: sneaking down to the brick-lined larders in the basement, filling a bag with whatever food he can find, hiding it away behind the sacks in the cupboard under the stairs, and then whisking it away in the morning when everyone's busy. It's his only possible chance. It all made sense in his imagination but now that he's actually doing it, it feels like a dream. A bad dream.

He finds the door. The girls' clothes are hanging from the hook. The knob's just below.

The door creaks as soon as he pulls it. Laurel's soft snuffling stops.

He tries not to breathe. He waits as long as he can, then pulls it a bit farther open. It creaks again.

He hears Laurel sit up.

"Pink?"

Out of nowhere he remembers what it was like being made to stand up in class at School.

"Who's that?"

He can't move unless he says something, and he can't just stand there waiting for her to go back to sleep. "It's me," he whispers.

"What are you doing?"

"I need a pee."

She snorts crossly and flumps back down onto the mattress. "Could you try not waking everyone up when you come back?"

"Sorry," he says, and slips out, banging the lantern on the doorframe.

"For God's sake!"

"Sorry!"

He clicks the door shut behind him. He's so full of guilt and terror they're like the gas inside a balloon: he's stretched out, about to pop. He wipes his hands on his pajamas and gives the lantern a few noisy cranks, conjuring a thin and brutally white light. He has to go through with it now. He patters downstairs, feeling invisible eyes following him. The Abbey's twice as big in the dead of night, and older too, and somehow alive. He turns the handle as he goes, dreading the thought of darkness catching up with him. Its noise sounds like a ghost groaning.

The fire's out in the big room. They won't light it again until the next evening, it's not properly cold yet. The cellars are freezing, though, and heavy and shadowy as a tomb. That's why they use them to store food. He hurries to the larders. There's a squashy sack full of plastic bags on the floor. He takes one out and starts filling it, too desperate to get this over with to think about what he's picking up. Apples. Carrots. Beans. Floppy skeins of samphire.

"Rory?"

He drops the bag. The food spills out and rolls around his feet.

Kate's in the doorway, wearing a raggedy dressing gown and fluffy slippers and carrying a tiny night-light in the shape of a cube. Its orangey glow falls mostly on her hands.

He stands stock-still while the apples slowly come to rest. He doesn't have a single word to say.

The slippers must be padded, because Kate makes almost no noise as she comes in, squats down, and starts picking things up. He ought to help instead of watching her scrape around on the floor, but he can't move. Some carefully built tower is about to blow down. Some structure he lives by is on the point of collapse.

"You know," Kate says, "if you think you need extra you only have to ask."

She props her arms on her knees and looks at him. He feels as tiny and worthless as a mote of dust.

"No one owns any of this," she says. "It's not like the old days." She puts the last couple of things in the bag and straightens up, swinging it thoughtfully from one finger. "Everything's for everyone. If someone's hungry, it's fine, you can have a bit more, as long as there's enough for the rest and you really do need it." She holds the bag out to him. "There you go."

She's waiting, so he takes it. Kate's like that. It's hard not to do what she wants. She has that particular sort of kindness that makes you feel utterly helpless.

"The thing is, though." She puts her hands on her hips. Pink's lantern hasn't been spun for a while so it's faded almost to nothing. The little night-light shows the torn pocket of Kate's dressing gown; he can hardly see her face at all. "We all have to know who needs what. Otherwise anyone could say, I need this, I need that, and it might not be fair. That's why you always have to ask. See?"

"Yeah," he whispers. He actually tries to say the word properly but he can't.

"Otherwise . . ." She pauses, thinking about it. "Otherwise it's like saying your needs are more important than everyone else's. Like saying, I'm hungry and I don't care whether everyone else is hungry too, me being hungry is the only thing that matters. Which is the thing we can't do anymore. Isn't it?"

"I know," he says. Being told off by Kate in her Nice way is actually worse than being told off by his mother in her tearful babbling Can't Cope way. His mother's telling-off doesn't go inside him like Kate's does, it stops on the surface.

She pats his shoulder. "That's all right. You'll know next time. And you're silly to go creeping around in the night. It's important to stay warm. Look at your feet."

He'd been looking at them anyway. He's wondering now what he's going to do with all this food, and whether Kate's going to tell everyone what he's done.

"Rory?"

He looks up towards her voice.

"Is something bothering you?"

For a piercing moment he feels how good it would be to tell her everything. Kate says she's not their leader but she is, or at least she and Fi are together, everyone knows that. She'd know whether Rory had imagined everything. She'd know what it meant that he thought he met an angry foreign man in the middle of the night.

But he can't do it.

"You haven't been quite yourself these last few days."

"Sorry," he says.

She makes a sympathetic hum. "It's not your fault. We've all been feeling terrible since what happened to poor Ol."

To Rory this sounds like another reproach.

"Do you sometimes worry about that?" she says, in a different tone: cautious.

"A bit," he says, when the silence has dragged on too long.

"We'd look after you," she says. "You know that, don't you? We'd make absolutely sure you'd be all right."

"OK," he says.

Unexpectedly, she steps forward and hugs him. Her gown is fuzzy and tickly and doesn't have the sour smell most of the clothes have picked up. "You'll be fine," she says. "I know you will. Now get yourself back in bed. We'll leave all this here, all right?" She eases the bag out of his hands and puts it down. "And what do you do next time?"

"Ask," he says.

"That's right. It's not like anyone would ever say no." She hugs him harder. He can feel her muscles. Kate's very strong. "We all love you and Connie," she says with bewildering earnestness. "We always will." He feels her strength and her kindness melting him. He should have told her straightaway. He opens his mouth to say *When I was riding over to Parson's—*

"Off you go now," she says, picking up the lantern and giving it a few revs. "Get warm."

And just like that the moment's gone. She's sent him away. He runs back upstairs, burning with confused shame and unexpiated doubts. Whatever he thought he was doing, he's made a total mess of it.

"World's longest pee," Laurel grumbles, as he eases himself back onto the cushions. He lies there completely stiff and silent, refusing to give any sign that he's there at all.

6

or a few breaths as he struggles awake he's forgotten everything. It's just another day. He rolls over, sees Pink by the door putting her trousers on, wonders what she's doing in his room, then wonders where he is. Then it comes back, all of it, a weight dropping on him, knocking his breath out and replacing it with panic.

He's going to have to do it today. He has to figure it out, by himself. Or he'll be killed like a rat.

"Wakey wakey," Pink says, seeing his eyes open. "Breakfast time."

They all eat together. It's more Eekonomical, which is the word for why it's better to light one fire instead of two and bring water to one place instead of lots of different ones and let one person clean and tidy up for everyone. While they're chewing the tough spelt bread Libby makes (everyone else's bread is worse) they talk about who's got to do what. Rory's seized with the wild idea that since his mother's not there no one will tell him to do anything and he'll be free to fetch the bag of food, find some clothes, and take them all over to the crest of the Lane without anyone noticing.

"What about Rory?" Laurel says.

He's not sure he's ever hated anyone as much as he hates Laurel right then.

"Gathering," Missus Shark says. "That storm will have stirred things up. Brought down a lot of cones too." She looks around the room. There are murmurs of agreement. "In the Borough Farm woods. Connie wouldn't mind that." Everyone looks at Kate, who nods.

"Look for mushrooms too," Fi says. "The woods are full of them."

"Eurgh," Pink says. "He'll get the wrong ones and poison everyone."

"You know which ones, Rory, don't you?"

"'Course."

"Get them all," Missus Shark says. "No need for separate bags. I'll sort them out for you."

It's not too bad, actually. He'll be by himself, which is the main thing, and in the woods, which means he'll be hidden and no one else should be working anywhere nearby. He can sneak off and no one will know.

"Pink should go with him," Laurel says. "She's a good forager."

If he could kill Laurel by looking at her, she'd be dead.

"Good idea," Kate says, and because Kate says it that's that. He barely hears another word. Pink's jabbering about something, he doesn't know what. He's sick with dread. He can almost feel the stranger's hands on his throat. What's he going to do, what's he going to do? His mother's coming back soon too and then he'll never have a moment to himself. Since Ol died she's been weird about keeping an eye on him all the time, and she'll have a hundred other jobs for him to do, mopping, weeding, going up the ladder to do the gutters, or just the endless exhausting labor of lugging water around. Missus Shark loads him up with bags and instructions, and Viola adds more—"Stay in the woods around Borough Farm, all right? Rory? Nowhere else"—and wherever he goes Pink won't stand more than two feet away from him. He's in such a state that he's dressed and out the door before he remembers the bag in the cellar.

He stops dead, staring at Pink.

"I forgot something."

Pink's already cross with him for not listening. "What?"

"Something. Wait here."

Pink follows him inside, pink wellies scuttling. "Where are you going?"

"I said wait here!"

"I won't!" she shouts back. He pushes her but she just pushes back. She's got a much older sister, she's used to asserting herself and refusing to be left out.

"I'm only getting something from inside."

"What is it?"

"None of your business."

"Is it a secret?"

"'Course it isn't a secret, stupid."

Pink dances along behind him, skipping away each time he rounds on her and tries to shove her back. "You've got a secret! You're acting funny. I'm coming too."

"No you aren't."

"Show me. I promise I won't tell."

Rory may only be ten but he knows enough about people to be quite sure that anything Pink promises not to repeat will be common knowledge before sunset. Short of hurting her, though, he doesn't see what he can do. "It's only some food."

She looks disappointed. "Why can't I come with you, then?"

It's always hopeless trying to argue with Pink. She's a Brat, Laurel always says so. Without another word he stamps downstairs and collects the bag from the larder cellar.

"What's in there?"

"I told you, food."

"Who's it for?"

"Shut up. Idiot."

She really is disappointed, though, and she's lost interest in needling him. There's nothing exciting about some vegetables in a bag. She goes quiet while they set off along the Burra Road, which is now so overgrown on the sides there are places you could hardly ride a bicycle along it. A skin of sand and mud has grown over the hard surface. Rory goes ahead, letting the twigs and brambles spring back behind him so Pink has to duck them ("*Ow!* Watch it!"). He's trying to think, but all he can think of is that before he does anything else he's got to get rid of her because she's so incredibly annoying he'll never be able to think properly about what to do until she's gone. The road bends around the Pond and comes to a muddy junction by a small house with nettles growing through smashed windows. A stony track leads up towards the ruins of Burra Farm. To one side are the trees. It's more or less the middle of the island. The sea's not far away—it's never far away—but standing here you'd never guess. They climb over a bent gate onto earth caked with dry pine needles.

"OK," Rory tries. "You go that way. I'll go round this way."

"I want to go together."

"Well I don't."

"Auntie Vee told me to go with you."

"You did go with me, didn't you. Now we split up. It's faster, we'll collect more."

"I don't want to."

It's no good. She refuses. She won't admit it but she doesn't like being by herself in the mess and shadow of the undergrowth, with things rustling around. She's a baby. She follows him, chattering. He can feel panic and despair beginning to pinch him. The morning's passing. He's running out of time. He thinks about knocking Pink out or tying her up or just running away from her until he gets clear, but he can feel the senseless desperation in all those ideas, they're not proper Plans. He could make a proper Plan if only he could think. But all the time she's chatting, chatting, no matter that he doesn't say a word in reply except telling her to shut up. She won't shut up.

"When we're older we'll have to get married."

"Shut up."

"We will. Laurel's too old." They're combing through the litter around the trees, looking for puffballs and chanterelles. "We're the only boy and girl. We could be king and queen."

"I'm never going to marry you."

"We'll have babies."

This is too much. "Shut up!"

"Yes we will! Or there won't be anyone, all the old people will die."

"You don't know anything about it."

"Yes I do. You need a boy and a girl to have babies."

"You're a baby yourself."

"It's about kissing."

He tells himself not to say anything. If he doesn't say anything at all she might give up eventually.

"I'll get the nicest dress from the Stash and we'll get married. It's like a big party. Everyone can eat whatever they want for a day. Then after the party you go upstairs and kiss and have babies. I know, Ol told me. You're just embarrassed 'cos you don't know anything about it."

He kicks a handful of pine straw out of the way.

"You could kiss me now."

Despite his resolution he can't bear it. "Shut! Up!"

"No one's looking."

He's going to have to knock her out. He'll say she tripped and hit her head. Maybe he'll kill her. He's angry enough to kill her.

"I saw Laurel do it with Ol. I know how you do it. Do you want me to show you? Don't tell Laurel I saw her. You won't tell, all right? Rory?"

"I will if you don't stop talking right now."

"If you do I'll say you're lying. Anyway I didn't really. I just said I did but I never. So don't tell her I did."

Or he could pretend to faint and wait till she ran away to get help. Pretend to knock himself out.

"But I do know how to do it. Look."

"Go away!"

"No one's looking. I want you to."

"I don't want to kiss you."

"Go on."

"I'd rather kiss a goat."

"Eurgh!"

"I'd rather kiss Doreen. I'd rather kiss Missus Grouse."

"You're disgusting!"

"I'd rather kiss one of Them."

That, finally, shuts her up. Maybe he said it a bit too fiercely. Maybe he actually meant it. Whatever, her mouth hangs open and she stares at him with an exaggerated shocked face.

"That's sick," she says. (It's what Ol used to say.)

He turns away, smarting with a kind of bitter triumph. "Yeah. Well. It's true."

"I'm telling your mum you said that."

"I don't care."

"I bet They taste all slimy. Eurgh."

"You've never seen Them," he mutters, furious at her stupidity.

"Yeah, well, neither have you."

"I might have." There's something irresistible about shocking her. If he does it enough times maybe she'll finally be quiet, or even run away.

"You never!"

"You don't know."

"You can't. Boys aren't allowed."

"Who says?"

"Have you?" She says it quietly, sort of breathlessly. "Have you really?"

"I'd never tell you, would I?"

"Please."

"Shut up."

"Please, Rory. I won't tell. Have you really?"

She's horrified, but she's also thrilled. He's made a mistake. He should have known what she's like whenever she suspects anyone's got a secret. He goes back to ignoring her completely. He should have stuck to that all along. She begs and cajoles and threatens and then starts whining, but he still refuses to answer, so she gets cross.

"You're such a liar. Liar liar. I know you're lying anyway. I know you never 'cos you can't, you'd be dead if you did. I know, They've got a special hole They suck boys into the sea with, soon as you look at them. You just think you're being clever."

He's so angry it's like a film in front of his eyes. Pink's a whining baby and he hates the way her voice sounds like it's coming out of her nose. When She talks it's water humming. Even the words She uses are different from Pink's, like it's not even the same language. She never whines.

"Anyway I won't marry you, I'm going to be queen all by myself, and when I'm queen I'm going to order all the boats out with big nets and catch all of Them and kill Them. And you can't be king because you have to stay inside like Ol was supposed to. I won't even let you go look at Them when they're all dead. You big stupid liar liar."

Rory's mouth goes without him meaning it to. "At least They're not stupid. And They make you look like a pig, so shut! Up! Now!"

"They're evil!"

He hates the way these ridiculous arguments make everything go cloudy. He forces himself to turn away and just breathe. That's when he notices that she's stopped yelling.

"You did see Them," she says. "Didn't you."

"None of your business," he says.

She puts her bags down—there's almost nothing in them anyway—and squelches over to stand right in front of him. "I swear, Rory. I swear I won't tell anyone. On my mother's life. On the Bible."

He moves away, raking with his fingers. It's slow work. Everything's slow work.

"When did you see Them? You really did. I know you did."

"Haven't you got work to do?"

"Please, Rory."

He gives her a superior look and says nothing.

"I'm telling Mum. If you don't tell me, I'm telling everyone."

How has he let this happen? Today's turning out like quicksand. Every step he takes sinks him deeper.

"Right now," she says, stamping a few theatrical steps away. "I'm going! Here I go."

She doesn't mean it, of course. But the mere sight of her moving away gives him a sudden brainwave.

"All right," he says, straightening up.

She squints suspiciously.

"I'll show you," he says.

He has the satisfaction of seeing her lumpy face wash over with awestruck wonder.

"But," he says. The brainwave's already beginning to fizzle a bit. He keeps talking, surfing it as long as he can. "You have to stay here. You can't come with me. Or it won't work."

"What won't work?"

"Seeing Them. I have to go on my own. If She's— If They're there"—he's horrified that he's spoken Her name in front of Pink—"I'll come back and tell you."

She's paralyzed with an incredulous thrill. "Really?"

"Yeah. But you can't come. You have to wait."

"I don't want to."

"Do you want to see Them or not?"

"All right."

"OK, then." He can't believe this is actually going to work, but when he takes a step back she stays rooted to the spot. "So, stay here."

"How long?" she says. Her voice is whispery and tight.

"I'll be back in a bit." He was about to forget the plastic bag, the bag of food. He grabs it quickly.

"Wait," she says.

"What?"

"I don't want to."

"Too late," he says.

She grabs his arm. "I don't. I'm scared."

This gives him the chance to use the only line that ever works on her. "Don't be such a baby."

"I'm not a baby!"

"Then why are you scared?"

"Is it safe?" she says.

"'Course it is. You just keep gathering stuff. I'll come back and tell you if it's OK. They might not be there."

"Wait!"

"Chickening out?"

"No!" she says.

"Right, then," Rory says triumphantly, and scampers away through the trees. She squeaks at him to stop but she's wavering, he can tell by the sound of her, so he keeps going. The bag bangs on his knees. She's not following. Another few steps and it'll be too late for her to change her mind. He puts in a burst of speed. He's done it!

Almost done it. He remembers about the clothes.

But it's easier to think now there's no idiotic chatter in his ears. He's on his own, he can work it out. He's going to have to get to the Stash, which is in one of the houses that belonged to the Club, across on the other side of the island. That's where they've gathered everything they found in all the different abandoned houses, all the clothes and towels and blankets and curtains and paper rolls. There are tons of clothes in there, that's not a problem. The problem is that there's almost always someone around that part of Home, working in the Drying Room or on the Beach or the old Laundry, and if anyone sees him it'll be a disaster. He's about to head that way anyway—he'll just have to be careful and hope for the best—when his brainwave surges again, prompted by a glimpse of a dirty white house at the edge of the trees.

The solution's so obvious and simple and perfect it almost bowls him over.

The dirty white house is The Larches. It's the one Molly and Ol used, because of all the houses that didn't get wrecked it's farthest from any view of the water. And since it's Ol's house, all his clothes must still be there.

It's not like he needs them anymore, is it?

Rory's brain is going at triple speed now. He's thinking how much quicker it'll be to nip into The Larches and then around the back way to the Lane instead of having to go over to the Club where anyone might see him, and at the same time he's remembering that the angry foreign man who attacked him seemed small so Ol's clothes will probably be the right size for him, and while all these thoughts are falling satisfyingly into place he's still managing to keep up a jog in case Pink loses her nerve and comes after him. He reaches the house, has a quick look around, and tramps through the weeds and long grass to the front door, feeling almost defiantly brilliant.

It's only been a few days since he was last here, playing with Ol. He expects it to look different now Ol's gone but it doesn't. Lots of the things they played with are still scattered around. Rory's bubble of glee pops. He tiptoes through the downstairs rooms as if he's afraid that Ol's going to appear at any moment, naked and ghastly and dripping. *You could have stopped me.* The stairs creak accusingly as he goes up. On the windowsill at the top there's a photo of Ol and Molly and Ol's dad, all grinning. He's passed the photo hundreds of times but this is the first time he's noticed that they all look dead, as if the faces have been painted onto their skulls. He averts his eyes and hurries to the room Ol used.

There's Ol's bed, and the old chest of drawers and the two built-in cupboards with slatted doors. The Manchester United mug and the *Top Gear* annuals are still on the table by the bed. Nothing's changed at all. The air in the room is very still. It's like one of those Egyptian tombs where the kings were buried with all their possessions.

And he's come to rob it. He starts with the chest of drawers. Pants and socks. For the first time he wonders what clothes the stranger wants. He tries to think about it but his brainwave's passed, crashed, and expired against rocks. He just wants to get out of here quickly. He pulls out another of the bags Missus Shark gave him and begins packing as if he was getting dressed himself, but with two of everything instead of one. Shirts and sweaters and trousers. He's about to go when he thinks of shoes, and a coat. He opens one of the cupboards.

There's a noise downstairs. The front door scrapes and Molly's voice calls, "Is someone there?"

Rory freezes, going blank.

"Hello?"

He stands as if he's forgotten how to move. He hears Molly come in the house.

Hide, he thinks, and slides into the cupboard, and pulls the slatted door closed after him, as lightly as he can.

"Who's there?" The stairs creak.

Rory realizes he's not breathing. He takes a few frantic gulps. He's squashed between hanging coats. He hears Molly on the landing.

She comes into Ol's room. He can actually see her, through the slats. He's looking right at her. She peers around with raw-looking eyes. Her shoulders are sagging and her hands look horribly thin. She comes into the room and sits down on Ol's bed. She puts one of her thin hands out and spreads her fingers across the pillow. She bows her head. She starts quivering, silently.

The handles of the plastic bags are starting to dig into Rory's fingers. His fingertips feel numb. He can't move them at all or they'll rustle. All he can do is watch.

He's never been able to understand how adults can sit for so long without doing anything. Sometimes Molly sniffles a bit and moves her fingers or tightens them into a fist, but mostly she just sits there for he can't guess how long while his legs seize up and his fingers start to burn and he realizes he needs to pee. He's not far from giving himself away out of sheer hopelessness when there's another sound outside and the door scrapes again downstairs. Molly jerks upright and wipes her eyes.

"Molly? Are you there?"

It's his mother, though he doesn't actually care who it is; all that matters is that Molly's scrambling to her feet and going out of the room, which means he can finally put the bags down and shift his feet. He carefully shunts a few shoes out of the way and folds himself silently down to sit on the cupboard floor.

The bad news is that his mother's coming upstairs. She and Molly start talking, just outside the room. The talking, Rory knows from experience, can go on for a very long time. He wonders whether he can pee without making a noise, right here in the cupboard.

"How did you get on?" he hears Molly ask. She's always polite like that. He can hear the strain in her voice, pretending she cares.

"Pretty well."

"They let you have something?"

"A twenty-footer. It's a bit banged up but it's not too bad. No fuel, though, they wouldn't go that far."

"Never mind. We'll sort that out for you."

"Yes," his mother says. "We will."

There's a pause.

"Molly," his mother says. Molly starts sobbing.

"Let's sit down for a bit," his mother says. *No*, Rory thinks, *no, let's not, please let's not do that*, but into Ol's room they come, Molly crying and shaking and looking like a limp wet rag—she used to be plump, but no one's plump anymore—bundled in his mother's sturdier embrace like a child. They sit down on the end of the bed.

He can see them both perfectly clearly through the slats, so clearly it's almost unbelievable that they can't see him.

"I'm sorry," Molly whimpers. "I should pull myself together, I know."

"Don't be silly."

"I just hoped . . . I thought . . ."

"You cry as much as you want to," his mother says, as if this was reassuring. But instead Molly sort of braces herself, sitting up, swallowing, taking deep breaths.

"We should have left," she says. "Shouldn't we."

"Hush," his mother says. "Don't say that."

"I don't know what I was thinking. I should have been braver."

"You did what you thought was best."

"A teenager. How could he have ever grown up here?" She turns to touch the pillow again. "I should have known. I should have known."

More sobbing and shaking.

"You and Ol had a good life here," his mother says, not very convincingly. "Who's to say it wasn't the right thing to do? None of us know what's going on out there. Do we? You mustn't torture yourself with what's past." She wraps Molly in an awkward cuddle. "You know, maybe Ol had more happy days here than most people have managed since . . ."

Rory's noticed before how none of the adults like saying anything about What Happened.

"I tried to make it easy for him," Molly says, between whimpers.

"You did. You really did. You were wonderful." Rory knows his mother doesn't really think this but it's another thing he's noticed about the adults, they spend a lot of time not saying what they really think.

Molly looks at the ceiling and heaves a long sigh. "Oh, listen to me. As if I'm the only one. I'm sorry."

"Just 'cause we've all been there doesn't make it any better," his mother says. "You remember that."

"I just wish . . ." Molly looks hesitantly at his mother. "I wish I'd had your courage."

"I don't know. Perhaps you did the right thing."

"But you've made up your mind?"

His mother nods.

"It's going to be terrible for us," Molly says, in a very small voice.

"I'm not sitting around waiting for Them to take Rory as well. I'm just not. Oh, Mol." Molly's bent over and scrunched up her eyes again. "I'm not saying that's what you did. Oliver was a teenager; it's different. You never had the choice. Rory's just a little boy."

"I know."

"You mustn't blame yourself."

"No. I'll try not to. It's just . . . Maybe you'll feel differently by the spring."

His mother lets go of Molly and sits straighter. Her face has gone hard as rock.

"I'm not waiting till spring."

"What?" Molly's changed in an instant, shocked out of her misery.

"I'm not waiting. We can't."

"But . . . Six months can't make any difference?"

"It might. I read that boys are getting to puberty earlier. Anyway, there's lots of calm days still at this time of year."

"But won't it take time to get ready?"

Rory's not really listening to them. He's too busy trying to get them to go away using just the force of his mind, not to mention the horrible squeezing distraction of his urge to pee, but for a moment he thinks: *Ready for what?* What's his mother talking about?

"Ready for what?" his mother says bitterly. "Whatever we find, it can't be much worse than this. I'll take my chances."

Molly turns away, abashed. "It could be. Mary's was worse."

"Maybe."

"It was. Last summer was worse here. At least we're at peace now. We're safe."

"Safe until They show up and flash their boobs at our children." Molly goes completely limp. His mother as good as has to catch her. "Oh no. Oh, I'm sorry. Mol, don't listen to me, I don't know what I'm saying anymore. I lie awake all night only ever thinking about me and Rory. Mol, please, I'm sorry." She rubs Molly's back clumsily. The look on her face is resigned irritation. "Come on now. It's doing you no good sitting here. Let's get you some food. You've got to eat, you're wasting away." She pulls Molly upright. "You've got to think about yourself now. For him. Oliver wouldn't have wanted you to . . ." The sentence peters out. Ol wasn't very nice to his mother, everyone knows that. Rory's not interested in what his mother's saying, though, beyond the fact that she's trying to get Molly to leave, which at the moment is the one thing he cares about in the whole world.

A squeaky shout comes from outside: "Rory?"

The feeling in the room changes instantly. Both women sit up and look out the door.

"Rory!"

"That's Pink," his mother says.

"She and Rory went foraging in the Borough woods."

For a moment neither of them move, and Rory can hear what they're thinking just as if it was written in cloudy bubbles above their heads like in the comics: *Rory must have gone off on his own.* The moment ends and they both scramble downstairs. Rory's beyond guessing how deep a hole he's in or how he's going to get out of it, but at least he can stand up now and stretch his legs.

"Pink!" his mother shouts.

"Connie?" Pink's amazingly loud. She must be at the edge of the woods but she sounds like she's right under the bedroom window. "Where are you?"

"In the house!"

Pink's in a total panic. Rory picks up the bags and then stops. He still can't go anywhere. The women are just by the front door. He's going to have to pee very soon, he can't help it.

"What's wrong?" he hears his mother shout. "Where's Rory?"

"He went off!" Pink shouts back. Molly says something, but her voice is naturally quiet and he can't hear. Pink comes scrambling up to the house.

"Where's he gone?" They must be just inside the front door. Rory can tell by the sounds that they're not outside. Pink's panting. His mother's voice is crisp with rising panic. "You were supposed to stay together."

"I tried but he wouldn't!"

"Where did he go?"

"He said to wait but I was on my own and I got worried—"

"Said what? What did he say?"

Oh no, Rory thinks. *Oh no. Please don't, Pink.*

"—and I did wait but it was ages so—"

"Pink!" It's like a slap. "Where is he? Where's Rory?"

"I dunno! It's not my fault!"

"What isn't? What's wrong?"

"He said he was going to Them!"

Oh no.

"Who?"

"He said, he was boasting and I said he never could but he swore he'd show me, he was going to find Them—" The women are trying to talk but there's no stopping the frantic babble now. "And he said wait here and he'd come back and he went off to talk to Them, that's what he said, I swear he did, I swear!"

There's another small moment of silence. Then they're all off running down the road, shouting together like the gulls. Rory stands at the window where Ol used to stand, wondering whether it would be better for him now to be underwater where it's quiet, being led along by a white hand. Then he grabs up the bags. He only just remembers to stuff a pair of shoes in before he bolts down and out of The Larches at the fastest sprint he can manage.

He runs along the road on the east side of Home, the ruined side, looking across to even more ruined Martin. The road here's full of rubbish as well as being overgrown. No one usually comes down this way, but he's not worrying about what'll happen if someone sees him. That's the least of his problems now.

He's going to have to say that Pink made it up. They'll believe him. Some of them will, at least. Pink likes saying things to get people into trouble, everyone knows that. Pink will know, though.

She'll always know that he lied. Just like Ol will always know that Rory could have stopped him drowning but didn't.

He's feeling a bit teary. For no reason that he can pin down, his life has spun out of control. Running faster helps a bit. If only he could run away for good.

At the smashed-up houses by the Old Harbor and the Hotel he turns inland, swinging past the School towards the church and Parson's. He hasn't been here for a while. The weeds have grown so tall none of the fields he remembers look like fields anymore, they're jungles of knotted green. There was a playground behind the school. It's vanished completely under bramble and bindweed.

"Boy!"

He'd only turned his head to look at where the playground used to be for a moment. Before that moment it was just him and the Lane and the weeds everywhere. Now, out of nowhere, there's a man. Rory skids to a halt.

The man's bald and very short, with a weird thin nose between fierce-looking and outsized eyes. He's wrapped in a big tartan blanket which looks exactly like the one they keep in the barn to help slide heavy things across the floor. His feet are bare, and a length of bare shin shows below the blanket. His toes are slightly curled. Rory notices all these things at once because this is the first new person he's seen for a year and a half: the first new person in the world. It's as utterly astounding as an alien invasion.

"This is food?"

It's the stranger, the shape in the dark. He's got that foreign voice. He skips forward. He moves bewilderingly suddenly and deftly, more like dancing than running. He looks left and right, swiveling his head like a bird. His scalp is pockmarked under a shadow of brown stubble. His face is scratched and rough. He's compact, hard, tense, entirely unlike every other person in the world. The air around him's almost vibrating with danger.

He snatches the bags like they're prey and pokes around in them.

"Is good," he says, and looks at Rory. His eyes are a bit too big for his face, and his head is in turn a bit too big for his body. His gaze is inexplicably overwhelming. Rory backs away as the man rifles through the bags. "Good," he says again. He picks out an apple, sniffs it, takes a quick bite. His teeth are stained barley-brown.

"You want?" he says, holding the apple out, and grins.

Hot, still panting, feeling the sweat around his neck, Rory's trying to make all of this come together. This stranger—a man—here on the road just down from Parson's; his mother, Pink, Molly; the trouble he's in; his life on this island, this world he inhabits. It's not working. It won't fall into place.

The man's grin disappears.

"This you say to no one."

This is audibly a threat, but Rory doesn't mind that, because there's no possible way he could put into words what's happening, not even to himself. He swallows and nods.

"Or," the man says, and hops forward and puts two fingers across Rory's neck, a knife. Neatly, he draws them from one side to the other. "You know?"

What he means is, *Do you understand?* Adults are always saying that to him. He never does actually understand, least of all now, but the right answer is always—

"Yes."

"Good. *Domani.* Day after this one. You bring more food. You bring," he points down behind Rory, towards the wreck of the Hotel, "there."

"Tomorrow," Rory says.

"*Ecco.* Tomorrow. *Domani.*" His whole face changes when he grins, like he's just got a joke. He bobs down and collects the bags. Even the way he does that isn't like anyone else in the world. The women pick things up slowly, laboriously. This man's fingers peck the plastic bags off the road like he's plucking an insect out of the air. "*Va bene,*" he says. "Go." He points the other way, up the lane towards Parson's.

"How did you get here?" Rory blurts out.

He can't believe he said anything. His face goes red. The man stares at him. Then he laughs. It's hardly actual laughing, more like a single squawk—*ah!* He pounces and grabs Rory's shoulder, but before Rory has time to be frightened the man turns him around and points up at the sky. A gull's circling, one of the big black-backed ones.

"Like this one," the man says, and squawks his laugh again. He spins Rory back to face the church and gives him a hard shove in that direction. "Go!" Rory stumbles forward. As he's collecting himself he's suddenly unsure what exactly he's supposed to be doing tomorrow. He turns back, saying, "But—"

The man's nowhere to be seen.

7

They find him not long afterwards. Or he finds them. He's gone up past Parson's, over the crest of the Lane, and he's walking down towards the Pub when he hears Libby shouting, "Rory? Rory!" so—as if nothing's happened at all—he trots around the corner to where she's standing on the wall overlooking the Beach and says, "Hi." She almost falls off the wall.

"There you are! Thank God."

"Why?" he says. You'd think it would be easy acting like nothing had happened, because it's just nothing after all, just being normal, but he's finding it almost impossible.

"Where have you been?"

"Nowhere," he says. That doesn't sound good. "Having a poo."

"Is that all?"

"Yeah."

Libby looks exasperated, but not with him. "Your mother's got the whole bloody island out looking for you."

"Oh," he says. "That's funny."

Word gets around quickly. Soon there's a little cluster of people standing around him there in front of the Pub. They're joking rather nervously with each other and with him. Eventually his mother comes running and all the chatting dies away. The cluster dissipates so she can tell him off in private. Libby and Fi give him sympathetic looks as they slink away.

He's been readying himself for the telling-off for a while, and anyway it's not like it's the first time. He stands with his eyes half

down (except when she says "Look at me," which is often), and lets
it roll over him. He mouths monosyllables when he has to. It's only
difficult when she makes him tell her what he said to Pink. "Nothing," he tries, and "Don't remember," but she's not having that, so
in the end he thinks of how Pink was bugging him and driving him
crazy and he starts shouting back at her about that as if it's all Pink's
fault, which, if you think about it, it really is, sort of.

"I don't care!" his mother shouts. She's getting breathless and
shaky now. "You never, ever make a horrible joke like that! It's a
horrible thing to say."

"She tried to make me kiss her."

"I said I don't care about what Pink did! Stop trying to blame
her for everything!"

"She wasn't letting me pick anything!"

"Rory!" She shouts right in his face. "Oliver's been gone less than
a week. Don't you understand you can't tell lies like that? How do
you think Molly would feel about it?"

Viola appears, which means they have to stop shouting and pretend to be a bit calmer. She's escorting Pink, whose face is blotchy
and puffy and downtrodden. Viola takes one look at his mother and
comes over to hold her by the arm.

"It's all right, Connie," she says. "No harm done."

Out of her aunt's sight Pink gives Rory a furious glare. Rory
returns it.

"You two," Viola says, "had better stop squabbling. I mean it.
We can't afford it."

Hate you, Pink mouths. Rory can't mouth it back because they're
all looking at him.

"Say sorry, Rory," his mother says.

"Sorry."

"Like you mean it."

"Connie," Viola says. "It's all right. They're just children."

"She wanted to kiss me!"

"I never!"

"Stop it!" both adults yell simultaneously.

In the end Viola squats down and spends quite a long time reminding them both about the big Rule, the crucial one. They were given a job to do, she says, which means they absolutely have to do it. It's only as her speech nears its end that Rory realizes what it means: he and Pink are going to be sent back to the woods to finish what they were doing, accompanied by the most stern and dire warnings about not even thinking about going anywhere else or doing anything else. Of course they are. You always have to finish what you're doing if it's to do with getting food.

Pink barely waits for the adults to be out of earshot before she begins hissing at him under her breath about him being a liar and how she'll always hate him and all that. He trudges along like she's not even there. That's the funny thing about being told off, when it's over it feels like nothing's really happened. It's just the same as when his mother gets all weepy and strange sometimes; it doesn't mean anything afterwards. You let it pass and it's gone.

Pink gets furious for a while, then when he goes on ignoring her she pretends to be upset. He concentrates on combing slowly through the woods. There are lots of mushrooms once you start looking carefully. Esme says it's the same as with the fish and the crops. She says technology drove them away but now everything's plentiful if you ask the spirits nicely, or something like that.

"Please," Pink says. Now, at last, she sounds a bit like she's really upset. He straightens up and looks at her.

"I'll forgive you for lying if you stop ignoring me," she says. "I swear."

His back's sore from bending over. He stretches out. He's been waiting for this moment and he's going to enjoy it.

"I'm not a liar," he says. "Unlike you."

Her eyes bug out and she's about to answer back but he silences her by pointing.

"You said you wouldn't tell," he says, nice and clearly. He knows he's right. He's full of things he knows about, things stupid Pink couldn't imagine in a million million years. "You swore. And then you told before I even got back. Now you'll never see Them."

He crouches down again and doesn't say another word.

* * *

When Rory's bags are full he starts back to the Abbey for lunch. Pink has to come with him, of course, because they promised to stay together. She's hardly got anything in her bags because of all the time she's wasted crying and threatening and begging. She won't get in trouble because no one really expects her to do much proper work, but still, it'll be embarrassing for her.

Lunch is fish, as always. The barbecue's a perfect way to use up any twigs which are too small for the fire. It's set up in a sheltered corner of the gardens. All summer long they've been sitting out there, people coming and going while one of the older ones looks after the fire. Today you can tell it's not summer anymore. The sky's clear and the light's yellow but there's a freshness in the breeze. Missus Grouse rubs her hands over the barbecue. No one else is eating yet. Dealing with the spelt is hard, slow work and chances are they'll be at it till dark without a break.

Rory hitches himself up onto a garden wall with his plate (Missus Grouse insists on them using plates) and scoops dribbly bits of fish into his mouth. The garden slopes away in front of the Abbey. Parts of it are almost completely impenetrable now, but he can see over the top of the thick dark bushes, across the Small Pond and the scrubby southern tip of Home. On the horizon sits the bump of Maries, with its broken radio tower on top like a burned-down skeletal candle.

"What's that boat?"

There's a sailing boat he hasn't seen before moored off the South Landing.

"Oh," Missus Grouse says, "I'm not sure."

Some awkwardness in her voice makes him look at her. She turns away to fiddle unnecessarily with her stack of kindling, though not before he's caught her watching him with a weird stricken expression on her face.

"It wasn't there before, was it?"

"Nothing to worry about," she says loudly.

Last autumn, he remembers, people quite often used to talk about what would happen if Other People tried to land on Home. Ol got excited and made them play complicated games involving making fortifications and stockpiling ammo, but Rory could tell it was serious. The women knew they were barely clinging on after everyone else had left, a colony of the weak, the old, the inexpert, or so they thought until winter came to teach them how resilient they could be when they had to. Libby was always imagining bands of pirates or cannibals (or was it pirate cannibals?) roaming the world taking whatever they could get. Kate, more boringly, worried about the Maries or Martin people. So for a long time it was always someone's job to spend the day on Briar Hill, watching the open waters around the edge of the world; quite often it was Rory's own job. No one ever came. By the time winter set in they'd given up worrying about it. Everyone had left and no one was coming back: that was the way the world was, so obvious in the end it didn't need discussing.

Until now.

"When did it get there?" he says.

"I've no idea. This morning, I think. Never you mind." She prods the coals. "And do be careful with those bones, you know Fi can use them."

Could it be the stranger's boat? But it's there in plain sight, obvious to everyone.

"I could go check it out."

"No. I said never mind. Come on, let's find you two something else to do."

Pink complains about being tired so Missus Grouse sends her off to find Viola. Rory's told to go and sweep out the stoves and fires in the Abbey. This is a stroke of luck. There's no one else inside except Ali, who's back in bed with her cough, so it's the perfect opportunity for him to snatch a bit more food. He doesn't try using a bag this time. It was stupid of him to think he could get away with carrying a bag of food around. Instead he has the idea of packing the pockets of his coat. He skims quickly around the cellars collecting things that don't smell: potatoes, raisins, a few dried figs. He takes just a little from each pile so it won't look like anything's missing.

Then he goes up and down the Abbey collecting the ash. He ferries it to the big scuttle downstairs. It's almost full by the time he's done, so he goes and asks Missus Grouse whether he should take a barrow-load to the shed behind the old Laundry. Fi makes them keep all the ashes to use as some kind of fertilizer on the fields. Before What Happened Fi was a gardener at the Abbey.

"All right," Missus Grouse says. "But mind you don't go wandering off again."

"I didn't wander off," he says. "I was just having a poo."

You can't hurry when you're pushing a barrow full of ash, because even with a tarpaulin tied as tight as you can you'll lose some if you jiggle around. So he walks slowly. The food in his pockets bumps his legs. He's got time to think now. He wheels the barrow around the back of the Club and past the collapsed shed next to the old Laundry. All he has to do is think of a safe place to leave the food overnight, then he can find time to collect it in the morning and take it over to the Hotel and no one'll know anything about it. There are hundreds of places where no one would ever look. Easy.

Normally when he's walking by himself he's thinking about Her, but today it's all the stranger. He finds himself wondering what else the man might need.

It so happens that he's thinking about this just as he's passing the Toolshed. His eye alights on its wonky sliding door, and straightaway he thinks: *matches*.

Matches are incredibly precious. Last winter he and Ol were given the job of turning over every inch of every building they could get into looking for boxes or books of matches. They've taken them from houses, from behind the counter at the Shop, from the Pub (lots), from the pockets of jackets left hanging behind doors, even from the office of the Hotel though Rory nearly died of fright getting in there. Every abandoned sailing boat they can reach has been searched for them. People whose hands aren't steady enough aren't even allowed to try lighting matches in case they break one. And their whole collection is stored carefully in the Toolshed, in a waterproof tin box with a lock.

Rory's not sure what the stranger would even do with matches. But he can imagine giving them to him. He can imagine this very clearly. *I thought you could use some of these.* And the stranger grinning in answer: *Good boy.*

He imagines this over and over.

He sets the barrow down by the Toolshed and slides the door across. It's dim inside. While his eyes adjust he feels along the ceiling to the left, where the key to the padlock on the tin box hangs from a nail behind a rafter. He's very proud of the fact that he's been told where the key is and Pink hasn't yet.

He unhooks the key and goes to unlock the box. There's no padlock.

He stands looking at it for a bit, surprised. Maybe someone forgot to lock it last time, or maybe they don't care anymore. He opens the box. There's all sorts of matches in there. He takes out one of the little purple matchbooks from the Pub. After he's replaced the key he looks at it outside, in the light. THE NEW INN, it says, and then a row of numbers, which by forgotten instinct he identifies as a telephone number a few moments before he can remind himself what a telephone number was actually for. The numbers look pointless now, random doodles or an indecipherable code. He puts it in the pocket with the raisins.

The ash goes in a shed a bit farther back. He tips it out very carefully. He loves its soft, cloudy slither. Quiet as secrets.

His mother says they're going back to Parson's that night. He's immensely relieved. He was dreading being shut up in a room with Pink and Laurel. They don't even hang around at the Abbey to eat with everyone, which is unusual. It's even more surprising that no one presses them to stay for supper. Perhaps they're all too exhausted. With the weather clear they all worked until dusk and now they're spent. But Rory thinks there's something else as well. He has the feeling everyone's being a bit quiet around him and his mother.

She's finished being angry, or maybe it's just that she doesn't have the energy for it. He's acutely conscious of the lumps in his coat as they walk back to Parson's but she never looks like she might notice. She's preoccupied. They have cold mashed vegetables mixed with a bit of salty fish oil and then they clean and tidy up and it's bedtime.

Rory's not quite asleep when someone thumps the door. He sits up in alarm, thinking of the stranger, but when a voice calls out it's a woman's.

"Connie? Are you still up?"

It's Kate and Missus Shark. Rory goes downstairs in his pajamas, wrapping a blanket around his shoulders like the stranger did. Kate's carrying the little night-light cube again. His mother sits them down in the kitchen.

"Is something wrong?"

"Rory," Kate says. She's put the night-light in the middle of the table. "You took a load of ash to the pile earlier on, didn't you?"

"What's he done?" says his mother.

"Nothing," Missus Shark says, "I'm sure."

"Yeah," Rory says to Kate. He doesn't like the sound of this. "You didn't see anything unusual up there, did you? By the dump?"

"No."

"What's this about?" his mother asks.

"Just a sec." Kate's not easily interrupted. "Did you see anyone else on the way there? Or on the way back?"

"No."

"What about hearing anything."

"Like what?"

"Anything you noticed. A bang, a loud noise."

"No." They wait. "Nothing like that."

"OK, so." Kate folds her hands and leans back. "Someone's been in the Toolshed."

"The lock on the matchbox was broken," Missus Shark said. Rory can't help glancing towards his coat. It's hanging on the wall just by Missus Shark's head.

"Broken how?"

"The padlock's gone," Kate says. "And the metal of the catch is twisted, someone must have snapped it right off. And there's a knife missing, and the bottle of lighter fluid. Someone rummaged around in the tools as well."

After a short silence his mother says, "I don't understand."

"No one's said they took anything," Missus Shark says. "We've asked everyone else."

"You don't know anything about it, do you, Connie?"

"No. No, of course not." She sounds angry for a moment, before the implications sink in. "But . . ."

"So then," Kate says. She doesn't have to spell it out.

"Well," his mother says. "Obviously someone must have been in there."

"Yes," Kate says, and "Exactly," says Missus Shark. Kate turns to Rory. Her shaved head looks like a statue in the gloom. "Are you absolutely sure you don't know what happened to those things in the Toolshed?"

"No," he says. "I mean, yeah. I'm sure."

"Hang on," says his mother.

Missus Shark leans in towards Rory. "Because if there are things you're worried you might need, it would be best to discuss that with everyone."

"Are you accusing Rory of stealing?"

"Nobody's accusing anyone of anything, Connie," Kate says.

"He doesn't know the plan," his mother says, very coldly. "I haven't told him."

"What plan?" Rory says.

"Never mind."

"It's just that nobody else went up that way today," Kate says. "The rest of us were busy all afternoon."

"Lighter fluid," Missus Shark says. It's a reproach. Anything flammable is precious.

"Perhaps someone came over from Maries," his mother says. She's beginning to get a little angry. "Have you thought of that?"

Kate slumps, sighing. "I don't know what to think," she says. "They might have. I just hate the idea of people stealing from each other. I suppose we'll have to start keeping a lookout again."

"It's better than thinking one of us took something and won't say so," says Missus Shark.

"Rory isn't like that, Asha, and you know it."

"All right," says Kate, standing up. "We're not here to cast doubts on Rory, or anyone else. I just wanted to ask if you'd seen anything, that's all. You're right, Connie, it's probably someone from one of the other islands. We'll have to think about what else needs locking up."

"The rest of us will," says Missus Shark, looking at his mother.

"If you remember anything," Kate says quickly, looking at Rory, "please tell me. All right? Remember, you can come and find me any time and we'll talk."

He can't make out her eyes but he knows what she's thinking. She's already found him stealing food. She won't say anything in front of anyone else, she doesn't need to. He can feel her disappointment without words.

"I don't," he says. "Remember anything, I mean."

After they've gone he's going to ask his mother what the plan is she hasn't told him about, but she says "Go back to bed, Rory," and he can hear in her voice that she's shaking with anger. He's safest by himself, under the covers.

For the first time in a long time he thinks about his father.

8

For more than a year Rory and his mother have been getting up
every morning soon after it's light and having breakfast and
then going to the Abbey for the Meeting. This morning it's
different again. The rhythm of the world is broken.

He wakes up to the sound of talking below, and when he goes
downstairs Fi is there. Both she and his mother look terrible, bleary,
anxious. He was going to get his mother to explain the plan she
wouldn't tell him about last night but he never gets a chance.

"You'd better come and see," Fi says.

They turn the wrong way at the door, not left over the crest of the
Lane towards the useful side of the island but right, past the church,
in the direction of the Old Harbor and the Hotel and all the worst
of the ruins. Rory's still cold after waking up in a hurry and when he
sees his mother and Fi setting off that way a pit opens in his stomach and he thinks, *They know about the stranger and now he's going
to kill me.* But they walk past the looted church and the overgrown
playground, past the spot where the stranger offered Rory the apple,
without saying anything. No one's talking. It's a breezy morning and
the air has the chill of the sea.

The houses around the Old Harbor were pillaged a long time
ago, when lots of people were still living on the island. No one likes
to talk about that first spring after What Happened, when the TVs
went blank and the ferry stopped coming. No one even likes to think
about it. The wreckage they're walking beside now is enough of a

reminder. Gaping doors and windows have filled with weeds but they're still dark, dripping, edged with broken wood or glass like they have teeth. Fi leads them between a collapsed fence and a row of ruins towards the Old Harbor quay.

"Are we going somewhere?" Rory says, suddenly nervous. Before he fell asleep he was thinking about his mother's plan, and some other things he's heard people say the last few days, and a nasty thought had struck him, though he'd dismissed it quickly because he knew it couldn't be right; now it surfaces again, even less plausible in the daylight, and yet somehow even nastier too. But he forgets it almost as soon as he's spoken, because they step out onto the quay and there's other people there.

Viola and Laurel and Missus Anderson are standing in a tight group by the shelter, except that the shelter's not there anymore. Instead of the wooden hut where people used to wait for boats there's a charred heap, shapeless as the mounds of bramble.

"There," Fi says. She's not pointing at the burned shelter. She's peering offshore, towards Martin, the same way Viola and Laurel and Missus Anderson are looking.

Out in the shoals between Home and Martin another black wreck has appeared overnight. A squat fishing boat is beached at a bad angle on the edge of a knuckle of rock. It's listing so far over that the triangle of sail on its stubby mast is being slapped by the tops of waves.

Before last winter there were a lot of wrecks. Usually it was bigger ships. He'd see them from his lookout post on top of Briar Hill, tankers so big it hardly looked like they were moving at all, drifting like clouds, passing out of sight unless they came to rest on the outer rocks at the very edges of the world. Occasionally something smaller, a yacht or a fishing boat, would float aimlessly into the Gap on a rising tide and end up foundering in the shallows or on the shores of one of the islands. Not anymore, though. The winter must have finished off the rest of the empty vessels, and no one's crazy enough to risk the cursed ocean now.

This wreck looks like a ghost ship. The rock where it's run aground is halfway across to Martin, but even at that distance Rory can see its boom lurching and slapping, a dead limb swinging in the wind. The hull's as black as the rock.

"Any sign of anything?" Fi says. She's digging a black leather case out of an inside pocket.

"Laurel thinks she might have seen something," says Viola.

"I'm not sure," Laurel says. "It could just have been a bird."

"What else did you think it could have been?" Fi says. She's from Scotland, which Rory thinks makes everything she says sound as if she's slightly disappointed. She opens the case. There's a pair of binoculars inside.

"I dunno," Laurel says. "For a moment it looked like there was somebody there."

"Really?"

"I dunno."

"Laurel's got good eyes," Viola says. Fi raises the binoculars and spreads her legs for balance. She examines the boat for a long time then passes the binoculars to Laurel.

"Can you read the name?" she says. "I can't quite make it out."

"What happened to the shelter?" Rory says.

"It burned down in the night," Missus Anderson says.

"It didn't burn down." Viola's tense and angry. "You make it sound like it did it by itself. Someone burned it down."

"Well done for sleeping through it, Rory," Laurel says, without turning away from the binoculars. "Everyone else has been up all night."

"Why'd anyone do that?"

"And," Laurel says in her sarcastic older sister voice, "*aaaand . . .*" He misses the point entirely. "Congratulations."

"That's enough, Laurel."

"Bee Ee Zee something?" Laurel says. "Is that an *E*?"

"That's what I thought," Fi says.

"Wait," Laurel says. She leans forward, as if that'll help. "There's one of those things on the E. One of those slopey lines. An accent."

Fi takes the binoculars. "So there is. Well done, Laurel."

"Does that mean it's French?"

"Must be."

"Oh no," Missus Anderson says, "someone found us."

"There's no need to panic," Fi says.

"It must have been Them?" Of all the women, Missus Anderson's most prone to what Ol calls—called—wittering. "Who did this? Someone's got on the island."

Rory's fists clench in his pockets. Adults never notice anything, but he suddenly feels like Laurel's staring right into his brain.

"That would explain the business with the Toolshed," his mother says.

"Possibly," Fi says, still watching the boat.

"They might have been right here," Missus Anderson says. She's wringing her hands. "While we were dealing with the fire. Right here, watching."

"We don't know," Viola says wearily. "You can't jump to conclusions. That boat might have just drifted here empty."

"But the shelter," Missus Anderson says. "You said yourself, someone must have done this. Who'd do a thing like that? It's such a waste."

Fi lowers the binoculars. "I don't like it either," she admits.

"They might not have anything to do with each other," Viola says.

"But there's the business with the Toolshed too." Fi doesn't witter and she doesn't snap at people. She's quieter than Kate but everyone knows she's the other competent one. "Think about it. Yesterday someone takes matches and butane, then in the night there's a fire. An obviously deliberate fire." She pokes her toe into the charred grey heap which is all that's left of the shelter. "That's never coincidence, is it."

Missus Anderson's eyes go wide. She stares out towards the wreck again. "But that means They must have been here since yesterday!"

"If it's Them," Viola says.

"Who else can it be? None of us would do a thing like that. Oh God. People sneaking around the island in the night."

Rory's throat is going very dry. What if they find the stranger? He'll think Rory told them about him, and then he'll kill Rory like he'd kill a rat.

"It would help," Fi says, "if we had some idea how long that boat's been there. You'd think someone would have mentioned it if they'd seen it in the last few days."

Rory sees his chance and grabs it before he can think. "It wasn't there yesterday," he says.

Everyone looks at him.

"So," he says, beginning to feel suddenly hot. "There's probably no one here. No one foreign, I mean." The way Laurel's looking at him is making him lose his train of thought. It seemed like such a good thing to mention but he's struggling to remember why. It's because . . . "If someone off that boat took the stuff in the Toolshed they'd have been here yesterday," he says in a rush, "but they can't have because it wasn't. It must have drifted in in the night." He faces Viola, slightly desperate now. "Like you said." They mustn't start searching the island. He's got to stop that from happening.

It's only when his mother says, in an alarmingly cold voice, "How do you know?" that he realizes his mistake.

"What?"

"How do you know? How do you know that boat wasn't there yesterday?"

He knows because he came around the ruined side of the island to deliver the bags of food and clothes to the stranger, and he'd have seen it among the shoals if it had been there. But he can't say so. Of course he can't. He was supposed to be picking in the woods with Pink. He told everyone he'd gone for a poo.

"I . . ." Every eye is turned on him and he can feel each one like a weight. He knows his face is going heavy. "Actually, I'm not sure. I just thought."

There's a silence.

"Thought what," his mother says.

"Thought I saw that, that it wasn't. But actually, I dunno."

"Where did you go yesterday?"

"Nowhere. Just for a poo. I," he scrambles to recover his footing but he knows it's too late even as he comes up with the lie, he can feel the ground slipping away beneath him. "I went up to that place by the north fields, you know, and I turned round to look at the sea on my way, and I saw it wasn't there. I mean I didn't see anything. I would've, if there'd been anything. I think. Maybe I'm not actually sure."

Laurel snorts.

His mother bends over him. "You need to tell us the truth, Rory."

"I am!"

"Where did you go after you told Pink that horrible lie? Where did you really go?"

"Easy, Connie," Fi says.

"Yeah," Laurel says. "Might be too hard a question for him."

"Laurel, shut up," Viola says.

Laurel turns angrily on her aunt. "Rory's been acting really weird lately. You know he has. Anyone can see he's lying."

His mother snaps at Laurel. "That's not helpful."

"I think," Fi says firmly, "we should go back to the Abbey and get this all sorted out."

He's got a bit of time as they walk over there to work out what he can and can't say. The only important thing is not to say that there's anyone else on the island. He clings to that one idea as hard as he can. It's not just that he's afraid of the stranger's threats. There's something else about his secret too, something which makes him want to keep it to himself, like Her. It's a thing he owns, in this world where no one has any possessions anymore. It feels precious.

It's a good thing he has a bit of time to think about all this because once they're all at the Abbey and finished with breakfast and cleaning up and tidying away Kate makes him stand up in the middle of the big room by himself, with everyone listening, and asks him all about yesterday. She smiles kindly and says it's to help him concentrate and not be distracted but he knows it's actually to make him tell the truth, because how can he make anything up with all the people in the world staring at him like that? Fortunately, though, she doesn't seem too interested in the bit where he does actually have to lie, when he says what he did after Pink's stupid jabbering made him run away. She cares most about what happened when he took the ash to the pile up by the Dump, and all he has to remember is not to mention going in the Toolshed, which is easy because he hardly went there at all, just took one tiny matchbook, which doesn't even count as doing anything, not really. Despite that he can feel how red he's going and he can hear himself mangling words. He tries not to look at Laurel but she's glaring at him and her eyes are accusing as plain as anything, *Liar*.

But when Kate finally lets him sit down again it turns out that she's got something on her mind other than whether or not he's telling the truth.

"Well," she says, "I think that's pretty much that. We have visitors."

Half of them are shaking their heads and muttering *that's impossible*. The others, like Missus Anderson, are somewhere between shocked and terrified.

"There's only two possibilities," Kate says. "Either one of us set that fire or someone else did. Rory's the only person who went near the Toolshed yesterday afternoon. The rest of us all know where each other were. And even if Rory did take the things from the shed, which I never for a moment thought he did, he was asleep all night and can't possibly have had anything to do with the fire, not that I ever thought you did either." She smiles warmly at him. She hasn't said anything to anyone about catching him stealing the food. She's on his side. If Kate's on his side then it doesn't matter what anyone else thinks, Laurel or Pink or even his mother.

Esme speaks up in her whispery voice. "Can we really say what's possible or impossible anymore?"

Fi, sitting next to her, rolls her eyes. "I don't think the fairies would have bothered breaking into the Toolshed and dragging all that crap down to the quay just to start a fire." Esme only smiles: she's impossible to offend.

Kate holds a hand up before people start taking sides. "Lots of things could have happened. It's most likely just someone over from one of the other islands, making trouble."

"It'll be those two girls from Mary's," Missus Shark says. "What are their names. Those sisters. I caught them messing with our nets in the summer."

"Or it could be people off that boat," Viola says. "From France."

"We'll have a look at the boat later on, when it's calmer," Kate says. "I'll row a boat out there. Someone should keep an eye on it meanwhile."

"Two people," Viola says.

"The important thing," Kate says, "is to work out what needs doing now. Viola's right, we should make sure two of us are always together. We'll need to lock the Stash and the barn. There's no need to worry, we just have to start being careful again, until we find out what's going on."

"This is an island," Missus Grouse says, as if no one else knows. "No one can arrive or leave except by boat. We should have patrols around the shore. If anything's going on we'll see it soon enough."

"What about that boat you brought over, Connie?" Viola says. Startled, Rory looks at his mother. She's gone rather pale and is shaking her head tightly at Viola. "Could someone from Mary's have—"

"Vera's right," his mother says, quickly. "We should start a search. I'll go."

Rory's remembering hiding in the cupboard and overhearing Molly say something about a twenty-footer. He wasn't paying attention at the time, all he cared about was not getting discovered. But now the nasty thought he had in the night rears up again. His mother went to Maries and came back with a boat? Why would she do that? She always hated sailing. It's one of the reasons she said she'd stay with Rory on Home when Dad and Jake and Scarlet went off to try to reach the Mainland and find out what was happening.

"Whatever's going on," Kate says cheerfully, "it won't take too long to find out. It's a small island after all." Kate can feel the nervous unhappiness in the room as well as everyone else can, and she's doing her thing where she tries to jolly them all out of it.

"It'll be those girls," Missus Shark says. "If you ask me they've been sneaking across from Maries and stealing things for months."

"What's the point of stealing fuel and then wasting it burning down a useless building?" Viola says.

Missus Shark sniffs. "Teenagers."

By now almost everyone has started muttering to their neighbors, but when Esme speaks they're all quiet again in a moment.

"The fire was the point," Esme says. "That must be why whoever it was took all those curtains and blankets and whatnot down to the quay. To make the fire burn brighter and longer. So bright it woke us all up. Like an offering."

Viola and Fi exchange knowing looks. Kate stands up before the gathering murmurs get out of control.

"We've dealt with worse than this," she says. "Remember what really matters. We make sure we do what needs to be done. Together." She has a way of making it sound like the worst thing any of them can do is start arguing with each other. "We'll have the meeting as usual. We need to lock up a couple of places and maybe send a couple of people to look around the island and keep an eye on that new boat. But we also need to finish the spelt." *Or we'll all starve this winter*: she doesn't need to say it aloud.

"First things first," Fi agrees, looking pleased.

"So." Kate stares everyone back into their chairs and then sits back down herself. "Let's sort today out." This is how the Meeting always starts. Everyone relaxes a bit. It's as if she's persuaded them that nothing unusual is happening at all.

Except Rory's mother. "We were going to discuss . . ." she begins, and glances at Rory. "That thing I wanted to talk about."

"Maybe not this morning," Fi says. "What with all this going on."

"No," his mother says. "I'd like to."

For a moment Kate's not sure what to say. "Well, I suppose we can see what everyone thinks—"

"I'd like you to decide today," his mother says, not meeting Kate's eye.

You? No one ever says *you. You?* Who's *you?* I'd like *us* to decide, that's what people would say. What's his mother doing pretending that she's not one of the people in the world?

The room is suddenly extremely tense.

"Surely it can wait until we know for sure what's happening," Viola says.

"We talked about this." It's his mother against the whole room.

Rory's never seen anything like it. She's bracing herself, ready for a fight.

Kate looks very uncomfortable. Everyone's waiting for her to make a decision.

"It's her right to decide," says Molly. This is the first time Molly's spoken up all day. Her voice is hollow with desolation.

"Yes," Kate says. No one can say no to Molly at the moment. "Of course it is. All right then."

Viola frowns into her lap.

"So," Kate says, looking at Rory again. "Um."

"Rory." His mother motions him to his feet. "We need to discuss something privately. Go home"—she means Parson's—"and wait, all right?"

"Not by himself," Missus Anderson says.

"You two can go with him," Viola says to the girls. They both start a *no* at the same time but Missus Anderson, of all people, cuts them off.

"I'll take him," she says. "I don't want any part of this decision."

The silence is as bad as Rory can ever remember it.

"Straight there," his mother finally says, "and lock the door. Stay in your bed and read. Understand?"

"You'll come back, Dorothy?" Kate says to Missus Anderson. "We need to—"

"Stick together," Missus Anderson says, in a flustered rush. "I know I know I know. I know we do. Why doesn't someone tell Connie that? Come on, Rory."

"I won't be long," his mother says. They always say that before Meetings or chats. It's nonsense. Adults talk for ages and ages and don't get anywhere. He hurries out after Missus Anderson anyway. He doesn't know how long he's going to need and if his mother doesn't find him at Parson's when she gets back he can't even imagine how much trouble he'll be in.

The wind's gusting up and the brownest leaves are beginning to fall. Summer went on so long he's forgotten what it's like to feel the air sting and to see the relentless heaps of nettles and grass and weeds slowing down, wilting. He lets Missus Anderson escort him all the way to Parson's and inside and even upstairs. She hugs him rather tearfully, which isn't like her, but he's only waiting for her to leave so he doesn't give it much thought. Once she's gone at last he collects all the food from the pockets of his other coat and puts it in the spare bag, before unlocking the door and dashing out again into the blowy morning.

He's only gone as far as the church, hardly thirty steps, when there's a sharp whistle above.

"Boy!"

It takes him a few moments to spot the bald dome of the stranger's head leaning over the parapet of the church tower. The stranger looks around—he must be able to see a good way from up there—grins, makes a *pssst* noise, and beckons Rory inside before disappearing from view like a squirrel diving into a hedge.

The church is empty and dusty as a barn inside. He never went there in The Old Days but he knows what churches are supposed to look like, rows of wooden benches and cushions and big candlesticks. The little one over on Briar still looks like that, peaceful and solemn. Here the benches were chopped up for fuel long ago and everything else was taken in the bad time after What Happened, when people grabbed whatever they could before leaving. The only things that make it feel like a church are the windows with their sooty patterned glass, and the tablets like gravestones around the walls.

A rope comes flying from the ceiling in the square space beside the entrance. Rory jumps at the sudden movement—it's like a snake uncoiling out of nowhere—and looks up. For a painful instant he thinks he sees Ol, but of course it's only Ol's clothes. The stranger appears around a hole where the rope disappears into the ceiling and then drops out of it. It looks for a moment like he's going to fall the whole way to the floor, but he's got hold of the rope somehow. He slides down it straight and smooth as an acrobat and lands lightly beside Rory. The clothes turn out to be a bit big on him, which has the effect of hiding the shape of his body so his head looks even bigger.

"Good," he says, snatching the bag. "Very good." He doesn't look dangerous at all today. He looks comical, with his goggly eyes and loose clothes, like a clown. Rory can't imagine why he was ever frightened of him. The stranger's excitable today, hopping from foot to foot as he picks through the bag, muttering under his breath in his own language. "Good boy!" He clips Rory on the shoulder. "Say to no one? Eh?"

"I didn't tell anything."

"Clever. So you live, hmm? I don't kill you?" He makes a bared-teeth grimace and then smiles like it was a joke all along.

"I got matches."

"*Come?*"

He doesn't understand. Rory takes the bag back and fetches the matchbook from the bottom. "Matches."

"Ha!" The stranger looks more amused than pleased. He holds the matchbook up to the light and reads the words. " 'New Inn,' " he says, carefully, making the Pub's old name sound silly: *nyeuw een.* "*Osteria nuova.*" He flips the matchbook back to Rory, forcing him into a fumbling catch. "I have," he says, and points up into the gloom at the top of the rope.

"You're hiding out up there?"

The stranger seems happy to talk. He seems happy in general, in fact. He bites the end off a carrot and makes appreciative noises.

"Hiding, *si si.*"

Rory looks up the rope. "Can you climb up that?"

The stranger's stuck for a moment before he understands. "Ah. Yes. You do." He puts the rope in Rory's hands. "Go up."

He's teasing. Rory's never liked being teased about how bad he is at sporty things.

"No thanks," he says sullenly.

"*Ecco.* No one does this. Good, ah . . ." He clicks his fingers to help himself remember. "Hiding! Good hiding." He grabs the rope back and waves it at Rory. "This, up. *Perfetto.*"

"What's up there?"

The stranger outlines a curvy shape in the air and sings "*Donnnnn.*"

"Oh. The bell."

"Bell, *ecco*. And me. *Uccellino*." He holds his hand out. It's very dirty, with ragged discolored nails. "*Uccellino*," he says again.

Rory shakes hands.

"You? Name?"

"Oh." Rory has a very strong feeling he shouldn't say, but he wants to, plus the stranger's big round eyes are almost bullyingly insistent. "Rory."

"Rory."

"Yeah."

"Clever boy."

Rory pulls his hand away shyly, making the stranger laugh.

"Or bad boy." The stranger pokes him, hard. "Eh? Bad boy? In island of women." He shakes the bag of food at Rory. "This, women don't know. *Shh*."

Rory's feeling obscurely ashamed. "I should get going."

"No no no no no," the stranger says, extremely fast so it comes out like singing, *nonononono*. "No, no. Listen. This night."

"I can bring more tomorrow."

"No. Food is OK. No more. This night you bring *bicicletta*." He mimes riding a bike, hopping with his knees bent like a deranged puppet.

"Bicycle?"

"*Si si si! Bicicletta*. You bring her."

"You want a bike?"

The man seizes him by the arms. His strength is amazing for how tiny he is. "Listen. You know. *Fuoco*." He lets go to mime again: with his empty hands he strikes an invisible match and then (puffing his cheeks and billowing his fingers) raises invisible flames. "*Fuoco*."

"Fire?"

"Fire. OK. You know, in the night, fire." He points in the direction of the Old Harbor. "You know this?"

Rory nods nervously. Of course it was the stranger who set fire to the shelter. Like Kate said, there's no one else it could have been.

"OK. There, where fire is. You bring, ah, bicycla, this night. Bicycla with light. Like you have before."

"I don't understand."

The stranger grimaces in frustration. "You. This night. Bicycla with light. There. OK?"

"I . . ."

"Good boy."

"I can't."

"*Come?* No no no. No no no." His face turns stern. "You do this."

It's gone too far. Until now it was feeling exciting, dangerous in an interesting way, like an adventure out of the comics; special, like the fact that no one else talks to Her. This is something else. He can't go out in the night on his own stealing bicycles. He's not allowed. "I can't!"

The man pushes him, hard. Rory staggers backwards. The man pounces after him.

"You and *mamma*," he says. "You have this house." He points up in the direction of Parson's. "I see you. Go in, go out. All the time, I see this." He's talking very fast, pausing only to chase down English words. "Day. Night. So, night, like this." He makes a pillow of his hands and leans his cheek on it, eyes closed, all in a breath or two: *sleeping.* "Long time. So, *mamma* like this, you go out. No one to see. You bring *bicicletta* with light. One thing you do, this thing. Then no more. Or I kill you. I kill you and *mamma*. In this house." He pulls a knife out from the waistband of the trousers. Rory recognizes it: it's the knife from the Toolshed. It glints a few inches from his eyes. Rory's guts turn to water. No one's ever threatened him with a weapon before.

The stranger stops his rapid patter and steps back, eyeing Rory curiously. He puts the knife out of sight.

"*Ecco là.*" He pats Rory awkwardly. "Good boy."

Rory's sniveling. He drags in a deep breath.

"They know you're here," he mumbles. "They're all looking for you."

The stranger grins. "Women. Is OK. I go"—he whistles and waves at the ceiling—"up."

"I can't keep taking things. They'll notice." The man waves a finger by his ear and shrugs: he doesn't understand. "They'll notice. They'll notice stuff missing. I'll get in trouble."

"No one see Uccellino," he says.

Rory wipes his nose. "Is that your name?"

"Mmmm?"

"Oochel—"

"Uccellino. *Si si.*" He smacks his chest. He pronounces it slowly. "Uccellino."

Rory knows he's got to get back. It hasn't been long but he can't take any risks.

On the other hand, he's standing here in the church talking to a foreign man who's arrived on Home. It's as miraculous as talking to Her, though not, he has to admit, as nice.

"Where are you from?"

"Where are—? Ah! From Trieste. Italy. You know? Italy?"

It's like he can feel the world spinning. There were, once, other places: he remembers (or half-remembers, or remembers now for the first time in so long that it's like making it up) seeing them, on weather maps on telly before the TVs all went dark, on the covers of books on the shelves at School before all that went away. There are Italians in some of the stories in the old comics, gangster stories. They wear long overcoats and say *you sleep-a with-a-da fishes.* It's all imaginary, all beyond the world, meaningless and impossible.

Sometimes the women talk quietly together about When All This Is Going To End. Rory wonders whether this is it, now, whether it's happening. There's a man from Italy on Home. It's like some point of view has suddenly zoomed up, up, away from the reality of the earth and the sea, up until the islands of the world are no longer earth and rock anymore but little flat green shapes in a big flat blue surround, with a name attached, The Isles of Scilly. *We're a dot on the map,* Dad used to say.

The man takes him by the shoulders, less forcefully. "I need help of you," he says. His eyes are so big and intense they're almost glowing. They're a funny color, too yellowy to be properly brown. "One time only. Very important." He says it *verrrry.* "For you is *facile.* Small thing. One hour this night. Women all," he mimes sleeping again, "*così.* For you is OK. No one see. Only women here?"

"Yeah. 'Cos of Them." The stranger looks blank. "Them. The people in the sea."

"Ah, *si si. Sirene.*" He sounds like he understands.

"Why didn't they kill you?"

"Hmm?"

"How come you're here? They didn't kill you?"

"Ha!" He thinks about an answer, drumming his fingers on Rory's shoulders. "Listen. So, you help me, then you know. Next day. We say. We say all things to you."

We? "Who's we?"

Oochellino smiles a broad sly smile and taps the side of his bizarrely straight high nose with a finger. "You help, then you know."

"It's not just you?" This is another extraordinary thought. "There's other people here?"

"*Shh.* Next day, you know. This night, *bicicletta.* OK?"

"So you want me to bring a bicycle to the Old Harbor tonight?"

"With light. Very important, light."

"Why? What d'ya need a bike for?"

"Ah ah ah." He taps Rory's temples with a finger. "You think." *Work it out for yourself,* he means. "Now. I, like this." He closes his eyes on his imaginary pillow again. He takes hold of the rope and starts shinning up it, gripping with knees and ankles. He makes it look as easy as going up stairs. "This night!" he calls, his voice echoing around the tower. Absurdly soon he's at the top. He disappears through the hole in the ceiling. There's a bit of clattering around and then the rope whisks up as if it were alive and vanishes after him.

Rory realizes he's still holding the matchbook. He shoves it back in his coat pocket as if it might burst into flame in his hands. He has no idea how much time has passed. He feels years older.

The rest of the day is a blur. He'd really like to get away from everyone and talk to Her. She knows a lot of things and likes answering questions. There's no chance, though. Once his mother gets back and they start on their jobs he's never out of her sight. The adults are talking about searching the island. He listens to Missus Shark guessing all the places someone could hide on Home. She never thinks of the belfry. Rory wonders whether he ought to find a way to warn Oochellino so he can tell the others to be careful, wherever they are. He can't stop thinking about them. Are they all Italians? Are they gangsters? How's he going to do what they want him to do tonight, fetch a bicycle with a dynamo and bring it to the Old Harbor quay? But the more he thinks about that the easier it seems. All he has to do is wait until everyone's asleep.

His mother's very preoccupied that evening, which is good since Rory is too. As they're walking back from the Abbey after supper she says, "Don't you want to know what we talked about at the Meeting this morning? After you left?"

"It's OK, Mum," he says. She's more likely to settle to sleep quickly if she doesn't get going on one of her conversations. He walks on a bit before he realizes she's staring at him. It's almost dark, the first evening of the autumn when it's really felt dark after supper. Kate insisted they take one of the little night-light cubes back to Parson's with them.

"Unless you want to say," he adds, sensing rather than seeing the look on her face.

She turns away. "Never mind," she says. "Tomorrow, why not."

"OK."

"Are you feeling all right?"

"Yeah."

"You've been very quiet the last few days."

He shrugs. He tries to walk a bit faster, to encourage her along.

"It's Oliver, isn't it," she says.

"Yeah," he lies.

"Have you been thinking about what happened to him?"

"A bit."

She catches up. "I'm not going to let it happen to you. I promise. You know that, don't you?"

"OK."

"They won't get you," she says. "Not while I'm alive. Never."

"Thanks, Mum," he says.

Again they go on a while before he becomes aware that she's looking at him peculiarly.

"You're a funny one," she says. It's what Dad used to say too. They never said it to Jake or Scarlet. It means he's not like his brother and sister, he likes the wrong kind of things, he's not into what they were into. Now he's feeling so much older the sting's gone out of the words, though. There's no pinch of shame anymore. He may be funny but it's because he's the only person in the world who talks to Them and knows there're Italians hiding in the belfry.

9

He pulls the curtains open a crack to monitor the darkness. He was worried he'd get sleepy but he isn't, not at all. As he came back down the twist of the Lane to Parson's after his poo he looked at the silhouette of the church tower. That was all it took to set his heart thumping and his stomach tingling like he'll never sleep again.

He waits. He mustn't start too soon. The bikes are kept in an outside room near the arched entrance at the end of the Abbey road, so even if he makes a bit of noise they shouldn't hear it inside the Abbey, but Kate is sharp-eared and pays attention, she doesn't stumble in and out of sleep the way the old women do. He's got to wait until he's sure she'll be fast asleep.

It's agony. He tries counting to a hundred and then works out that even if he counts as fast as he walks that's only a hundred steps, not even as far as the Club, which is no time at all. His mother's rustling and huffing in bed next door. He can't even think about starting until she's completely quiet. He makes himself lie motionless, as if that'll help her settle. The effort makes his legs ache.

Eventually he can't stand it anymore. He pushes the blankets back and sits up. His mother's breathing in long deep puffs. He counts twenty of them and then eases himself out of bed. He creeps downstairs as if the floor's carpeted in nails, gritting his teeth each time he puts his foot down.

He can't believe he's doing this.

Yet when he makes it to the kitchen at last and starts pulling warm layers over his pajamas he's overwhelmed by an ecstasy of exhilaration. It's a hundred times more pure than anything he ever felt during one of Ol's mildly naughty, not-quite-forbidden escapades. A grandeur's descending on him. He's stepped into the panes of the comics, among the superheroes and their exquisite perils.

He finds the night-light, checks its charge—it gleams cloudy warmth for an instant—and pockets it. He's sure he can find his way to the Abbey under anything but the most absolutely black night sky, but it won't hurt to have a tiny bit of extra light, especially in the bike shed.

Getting out the door is the hardest bit so far. The lock snaps and the hinges rattle. *I'll say I needed another poo,* he's thinking, convinced that every slither of the wind is actually the sound of his mother getting up and coming downstairs; but she doesn't. It's still hard to make himself go out. Once he's started there'll be no turning back. He'll be doing something he's never done before. An unimaginable line will have been crossed. If he gets caught everyone will know. He's not even sure exactly what they'll know: they'll just *know.*

He counts as far as forty-one and then suddenly it's too cold just standing there and he's off, jogging up the bend in the Lane. The night's immense and full of noise. He takes the night-light out straightaway. It's no brighter than a candle but it's something. When he gets to the crest of the Lane he can see a faint glow on the water of the Channel. It glistens even in the dark, like Her skin. All the distances stretch out. It feels like it's taking twice as long to get to the Club as it ought to. The deep night changes everything, it's not the same island. He's not the same Rory. Everything has changed since Ol died.

At long last he catches the smell of the pines over the Abbey road. He'd like to hide the light entirely as he approaches the Abbey: what if someone's looking out a bedroom window? But it's far too dark under the trees. Now the arched gateway comes up too quickly. Everything's suddenly happening too fast. Someone could easily be awake, listening. . . . He steers the night-light towards the screen of ivy opposite and jerks the shed door open in a clumsy rush. The wind catches it and it bangs against the wall, *thwack*. He jumps and swears. He pulls out a bike, knocking over the one next to it. The noise it makes is a metal shriek. Without stopping to close the door he jumps over the saddle. The light whirs into existence in front of him, quickly blazing white as he races away. He's panting. It's like swallowing ice in his lungs. He skids past the signpost at the bottom of the Abbey road, not expecting the turn: he's panicking, he's forgetting where he is, what he's doing. By the Club he stops and holds his breath, looking over his shoulder, listening for the sounds of pursuit.

Nothing, though.

Oddly, it's right then that he wonders for the first time what his mother was going to tell him. Up until now he hasn't been able to see beyond tonight, but all of a sudden he can picture himself getting the bike over to the other side of the island, dropping it off for Oochellino, going back to bed, waking up the next day and then . . .

What's the point of his mother going to Maries to get a boat?

He doesn't want to pass Parson's so he turns off behind the Old Laundry and rides up past the Dump on the middle road instead, even though it's broken and stony and clogged with twigs and leaves. As he comes down onto the ruined side he spots a small light off in the distance, on Martin. He stops to rub his eyes and confirm it's really there. There's no one left on Martin after the fire, that's what he's always been told.

There's something odd about the light too, the way it's bobbing around, winking brighter and dimmer.

With a delicious tangle of fear Rory realizes his mistake. The light's not on Martin at all. It's much closer. It's the light of a torch, not a distant window. It's on that wrecked boat.

It goes out. The blink of darkness sharpens his ears and he's sure he hears the fragment of a voice across the water.

The other Italians aren't in the belfry. They're on the ghost ship. They've been there all day, probably, lying low, while Viola and Fi and everyone stood around on the quay and stared through binoculars and wondered what to do. All at once—and it's so obvious he can't believe the others don't know this too—he understands the fire. Esme was right. The only reason to burn the shelter was to make a big fire. It wasn't an offering, though, any more than it was teenagers from the other islands being vandals. It was a beacon.

He's about to assist an invasion.

He stops. The headlight fades to nothing.

When Ol used to make him play games with forts and trenches and ammo they'd often pretend that someone was the Traitor. Usually it was Missus Anderson because she's actually from Maries not Home, plus Ol didn't like her. They'd sneak around looking for her and pretend to toss ammo if her back was turned.

It would never have occurred to Rory that the Traitor would turn out to be him.

Right now—at this exact moment: it's the instant of choice—he should turn around, cross back to the Abbey, and wake everyone up, shouting, *They're coming! Invasion! Enemy alert!* Kate would know what to do. They'd barricade the weak ones in the Abbey and the rest would go out on guerrilla warfare. He'd be the one who saved the island. He'd be the hero.

After a long moment he cycles on.

He's not so sure of his route on this road. People only come here for wood and he's too small for that job. He has to maneuver round holes and rubbish, and the dynamo almost goes dark when he does. It's the noise that lets him know when he's reached the small broken houses near the School and the Old Harbor bay. He's closer to the sea here and the suck and push of waves abruptly sounds as if it's right by his wheels. He dismounts and pulls out the night-light. There's darkness in every direction. No one's there.

"Good boy."

He jumps out of his skin. "Who's that?" he blurts stupidly.

Oochellino steps into the faint radiance. In the shadows he looks terrifying again, monstrous, like he's wearing a strange round hood with blank holes for eyes.

"Verrry good. I know you do this. Now. *Subito.*" The man snatches the bike and vanishes with it. There's a clattering, the rubbish in the road being kicked out of the way. "Here," the man's voice says. "With me." Rory hears the bike clank down somewhere out near the water, on the quay where the fire was.

"Where . . . ?"

Oochellino reappears and grabs him. "*Subito!*" He tugs Rory away.

"What—"

"*Hsss!*" He turns to face the sea and whistles twice, sharp whooping whistles. "Go. Like this." He beckons Rory to follow him.

The stranger steers him beside the ransacked houses and out onto the quay. He doesn't hesitate. It's like he can see in the dark, an animal. He whistles again. The offshore light reappears. It's an electric torch, winking unsteadily towards them.

"Who's that?"

"*Hsss!*" It's like *shh*. He yanks Rory another step or two and there's the bike, wonkily propped up on a sort of trestle made of bits of driftwood. "You." He pulls Rory down to a crouch and places his hand on the pedal. "Like this. Go." He starts spinning the pedal, still clasping Rory's hand. The front wheel's lifted off the ground and spins freely. A weak light appears, pointing out towards the shoals. "*Ecco*. Light. Go go go. No stop."

"You want me to—"

"No stop!" Oochellino pumps his hand harder on the pedal. "Light!"

It's obvious what he's supposed to do. The bike's headlamp is aiming straight out towards the wreck, where the other light is.

The unmistakable bumping and rattling of a boat comes out of the darkness offshore. Someone there calls out *Hoi!* It's hard to make out among the thumping and scratching of the invisible waves, but it's another man's voice.

"Good! Like this!" Oochellino bobs down and pushes Rory's hand faster. His arm's tired already. It's an awkward way to crank the pedals. He understands why he can't stop, though. Out there in the dark someone's taken the dinghy off the wrecked fishing boat and is lowering it into the shallow waters. They need a light to aim at or they'll never find the Old Harbor beach through the shoals and sandbars and tiny reefs. Really what they need—Rory remembers his father explaining this to him, trying to get him interested in sailing by talking about navigation—is two lights, one above the other, so they can line them up and stop themselves drifting to one side or the other.

Something big swishes in the trees behind him. He jerks around, startled.

"Not stop," Oochellino calls from high up. He was right beside Rory a moment ago. It's like he's floated into the air. The branches shake again. It must be him. He's climbing a tree, in the dark.

Up there, a tiny light flares.

"*Via via via!* Go!" Rory's let the headlight run dim and wan, a harvest moon. He sets to the pedal again but keeps an eye over his shoulder. Perched in the branches, Oochellino has struck a match. He pulls a candle from one of Ol's pockets and tries to light it, cursing in Italian as the wind blows it out. From offshore comes a familiar muffled creak. Oars.

They're coming.

On his third try Oochellino coaxes the candle flame into life, sheltering it between his palms. He holds it up. By its light Rory can see his weird face nodding. "Good!" he calls, half a shout and half a whisper. *Crrrk,* the oars say. Is he imagining it or do they sound closer already?

He grits his teeth against the soreness spreading over his shoulder and keeps turning the pedal. He doesn't ask himself why he's doing it anymore. He looks back to see how Oochellino's managing with the second light.

There's another light. A yellowy elegant one, wobbling among the hedges up towards the top of the Lane.

Someone's coming. With a flashlight.

An instant later he hears a shout, a woman's voice. Kate's voice: even muffled and at a distance, it's her, he can tell. Oochellino hisses something angry and brief. His candle snuffs out. The new light wobbles faster. Kate's running now, down the Lane, towards the Old Harbor: towards them. She must have seen something.

Rory seizes up in complete terror. He jams the wheel to a stop. The light dies.

"Who's there?"

It's Kate. Of course it's Kate. She always knows what's going on.

She's going to find him, all of them. Rory's mind has gone blank except for the one word, *Traitor*.

"We saw you!" And it's Fi too. Both of them are coming, shouting from a distance but approaching quickly. Fi doesn't anger easily but when she does she goes crazy, he's seen it. Their torchlight reappears as a glow behind him, screened by the trees behind the quay but making a segment of the sky above flicker in and out of darkness. The noise of the oars has stopped. The Italians are out there, completely benighted. Oochellino's gone invisible and silent. He could be anywhere but they'll never find him. Only Rory's stuck. If he tries to squeeze back past the ruins to the road they'll hear him. They'll turn their torch towards the noise and they'll spot him straightaway.

He's trapped.

He can hear Fi's and Kate's feet now, running past the church. They slow down as they approach the Old Harbor.

"It was just down here." That's Fi, talking to Kate. They're on the shore road, on the far side of the broken fence and the trees, barely twenty steps away.

"Who is it?" Kate shouts. "Don't be silly. We just want to know what you're doing. No one wants any trouble." The torchlight swings into the trees. It's too feeble to reach through them to the quay but it almost makes Rory's heart stop. This is the worst thing that's ever happened. He doesn't care what he has to deal with for the whole rest of his life if only this could somehow not be happening, if he could be back in bed where he's supposed to be—

He's got the bike. His hands are on the bike.

"Was it on the quay?" Fi says. "I thought it was here somewhere."

"Please!" Kate shouts. "Just talk to us!"

Rory hears Fi's snort. "I don't think they want to be friendly," she mutters.

"Let's check the quay," Kate says. Their torch swings away from the trees and picks out the overgrown ruins. This is it. They're going to come out by the water and they'll see him. He's done for, unless someone does something.

The heap of driftwood Oochellino used to build his trestle is right by his hand. He grabs a loose stick, stands up, reaches back, and hurls it as far as he can in the direction of the abandoned houses. There's an instant of terrible silent suspense and then—

"Who's there?"

The stick has thunked against something, roof or wall or window. It rolls down, clattering, and goes still.

The torch has swung away in that direction. Carefully, infinitely carefully—if he knocks the bike it's game over—Rory gets hold of another stick.

"Hello?"

"In the houses somewhere," Fi mutters quietly. Rory lobs the second stick, as far as he can. It thuds, quieter than the first, but hard enough.

"We can hear you!" Kate shouts. "We saw your light!"

They're moving that way. They're not coming out onto the quay anymore.

"Careful," Fi says.

Rory finds a couple of small stones. He flings them in a handful. *Rat-a-tat*: they patter against slate or stone.

"Please don't try and hide!" Kate says. They're both definitely moving away, down the road, towards the sounds. "It's dangerous in there!"

Now, Rory thinks. Now. He's got the bike. He just has to get out onto the road and he'll be away, they'll never catch him.

He sees it all at once. It's as if someone's reached up into the sky and switched on a light. He sees where everyone is, Oochellino hiding in the tree, the other Italians in their boat listening to the unexpected people onshore, Kate and Fi pressing together wondering who's sneaking around in the dark. In a flash he sees what to do.

He reaches a sweaty fist into his pocket, pulls out the night-light and switches it on. There's a big chunk of slate near his foot. For good measure he lobs that into the darkness as well. It comes down with a sharp splintering crash. Kate and Fi gasp: they're already farther away down the road, perhaps sweeping the torch into the nettles and bindweed between the houses. He's got to be quick now, quick quick. He puts the night-light down at the very edge of the quay, over the beach, right in front of the bike. There. It's nothing like as bright as the bike light but it's better than nothing. Now.

He picks up the bike. The driftwood rattles.

He can't hesitate.

He carries the bike to the back of the quay and faces the alley by the ruined fence. He's about to make a terrible racket but he has no choice at all now.

He can't ride through the mess in the alley. He gulps and blunders in.

The crashing and crunching around his feet burns his ears. He hears Kate and Fi stop. One of them says something to the other. He pushes on.

"Back that way."

"Who's that? Stop!"

"They've got a bike!"

He doesn't know how but he's out on the road. His hands are shaking. He almost tips over in his hurry to mount the bike but he's on. He kicks for the pedals desperately. The feeble torch is swinging in his direction but they're too far off. He's moving, he's done it. The headlight grinds awake. "Wait!" Kate shouts. "Please wait!" Like she forgot to be polite. He stamps down hard and points the bike up the Lane. He's away. He risks a glance over his shoulder. They're chasing, Fi and Kate, running away from the Old Harbor. He's got to keep them moving that way so the Italians can land. He's having brainwaves again, he can feel everything go sort of slowly, as though he knows what's happening before it happens. He eases off a bit, letting them think they might be able to catch up. Kate's shouting things about being sensible and only wanting to talk and no one being in trouble. She sounds badly out of breath. Maybe if he pretends to fall off? He dismounts and drops the bike in the road: it goes dark. The chasing torch waggles eagerly. He lets it come closer and then when they're close to the church he hops on again and speeds away, quickly at first, then struggling as he gets to the steep towards the crest of the lane. He lets them close in again while it's uphill, and then at the last moment he's away racing down the other side of the island towards the Pub, the light white as fresh paint in front of him, the air clean and cold, glory in his heart. He dismounts just before the bottom of the slope and throws the bike over the hedge into the mass of bramble beyond, then squeezes himself down into the niche under the ivy at the corner of the Pub. He holds his breath and curls tight as Fi and Kate come gasping by. He lets them go past him, down to the road by the Beach. They stand there, mumbling as they try to catch their breath, and he slips out as quiet as anything and tiptoes back up the Lane. It's dark but it doesn't matter, there's a trace of hidden moonlight in the clouds and this is his territory now, he could walk the length of the Lane with his eyes shut. No one's coming after him. Why would they? He's invisible in the night, and as far as Kate and Fi know the traitor on the bike has raced away in completely the other direction. He feels his way to the door of Parson's and lets himself in.

It's so still inside. It's like nothing at all has just happened. His mother's snoring. He peels off his shoes and warm clothes, one by one, putting them back exactly where they came from. He creeps up the stairs and slides himself into bed, marveling at himself and at the sheer wonder of the world. A while later, lying with eyes wide open, he hears Kate and Fi come down the road outside his window, talking softly. He's still flushed and sweaty and his hands must be filthy and if they come in to wake them up it'll be obvious he's been outside, but they don't. He hears what Kate says. She's got a strong voice even when she's murmuring. "We'll never find anything in the dark anyway," she says. "Leave it till morning. Let poor Rory sleep."

10

Wakey wakey."

He blinks. Daylight's come out of nowhere. He's missed something.

"Come on, sweetheart. Up you get."

His mother's sitting by his feet. There's a sound of rain against the window.

"This isn't like you. You're usually my alarm clock." She jiggles his shoulders.

He's overslept. He's facing away from her. His eyes open wide as he thinks of how filthy he must be under the blankets.

"I've put a bit of warm water in the sink." She bends over and kisses his cheek. "All right?"

He has to pretend everything's normal. He makes himself stretch and yawn, though he keeps his hands hidden. "All right, Mum."

"That's better. I let you sleep in a bit." She stands up. "It's going to be a bit of a big day."

"Is it?"

"We're all going over to Briar to say good-bye to Oliver. Remember? And there's something else we have to have a little chat about. Come on then, get yourself going. I'll start some eggs. We can have them with a bit of milk."

"Nice," he says, though he's hardly listening. It's gradually coming back to him just how far from normal everything else is. He almost can't believe his mother doesn't know. Talking about breakfast, as if it's just another day.

She goes downstairs, which allows him to bring his hands out and inspect them. They're pretty bad, but if there's water in the sink that's OK, he can clean off before she sees anything. The rain's that kind of wind-driven spitting drizzle that plays intermittent bursts of percussion on the glass. *Tappitytaptap,* it goes, answering a gust. *Taptaptaptaptap.* He turns to the window idly.

There's a face outside.

Tap tap tap. It's Oochellino. He's pressed up against the smeared glass, tapping. The rest of him is sort of folded up underneath, sideways. He's balancing on the window ledge, high off the ground.

This is insane. His mother's right downstairs. How can she not notice a man clinging to the side of the house? How can Oochellino even be clinging there at all? The ledge isn't much wider than Rory's arm.

Oochellino jiggles the window and points upwards. *Open it.*

Eggs crack downstairs.

Stunned into obedience, Rory pushes the catch and slides the bottom half of the window up. His room fills with the sounds and smell of a wet, blowy morning. Some incomprehensible arrangement of cramped limbs is keeping Oochellino upright and attached to the ledge. His feet are bare, and the toes are curling over the slate almost like fingers. A hand appears and passes something through the window.

It's the night-light.

"What's going on up there?"

"Nothing!"

"Did you just open the window?"

"Yeah."

"It's pouring out there!"

The hand waggles the night-light. Rory takes it.

"Good boy," Oochellino whispers. "Verrrry good."

"What on earth are you . . ." Her footsteps come to the bottom of the staircase. "Shut it, for goodness's sake!"

"Sorry!" He's gone to block the door, panicking that she's going to come up and see. When he turns back Oochellino is gone.

There was no sound at all. No thump of someone dropping to the ground, no rustle of clothes. (He's got a different coat and trousers from somewhere. He was wearing something dark and waterproof, not Ol's stuff.)

After another moment of paralyzed astonishment, Rory closes the window.

"What did you do that for?"

"Sorry. It felt a bit smelly in here."

"Go on, get yourself dressed. Hurry up."

"OK. Sorry."

He hears her go back to the kitchen. He wipes spits of rain off his hands.

A moment later he hears her say to herself, "Where's that night-light gone?"

He checks the kitchen surreptitiously while he eats. He's put the night-light back (he took it to go out for a pee in the night, he says). Everything else is where it's supposed to be, the clothes, the shoes. His hands are scrubbed and he's splashed the dried sweat out of his hair. The only thing he won't be able to replace as if nothing happened is the bicycle, but he can't see why that's a problem; they already know someone stole a bicycle, it doesn't have to be back where it used to be. So when Kate arrives he's calm, he's safe, he carries on with breakfast while she shakes out her umbrella and unwraps her scarf. He's eating scrambled eggs with a fork, separating them into tiny lumps and chewing them morsel by morsel.

Kate's come to tell his mother what happened in the night. He keeps his eyes down and concentrates on chewing, the way he's supposed to.

"Is there any damage?" his mother asks.

"We've locked everything we can think of. Fi thinks there's some stuff missing from the Stash. As far as I can see nothing else has been touched."

"Why would they do this?"

"Who?"

"Isn't it . . ." His mother sounds peculiarly halfhearted, as though she doesn't care as much as she feels she ought to care. "I thought it's those people from Mary's?"

"I don't think it is," Kate says as Rory concentrates on spearing another lump. "It didn't feel like that. It felt like it was one person. Very frightened. Fi thinks the same. I think it must be something to do with that fishing boat."

"You're probably right."

Rory chews. No one's looking at him. To stop himself going red he concentrates on the taste in his mouth.

"I think it must have been an outsider. Why wouldn't she show herself otherwise? No one's got anything to hide, and it's not like Fi and me are so fearsome. But if she's maybe come from the Continent, something like that . . ."

"Mm," his mother agrees, vaguely. "Well. Whoever she is, she'll have to show her face eventually."

"Connie," Kate says, and Rory knows at once that this is what she's actually come to say. She's put on her calm voice, the one that makes other people stop and do what she tells them. "I'm asking you to reconsider."

Rory looks up, surprised. His mother's being told off.

"Not now," she says.

"Until we're sure of the situation. Surely it would be better to wait until spring anyway. Rory's not eleven for a while, he can't possibly—"

"I haven't talked to him about it yet."

Rory's looking back and forth between them. His mother looks ashamed. Kate looks surprised, and disappointed. "Oh," she says.

Now they're both looking at him.

"What," he says.

Kate stands up slowly. "I'm sorry," she says. She doesn't sound sorry at all. "I'd have thought you would have by now."

"Well," his mother says, sounding bizarrely like Pink when she's being told off, "I haven't. We were going to talk this morning."

"Perhaps I'd better leave you two alone then." Kate picks up her umbrella. "But please, Connie. Think about waiting for a few months. It's winter soon, and you're such a help, both of you."

"Do you think I haven't thought about it?"

Rory's never heard anyone snap at Kate like that. Shocked, he waits to see what the punishment will be. Kate just opens the door.

"Sorry," his mother says.

"Just give it some time," she says. "Come along to the Abbey whenever you're ready."

"Of course."

And out she goes, leaving Rory and his mother staring at each other across the table.

"There's something I have to tell you," she says.

He can't say anything. Before Kate came in the only thing he was worrying about was keeping his secret stuffed so far down inside himself it wouldn't show. Now he's not thinking about that at all.

"Put your fork down, please," she says.

He puts his fork down.

"We. Um." She pushes her hair back and takes a deep breath.

"What," he says.

She reaches across the table and takes one of his hands in hers. She feels cold.

"We can't stay here, Rory," she says.

"In Parson's?"

"I'm not talking about Parson's. We can't stay here. On this island, these islands. We're going to go away."

He stares, waiting for her to say something that makes sense. The whole room, himself included, seems to have turned to stone. He feels numb. Time isn't passing. The air's gone solid.

"I know," his mother says, in an attempt at a gentle voice. "It's a big change for you."

He doesn't say anything. This isn't a conversation anymore. It's an execution.

"We'll find a better place." She squeezes his hand. "I know we will. I promise. All right?" She smiles, weakly, nervously.

His hand doesn't feel like it belongs to him.

"What do you think?"

What he's thinking is *No*.

"No," he says.

The smile vanishes. "Rory."

"I'm not going."

She's making an effort not to lose her temper. "It's all decided, Rory."

"You can't."

She looks down. "We have to."

"No we don't. Why? Why do we have to?"

"Because They'll kill you." The gentleness has gone the way of the smile. She's getting louder. "They will. Is that what you want, to wait till that happens? Because I don't. I'm not going to."

"Yeah? Well I'm not going."

"Rory—"

"I don't want to!" He tears his hand away and pushes back his chair so hard it falls over. The noise makes the air ring. It unlocks the room. Time starts beating again, painfully fast. He can feel it in his chest.

"Sit down. I said sit down! And pick up your chair!" She shouts the last bit so loudly he flinches. He crumples onto the floor and holds his head in his hands.

After a little bit she crouches next to him.

"It's not far to the Mainland," she says. "We'll wait for a clear day and we can get all the way there in just one day. And when we get there—"

"You can't get there! No one can! We'll die!"

His mother doesn't answer. She takes a few slow breaths and goes on as if he hasn't said anything. "You probably don't remember, but the Mainland's big. Really big. You can't even guess. There'll be all sorts of things there we don't have. They've probably got telly and computers. That'd be good, wouldn't it? You'll like that. We might even find Dad and—"

"They're dead!" The sea is death. He's always been terrified of sailing. Hundreds of times he's imagined his father and brother and sister drowning, flailing around in freezing heaving grey, nothing to see, nothing to hold on to, then sinking, nothing to breathe.

"We don't know—"

"They are! They're all dead!"

"Rory." She hugs his shoulders. He's too riven with horror even to twist away. "All right. I don't know what we'll find. But we can't stay. I've made up my mind. I'm getting you away from these islands, no matter what."

"But there isn't anywhere—"

"No. Matter. What."

She wants to take him off the edge of the world. She wants to tear him out of existence, away from everything there is, gathering and foraging and reaping and baking and fetching and carrying and eating and sleeping. And from the wonderful things too, the comics, the Italians, Her. The whole of his life. The sea is its boundary. The sea is where life runs out. She's going to kill them both.

"We'll have a few days," his mother's saying. "We'll get everything we need ready and wait for a nice calm bright day. I know it's a bit of a shock but you'll get used to it. And Rory. Look at me, please."

He can't. He won't.

She sighs. "All right, then. But listen very carefully. We're going to do this. I'm not letting Kate or anyone say otherwise. It's very important you understand that. I'm sure Kate's going to have all sorts of terribly good reasons why we shouldn't, but I don't want you listening to her. They're all just thinking of themselves. They don't—"

He's lurching to his feet before he knows what he's doing. He springs up so fast he tips her over; she drops to the floor in a tangle, with a little gasp. He's bellowing, running for the door. "If it wasn't for Kate we'd all be dead!" He kicks his shoes on and pulls his coat off the hook. The other coats all fall down with it. His eyes are stinging. "I won't go anywhere with you! I won't go anywhere!" He flings the door open.

"Rory, stop right there."

"I won't!" He's out, sprinting up the Lane. He has no idea where he's going. He's driven by rage and grief and they're equally blind.

"Come back here at once!" She's yelling from the door. "Rory!" He won't stop. He won't let her take him away. He'd rather stay here until She takes his hand and leads him down under the waves to show him all her treasures. He runs out of his mother's sight as fast as he can. He never wants to see her ever again.

* * *

There aren't many places to run to. It's a small island.

He ends up in the Castle ruins, squatting out of the wind with his back against a wall. Fast clouds race low overhead, taunting him with freedom. He's out of breath and his chest hurts. He couldn't run much farther anyway, there isn't much island left beyond. He'd love to go down to the cove and wait for Her but he can't, his mother's bound to be following him. He heard her calling furiously as he ran. *Rory! Rory!*

Anyway his legs are tired and he's hot and shaky and his heart's broken. He just wants to sit on wet earth and stone.

He knows his mother's lying about finding somewhere with telly and computer games. That's just trying to make him want to go. He knows it's a lie because the women used to talk about it all the time, that first summer. No one actually knows What Happened but everyone knows it was terrible on the Mainland. *We're the lucky ones,* Kate used to tell them, even in the winter when they were all desperately hungry and getting sick. And however bad it is on the Mainland, the sea is worse.

He squeezes his head between his knees and folds his arms over them to make everything go away.

After a while he hears his mother coming. There are steps coming up the path, scratching against the stiff heather. He wraps himself tighter into his ball and stares balefully at mud.

The steps come around the roofless walls into the ruin. They stop. She doesn't say anything. He doesn't care what she says or does, he's not going to look up or talk to her.

They stop for a surprisingly long time. Then she comes and stands right in front of him. He grips his sleeves and presses his knees harder against his head.

"Hello."

He jerks his head up as if he's been kicked.

Someone else is standing there.

She's got her hands stuffed down in the pockets of a navy blue anorak, which makes her shoulders hunch. The hood of the anorak is pulled up. She's wearing scuffed black wellies and crinkly waterproof trousers. She could be any of the women rugged up for working outside, but she's not. The face in the hood is a strange face. It's dark with something more than just the shadows inside the hood, but its eyes are clear and sharp as sea spray.

An expression of inexplicable wonder fills those eyes for a moment, and she murmurs something to herself in a foreign tongue.

"Who are you?" Rory says, because someone's got to say something. The woman goes on staring at him as if he's the most amazing thing in the world, not the other way around. He gets it. He gets where she must have come from. She probably doesn't speak English. "Italian?" he says.

The wonder blinks away.

"I don't have a country," she says, in English, though the sounds are slightly wrong: *cahnntry*. She's a foreigner. "My name is Silvia. Do you remember me?"

"What?"

"Silvia," she repeats. She pushes back the hood. Her hair's greasy and completely black and her skin's the color of the autumn heath. She's young, not an old woman but young like Kate. She says it again, as if reminding him of something: "Silvia. No?"

He's too baffled to answer. She smiles. Her teeth are yellowed but they look bright in her dark face.

"What's your name, my friend?"

"Rory," he says.

"Rory." In her mouth both *r*s have a tiny musical up-and-down roll. "Of course. Rory."

"It's Scottish."

She makes her eyebrows arch. Her face is quick and lively. "Ah. Well, then. Thank you, Rory."

"For what?"

"For your light. So we could row to land. Lino says you were very brave, very clever."

"Lino?" Saying it makes him understand: Oochellino. She's his friend.

"Little bird," Silvia says. "You know that's what it means?"

If it wasn't for the ache in his heart he'd think he was dreaming. He's trying to remember that he just ran away from his mother and is waiting for her to catch him up and yell at him. It doesn't connect. It's like the strange young woman has stepped out of thin air.

"*Uccello* in Italian is 'bird.' So, *Uccellino,* that's, like, 'little bird.'"

"Oh," he says. "OK."

She hasn't taken her eyes off him. She's very still. Everyone he knows in the world always stands slightly bowed, aware of the world's weight. Not this woman.

She tilts her head a fraction. "You were running here," she says. "You look angry."

"I wasn't."

"You are like this." She hunches her shoulders up and makes a tight-lipped sulky face. "Something's wrong, I think."

"I'm all right."

"Really?" Her eyebrows bob again. "OK then."

Across the heath comes a wind-muffled shout: *Rory?*

It's his mother. He's not dreaming. He crouches tighter against the wall even though he's perfectly well hidden. "That's my mum," he says.

Silvia's taller than the ruined wall. She doesn't duck. She doesn't even look away, or show any surprise or alarm at all.

"Near the beach where we land," she says, "there are many buildings together. Brown. With all the broken windows."

"You mean the Hotel?"

She snaps her fingers. "A hotel, of course. Do you know, inside the biggest building, there are stairs down?"

Rory? Rory!

"Yeah," he says hurriedly. He's not sure he knows anything at all at the moment but if she doesn't stop talking to him soon and go away his mother's going to find the two of them.

"Down there is a room. That's where we are."

"Who?"

"Me and Lino and Per."

"Who's Pear?"

"Our other friend."

"Why's he called Pear?"

"Hmm?"

"Like a fruit."

She takes a moment to get it. "No, no. Pee Ee Are. Per." She smiles again. "He doesn't talk so much. I'd like you to meet us. Can you come there? By yourself?"

"You're like a gang?"

She makes a face like laughing, though without the sound. "That's good. A gang. The four of us."

"There's another one?"

"Of course." She juts her chin at him. "You."

Rory!

"My mother's coming," he says.

At last she crouches down and hides herself. She crouches very close to him. She smells of somewhere else, beyond the world. Her cheeks have little scars and scratches. Close up she feels magnetic, as if he couldn't move away unless she let him.

"You should go out," she says quietly, without any hurry. "Or your mother comes here and sees me. That would be difficult."

"What are you doing here?"

"We talk about it when you come."

He shuffles across to the empty window cut in the wall and peeks out. His mother's just come over the horizon. She's calling in different directions, spinning and staggering as if she can't hold her course in the wind.

"Now you should go," Silvia says, gesturing out of the Castle with a roll of her eyes. Her eyes are what make her look so strange and young and magnetic. They're pale and faintly green, too light for the rest of her. Rory can't help staring.

"How come you speak English?" he says. "You're not from here."

She looks away for the first time. "I had a good teacher," she says. "Go now."

"Rory!" His mother's quite close now. "Are you hiding in there?"

He takes a deep breath.

"See you later," Silvia says very quietly.

He stands up.

* * *

Everyone's unhappy. The whole island's gone wrong, it's not just him. People have whispered conversations which stop when they see someone else coming. No one seems to want to talk to him and his mother at all. Kate and Fi and Missus Shark and Ali have gone off to search the island. The rest of them all look thin and weak and old, even Laurel and Pink. Leaning over the grindstone, carefully dribbling grains into the hole in the middle while his mother and Viola take turns spinning the heavy wheel, Rory suddenly feels the sheer desperate hopelessness of the work. It's such a feeble trickle of flour oozing out from the grooves, even though the stone goes round and round and the women grimace and rub their arms. How could he ever have thought these were all the people in the world?

At lunchtime Laurel plonks herself down on the garden wall next to him while he's eating his fish. The sailing boat his mother went and got from Maries is still anchored off the south end of the island. They stare that way together.

"So where are you going to go?" Laurel asks.

"Dunno."

Laurel heard everything that happened. There was lots of arguing at the Meeting, she said, especially when his mother asked for enough fuel to cross over to the Mainland. Diesel's about the most precious stuff they have. They've been all over every room and every cellar and cupboard of every abandoned house and barn and shed all across Home, collecting every drop of diesel from every tank and drum they could find, hoarding it, saving it for life-and-death emergencies and for tasks they can't muster strength for even when they push themselves to the edge of collapse. The four-wheel-drive ATV is the difference between survival and extinction because they haven't yet found any other way to pull a plow. They push the ATV to and from the fields and barely touch its throttle on the downhill passes but even so everyone knows that one year it will drink the last of the fuel. Rory doesn't know how much closer his mother's request will have brought that year. A lot closer. She's asked the people of Home to sacrifice their future so that two of their number can abandon them. Laurel doesn't have to spell any of this out.

"I heard people on the Mainland eat each other," she says.

He wants to tell her to shut up but he doesn't have the heart for it. His fish tastes of nothing. The whole world feels flat, like it's already been taken away. The only things in the world with any life, any weight, are Silvia and Oochellino and Her, and they feel like people in the comics, so brilliant and beautiful they don't touch anything else.

"Are you still coming to say good-bye to Ol?"

"Suppose."

Fi and Missus Shark come back from their search. They haven't found anything. He overhears them talking about the Hotel. They've searched it but they haven't found the Italians. He can imagine Silvia and Oochellino pulling their anoraks around them and saying magic words and making themselves disappear. People don't go to the Hotel. It was ruined very early on, when everyone started fighting over vanishing supplies. Something bad happened there. Esme says it's an evil place. Ol dared Rory to explore it once but even if he hadn't been terrified he wouldn't have been able to get very far into its wilderness of rampant nettles and smashed gutters, and that was last winter before things got even more overgrown.

He'll find a way, though. He's finished with his mother and all the weary old women. He's going to go and join the Italians.

Kate and Ali come back. They haven't found anything either. They discuss who's going to row out to the wreck. Rory almost smiles to himself, because he knows they won't find anything there either. The gang are safely ashore, thanks to him.

"Laurel, can I chat with Rory for a minute?"

It's Kate. He didn't see her approaching. Laurel slides off the wall without a word and goes inside to wash her hands.

"Hi," Rory says.

"Rory." Kate settles beside him. No one else is in earshot but Doreen, who's taking her turn looking after the fire, and she's deaf as a post. "What's going on?"

Rory feels his cheeks go scarlet.

Kate leans close. "I understand you might not want your mum to know. This is just us talking now."

He clamps his jaw tight and stares at his feet.

"More food's gone missing," she says. "Fi's quite certain. And I went and had a look around Parson's just now. Just me, Ali wasn't there. I noticed one of your coats smelling of apples. I had a look in the pockets and found this." She unfolds a hand and shows him the matchbook from the Pub. She tucks it away again immediately, like a secret.

She stares at him for so long he has to say something.

"I dunno how that got there."

Kate looks away. "All right," she says, wearily. "I just want you to know that I know something's up, that's all. And I think you'll feel better if you talk about it. No one else will have to hear about it."

"There's nothing," he mumbles.

"Because any day now you might be—" Her voice catches. She says the last word in a sort of hiccup. "Gone." He looks up and is horrified to see her eyes turning wet. She leans in again quickly and gives him a fierce hug, stinking of sweat and dirty clothes, and then hurries away.

Laurel passes her on her way back.

"What was all that about?" she says.

"Nothing."

It takes much longer than usual to get all the jobs done because they're having to think about locking up behind themselves. Nevertheless, it's been agreed that this is the afternoon when they're going to gather together and cross the Channel to the church on Briar to say good-bye to Ol, whatever that means, and once it's been agreed everyone has to stick to the plan.

No one wants to. It's obvious. The bad feeling hasn't gotten any better as the day's gone on.

"We ought to put it off," Viola says, but she's muttering to herself. They have to do it for Molly. No one wants to be the one to tell her that Ol doesn't matter anymore.

So once everything that needs doing has been done they all gather on the Beach, hauling dinghies down from the sheds, some on trailers, some dragged across the sand. The tide's below halfway and falling. The wind's beginning to ease. Rory's been watching the wind all afternoon, hoping it'll blow harder and harder, all winter long, forever in fact, but the chop in the Channel is already softening to ripples. It's just the evening calm, he tells himself; it'll blow back up by morning. But what if it doesn't? What if the very next sunrise comes clear and still, and by this time tomorrow, the very next afternoon, he's gone, gone from Home and everyone he knows, gone from Her with her beautiful arms and her voice like water humming, gone from the miraculous superheroes who want him to be in their gang? What if by this time tomorrow he's dead? No one survives the sea. His mother must have gone mad. He can't look at anyone. People try to chat with him and he can't answer. The dread of what might come has sucked his insides away. His mother tries to hug him while they're standing on the beach waiting for the older women to get into the dinghies. He twists away from her arms.

"Rory!" she snaps, angry and embarrassed.

"Let him be for a bit, Connie," Viola says.

Every other conversation stops.

They all clamber in eventually and get themselves launched. It takes five boats to carry them all. Rory's in the biggest one with Laurel and Pink and Viola and his mother. The two women sit side by side with an oar each. They push out past the Harbor wall, around the rusting wreck of the ferry with its wide skirt of trailing seaweed, into the Channel. The sky's still a jumble of speeding clouds, though there's a flare of western light between them and the brow of Briar, touching the overgrown hill with gold. He's sitting in the stern with Pink, opposite his mother.

"Listen to me," she says in an angry half-whisper, rocking backwards and forwards with the oar. "This afternoon is about Molly. We're doing this for her. So I want you to stop sulking and—"

"Oh!" It's a shriek from the first boat. It's Missus Grouse. She's pushing herself up unsteadily from the bow, pointing. Everyone turns to look.

"Oh my God," Viola whispers.

Every oar's hanging motionless, dripping, and every head is equally motionless.

There's a conical spur of broken rock down the Channel. At low tide it's attached to the beach outside the Club, part of Home. The rest of the time, like now, it's a tiny black island of its own, with a fringe of barnacles and unkempt grass and a barren top.

On that top a naked girl's sitting. She's silver-white, her long tangled hair the colorless blond of stubble or bone.

It's Her.

Missus Grouse's cry echoes away in the horrified silence. Then Rory's mother leaps up. The oar crashes out of her grip and the dinghy yaws. "Don't look!" she shouts at Rory, and throws herself on top of him, almost knocking him overboard. "Don't look!" He's being squashed under her. He's suffocating. He hears Missus Grouse shout "Get away, you horrible thing!" and then everyone's shouting at once. He squirms and shoves and finally manages to push his mother off. She scrabbles at his shoulders, trying to force him down into the bottom of the boat, but before she gets hold again he manages another glimpse of Her, watching them from her perch, her legs folded under her, the afternoon light making her shine. Molly begins to howl. Kate's bellowing instructions to all the boats: "Keep going! Ignore it! Keep rowing!" Rory's mother grabs his head and jams his face into her shoulder, gripping him tight. He pushes and struggles but she won't let go.

"Connie," Viola says, "it's all right. Careful with him."

"Shut up!" his mother shouts.

"Shall I row, Auntie Vee?" says Laurel.

"Connie, you'll suffocate—"

He manages to yank his head away to get a breath. She whacks his ear painfully as she tries to get hold of him again. He curls himself up on the bench and yells "Leave me alone leave me alone leave me alone" at the top of his voice. It echoes between the islands.

"Keep on." Kate's voice is clear across the water. "Don't give it the satisfaction. Don't even look at it."

It, he thinks. A savage rage is curled up in his chest. *It.* He's thinking of how She slips featherlight from the sea and lies on the rocks with her hair slowly drying out and tells him stories about the big house she used to live in and the books she used to read (he loves imagining houses and books under the sea). And now Kate's calling her *it* like she's a thing, a fish, and they're falling over and screaming at each other because they're frightened of her even looking at them.

"What was They doing watching us, Mum?" Pink's like a frightened baby.

"Just ignore it," Viola says. "It can't hurt us. It's all right, it's gone now."

"No one's ever seen Them in the Channel before, have they?" his mother says.

"I don't know why you care," Viola says.

Rory listens to himself breathing. No one tries to touch him. Eventually the boat scrunches against sand.

"All right, Rory love?" his mother says, cautiously. He stays curled up.

"Let me," Viola says.

"He's my son, thank you very much."

"For God's sake, Connie. I'll bring him along soon, I promise."

He listens while they all stumble out of the boats, all the old women. Some of them are talking about him. The voices ebb away across the beach eventually, though he's aware of Viola sitting beside him. She rubs his back from time to time.

"I'm so sorry," she says, when everything else is quiet.

He has no idea what she means but it's better than everyone shouting at each other, and her hand feels nice on his back.

"Why don't we go up," she says. "You were Ol's best friend. He'd have wanted you there."

"I don't care about Ol."

Her hand hesitates only for a moment.

"Do you remember Hugo?" she says after a while.

Hugo was Laurel and Pink's brother, the middle one. He's dead, of course. Lots of people whose names he remembers are dead, so many that it's not really even like remembering, any more than you'd remember the slice of a loaf you've just eaten or the piece of wood that just burned in the fire.

"I think about him every single day," Viola says. "Things he said. His little face."

He tells himself he doesn't care.

"I'm not whining about it. You lost your father, and Scarlet and Jake. It's the same for all of us. We can't spend all our time grieving, I know that, but sometimes we have to remember. It's not for them, it's for us, you see. They're at peace now; they're all right. It's for Molly. That's why we're doing this, to help her feel not so alone." She bends over him. Her hair tickles. "Can you do that, Rory? For Molly? And for all of us? Just for this one afternoon?"

He lifts his head. The light makes him blink. He looks back down the Channel but She's not there anymore.

"There you go," Viola says. "You'll be all right now. Come on."

He lets her take him up to the church. It's tiny, much smaller than the one on Home, but you can still use it for things like this because it's OK inside, though it's almost swamped now by the jungly growth spilling out of the hedges behind it. Even in The Old Days hardly anyone lived on Briar. They didn't go wild and smash everything up after What Happened, they just upped and left quietly, going off to be drowned, like he's going to be whenever his mother thinks they're ready. In the church windows are pictures made of colored glass, flowers and waves and puffins, and words from some kind of poem: THEY TOIL NOT NEITHER DO THEY SPIN. Rory has to sit on the high-backed benches next to his mother. She tries to hold his hand but he snatches it away and stuffs both in his pockets. She bends and hisses in his ear. "Stop. Sulking." Missus Anderson turns round from the bench in front and glares.

Kate stands up at the front of the church and starts talking. Molly begins sobbing almost straightaway. Rory doesn't pay attention to what Kate's saying. She talks about being sad. They're all so miserable, all the women, so miserable and hopeless, but they're wrong. They live surrounded by wonders; they have no idea. He spoke to Silvia only for a little bit but whoever she is he knows she'd never be like this, sniveling and talking rubbish about how Ol's constant good humor was a beacon in the dark days. Kate's not saying anything about Ol being a bully who made jokes about everyone behind their back.

Other people get up and talk about Ol. Even Pink. She's red-eyed and mumbly and all she says is "You were my best mate, Ol, and I really really miss you!" before bursting into tears and sitting down. Molly gives her a feeble smile and hugs her.

"Rory?"

Kate's looking at him. Everyone is, in fact.

"Do you want to say something?" Kate asks. His mother kicks his foot.

"Let's not mind about Rory," Esme says peaceably, but his mother kicks his foot again and gives him a sort of nudge. He stands up.

"I don't want to go," he says.

Every face is turned to him. Every face loses its encouraging weepy smile at the same instant. Some wince, some look horrified. Most just look away, anywhere else.

"I want to stay here," he says. "I won't be like Ol. They won't kill me. I know They won't."

His mother's up and dragging him to the door. Viola tries to stop her; she elbows her out of the way. Before she shoves him outside he catches a glimpse of Molly's face. She looks like people in the comics when they're being shot, wide-eyed and grimacing: *aaargh!*

His mother spins him against the outside wall. "How can you be so bloody selfish?" Her breath puffs over him, smelling fishy and rank. "Can't you ever think of anyone except yourself? Stay out here." She jabs her finger into his chest. "Right here. Until we're finished. You can say sorry to Molly afterwards."

Kate puts her head around the church door. "Connie—"

"Leave us alone!" his mother spits. Kate frowns but withdraws inside.

"Right here, do you understand?" She's breathing hard. She's doing that thing where she's shouting but whispering at the same time.

"One step from here before we come out and I swear you'll be in some proper trouble. You hear me? Not one step." She goes back in the church, slamming its door after her. A battalion of small birds scatters out of the wild hedge, startled.

He gulps back the threat of tears. He's tingling all over, like he's on fire. At least he's finally on his own. He can hear the talking start again inside, without him.

On his own.

He looks along the deserted road back to the beach.

He's going to be in the worst trouble he's ever been in, he realizes, but he doesn't care. He may never get another chance. If it's still calm in the morning there may not even be a tomorrow.

Silently for the first few steps, then at a run, he goes down the road to the beach.

He's taken the smallest dinghy, *Rat*. He's halfway across the Channel when he hears the first wild shouts from Briar. He braces himself and rows harder.

Some of them have got in the boats and started across by the time he touches ashore on the Beach. They're all waving at him and shouting. They can't row nearly as fast as he can run, though. He'll be far out of sight before anyone else gets across to Home. He doesn't bother pulling *Rat* up onto the sand, he just jumps out as soon as he can, sprints across the Beach, and then into the Lane and up over the hill.

He's a tiny bit worried about where exactly to go once he reaches the Hotel. He doesn't actually know his way around in there at all. But as he's puffing and panting his way past the Old Harbor towards the vast shattered warren of scarred buildings on the promontory, he rounds a corner and there's Oochellino in the middle of the road, beaming, the evening sun crowning the patchwork of stubble on his scalp.

"Clever boy," he says.

11

ochellino leads Rory over the foreshore rocks to a side door almost lost behind a rusting pile of big metal drums on wheels. Rory can just about hear people shouting in the far distance. Oochellino completely ignores it. The door says STAFF ONLY. It opens into a place of broken steel machines and dangling black tubes, pipes and taps and spouts, gloomy in the light of a high mold-spotted window which is cracked all over so the glass looks like spiderwebs made of ice. At the back of that room's another door, open. The corridor beyond it is totally dark. Oochellino steers Rory into it. He puts Rory's right hand on the wall and makes him walk along like that, following only a step behind. It's dark as death, as nothing. He could be walking into empty space. Only Oochellino's mutterings and prods keep him moving. They negotiate a corner and go on for what feels like an eternity.

Then Silvia's voice calls out "Lino?"

"*Si. E il ragazzo.*"

And then there's light, a thin rectangle of it around the frame of a closed door ahead. A moment later and it swings open. They must have a fire going inside, though there's no sound. The room beyond glows with a deep shimmering orangey warmth. Silvia's standing in the doorway, the greasy tumble of her hair unhooded, her face in shadow.

Absolutely none of it feels like it's really happening.

His brain tells him they've snuck into a concealed room in the downstairs floor of the main Hotel building, and he's hidden there while his mother and everyone else start running around the island looking for him. His heart tells him he's crawled through lost caverns into some space not of the earth, a tomb of strange gods.

"Welcome," Silvia says. Rory notices how pretty her accent is. It lilts like a dance. When she speaks English she turns it into a different language from the one everyone else in the world uses. She makes Pink sound like a goat. "Come in."

The room beyond her is a low-ceilinged oval. Big fancy armchairs are arranged around glass-topped tables. A complicated chandelier of twisty metal and crystal droplets hangs in the middle. The glass and crystal and metal sparkle and glimmer with reflected firelight. The whole space is swimming with the light, though Rory still can't hear or smell a fire. Silvia steps back from the door to let him past and the mysterious light catches her too. Her eyes glint like an animal's.

"Come and join us," she says. Oochellino says something in Italian, and she smiles.

He gets one step inside the doorway and stops. It's not fear, exactly, or astonishment. He can't get as far as being frightened or astonished. It's more like the whole scene has stopped happening to *him* at all.

There's another man sitting in one of the armchairs. He's enormous. He's wearing heavy shapeless overalls and his hair goes everywhere like a Viking's. He's holding a bulky walking stick between his knees, and the top of the stick is on fire.

Except it's not. There's no heat or sound. There's no fire anywhere in the room. A sort of orange-red smoke is wrapped around the head of the stick, curling and winding. It glows like bright embers.

"Sit." Oochellino's dropped himself into one of the chairs. He's so short he has to tuck his legs underneath himself. There are piles of clothes beside the chairs, and some open canvas duffel bags. The weird glimmer from the big man's stick flickers like the flame of a candle and makes everything appear to be moving: everything except the big man himself, who sits stock-still and stares at Rory.

"This is Per," Silvia says. "And Rory. Per doesn't speak English so much."

"What's that he's got?" Rory says.

"Ah." She sits in a chair next to Oochellino, leans back, stretches her legs out. "You know, Rory, there are many stories in this room. Long stories. Yours too, I think. We don't have time to tell them today. Maybe another day."

He can't take his eyes off the walking stick with its twisting halo of soundless fire. It's not like a walking stick at all. It's too big, even for a huge man like Per. Plus it's carved. There are patterns on it, almost like writing.

"So." Silvia spreads her arms. "Do you think anyone will find us here?"

"Is that magic?" Rory says.

Oochellino makes a *hmm?* sound. "*Magia*," Silvia says, and he nods. Per grunts and, without letting go of the stick, gestures towards an empty armchair.

"It is," Silvia says. "Haven't you seen magic before?"

Rory takes a couple of steps towards it. At once Per barks something rough-sounding.

"He doesn't like anyone to go too close. Sit down, please."

All the chairs are too big for him. He sets himself down nervously, perching on the edge.

"Now," Silvia says. "We must all say thank you." She's the leader of the gang, clearly. "Lino tells me you help him very much when he arrives. And you tell nobody."

"*Si si*. Good boy."

"And then last night you were very clever. We watch you from the boat, me and Per. We don't know what's happening but we see the other people go away, then Lino goes like this again"—she whistles—"and we know it's safe."

"It was easy," he mumbles.

"How old are you, Rory?"

"I'm ten."

"Only ten!"

"Yeah."

"You should be proud of yourself." She sits up smoothly and leans towards him. "So you were born ten years ago," she says. "Look at me. Look at my face. Did you ever see me before?"

This is such a strange question he almost asks her to say it again, thinking she must mean something else, but he doesn't dare.

"No," he says.

"Think carefully," she says. "Maybe imagine a younger girl. A gypsy girl, like me." She pinches her cheeks: *look at my skin,* she means.

"Are you a gypsy?"

Oochellino chuckles. Rory feels himself blushing. Now that he's said it, it sounds rude.

"I told you," she says, "I have no country. The gypsies came from the east a long time ago and we're still traveling."

He thinks she probably means *yes* but he's in no condition to be sure of anything.

"I didn't know there were any real gypsies," he says.

Oochellino hoots with laughter. Rory's embarrassed again, but Silvia doesn't seem to be put out. "You never met a gypsy girl, then," she says. He shakes his head. Silvia sits back as if she's not quite satisfied with his answer. "Let me show you something," she says. She's reaching her hands to her collar. She digs around inside the front of her sweater and pulls out a tiny bag, a pouch, fastened by a cord around her neck. She loosens the top of the bag and takes out some small dark things one by one, one two three four five of them. "Here. Look."

Oochellino mutters something inquisitive. Silvia shushes him and beckons Rory towards her. "You know what these are?" She holds them out in cupped hands.

Rory has to kneel to look properly.

"Acorns," he says. He's a little disappointed. With the atmosphere in the room, the light, the hush, the secrecy, and after the way she offered her hands so carefully, he was expecting something wonderful: gold dust, dragons' teeth. "Aren't they?"

Silvia's watching him intently, as if waiting for a different answer. He doesn't know what else to say.

Per makes a sarcastic-sounding grunt, *hmph.* Rory feels like he's failed some kind of test. He stands up and digs his hands into his pockets.

"I better go," he says. "Everyone's going to be looking for me."

"OK," Silvia says. She tips the acorns back into the pouch at her neck and hides it in her sweater again. "We don't want them to look too much."

"I can try bringing more food if you like."

Oochellino chuckles again and says, "No no no." He hops out of his chair and takes a plastic bag out from behind it. He opens the handles to show Rory. It's packed with things from the cellars. "Lino does this now."

Rory stares in confusion. "How did you . . . ? I thought they locked everything."

"Hmm?"

Silvia translates.

"Ha!" Oochellino pulls something from Ol's pockets, a jingle and flash of metal. "See." It's a bunch of keys. He rattles off something in Italian.

"He says old women are forgetful. They leave things lying around."

"*Si si*. Woman with *aspetto*, like this." Lino pulls a startlingly good impression of Missus Shark's crabby beaky face.

"You stole those from Missus Shark? And then went in the cellars?"

"*Cantine*," Silvia explains to Lino.

"But someone's been there all day."

"No one sees Lino," Silvia says. "It's his gift. He sees everything and no one sees him."

"*Come civetta*," Lino says, and hoots.

"Like an owl."

Rory remembers how he balanced on the window ledge in the rain and then vanished without a sound in the blink of an eye.

"*Ecco*," Lino says, snapping the keys away like a conjuror's trick. "Food, clothings, is OK now."

"But maybe," Silvia says, "you can help us find what we're looking for."

Per leans forward sharply. It's the first time he's moved. Under his massive eyebrows his look is pitch-dark. "*Shh!*" he growls.

"No," Silvia says. "I know it's OK."

"A boy?" Per says. So he can speak after all. He sounds the way you'd imagine a bear might sound. He's foreign too: the word comes out like *beuy*.

"I know this boy," Silvia says. She's half Per's size but she sounds absolutely in charge.

Per slumps back in his seat. "Crazy," he mutters.

"What are you looking for?" Rory says. "I can help. I know everything here. Better than anyone else."

"It's not here," Silvia says. "Not on this island. It's in England."

There's quite a long silence.

"You're trying to get to the Mainland?" Rory says.

"We were caught in a storm."

"You mean . . . You were in a boat?" Of course they were, he knew that already. But it's unthinkable. The sea's cursed; no one survives it. "What about Them?"

Silvia cocks an eyebrow.

"I thought They don't let anyone . . . They kill everyone who goes to sea. All the men."

"*Ahh*," Silvia says. "The *sirene*." Hearing the Italian word, Lino echoes her: *ahhh*. It sounds like Silvia said *sea-rainy*. "Well, Rory, you see. Pear has a gift too."

"Don't say," Per grumbles.

Silvia props her arms on her knees and fixes Rory with her weirdly gripping stare. "We come a long way. Longer than you can imagine, Lino and me. We come to the sea, we find Per and his boat. And his gift. Now we're sailing to England to find the most important thing in the world."

"Don't say. He's a boy." *Hissa beuy* is how it sounds.

"Not just any boy," Silvia says sharply, and though Per must be three times her size Rory gets the feeling he's just been told off.

"What's that?" Rory says. The mystery is indescribable. He can almost feel the black frame of the panel around the scene, the vivid ink light filling the panel, the wide-eyed boy in the superhero's lair.

"The most important thing in the world? It's a ring."

Per snorts angrily. "Crazy!" But Lino, who's been following the conversation as best he can, frowning, nodding, bubbling with contained excitement, now hops onto one of the tables, gesturing happily at the three of them. "*Si si si!* We are 'obbits! Big 'obbit, small 'obbit, lady 'obbit!" He laughs delightedly. "We go to find ring. Ring of biggest power! Biggest *magia*."

The light in the room wavers suddenly, like it's liquid and someone's stirred it. "Stupid talk," Per says. The glow at the end of his stick is contracting, dimming. "They want to go. Take the boy out. Boy!" He makes sure Rory's looking at him, and makes a zipping motion across his closed lips.

"Is good boy," Lino says. "Not say to people."

"I won't tell anyone," Rory says. "I swear I won't."

"I know," Silvia says. "Now you should go."

"Can I come back?"

"I think you will," she says, standing up.

"I don't know how I can help," he says. He doesn't want them to send him back to the open air. He doesn't want this to be over. "I don't know about the Mainland."

"Maybe you know more than you think," Silvia says.

Dread of what's waiting for him outside comes all in a rush. "I don't even know if I'm going to be here for long. My mum wants to take me away. She thinks They're going to kill me if we stay. I might not even be here tomorrow."

Silvia crouches in front of him. She's so close and so intent it's like she's trying to hypnotize him, or searching for a secret hidden in his face. "You know I tell you Lino has a gift, and Per has a gift? I have a gift too. A gypsy gift. Do you know what the gypsies are famous for?"

"Stealing?"

Lino hoots with laughter again, absurdly loud in the dusky stillness of the room. Rory flushes, deeply and instantly ashamed. She just grimaces for a moment.

"Telling fortunes," she says.

"And stealing!" Lino says, in his best careful English. "Clever boy!"

"*Pssh,*" Silvia hisses at him, not angrily. "Telling fortunes. Reading hands, tea leaves. Ball of glass. What do you think, Rory? Do you think Silvia knows the future?"

The best he can answer is, "Dunno."

"I tell you, I have the gypsy gift. I see the road ahead. What I see tells me I think we meet again, you and me." The room's noticeably darker, as if the light from Per's stick is being gradually swallowed by a rising tide. Her eyes are glinting.

"Not long," Per says.

"When are you going to the Mainland?" Rory says. He can feel this whole enchanted scene slipping away, sinking like the light.

"When the time is right," Silvia says. "We don't hurry. We find another boat, we wait for the wind, we go."

"Quick now," Per says.

"*Via via via.*" Lino turns Rory around and marches him into the black corridor.

"Good-bye," Silvia says behind him, but already he's at sea in the dark again, just trying to keep his footing as Lino nudges him along from behind, and he can't answer.

The outside door groans open. It's dazzling outside. He's amazed to see the island, the world he knows. The dazzle fades quickly. It's late afternoon, shady and chilly on this east side of Home. Everything smells of the sea, vivid and wild.

Lino pushes him out, not roughly. "Go to mamma," he says.

If it wasn't for the small man behind him, his odd round head poking around the door, Rory would be telling himself he'd imagined the whole thing.

"She like you," Lino says, grinning.

His mother? What's he talking about? "Who?"

"Who. *Cretino.* Silvia. She like you. I see this." He winks. Rory looks away, heartsick. He doesn't feel like being teased.

"Can you do magic?" he says.

Lino frowns as though he doesn't understand, then shrugs.

"Can you make it windy? Really windy? So it's too rough to sail anywhere?" But Lino's wide eyes are blank. He doesn't care.

"Go to mamma," he says, and pulls the door shut with a bang.

Rory was right. It's the worst trouble he's ever been in.

Ali's the one who finds him, up at the top of the Lane. She takes him back to the Abbey where he gets told off by Missus Grouse while Laurel and Pink go off to get word out to everyone else who's been looking. Kate arrives first and tells him off some more, and goes on telling him off in front of everyone else as they come in. Finally his mother arrives. She's red-faced and red-eyed and breathing like she does when she wakes up from a nightmare. She doesn't say anything at all, just grabs him by the wrist and drags him outside. Some of the others try to stop her. Viola says she and Rory ought to stay over-night at the Abbey and then his mother blows up at Viola so badly that everyone else sort of falls out of the way like it's an explosion, even Kate. So Rory gets hauled back to Parson's and sat down at the table, and that's when the real telling-off begins, complete with shaking and slaps and tears and his mother doing her thing about how she wishes she'd died at the beginning of it all, right after What Happened.

It's somewhere around the middle of the telling-off that Rory gets his unbelievably brilliant idea.

12

ext morning: the last of his childhood, though he doesn't know that yet.

The first thing he does is go to the window and push aside the curtain. The sun's coming up bright in a clear sky but the tops of the hedges are fidgeting and he can hear gusts.

He was awake long into the night. First it was because he was buzzing with choked rage, later because he was praying for wind and rain. The only clouds he can see are worryingly thin and high but at least it's nowhere near calm. One day is all he needs. One morning, if he can just find a way to be left on his own for a bit. He'll have to be on his best behavior. If there's no other way, he can always say he has to go for a poo. His mother won't follow him to the toilet, surely.

He goes downstairs determined to be obedient and helpful. To his surprise his mother's acting normal as well, as if she hadn't spent the previous evening screaming at him and telling him she wished he'd gone off and died instead of Jake and Scarlet.

It soon becomes obvious, though, that today's not going to be a normal day.

The breakfast his mother's making is what gives it away. It's the porridge Libby taught them to make with milk and the half-wild oats. There's a whole saucepan of it on the stove, enough for six. She's standing there stirring large handfuls of dried apples and pear into it, so much sweetness he can smell it while he's still on the stairs.

"Who's that for?"

Her face is full of lines and her eyes are tired but she gives him a determined smile.

"You and me," she says.

"All of it?"

"Every little bit." She must have used the whole tin of milk. They only filled it yesterday.

"Shouldn't we share that with someone?"

"I don't feel like seeing anyone."

"What about the Meeting?"

"Sod the Meeting," she says, stirring. "Sod the lot of them. Come on, I think this is ready."

She's used all the dried apple and all the dried pear. He can see the jar on the counter where they keep it and it's empty. At the end of a particularly long or particularly exhausting day they'd sometimes open that jar, take out one strip, tear it in half, and share the half, enough for two bites each.

He's beginning to feel worried.

"Shouldn't we be Eekonomical?" he says cautiously.

"You know what? I'm tired of economical. I've had enough of it. Don't you think?"

He doesn't know what to think. This isn't at all how he'd imagined the morning going. This isn't how he could imagine any morning going. She's breaking six different Rules at once.

"Eat," she says, spooning it out.

It's good. It's painfully good. It goes on being good after the five or six mouthfuls, which are what meals are supposed to consist of. It gets better, if anything.

"What about . . ." He doesn't quite know how to put it. He has to be on his best behavior, he doesn't want to set her off, but he also wants to know what's going on. "What about everyone else?"

His mother puts her spoon down carefully. "Everyone else," she says, emphasizing the words like Ol would do with a rude joke, "has decided I'm being selfish. Everyone else doesn't think I know what's best for my own family. I don't give a damn about everyone else. Actually."

The sweetness in his mouth turns ashy.

"We're not leaving today," he says, "are we?"

"The sooner the better."

"But." His stomach's turning. "It looks really windy."

"We can manage a bit of rough weather." She smiles at him, and suddenly he sees a sort of skin over her smile, and over her eyes, a glaze, a strange mask. "You're a good little sailor."

For a start, this is nonsense. He's always hated rough sailing. Everyone knows that. Jake and Scarlet were the good little sailors. And Dad. She hates it too, she always has. She and Rory stayed home and watched telly when the others went out for a sail, that's how it worked. But as well as being nonsense there's a terrible threat in it.

"I don't like it when it's rough." He's got to stay calm. Best behavior.

"Rory." She reaches across to pat his hand. She's not getting angry. She's alarmingly calm herself. "There's nothing more to discuss. You and I are finished here."

"But—"

"Eat up now, and we'll go and choose you some clothes."

She leaves the saucepan on the stove, and the dirty spoon and bowls on the table. She doesn't even give anything a quick rinse.

She won't let go of his hand, all the way down the Lane. She acts like it's nice handholding, like she's not pulling him along, but she won't let go.

Gulls ride the breeze silently overhead. When they spread their wings wide they sail east, in the direction of Martin, and the Mainland.

"It's really windy," he says.

She doesn't break her stride. She doesn't look or sound like she's going to lose her temper. She's frighteningly steady. "We're going, Rory," she says in her normal voice. "Try and get used to it. Tomorrow, maybe, or the next day. As soon as I've got everything ready."

A tremor of relief ripples through him. "So not today?

She smiles. "Why? Are you in a hurry?"

"No!"

"Maybe," she says. "We'll see."

"Not today," he says. "Please."

"I don't know," she says, like it's a joke. "It looks like quite a nice day for a trip."

"I bet it'll be calmer tomorrow."

"Oh? Do you?" They come down to the Pub and turn along the back of the Beach. Looking down the Channel, under the rust-colored ferns on the two hills of Sansen, the Gap's crisscrossed with whitecaps, sparkling in brilliant sun. "Little weather forecaster, are you?"

"Look how windy it is in the Gap."

"All right then, how about tomorrow? Shall we agree on tomorrow? Mister weather forecaster?"

He doesn't know what to say. He doesn't think she's listening anyway.

"I'll need today to get loaded up anyway," she says. She's working it out aloud to herself. "I did the fuel yesterday, that was the really tricky bit. The rest's just bits and pieces. I'll bring the boat round to the quay here when the tide's up. That's the easiest way, isn't it? We'll do it like that."

When they get to the Club she turns off and goes down the side road to the row of tall weathered wooden houses overlooking the Channel.

"Are we going to the Stash?"

"Of course," she says.

These houses were built by the Club for posh holidaymakers. They're too cold to live in with their big windows and high ceilings and being right by the water, but they're solid and dry inside, so this is where the Stash is. Kate's been talking about moving it to a place they can lock—the keys to these houses are long lost—but that's a job for later, when they can spare the labor.

All the household things they've salvaged from all over the island are piled up here. Coats, shoes, sheets, towels, cotton bags, blinds, strips of carpet, dishcloths, all kinds of clothes. The bulkier things are downstairs. She picks out a couple of suitcases and hands one to him.

"Let's fill one each," she says.

You don't just go in the Stash and take stuff. That's not how it works. It's unthinkable. "Did they say it's OK?"

"Never mind that," she says. "We've got as much right as anyone."

The clothes are upstairs, in what used to be the main bedroom. The stairs are carpeted, thick with dried dirt but still fascinatingly soft, so Rory and his mother don't make a sound as they go up. The curtains across the big window facing the Channel and Briar are drawn. His mother pulls them back, revealing green streaks of lichen on the glass. Dust dances in the sunlight.

"Right," she says, putting her hands on her hips and examining the neatly sorted piles. "Warm things are what we need. Good boots first. Let's try those ones on you."

"I knew it was you," Fi's voice says. Rory and his mother both flinch.

Fi's leaning in the doorway. Her bare feet made no noise at all. She must have been in one of the little bedrooms at the back. She looks glum.

"Obvious all along, really," she says, folding her arms. They're big strong arms. She's broad-shouldered, built for garden work. She's blocking the doorway.

His mother tries to draw herself up straight but she's been caught red-handed and all three of them know it. "We're taking what we need," she says. "Same as anyone would."

"That's rubbish, Connie, and you know it."

"Oh, so you and Kate own all this now, do you?"

Fi shakes her head. "You know, if you'd only asked, everyone would have been happy to let you have whatever."

His mother looks like she's trying to think of a response before giving up. She turns back to Rory, holding up a pair of brown walking boots. "Try these," she says. "They look about right."

Rory's face is burning. He can't look at Fi, but he can't pretend she's not there either.

"Maybe you could at least try to think about how much you need," Fi says. "I have to say, I thought you'd be finished by now."

"What are you saying?" His mother's sorting through trousers now.

"You know what I'm talking about."

His mother drops the suitcase she's holding abruptly, and for the first time that morning Rory can hear her beginning to crack. "No, Fi, I actually don't know what you're talking about. Actually, I'm a bit tired of being told what I'm thinking. Who made you the island police? Why don't you leave us alone?"

"Well, that's an easy one." Fi's accent gets more Scottish when she gets riled up. "Because someone's got to make sure you don't clean out the whole Stash."

"Two bags!" His mother's gone very shrill. "That's too much to ask, is it?"

"Two bags today," Fi says.

There's a pause. His mother is breathing too fast, too noisily.

"What does that mean?" she says.

"You think no one noticed what's gone missing the last couple of days? Why do you think I slept here overnight?"

Another pause. Rory can't stop himself thinking at once of the piles of clothes in the mysteriously firelit room deep in the ruins of the Hotel. He fumbles at the laces of the boots.

"Are you accusing me of stealing?" his mother says.

"Actually, I'm standing here watching you steal with my own two eyes."

His mother takes a couple of hasty steps towards Fi, who doesn't flinch, of course.

"Rory and I are taking things we might need." She's trembling with weak defiance. "For whatever we'll find. Because we're not going to sit on this godforsaken miserable island until he dies. It's one bag for each of us, and if you and Miss High and Mighty Kate think that's too much you can go and fuck yourselves. For a change, instead of fucking each other."

Rory just wants to run downstairs and away and out into the fresh air where things like this don't happen. He can't though, he's stuck watching it. Some part of him is imagining what it's going to be like tomorrow when his mother finds out she can't leave the island after all. He has an overwhelming suspicion that there'll be no family anymore, he's going to have to go and live in the Abbey, with Kate and Fi and the others who are in the right, who are Eekonomical, who Can Cope.

"So where are the other bags, then?" Fi's just leaning in the doorway, tapping her fingers on her arms. "Already on your boat? Which, by the way, other people gave to you, out of kindness."

"There are no other bags. If other stuff's missing then someone else sto— Someone else took it. Someone else might not be a perfect saint."

"Have you got Asha's keys?"

Asha is Missus Shark's proper name.

"Rory was in the garden when she lost them." Fi's still looking at his mother. "She says she only put them down for a few seconds. And there's food missing too, from the cold stores. Which were locked."

The silence is horribly cold.

"No, of course we bloody don't." His mother comes to stand beside him. She hugs his shoulders. Her hands are trembly. "Of course you're not a thief, Rory," she says, much too loudly. "I can't imagine what sort of person would think—"

"Just," Fi says, very sharply, and with the unmistakable fervor that means she's close to blowing her top. "Just give the keys back before you go. If that's not too much trouble. You could leave them somewhere we'll find them, if you want to go on pretending you don't have them. On the dock, maybe." She turns away. Rory and his mother listen as Fi goes down the stairs and outside. She closes the door quietly behind her.

His mother slumps on the floor and starts crying.

After a little bit Rory sits down and tries on a different pair of boots.

When they're finished they haul the suitcases downstairs and outside. His mother's hardly spoken and Rory doesn't dare say a word, not even to ask where they're going next. Although he knows Fi was wrong to accuse her of stealing the keys and the food and the other clothes—Lino did all that, of course—he also knows that in some more important way Fi was right. Fi and Kate may be irritatingly bossy but he doesn't have to think about it to know that the way they do things is the right way, the proper and just way. He's never seen before what happens when someone smashes the Rules.

"We should have done this months ago," his mother says, as they wheel the suitcases back to the road.

He thinks she's gone properly mad. Everyone knows that every single person who sailed away from the islands has never been heard from again. He's gripped with the abrupt fear that there's a flaw in his brilliant plan somewhere, that it's going to go wrong and she really is going to end up forcing him out to sea to die cold and terrified and helpless. He can't let it happen. He's got to get away from her. Just for a little bit, surely that's all he'll need.

She turns back towards the Beach.

"Where are we going, Mum?"

"We'll leave these on the quay. Or maybe we should take them up to Parson's and lock them in there, that bitch might come back and go through them. No. She wouldn't." She's muttering to herself. He's not sure she really knows he's there. "We'll put them on the quay. Then tools. I'll do the Toolshed next. Keep up!" She's pulling her suitcase faster than he can manage. "We'd better get a move on." They follow the curve of the Beach around to the Harbor quay. The tide's coming up. Already there's water between the wrecked ferry and the end of the quay. Whether it's deep enough yet to bring a sailing boat he's not sure. The boat's down at the south end of the island and you can't sail anything more than a dinghy up the Channel until at least half-tide. There must still be time to figure something out. He just needs to keep an eye—

His mother drops the suitcase on the road with a shriek.

He can never see how She does it. It's as if the sea has a hand, or a wing, something which comes out and unfurls, and when it's finished unfurling it's Her instead of water. There are only little waves in the Channel but one of them rustles against the rust-flaked bow of the ferry and stops being a wave, stands upright, becomes a glistening white girl.

His mother makes a strangled noise, grabs Rory, and shoves him to the side of the road. "No," she whispers, hoarsely, and then—as he tries to keep his balance—"No!" she shrieks. "Don't look!" He did look, for a moment: he thought he saw Her waving to him, unless it was a trick of the sparkling morning light. He's dropped his suitcase too. His mother's pushing him violently back along the quay road. "Oh God," she's saying, "Oh God, oh God." She gets him as far as the back lane, which leads to the north fields. It's almost swallowed between banks of gorse with their sun-yellow flowers, but she shoves him into the opening, out of sight of the water. She's clinging to his wrists. "Oh God. What am I going to do? Think. I've got to think." She looks as if she thinks it's the middle of the night, not a clear autumn morning. Her eyes are hunting around without seeing anything.

"Mum? What's wrong?"

The glaze over her face has hardened.

"Sit down," she says.

He does.

"Let me think. God. Are you all right?" She stares blindly into his face. "Do you feel all right?"

"I'm fine."

"Are you sure?"

"Everything's fine, Mum."

"Let me . . . I know. I've got it." Her hands start ticking things off in the air. "I'll . . . Yes. Bring the boat round. Leave him in Parson's. I can manage. That's it." She pulls him to his feet again. "That's right. No, not that way."

"Mum?"

"Up this way." Holding him by the wrist, she starts scurrying up the back lane.

"What are we doing?"

"We'll take you to Parson's." She rounds on him suddenly. "You've got to stay there!"

His heart leaps. He tries not to let it show.

"You've got to! Just for once, do what you're told!"

"I will," he says. "I swear."

"Draw the curtains. I'll lock the door. It'll be all right."

"'Course it will," he says.

The back lane's badly overgrown but she won't slow down. Whips of bramble spring back from her shoulders as she hurries them along. They come to the top of the ridge and turn aside onto the mud track leading across to the Lane. His mother keeps saying the same things. She's telling him he has to stay in his room and wait for her. He tells her he will but he's not sure she's listening. When they get to the house she goes around closing all the curtains. She pulls their edges too hard, as if she's trying to zip them up.

"Where are you going, Mum?"

"Never mind. You stay here."

"All right."

"Upstairs."

"All right."

"In your room."

"I will."

When she goes out she listens while he locks the door behind her. Then she shouts through the door telling him to head up to his room. Even after he does that he hears her rattling the door to make sure it's really locked. He decides he'd better wait a while before he goes out. He tries reading a comic but it's hard to concentrate, he's turning pages without really looking.

Better to go while he can, he thinks.

He lets himself out a window, listens, then sets off down the Lane to the Hotel.

He's hoping Lino will appear out of the bushes before he gets there, but no. This corner of Home is the same as always this morning, a sad wasteland abandoned to the unstoppable avalanche of weeds. Even in clear sunlight the remnants of the Hotel look creepy, dark with ivy and full of blind alleys. He picks his way onto the rocks above the shoreline, remembering the way Lino led him before. The black boat's still grounded on its shoal. Rory promises himself he'll take a dinghy out to explore it sometime after they're gone. The thought surprises him with melancholy.

He finds the old service door and bangs on it. No one comes straightaway, so he pushes it open and leans into the machine room. "Hello?" he calls. "It's me. Rory. Is someone there?" He cups his hands around his mouth. "I've got an idea!"

Silvia jiggles up and down on her toes, thinking. She and Rory are outside the service door, in the alley between the main Hotel building and one of the blocks of what used to be seaside rooms. The walls are close together but the sun's at just the right angle to flood straight down between them. She turns her face up to it, closing her eyes.

"Wonderful," she says, finally. "It's perfect."

He knew it would be, but he feels a happy glow anyway.

She blinks her eyes open and looks seriously at him. "You see?" she says. "I always know you can help us."

"Yeah," he says, tongue-tied.

"Lino is out watching. I'll tell him when he comes back."

"The only thing is."

"What?"

"It's my mum. She's acting weird today. I think she might try something right away. So maybe you should, you know. Soon."

"I understand." She's communing with the sunlight again. "I don't miss my chance. I never do."

"OK then."

"This boat. Where will it be?"

"At the Harbor. Not this one." The Old Harbor's right by the Hotel, he doesn't want her to get confused. "On the other side."

"Lino will know."

This strikes him as likely.

"We will get ready, then," she says.

It occurs to him that they're saying good-bye, sort of. He feels abruptly shy.

"I better get back," he says.

Silvia ruffles his hair, which makes him even more uncomfortable. "You are a lucky charm for us, I think."

He wonders if this means *thank you.* "That's OK."

"I have a feeling," she says, ducking into the shade so she can look at him without squinting, "we will meet again."

"Yeah?" He's obscurely flattered. Silvia's not at all nice-looking, with her freckly tea-colored skin and her incredibly black and greasy hair, but she's very thrilling in a way he can't explain to himself.

"Maybe after we finish our journey I come back here. Do you think these women would let me join them? It's a good place."

He's astonished. The idea is unimaginable in about ten different ways. "Here?"

She laughs. "You don't think so?"

"There's no . . ." No TV. No computer games. No chocolate, no power, no money. No supplies, no upstairs toilet, no rest from work. And winter's coming. Last winter they all nearly died. Missus Stephenson and Missus Hatchard and Missus Anderson's baby did die. The baby's buried in the Abbey garden.

"You have peace," Silvia says. "And best of all." She leans down to him and speaks in a stage whisper. "No men."

From inside the Hotel comes a rough shout. Per.

Silvia winks at him. "See?" Before he can say anything else at all, even *good-bye,* she's inside the door and gone.

He picks his way back over the rocks, thinking, *Well, that's done.* His brilliant idea has worked perfectly but he's feeling strangely empty.

He wonders whether Silvia really will come back. His life might be completely different by then. He might not be living with his mother. He might have become a proper part of the Commonwelf. This is a word Kate uses sometimes: it means the way they all live together by looking after each other and sharing everything and Coping, instead of freaking out and stealing stuff. It's obvious that he and his mother won't be able to go on like before, not after she swore at Fi. What will happen instead he can't imagine. One thing he knows for sure, though, which is that if Silvia really does come back he'll be here on Home to greet her. At one stroke his brilliant idea has provided her and her gang with the boat they needed and put an end to his mother's plan to take him away. When his mother finds out that the sailing boat's gone, that'll be it. She can't possibly go back to Maries and tell them, *Sorry, I lost that first boat, can I have another one?* And even if she does there's no possible way Kate and the others will let her have another whole can of diesel. And even if they do—he's thinking it all through again, as he scrambles past the Old Harbor and back onto the Lane—it can't possibly get sorted out quickly, and the leaves are turning, the sun's staying lower, there won't be many clear days left and however mad she is she won't dare go to sea in winter. He'll still be here, Home, tomorrow, and the next day, days and days, all winter long, and by spring he'll have figured out a way to explain that he's not like Ol. They're not going to kill him. Perhaps he'll ask Her himself. Why not? He could ask Her to promise that They'll never drown him. He knows She wouldn't, She's his friend. She's not a monster or a villain. She's not mean. She likes talking to him, She always says so. She's—

She.

(He stops in the road.)

She's standing outside Parson's.

There are gulls flying around overhead, the sun's beaming down, and the breeze is blowing, everything's doing what it normally does, and there's a fish-white naked girl standing on the road outside the front door.

"Is this really your house?" she says. Her voice comes from between her lips but also from somewhere else, some other shore where surf is rolling and retreating. "It's so tiny. I never thought you'd live in one of the doll's houses."

He blinks his eyes to make the hallucination disappear. He'd rub them too if it wasn't for the fact that he can't move his arms, or in fact anything else. He can't even close his mouth.

"Where I used to live," she says, reaching out a finger and touching the door experimentally, "there was a room which was wider and higher than your whole house." Her finger slides over the nameplate below the dolphin knocker. "Parson's," she reads. "That means a priest lived here once. Oh, because it's close to the church. Of course."

She steps back to look up at the window of his mother's room. Her feet leave small wet prints. "This is the right one, isn't it?" It's more a statement than a question. "I can smell you on it. And that woman."

He manages to get enough control over himself to permit speech. "What are you doing here?"

"Talking to you. You like it when we chat."

"I thought you couldn't . . ." He's churning inside. The two of them are just standing in the middle of the road. What if someone sees?

"Oh," she says. "You mean, what am I doing *here*." She waves to encompass the surroundings, brambles and twitching leaves and peeling paint.

"You're supposed to be in the sea."

"I am," she admits. "But I still remember all this. My father was a man. I never told you that, did I?"

He's not properly listening. (Anyway, it's not like her father would have been a woman, is it?) He wants her to go away. He shuffles closer as if he can shoo her up the road like a chicken. "Someone might come!" he says in a thick whisper. "What if they catch you?"

She smiles her funny lopsided smile. "We catch you. Not the other way round. Did you know these islands are sinking? Centuries ago it was all land from south to north and east to west. There are stone walls under the water that were once around fields. The land's been falling all that time. One day your house will drown. And that church, all the way up to its tower. Then I'll lie in your bed."

He's trying to shake her voice out of his head. It's like water, it looks soft and weak but it can throw you around as if you're made of paper. He's having an unwilling yet irresistible vision of her in his bed, a sort of smooth cold sheet against his skin. "Please go away," he says. "They're going to come and work in the north fields soon. Just over there."

"I saw them yesterday. Lots of them." He can't make her listen. He's all cramped and squeezed with dread but she's talking as calmly and dreamily as if she's lying on the rocks in the cove. "And you, for a bit. You were all in little boats together, going west. You must have seen me as well? Everyone was looking. That other woman covered you up so I couldn't see you. They're afraid you love me, aren't they." She brings her arms over her head and then slowly lowers them, like a step in a dance. She comes so close in front of him that he can smell her briny tang and she can lower her voice to a murmur. "But you don't, do you?"

"'Course not."

"Not yet. One day, though. It's coming. It's like the land sinking." She holds a hand out level and then lifts it slowly up, past his shoulders, over his head.

"Please," he says. "You've got to get out of here."

"I've been looking for you, you know. You haven't come to see me for days. I thought after I looked for you yesterday you'd come."

"I couldn't!"

"Then I remembered how to walk on the roads." She dances away, placing one foot behind the other very deliberately, and then strides back, demonstrating. "I walked a long way once. Miles and miles. My mother would be terribly angry if she knew I'd gone walking again. Did you know that when she's angry the storms blow and the sea rises up and throws your ships around and breaks them in pieces? And the people come drifting down. They look so relieved, I always think. Not sad at all. Like this." She makes a blank-eyed, heavy-lidded, openmouthed face, the corners of her mouth gathered in the beginning of a slack smile. "It looks like bliss, doesn't it? As if they know they've left the horrors of the road behind." She looks down at her feet and curls her toes to poke at the tarmac. "Although this one seems all right."

He wants her to go, desperately, before Something Bad happens, but at the same time he doesn't. And anyway it doesn't matter what he wants, it's like wanting the tide to go up and down; it's not up to him.

"She shouldn't be angry anyway." She stretches her arms again. "She's only afraid I'll get hurt again, but nothing can hurt me anymore. I'm like the drowned people; I'm safe now. Did you know she loved my father so much she kissed him and filled his mouth with the sea so he wouldn't have to go on suffering?"

She waits for his answer, studying him with a serious look. He's completely sunk in whatever she's saying. He's trying to struggle up to where he could take a breath and scream, *Help! Go away!* but he can't do it. "No," he says.

"She did. I remember"—a flicker of something other than tranquility disturbs her smoothed-out features—"it made me sad once. That was when I still lived here, where all the unhappiness is."

"Here?" he says. He's kicking and flailing and fighting inside, but it's no good, it's not even breaking the surface.

"Not *here*, silly, not this house. Above, I mean." She opens her arms wide and executes a sweetly balanced pirouette, hands fluttering to indicate the world around them. "Here. It wasn't always unhappy. I remember lots of good things. But." She comes to rest, drops her arms; her face tightens. "It's like a road. Wherever I start remembering it always seems to come to the same end, where the two men hurt me." She crosses her arms over her chest and steps back, troubled. "I've never spoken about that before."

He has the impression of a small cloud passing over the sun. He'd look up to check but he can't take his eyes off her face.

"It's not a good thing to talk about. They hurt me inside and out, one after another. Just because they wanted to. It was in a small house like this one. In a room full of faces. You'd never hurt me, would you?"

It sounds like a threat. "'Course not," he croaks.

"You'll want to, though. You will. I saw the way all those women in the little boats were looking at me. I know what faces like that mean now. They all wanted to hurt me."

"I wouldn't. Never. I swear."

"I don't listen to boys' promises." All of a sudden she's ocean-cold. He can almost feel it in his flesh though he's not touching her (he'd never touch her, he wouldn't dare). "Not anymore."

"I'm different from them," he says. "Let's not just stand here."

"Are you? There was another boy once who told me he was different from other people. He betrayed me too."

"Please," Rory says. He's actually frightened of her now. In her eyes he can see what it would be like to drown, the throttling weight, the terror. "You've got to go."

"Now you're scared," she says. "Is that why you haven't come to talk to me? Because you're afraid of me?"

"No," he says.

"They've taught you to be afraid of me."

"It's not like that."

"You don't want me here, do you? You don't want to see me."

"No! I just—"

"They can't stop you. It doesn't matter what they tell you, one day you'll love me and you'll come to me and stay forever."

Her eyes and voice are all *drowning, drowning* and yet the words fill him with a different kind of breathlessness, bliss. He's in turmoil.

"Did they bring those people to the island? Is that why? To drive me away from you?"

"What?"

"Don't let them, Rory." She's changed again. Suddenly she's entreating him. She clasps her hands. "There's terrible danger. That's what I've been wanting to tell you, but you wouldn't come."

"I wanted to. I tried."

"I can feel the fire in the air. It's hungry. It's waiting, getting impatient. It came with those people on their boat. We couldn't come near them; the fire drove us away. I remembered it as soon as I felt it. It's a very bad thing. You have to believe me. You believe me, don't you?"

"Yes. 'Course."

"Everything bad that happened to me started the first time that fire came. You mustn't let it come here. You have to tell everyone. Tell them to make those people go away. Rory?" He wants to understand her. If he could work out what she's saying he could tell her *All right, whatever it is you want me to do I'll do it,* and then she'd be finished and she'd leave. But he can't keep up with her. "Whatever they think, they're better off without it. I *know!*" The morning's definitely clouded over. She's not glistening anymore, she's gone the white of dead flesh, and her hair's blowing in matted strands over her mouth. "It came into my house. It turned kind people bad. Then it gave itself the body of an animal and tried to kill us." She shuts her glassy eyes for a moment and shivers. "It wants to come in again. I can feel it. It wants a house. Whatever you do, you mustn't let that happen." She reaches out and almost, almost touches his face. He's weak with an overwhelming combination of confusion and terror and crushed delight. "I love you," she says. "I want you to be safe with me. Where it's always quiet."

His blood's whistling in his ears like the sound a shell makes. He hardly knows she's stopped speaking. Her head turns away and she brushes hair from her mouth just like Laurel does, like a real girl. She's gone quiet at last, and in the silence he can hear—

His limbs turn to lead.

She frowns a little and then looks over her shoulder, and says, "Is that someone coming?"

The next few moments are like falling off a bike. You know it's going to happen just before it happens. There's the first wobble and slip, that's how you know; then you're watching and waiting for everything to collapse into chaos around you. He hears steps on the road: that's the wobble. *Someone's coming.* The realization hits him fast and slow at the same time: too quickly for him to do anything about it and yet slowly enough to feel every tick of imminent disaster. He looks up the Lane, where—

His mother drops the bag of tools and screams. The tools fall, *clank, rattle.* She goes as white as Her. She stops the scream and stumbles forward, waving her arms. The stumble makes her kick the bag. A spanner slides across the road, *clank.* She trips, picks up the spanner as her hands hit the road. She's trying to shout something like *No.* The crash is over now, Rory's mangled and stunned and at that stage where you're lying on the ground thinking *How did that happen?* but still can't do anything. His mother lurches upright and flings the spanner. It hits the door of Parson's, *thwack.* Rory flinches and looks around. No one's standing by the door. In the space where She was a moment ago there's only a wet patch on the road. "Get away!" his mother screams. Rory keeps turning and discovers that She is getting away, light on her bare feet down the road. Then he can't see anything because his mother's on top of him and wrapping his head in her arms. She smells of diesel. He can feel her heart beating, much too fast. "Go away!" she screams, again and again, and at the same time she's scrabbling at the door with the key and then pulling him into the house. He can't quite breathe or think but in the middle of it all he still has a moment of clarity: the thought comes to him that maybe sailing off to be drowned would have been the better option after all.

Her hands are shaking all the time. She keeps almost tripping over herself. She's made him sit down at the table. "Don't get up!" she keeps saying, though he's not trying to, he's trying to stay very quiet and very still. She makes him put his hands flat on the table. "Like that," she says. "Don't move!" The dirty porridge bowls are still there. She drags a chair to the front door and tries to wedge it under the handle, then heaves another chair on top of the first one. They both tip over. She kicks them and starts crying, but even though she's crying she keeps going round and round the kitchen, pulling the curtains, saying *Don't move, don't move.*

He's never seen her this bad.

Libby comes and knocks on the door.

"Go away!" his mother screams.

"Connie?" The door bumps in against the chairs. His mother lunges at it and slams it shut.

"Don't come in!"

He can hear Libby and someone else talking outside. His mother opens the door a crack, puts her mouth to the gap, and shouts, "Leave us alone!"

"Connie—"

She slams the door shut and then bangs her fists on it. "Why can't you leave us alone?" She slumps into a chair across the table from Rory, drops her head on her arms, and starts crying properly, like she used to most of last year.

After a good long time Rory thinks he'd better say something.

"Mum?"

She lifts her head to look at him. She looks raw and wasted. She looks a bit like Molly did the evening after Ol died.

"It's OK," Rory says. "Should we calm down a bit?"

She gets up, comes around the table, and hugs him fiercely.

"You're all right," she says. Her voice has sort of lost its inside: it's the shell of a voice. "You're OK."

"I'm fine, Mum."

She unwraps her arms and peers at him. "What's your name?"

"Uh. Rory?"

"And where are we?"

"What do you mean, where are we?"

"What's this house called?"

He hesitates before answering. "You mean Parson's?"

"All right. All right all right." She sits down again. "Don't panic." He's pretty sure he's not the one who's panicking, but never mind. "We can do this. What we need is somewhere." She's picked up the dirty wooden spoon and is rolling it back and forth between her hands, quite clearly with no idea what she's doing. "There must be somewhere."

There's another knock at the door. His mother ignores it.

"Connie? Please let us in." It's Libby again.

"With a lock," his mother mutters. She looks around the room as if she's lost something. "And no windows. Think. Think."

More knocking. "Is everyone OK in there?"

"I think someone's outside," Rory says. His mother sits up and stares at him, then goes to the door. She smooths her hair out a bit before opening it a little.

"Sorry," she says, in a blankly polite voice. "I got a bit of a fright. Can you give us a few minutes, please?"

"Rory?" That's Missus Grouse.

"Rory's fine," his mother says.

"I'm fine," Rory calls. It's horrible when other people are around to watch his mother cracking up. He tries to make everything sound normal. "It's all OK."

"Just a few minutes," his mother says. "If you could wait for us at the Abbey. We'll be along in a bit." She closes the door gently and leans against it, listening.

There's some murmuring outside. Then they start drifting away up the lane. He can tell they're going that way because he can hear Missus Grouse's grumbling even with the door closed. His mother stands pressed against the door, barely moving. After a little while she opens the door a crack, very carefully, and listens some more, holding her breath.

Finally she turns and looks at Rory.

"All right now, Mum?" Very carefully, he tries moving his hands. She doesn't shout at him, she just goes on staring.

She snaps her fingers. "Got it."

She's no closer to getting back to normal.

She frowns. "But that would be stupid. No. Wait. Yes."

"Mum? What are you talking about?"

"Yes," she says. She plucks at the ends of her hair. "Yes. That's the place. It didn't open the door, did it?"

Rory takes a few moments to realize this is a proper question, meant for him.

"What?"

"No. It didn't. You saw it through the window, didn't you, so you climbed out. That's what happened. Isn't it?"

She's talking about Her. He knows he can't say anything about being outside already when he saw Her, so he says, "Yeah," and then, remembering that she made him swear about a thousand times not to go outside, "Sorry, Mum."

"No. No no no no." More violent hugging. "Don't say sorry. It's not your fault. You can't help it. That's how They do it. We just have to make sure you can't see out." She tugs him upright. "Let's go."

They're going to the Abbey already? He's been hoping she'll have time to calm down before everyone else has to see her. She notices his hesitation and composes herself into a terribly fake reassuring manner. "Off we go," she says, with the kind of false brightness people use when they say *This'll hardly hurt at all*. "Wait, let's get some of your comics, there's an idea."

"OK," he says, turning to go upstairs.

"No!" She just about stops herself from shrieking. "I'll do it. Sit! Down. Don't move."

She keeps shouting from his room above. "Are you still sitting there? . . . You haven't moved, have you? . . . Stay right in that chair!" Rory concentrates on the fact that this'll be over soon. He'll ask Kate if he can stay in the Abbey tonight. They'll see what his mother's like and they'll have to let him. She comes back down with a stack of comics in the spare plastic bag. "There," she says, twisting the top of the bag and looping the handle over his wrist. "That'll keep you going. It won't be for long anyway. It's for your own good."

He discovers what she means very soon.

She marches him down the Lane with his head in the crook of her elbow. He has to walk hunched over and scurrying. The comics bump uncomfortably against his knees. They get to the Pub and turn right instead of left, and that's when he knows something's wrong.

"Mum?"

"Careful. Watch where you put your feet."

"Where are we going?" Left is the way past the Club to the Abbey road. Right doesn't go anywhere, just around the back of the Beach to the quay.

"It's only for a little while, I promise."

"What is?"

"I'm putting you on the boat."

He stiffens. His legs lock. "You can't."

She drags him forward again. "Not for long."

Out of the corner of his eye he sees a grimy battered-looking sailing boat splattered all over with gull poo and the smeary fuzz of lichen, tied up inside the quay by the ferry steps. It's the boat that used to be off the south end of the island. She's brought it round, while he was off explaining his brilliant idea to Silvia.

His brilliant idea.

"I'll stay in Parson's," he says. "I won't look outside. I swear."

"There's a cabin at the front," she says. "I'm going to have to lock you in there. I'm sorry, Rory, but you understand why, don't you?"

"I won't even look at the windows. Please, Mum."

"It's the only safe place." She's got hold of him really hard now. "It's not for long. I just need to collect a couple more things."

She's marching him along the quay. A gull takes off from the boat's railing as they approach. At the top of the steps he makes a proper effort to break her grip. She grabs him harder than he'd have thought possible. A moment later and she's wrestling him down, and it's all he can do not to fall off the steps completely. He can hear himself protesting increasingly desperately. A sense of unspecified disaster is beginning to take hold. He can't exactly let himself think about why it's so but he knows with perfect certainty that he shouldn't get on this boat. It's not making any difference. She won't listen to him. There's a moment of teetering clumsiness as she brings him alongside and then they're aboard, the deck wobbling, the bitter stench of fuel everywhere. They're almost fighting each other now. He's too little, though. The bag of comics has gotten itself wrapped around his arms like a ball and chain, she's got hold of his wrists too, and once his hands are trapped there's nothing he can do. He loses his footing in the steep companionway which goes down to the cabin and for a moment he's actually dangling and kicking before she drops him into a stripped-out space of stained plastic and bits of foam padding. There's no way out. He thinks he's crying now as he pleads with her, he can't tell. She comes down after him, picks him off the floor, and carries and shoves him through a narrow space between two moldy bunks to a tiny door. Here she stops, finally. They're both gasping.

"You'll have your comics," she says. "It won't be for long. I'm sorry, Rory sweetheart."

Unthinkable consequences are spinning around his head, so vast and black he can't speak. She opens the tiny door of the forward cabin. Beyond it is a dim squashed space rank with condensation and neglect.

"Mum, listen to me."

She bundles him inside. There's a hatch overhead but it's almost black with age and dirt.

"Don't shut me in here," he says. The fight's gone out of him. It's too serious for fighting now.

"I'll be as quick as I can," she says, very shakily.

"Mum!" She slams the tiny door. He hears the latch rattle. He hears a padlock click. "Please!"

It's a bit like the silty water in a rock pool. When you swirl it around the sand gets caught up in the water and the whole pool goes cloudy, you can't see anything. You have to not touch it for a while. If you wait and don't do anything the sand settles, and then you can see all the way to the bottom, crystal clear.

He sits quietly for a while after she goes, and so he begins to see what's going to happen.

He whacks the door and the hatch a few times each. The door feels flimsy but it's not flimsy enough. He ends up hurting his hands. Perhaps he could try harder but he doesn't. He sits again, wondering why.

Eventually, of course, they come.

It all happens very quickly. He's been thinking about what he'll do when it happens: sitting in his damp dull prison, thinking. Or trying to. In the event, when he hears low urgent voices and then feet on the steps, and then the boat wobbles and scrapes as they jump aboard, he just goes on sitting, holding the bag of comics on his lap. He's amazed at himself and at the world. Three voices chatter hurriedly around the boat. Lines rattle. Once steps come close and the locked door shakes, for a moment. The fenders squeal. Motion grips the boat. Quietly, he takes one of the comics out of the bag. There isn't enough light from the filthy hatch to read by. He opens it anyway and stares silently at the pages and has the sudden knowledge that everything's inside out. The comics were once more vivid and wonderful than anything in the whole real world; now they aren't. His life has become a story instead of a life.

He remembers thinking once that this was what he always wanted.

II

※ ┅ ❧

Fantasyland

13

What's weird is that he never says anything.

Briar Hill, a bright autumn morning, a few days ago, gathering blackberries and sloes: he watched Ol walk away to his death, knowing he ought to stop him but not knowing how. The right moment kept slipping by, too fast to catch.

It's the same now. If he'd just shouted out *then*, a moment ago—*Help! Let me out!*—this whole unthinkable turn of events might have stopped and gone into reverse. But he never does, because *now* the moment is gone.

There was a point soon after they were under way when he heard shouting coming across the water, voices screaming from the island. That was the moment. He could have jumped up and banged on the door. He can see himself doing it, the sequence of actions, panel by panel. Bang, shout: *Hey! I'm in here!* They'd have realized what they'd done and let him out, and then something else would have happened, over the page: they'd have dropped him off at the beach on Sansen, maybe, or put him ashore in the dinghy. If there is a dinghy.

But it didn't happen. He was waiting for it to happen and it never did.

He has a little cry. Not for long: he's feeling too sick. They must be out beyond the edge of the world by now. In the no-man's-land, the vacuum. The graveyard. They're a speck in the big grey swell. There's no engine sound. They're sailing. The boat's wallowing and lurching in that queasily sluggish way which means the wind's behind. The comics slide around on the dismal bunk. Feet bang overhead and from time to time vague shadows further blot out the grimy light from the hatch.

At one stage the locked door rattles sharply and he hears Silvia say something in Italian. Obviously this is another moment when he ought to shout out—*It's me!*—or *was* another moment: it's gone almost as soon as it happens. What could he say, anyway? They're not going to take him back now.

Or ever, perhaps. Like Ol.

Eventually he hears muttering and scraping at the door and then a couple of very loud whacks, so loud they make him forget his nausea and sit up cross-legged on the bunk. After the fourth or fifth whack there's a metallic pop, and a crack appears in the door near the handle. One more whack shakes the handle loose. The lock falls out, the door bangs open, and there's Silvia, a mallet in one hand and a screwdriver in the other and a look on her face as close to surprise as Rory will ever see. The sea sounds twice as loud with the door open.

Her look changes to a dry smile.

"I had a feeling," she says.

They don't turn back. Rory climbs unsteadily up the companion-way and looks over the stern and there's nothing there but waves, dazzling hills of water. Lino whoops at him and slaps his back. Per, at the wheel, still gripping his massive walking stick, only scowls. He doesn't know what they're saying to each other but he can tell from Per's face that he wouldn't turn the boat around even if they asked him to. The hills rear up behind him, dark on their shadowed side, relentless, wave after wave. He's not so much seasick as plain terrified. The boat bangs and squeaks and judders and plunges off the back of each wave like it's going to fall forever. It's not even that windy, it's just the ocean swell. He always hated it, even when he hadn't just been kidnapped. He retreats below and crams himself into a corner of the main cabin, bracing himself against cold plastic.

"I don't like it either." Silvia sits beside him. "We're people of the roads, my people. Not like those two up there." Lino's scrambling all over the deck. They can hear him going back and forth all the time; it's like listening to mice in the ceiling. "Per was a sailor, you know. It was his job. He worked on the big boats, all over the world. And Lino grew up by the sea. Like you."

Perhaps she's trying to make him feel better by sitting and talking with him. He's too sick and miserable to notice.

"It doesn't help you so much?" She ruffles his hair, like she did earlier that morning, outside the Hotel. It can't have been the same day, he thinks, or the same world. How'd he end up here? "That's OK. I think it's right to be afraid of the sea. It's the opposite of us. Those two, they're the strange ones."

He's hardly said anything to her. What he wants to say is *I want to go home.* He wants to whine like Pink. But you can't talk to Silvia like that. She's not his mother. They don't care what he wants. He's caught up in their journey, small and useless as a burr. He's not going home. He won't be at the Abbey later on, or in his bed after that. His mother's not going to tuck him in tonight.

Silvia watches him for a moment and then just carries on.

"I was born a long way from the sea. Do you know Romania? No? That's where I was born. In a house on wheels. A car like a little house. What's the word in English? Anyway. So I was even born on the road. Nineteen eighty-four. How old are you?" She only waits a little. "No, I remember. Ten?"

He nods, finally.

"Only ten," she says to herself, like it's hard to believe.

Why's she talking about this? Why isn't she saying sorry to him, telling him it's all been a stupid mistake, explaining how she's going to fix it and put him back where he's supposed to be?

She pulls her knees up on the seat next to him and settles close. "You don't know about the history in Europe, then. You're much too young. Romania, where I was born, it's a country in east Europe. Thirty years ago, this whole part of the world, it's a completely different place. The Iron Curtain. Have you heard about the Iron Curtain?"

He shakes his head. No one's ever talked to him like this before.

"All the countries in this part of Europe, we were like little children, and Russia is the mother. Yes? Telling us what to do. Saying, No, you can't leave the house, you can't go outside to play, you stay here where I watch you all the time. In Romania all the people are like that, like children. And my people, the Roma, we're the smallest. The slaves of slaves. The Russians spit on the Romanians and the Romanians spit on the gypsies. Then one day, when I was a small child, Russia got sick and died. All the children were left with no . . ."

She looks at Rory and thinks better of finishing the sentence.

"So, all those countries, Romania, Czechoslovakia, Yugoslavia, they don't know what to do. No one knows what's happening, what rules there are now. For the Roma, my people, there was nothing. No money, no work, nowhere to live. My parents disappeared maybe, or died, I don't know what happened. I live in the streets. In a little box, under a bridge. This is the oldest thing I remember. My box, and water coming from a broken pipe. I remember the sound of dogs. Trucks crossing the bridge in the night, *brrrmmm*. I live like that, by the road. Can you imagine?"

She waits quite a long time, watching him fixedly.

"You feel sad without your mother?" she says, eventually.

He gives a stiff little nod.

Perhaps she's finally noticed what she's done to him. But she doesn't do any of those things grown-ups usually do when they're pretending to comfort you: no hugs or pats or *poor-you*s. She shrugs, looks at her nails. They're filthy. Then she goes on talking about herself.

"You know I'm an orphan? It's the same word in Romanian. *Orfan*. I remember the day people came and took me to the orphanage. Nineteen ninety. I'm six years old.

"It's very young, yes? They come with a big white car and take me from my box under the bridge. I scream, I fight like this." She waves her arms wildly in the air and makes her greasy hair flap around. "That night I'm locked in a room with other girls. All white Slavic girls. All our hair cut off. They say horrible things to me, pinch me so I can't go to sleep, blame me every time there is a noise. I didn't even have a mother but I cried for being alone."

Despite himself he can't help imagining this story, a little bit.

"You know they throw me out?" She catches his eye and smiles like it's a joke. "It's true. When I'm maybe eight, maybe nine, they decide they don't want a gypsy girl. That orphanage, it's the worst place I ever go to, but they think it's too good for me. They put me back in the same white car, drive me to a place where Roma are, and they open the door like so and—*pffwwt!*—out, like rubbish. Drop by the road, drive away. I was not as old as you are now."

The boat drags, yaws, slips downhill again. Loose things clatter around the cabin's galley.

"What happened?" he says.

"Hmm?"

"What happened then?"

She points at herself, arching her thick black eyebrows.

"You want to hear Silvia's story? It's a long story. I've come a long way."

"OK," he says.

She looks at him curiously, as if she's making her mind up about something. "Or maybe you want to know what a small child did, all alone?" He blinks, suddenly tearful. "Except you aren't all alone. No? I told you, I think your road and mine, they go"—she points the index fingers of both hands and lays them beside each other, like the rails of Jake's train set—"like this."

She doesn't care at all about what's happening to him. He's so astonished by this that it's somehow impossible for him to weep for himself, it's like she's changed the rules.

"I wasn't all alone either. The Roma took me in. They know I belong to them. I live in their camp for a while. An old woman looked after me, made me say she was . . ." She frowns. "The sister of your mother, what do you call this? I forget the word."

Rory has to concentrate to help her. "You mean aunt?"

Silvia snaps her fingers. "Of course. Aunt, she makes me say she's my aunt. We all live in tiny dirty houses. No floor or water. No one wants to see the Roma so there's no work. I remember one night people come with dogs to make us go away, they want the field we live on. But our dogs were bigger!" She grins at him. "Or maybe hungrier. Another old woman, she took me into towns with her to beg. In the towns I have to pretend I am her daughter's daughter."

"That's granddaughter."

"Granddaughter, thank you. I have to go like this"—*cough, cough*. "Pretend I am sick so people will give more money. And sometimes people come to the camp and give my aunt money to tell their fortune. That's how I lived. But it was better than the orphanage. My hair grew back!" She tugs it and smiles, sharing a joke.

It's too much. He stares back at her. Her smile disappears and she studies him for a while. Then she edges closer to him, sliding along the seat, bracing her legs against the plastic table in the middle of the cabin, leans close and says:

"Tell me, Rory. Do you believe in fate?"

She's talking almost in his ear. He's been stolen from his home, he's nauseous, he doesn't think he's ever going to see his mother again, and instead of curling up and crying his wretched heart out he's talking to a mysterious gypsy about fate.

"As soon as I saw you," Silvia goes on, "I know our roads run together. Do you believe that?"

Does he? Does it really matter what he believes? He thought he was only ten and nobody cared what he thought about anything, let alone destiny.

"Dunno."

"But it's true. Everyone carries their fate with them." She's murmuring, like she's sharing a secret. Every time the boat pitches he's pressed right up against her shoulder and he can smell the grassy dirty musk of her hair. "Everyone likes to think they're free, you know? Like they do what they want. In Romania, Bulgaria, everywhere, people said this all the time. *Now we are free. Give us more freedom!* Like they can choose their fate. But it's not true. Your fate is outside you. But like a shadow, you see. Attached. It's like this for everyone, even children. I see it when I look at you. The first time, in that old place, in the rain. I see this . . ." Her voice drops to a whisper. "Big shadow. Covering you." She turns to stare at him, very close. "Do you believe this?"

He can certainly feel a dark cloud above him but he doesn't think that's what she means.

She settles back and folds her arms. "When I was nine years old, in that house in the field, with no floor? And people came to hear their fortune? They came to the old woman, the one who calls herself my aunt. But it's me who knows the answers." She watches him as if she's afraid he's not listening properly. "It's true. Nine-year-old girl. There was this man one day, a farmer, big man. He comes to the camp. His son's getting married, he wants to know about the girl. You know, is she healthy here"—Silvia taps below her stomach—"will she bring boys, will she love other men, all this. The old woman sends me away to fetch a handkerchief and put his money away and when I'm coming back I look in his face and I see his fate, so I say don't worry because he will be dead before the wedding." Silvia smiles grimly. "He was very angry. My aunt too. She beat me afterwards. The man took all his money back, says I curse his son. But I'm not talking about the son, I mean the man. In two months he was dead. The old woman too. While she's beating me I tell her she will die soon after the man. Four days after we hear the farmer is dead, my aunt is drunk in the road and a truck hits her. Do you believe me?"

One look at her face is enough to tell him that doubting her isn't an option.

"It's true. Everyone in the world has a road they travel. Sometimes I see ahead, one turn maybe, two turns, or up or down. Sometimes the end. When I was little, like you, I think everyone can see like this. In that camp I learn, no, I am special." She shakes her head. "You know how I learn? Because the others, the men, they start to bring more people to our camp. To take their money! They make me work. This is how stupid people are. 'Look, here is Silvia, she has a gift, how can we use this gift to get money?' Then the men take the money and buy vodka and cigarettes. More vodka and cigarettes, that's how I find out I'm special." She looks away, brooding.

Rory has two feelings inside him and no way of making them join up. On the one hand he's been kidnapped, betrayed by a horrible failure of his own brilliant idea, helpless and lost, and he's never going to see Home again. On the other hand he's on a quest with a gang of superheroes.

"You mean," he says, when it becomes apparent that Silvia's backed herself into some kind of dead end, "you can see the future?"

"Yes," she says, as if he's just asked her whether she's tied her shoelace.

He makes an effort to process this. "So . . ."

"Now you're going to ask, 'What will happen next?' " That's exactly what he was going to ask, but now he has to pretend it wasn't. "It's not like a book." She mimes turning pages, peering at the next chapter and going *ahh!* "It's not all written like this, waiting for us to come to the right page. If you ask me when we're going to reach land, I send you up to ask Per. I don't know the next page. I know everyone in the world has their own fate. Your fate belongs to you, mine to me. Even if they go like this." She makes the train tracks with her fingers again. "Sometimes the shadow of it falls on your face and I see it there. I'm not like the girls on TV who tell you the weather." She chirps, " 'Tomorrow morning will be rain, then in the afternoon sun.' " She shakes her head. "Not like this. The men, the Roma, they take me to watch horses race in the fields and they ask me which one will win. They want to bet and make money! And when I don't know they beat me. Do they beat you all the time? Those women, on that island?"

"No," he says.

"I didn't think so. You have nice easy life, I think. Big house full of food and many women to look after you. And then—" She snaps her fingers close to his face and waves around to indicate the decrepit cabin. "This."

He grips the back of the seats more tightly.

Silvia sighs. "But this is your fate, you see. Maybe it's not so bad too. You tell me that your mother is going to take you away, yes? She's afraid you will grow older and the *sirene* will take you, so she wants to carry you from that island in this boat? So if not for this you go with her, and then either you drown or you starve. You don't believe me? It's true for certain. Even if you cross the sea and don't drown, when you come to land you die. Me and Lino, we come across half of Europe this year. I know what's happening everywhere. You and your mother, just two of you, on land? *Ai.*" She puffs her cheeks out and shakes her head. "You are lucky that isn't your fate. You are lucky the storm blows me and Lino and Per to your little island."

Black thoughts sting him. "How's it lucky?" he says, as sulkily as he dares.

"Hmm?" She wasn't expecting him to say anything.

"How's it lucky? If it's fate. It's not luck if it's fate, is it. It can't be both."

She's startled for a moment, and then she laughs. "Philosopher," she says.

"Didn't you know there was going to be a storm?"

"No. I told you, I'm not a weather girl."

"So what's the point? What's the use of seeing the future if you can't . . ." He blurts this out in a little fit of anger, enraged that she's making him listen to her story and telling him how nice his life is when she ought to be apologizing for kidnapping him and doing her best to comfort him like grown-ups are supposed to do for children when they're sad. The fit drains away very quickly under the force of her stare.

He's never seen an adult stare the way Silvia does, not even Kate. The thing with adults is you can tell they're not really interested when they talk to you, they're actually thinking about something else. Not Silvia.

"Little man," she finally says. " 'What's the use?' For men it's never enough to know anything. Always everything is to *use*." She flicks her eyes upwards, indicating the deck, where Lino and Per are. "Like them," she says, with heartfelt emphasis, as if she's exposing their most terrible secret. She slides close to Rory again, holding her balance as the cabin rocks and shudders. "I told you I have a gift? You remember?"

"Yes."

"My teacher, who taught me to speak English, liked to explain this word. *Gift*. It's not *tool*. It's not *power*. It's"—she cups her hands and presents them to Rory, as if offering him rainwater—"like this. A thing given. A free thing. Not for something else. You understand?"

She can tell from his face that he doesn't. She leans back and shrugs.

"Let me tell you about Lino," she says. "Then maybe you see what a gift is. I told you, his name means *little bird*? It's not his real name, of course. Not from when he was born. He has a proper name, Antonio I think. But his mother and father call him Uccellino from when he is a small child. Because even when he's this small he likes to climb up things and jump. All the time. He climbs from . . . What do you call the bed for a baby?"

"Cot."

"He climbs from his cot and jumps out to the ground. He climbs onto chairs, tables, jumps off. Like he wants to fly. When he's a bit older he climbs where the books are, high up. He's from a nice family. Nice house, lots of books, up to the ceiling. They find him"—she stretches a hand above her head—"here. Curled up on the edge. He's like this all the time. At first the nice family think it's a joke, it's funny, their little boy who likes climbing up things. They give him a special name. On the floors they put . . ." She pats the frayed foam padding of the seat impatiently.

"Cushions?"

"Cushions. They put cushions so he can jump and not hurt himself. They watch him, make videos, show their friends. Then one day he breaks his arm jumping from a window in the house. Now it's not a joke anymore. They're angry; they're frightened. They tell him to stop but he doesn't. He dreams all the time that he is flying. So they take him to doctors. Still he doesn't stop. They find him sleeping on the roof. If he falls off the roof sleeping he will break his head open, so they put bars on the windows, they lock him in his room, OK, but he has to go to school, he has to play outside, they can't stop that, and all the time he's climbing trees, climbing walls. High, high up, as far as he can go. So the nice parents and the doctors, they decide the boy is mad." She swivels a finger in the air beside her head. "They send him to a place, I don't know how to say it in English. For mad children."

"Loony bin."

She raises an eyebrow slightly, but goes on. "It's a nice place, I think. Not like my orphanage. His parents love him; they have money. They come to see him every day. So this is where he grows up. A locked room with bars on the windows. Hands tied like this when he goes outside to play, so he can't climb. When he can't climb his dreams get worse. He dreams he's a bird, flying everywhere. Then, one night, he wakes up, it's dark, and he's outside, high above the town. He can see it all there below him. It's not a dream, he's sitting in the branch of a tree. He's far away but he can see the window of his room in the . . ."

"Loony bin."

"He can see the bars on the window. It's summer; the glass is open. He can see his bed inside, where he was sleeping, but he's not in the bed, he's holding the branch of a tree with his feet. Then. He jumps."

Rory watches her make a long gliding motion with one hand. She looks at him as if to check whether he's understood.

"Then what?"

"He jumps. From the branch of a tree, high. He doesn't fall. He flies, like in his dream. All over the town."

Rory doesn't say anything, so she shrugs again. "Then he wakes up again, in his room, behind the bars. But he's naked. His night-clothes are lying on the bed and he wakes up on the floor."

She seems to have finished, so Rory says, "Wow."

"Let me ask you a question."

"OK."

"You met Lino on your island?"

"Yeah."

"After the storm."

He remembers: in the afternoon the sky turned green and then black, and that night he was in the Abbey because his mother had gone to Maries, and that's when Lino jumped on him in the dark. "Yeah."

"Then later you saw our boat on the rock and you helped me and Per come ashore."

"Yeah."

"And Lino was with you already." He nods as best he can. His neck's getting stiff and achey from the way he's bracing himself against the boat's constant heaving. "So how did Lino come to your island?"

"Right."

She pauses.

"That's my question," she says.

"Oh."

"You have to learn to think if you travel with us. Think. Me and Per came after, on the boat, when Lino lit a fire to show us where he was. How did Lino come? There is no other boat, no planes, no cars."

He remembers Lino pointing up at the sky. *Like this one.*

"Flew?" Rory says.

Silvia smiles at him.

"So Lino can fly."

"Sometimes Lino is an owl," she says.

"He can turn into an owl?" The boat tips down the back of a particularly steep wave and thuds into its base, jarring the breath out of Rory's chest. Even Silvia grits her teeth for a moment. They hear Lino whistle out on deck, *Mamma mia.*

"No," she says. "He can't turn into an owl. Listen to what I tell you. I said: sometimes he's an owl. You see how it's different?"

Rory says he does, though he really doesn't feel like being interrogated at the moment.

"Lino has a gift, you see, like me. Not a power."

She's looking at him expectantly, so he says, "Oh."

"So maybe I shouldn't tell you that I can see the future. Not like that, 'I can see the future.' I should say instead: sometimes I see the future."

She doesn't say anything for a while after that. It's awful when there's nothing to distract him, so eventually he asks her:

"What am I going to do?"

What he means is *Who's going to look after me, where am I going to sleep, what will there be to eat, where is my home now?* But she grins like it's a joke, snapping out of a distracted trance.

"You ask me this because I'm a gypsy?" She holds a hand out. "First you must cross my palm with silver."

He stares down, feeling horribly small.

"Ah." She relents. "I understand. Don't be afraid." She rubs his arm encouragingly. "We take care of you."

"Will I get back home?" He'd do anything not to cry but he feels so bleak all of a sudden.

"This I don't know," she says, mistaking his whimper for an actual question. "But listen. Home, it's not always where you think it is. Especially when you're young. Home is the place where you come to rest. It's maybe far away from where you begin, where your mother and father are. For me it's not the orphanage where they are cruel to me, or the camp where they beat me all the time. It's very far away. For you too, maybe it's not that small island." He looks up and finds that she's once again staring at him with alarming intensity.

"Am I coming with you then?"

She looks around with an expression that says *Isn't it obvious? Here you are,* before relenting again. "For sure we're not going back. We will be OK. All of us. Me and Lino, we walked a long, long way together. Across Italy, France. We know what to do." She taps him with the back of her hand. "You can help us in England. You speak better than me, you can help talk to people. Hmm?"

"OK," he says, shyly, unable to imagine any of this.

"And you have a gift too."

"I don't. Do I?"

She's clearly not joking now. "You don't know it. But you do."

"I'm just normal."

"Don't argue with me," she says, without rancor. "I see it." She lowers her voice a little, though there's no possible way Lino or Per could hear anything over the thrum of the sea and the boat's spindly rattling. "I recognize you." She nods at him as if to contradict his blank stare. "I see the truth."

The bleak feeling recedes a bit.

"Maybe I can help you find . . ."

"I think you can," she says.

"That ring. You talked about."

"Like I tell you," she says. "Our roads go together."

"Where is it?" He's muttering too, without realizing. "Is it hidden?"

She shrugs. "In England."

"England's big, isn't it?"

"Close. I know we're coming close."

"How d'you know?" She frowns at him, and he realizes it's a stupid question. "What happens when we find it?"

"Ah." She barely mouths the word. Her eyebrows lift high. It's another shrug, but a mysterious one: *Who can say?*

"Are you going to . . ."

"What?"

"You know. Rule the world."

There's a startled pause, and then she throws back her head and laughs and laughs, shrieking girly laughter. Lino comes scurrying to the hatch and puts his head in to see what's happening. Rory turns away, cruelly ashamed, sick to his stomach and his heart, while Lino and Silvia have a rapid conversation in Italian, she struggling for breath still. She must be explaining what Rory said, because Lino barks his own delighted laugh when she reaches the punch line. "*É vero!*" he says. "'Obbits!" He scampers down into the cabin and says something to Silvia.

"He says I make you sad," she says. "He tells me not to laugh at you."

Rory won't speak.

"Maybe you're right anyway." Now at last she sounds like a normal adult, trying to cheer him up, not really meaning what she's saying. It unlocks his misery at last and he starts to feel properly sorry for himself. He starts sniffling. Lino makes a long sympathetic noise, *ehhhh*.

"You come look," he says. It's the way people talk to Pink when she's crying about something stupid, trying to distract her. "Eh? Up. I want you see." He waggles Rory's shoulders gently. "Come with Lino. England!"

Silvia starts up and squashes her face to a grimy porthole.

"No no no. Come, up."

"Leave me alone," Rory mumbles.

But it's impossible to sulk at either of them. Silvia doesn't care enough, and Lino doesn't understand, and anyway he keeps on jiggling and cajoling Rory until there's nothing for it but to wobble to his feet, clinging to handholds as he goes, and follow the man up the companionway ladder. One look at Per, unmoving at the wheel, brandishing his walking stick in the air like a weapon, his long hair and beard matted and dark with spray, and he stops feeling sorry for himself again. He doesn't dare.

"*Ecco*," Lino says, crouching and pointing ahead, between the underside of the boom and the port bow.

It's a cloud-colored smudge, but big, solid: a barrier in the sea, a wall on the horizon. The Mainland.

For a year and a half it's been no more than a thumbnail blur in the far distance on a clear day. As far as Rory's concerned it's been as remote as the moon: a place they say people once went to, in The Old Days, but now separated from the world by a vast and deadly waste. Now here it is, in sight and in range.

His thoughts flip back suddenly to a different life, a different Rory. He's getting into the back of a car, holding a bag of chips. At the same time his sister's opening the front door of the car. She has a bag of chips too but hers have vinegar so they stink. They're taking her to look at a big school on the Mainland. In front of their car is a whole row of other cars lined up along the side of a paved street; the street is lined in turn with shops, all bright clean colors with clear windows full of stuff. The backseat of the car is ridges of fuzzy fabric, and they catch his trousers as he tries to slide in: that's the exact moment he's remembering, the pinpoint, but knotted around it are a hundred other impossible things, chips, vinegar, cars, brightly colored stuff, school, his father and his sister, the Mainland, the whole business of arriving and leaving and traveling. In that moment all those things seem not only possible but ordinary, boring almost. But they're not, they're all as fantastic as flights to the moon.

And yet there it is. It's where they're going.

The Mainland disappears as the boat staggers down the slope of another wave. Rory clutches frantically at a cleat. He wants to retreat to the cabin but Silvia's pushing up below him, trying to come out and see as well. He squirms around and finds himself looking up at Per.

There's a flicker in the air around his stick, an orange flash.

If anything Per looks even bigger than he did on dry land, bulked out by a puffy jacket and a set of stained and oily overalls which have gone on over the rest of his clothes like armor. His lips are moving, silently. Over his head things like scraps of flame torn from the edge of a fire shimmer in and out of visibility at the speed of an eyeblink.

"Stowaway," he barks, without averting his squint-eyed stare from the horizon even for a moment, so that it's a good while before Rory realizes that this is an English word, directed at him. Silvia's nudging him out by Per's feet, into the cockpit, exposed to the swing of the sea and the spitting air.

"Say hello," she says.

"Heya," Per says, without looking and without warmth.

"Rory is traveling with us." The boom twitches and clanks above his head.

"Another mouth," Per says. The top of his stick sways as he leans on the wheel. Twists and curlicues of sunset light appear out of nothing and vanish as soon as they appear.

"Small mouth!" Lino says, pulling himself up to sit on the edge of the cockpit, where he balances with acrobatic ease. "Little food. Easy."

"What is that?" Rory blurts out. Now that he's out on deck he can see that the phantasmal ribbons in the air are all around the boat, circling the hull too quickly for the eye to catch up with them.

Per looks down at him at last and sees him gazing at the stick.

"You never touch it," he says. *Neffer* is how he says it.

"Per is keeping us safe from the *sirene*," Silvia says, or shouts; human voices are nothing next to the cacophony of sailing. She's halfway out of the hatch, clinging on as she searches the horizon for the Mainland. Rory jams his back against the side of the cockpit as hard as he can, wedging his feet and hands against anything solid he can find, as the sea rears up and all but rocks their pathetically little boat sideways. The grey surface with its windblown dusting of spray heaves and slides around them. Silvia works herself round to face him. "I told you he was a sailor? His ship was wrecked, like many others. He got in a tiny thing   I don't know the word. For saving people. Like a tent floating. He was there for a day and a night, by himself, in the middle of the sea, waiting to die. He was bored waiting so he opened the tent to let the *sirene* find him and kill him and he saw it there, floating in the sea. This wood."

"Wood?"

"Piece of wood."

"That stick?"

"Stick. He picks it up from the water and it speaks to him."

"No more," Per grumbles. He sounds angry, but then as far as Rory can tell he always sounds angry. Rory's looking at the stick. He didn't use the right word. It's far too long and thick for a walking stick, even for a man the size of Per. It's too heavy, too serious. The lines carved into it look serious too. They're not scratches, they're like words, but not written in proper letters, not the kind you can read. The stick is in fact—the word pops out of the pages of books or the panels of comics—a *staff*. A magic staff, like wizards carry. Per's a wizard. He's making the air dance with fiery light and keeping the sea-rainy away. Per's a wizard, and Lino can turn into an owl, and Silvia knows the future.

"Is good," Lino says, patting Rory's shoulder energetically. "Boy will be *interprete*. England boy."

"Have to land first," Per says.

"Do we have enough time?" Silvia asks him.

"*Mmf*," he grunts. "Perhaps."

"Eh." Lino makes the sound into a little jolt of reproach. "Easy, easy. Look how near! England!"

"Perhaps," Per repeats. "Go watch."

"*Si si, capitano.*" Lino trots to the bows as easily as if he were jogging down the Lane by the church.

Silvia glares at Per. "If they leave us before we reach land you will have to let me sail."

Per dismisses this with another grunt. He's got a very expressive collection of grunts. This one manages to pour wordless scorn on the mere thought that someone other than him might be competent at the helm.

"Do you know this coast?"

"No," Per says. "Doesn't matter. No time to find haven. First strand we see."

Silvia looks worried. The sail loosens, slams tight, cracking the boat into the side of a wave with a ferocious thump.

"I want to go back down," Rory says. Per grunts a laugh.

Silvia helps Rory to the ladder. "Not much longer," she says in his ear as he lowers himself past her. Things are clattering around in the cabin as if the whole boat's about to shake itself apart. He realizes he doesn't care about being kidnapped, doesn't care about his mother, doesn't care about never going home, doesn't care about anything except getting out of this sea and off this boat onto solid ground. Anywhere will do, though he really hopes they end up landing near that place with the bags of hot chips.

"*Vieni,*" Lino says, appearing in the hatch again. "Come. See."

The swaying and thudding's been less violent for the last little while. Rory uncurls himself from the seat where he's been lying praying for the voyage to be over and heads back to the ladder. This time he hardly has to hold on at all.

The sun's gone a long way west. It's right behind them. It's striking the Mainland cliffs full in the face, turning them the deep and glowing color of rust. They're so huge they look like they're about to topple over. The waves battering their base are hardly more than a white pencil line rubbing itself out and redrawing itself. They could swallow the islands where he lives like a whale.

(Lived.)

The boat's passing a cluster of offshore rocks, like the western rocks beyond Briar except on the same scale as the cliffs: even the smallest one's twice the height of their mast. One of them's topped by a lighthouse, a looming pillar of deserted stone. Beyond the lighthouse is an even more enormous dead thing, a massive tanker impaled on a claw of rock. The wind and waves have pinned it there, as if to mock the failed light.

None of that's what Lino and Silvia are staring at, though. She comes behind him and steers his shoulders to look the right way. "On the top," she says. "See them?"

The clifftops are a stark horizon, rust below, clear blue sky above. Something moves along that line.

"Three," Per says. "Watching us."

As he says it, Rory sees them properly. The silhouettes turn the right way and they're lined up one behind the other. They're horses and their riders picking their way along the flat land above the cliffs, tracking the route of the boat.

A glimmer in the air makes him blink. The ghostly fire's still circling the boat. Per's still holding his staff up with his free hand. His arm must be getting tired. He looks drawn and tense.

Lino bounces on his toes and waves vigorously towards the horses, provoking a burst of cross Italian from Silvia.

"Have to land," Per says. "No choice. Time going out."

"Where?" Silvia says, and Rory sees what she means. The coast is steep brute rock as far as the eye can see.

Per grunts a shruggy kind of grunt. "Lino's looking." He eases the bow northward to run parallel with the line of the coast, away from the rocks.

"What's wrong?" Rory asks Silvia.

"We need a place to come to land."

"What if there isn't anywhere?"

"Then," Per says, with heavy satisfaction, "all dead."

"Ignore him," Silvia says, settling close to Rory. "You know the problem with Per? He's from . . . *Danmark*?"

"Denmark?" Where Rory remembers this from he has no idea.

"Yes. Northern. Cold and dark all winter. These north people, the cold gets in their blood, I think."

"*Donne*," Lino shouts over his shoulder, from the bows.

Silvia translates: "Women."

Rory peers at the high silhouettes. Other people. The Mainland must be full of other people, like the islands used to be. "How can he tell?"

"Lino has very good eyes."

"Women," Per says, lingering over the word. *Vimm-en*.

"The men would stay away from the sea," Silvia says, nodding to herself. "Let's hope." Seeing Rory's look, she explains. "Women are safer. Even more safe if there's only three."

"Are they enemies?"

"Everyone you don't know is an enemy first," Silvia says. "You walk as far as me and Lino, you learn this."

He's remembering horses. There were two, on Home. They lived in a field between the Abbey road and the Pond. Fields were flat then, and green, just grass: you could see all the way across, walk all the way across even. The horses had coats to wear, and their own shed. He can picture himself and Scarlet climbing over a gate and walking across that flat green grass, each with an apple cut into quarters. The huge beasts came over, frightening him, but Scarlet stood there with her palm out flat and let them snaffle the apples with their funny furry lips. How could they have given food to animals? But he remembers: there was so much food in The Old Days. You took a boat across to Tesco on Maries and came home with bags and bags of it. He can't stop remembering. It's as if the islands were a prison, and while he was jailed there he couldn't think about anything beyond its walls. How could he ever have made himself believe that those specks on a map were the whole world, and those coughing wheezing women all the people in it? The Mainland's vast and seems to go on forever, sweep after sweep of cliff marching off into the hazy distance. With it comes a whole universe of things he can suddenly think about again, chocolate and TV and computer games, and people most of all, so many people you didn't even know everyone's name. Scarlet loved horses. (His father called it *a phase. It'll be boys next*, he said, winking.) Maybe that's her, up there, right now, watching him arrive. Maybe she and Jake and his father didn't just sail off the edge of the world into oblivion. Of course they didn't. They'd have sailed to this enormous solid shore same as he's just done, and found horses and who knows what else, bags of food. Cars. Shopping. Chips. No wonder they never bothered to come back.

Per leans across the cockpit and yanks a line. The boom strains tighter and the boat heels alarmingly, furrowing deeper into the surf.

"No time," he says.

He sounds strained. Rory turns in alarm and sees that he's lowered the staff at last. His arm's shaking beside him. The fire in the air seems fainter. Silvia grips the rail, looking alarmed. She's about to say something when Lino shouts.

"*Ecco!*" He leans over the bow, pointing.

The coast is headlands and promontories, shouldering into the sea one after another. They've sailed far enough towards one to see into the bay between it and the next, the hollow between the shoulders. A strip of sand is showing itself below the cliffs.

Per growls something incomprehensibly guttural, though just by the tone of it you can tell it's swearing, and bears away from the wind at once, setting course for that fragment of beach. "Watch for rocks," he shouts. (*Votch'fer Ox*: English words sort of hop up and down when he says them, like they're in an ocean swell too.) Silvia hauls herself uneasily along the rails to the bow. Suddenly there's a lot of busy shouting and pointing and tightening and winding. Rory knows at once he's in the way. He retreats hurriedly to the cabin and sits there alone, listening to the noises overhead.

He shouldn't be here. It's evening; he should be finishing off his jobs, then going to the Abbey for supper. He's small and far from Home, on a quest he doesn't understand. When he pretended he understood it they just laughed at him.

He goes to the tiny forward cabin where his mother locked him in. The comics have scattered all over the place. Kneeling awkwardly as the boat rolls under him, he starts gathering them up, packing them away in their bag, getting ready, though he has no idea at all what he's getting ready for.

14

Calm.

After so long lurching around in the swell the stillness makes him dizzy. Things bump against the hull, to remind him that he's still afloat. He's never felt so relieved just to be alive.

Per's steered them into a sort of harbor. Really it's just one end of a long flotsam beach, with a stone quay hooking out from the rocks to make a pocket of shelter. They've come to rest in that haven along with lots of other lost floating things. The sea's completely still here, and completely invisible, carpeted in a scum of kelp and algae and shapeless plastic lumps bulging like weird fungi. A few identifiable objects poke out of it, sad islands: oil drums, tires, a red lifejacket, the upturned hull of a dinghy, a lobster trap enmeshed in the corner of a net. A slipway runs out from the shore into the carpet of rubbish, or used to: sections of it have collapsed. At its top there's about half of a tumbledown brick shed, roofless and charred. Behind that, on the shore, rising out of a swamp of ground-hugging weeds and rusting cars, there are other ruined buildings, houses, caked in moss and crawling with ivy, what's left of their roofs splattered with bird poo. At the tideline a froth of congealed scum stretches all the way around the crescent beach, backed against a bulwark of driftwood and plastic junk, buoys, shopping bags, nameless chunks of faded something-or-other. There are three boats lying on their sides along the beach, two fishing boats and a yacht with a broken mast, each of them skirted with a puddle of livid weed. Everything, absolutely everything Rory can see, looks as if it's just been dropped or thrown away. The land rises up behind the beach, covered in the bitter green of unchecked summer growth, and goes on rising, and rising. There's so much of it. On the islands the hilltops and heaths are scoured by wind and the sea's always over the next crest no matter where you are. Here the land is massive and solid and looks like it goes on forever. It's incredibly silent. It has no interest in the water. It's like a monstrous back turned to the sea, ignoring it. It's not in motion. It's windless, heavy. Dead.

There's a dead man too.

It takes Rory a while to spot him among all the other rubbish on the beach. It's only because the rest of the gang have gone quiet and are all facing the same way, looking at something, that Rory sees him at all; and then it's another while before the upright length of wood and the flabby blotchy thing stuck to its seaward side arrange themselves into identifiable things: a limp bloodless man tied to a post. At first it looks like he's been decapitated, but that's just because the sagging blob at the top is only barely recognizable as a head.

"Welcome to England," Silvia says, breaking the silence.

"I go look." The boat's drifting near the quay, bumping its way through bobbing filth. Lino hops onto the starboard rail like a squirrel, steadies himself, and then springs across the gap as though he doesn't weigh anything at all. He lands on his feet, grinning.

"First!" he says. "Like Cristofero Colon." He mimes planting a flag.

"Hey, Columbus. Take this." Per tosses him a length of rope.

"*Si, capitano.*" Lino makes the end fast to a ring of rusty iron.

"We don't fly," Per says, and Lino chuckles.

The two of them don't even seem to have noticed the corpse, the dead land, the disgusting ruin spread around them. On the contrary, Per's almost cheerful, by his standards. Rory looks back along the beach. A crow's perched itself on the dead man's shoulders and started to peck.

He loses his balance and drops to his knees, about to be sick. Per snorts.

"Better send this boy home," he says.

Silvia's pushing a duffel bag up from the cabin. "Rory comes with us," she says. "I told you."

Per shakes his head, but doesn't argue. "New boyfriend," he mutters under his breath, but only after Silvia's gone back below to fetch another bag.

The three of them—Lino's gone off somewhere—are ferrying their small pile of belongings from the quay to a patch of weed-split concrete farther up in the wreckage of the town when Per stops and looks up at the headland above, shading his eyes against the descending sun. He points with his staff. He hasn't let go of it for a second, no matter how full everyone else's hands are.

"Look," he says.

On the brow of the headland, overlooking the town and its crescent bay, two mounted people are silhouetted against the late-afternoon sky. Rory can see the horses whickering and fidgeting.

"Only two now," Silvia says.

"One went for more," Per says.

"Maybe."

Per foots his staff on the ground and leans on it with a satisfied grunt. "Women," he says. "Let them come."

Silvia's frowning as she stares up. The two riders are facing down towards the town, unmoving. "They're not afraid of us," she says. "They just watch."

Per laughs, just a shake of his shoulders. "Teach them fear," he says. His fingers flex around the staff. Silvia glances at him as if surprised.

"We won't make any trouble," she says. "OK?"

"Coming now," Per says, nodding up at the riders. He's right, they're moving off, turning the horses unhurriedly. The silhouettes are hardly more than hand-sized up on the ridge but Rory thinks he sees a long ponytail bouncing as one of them forces her mount into a trot.

"I don't think so," Silvia says. "They see the boat long ago. If they want to stop us they can come to the shore before we arrive. I think they wait for more of them."

Per straightens his back. "Be ready, then."

"What are we going to do?" Rory says.

It's the first thing he's said since he stepped ashore. He feels like just another piece of luggage.

"Where are we going to sleep?" he says. "What've we got to eat?"

Silvia looks at him as though noticing for the first time that he's tired and frightened and small. He'd be hungry too if his stomach wasn't still so upset by the crossing that the thought of eating makes him want to be sick.

Per sighs, picks up his staff and a bulky sack, and walks away.

Silvia puts her hands on her hips. "Come," she says. "Let's find a place to stay."

He stands where he is. He's looking at his toes because he's afraid he's going to tear up like a baby. He doesn't want it to be like this. The Mainland's nothing like what he remembered. It's like the worst bits of Home, the ruined side, where everything's smashed up and lying around overgrown, but there's so much more of it. And the superheroes in the comics don't grunt and squabble and haul bags around.

Silvia sits down by his feet. "Now you miss where you come from, yes?"

He doesn't want to say anything to her.

She rolls her neck, unstiffening. "You know something, Rory? I look at you and I see myself."

By now he ought to be used to her never saying what you think she's going to say, but it startles him yet again.

"I was nine years old," she says. "I think. Maybe ten. The same as you. One morning I wake up and I'm all on my own. I remember it like yesterday, how it feels. Who will look after me? What can I do? You can't imagine the next day. You think it's impossible, you're not going to live. I'm not talking about when they took me away from the orphanage. That time they put me with people at least. I'm talking about another part of my story, one I don't tell you yet. When I'm far from where I came from, in a strange country, no friend, no family, no one. I lost that morning the only person I loved, like mother and father and sister and brother all in one person. I was a small girl completely alone in the world. You don't believe me? It's true." She taps his legs, almost in irritation. "And for me there was no Silvia Ghinda talking to me, telling me, I know what it's like for you. No one at all. Only one person I met that day who spoke to me."

This is such an odd thing for her to finish with that he looks around after a while to see whether something's interrupted her. He finds her staring at him, the late sun making her face glow rust-colored like the cliffs.

"But you don't know about him," she says, "do you."

"Me," he says, "No, why would I?"

She sighs. "Anyway. And after all that, here I am. Twenty years later and many hundred kilometers away. Still living, you see. You too. You will go on. Some days you feel you've come to the end of the road, you can't go anymore, but the next day it's different. OK?"

"OK," he says. It's very hard not to say what she wants you to say when she's staring at you.

"Me and Lino, we travel a long way together, I told you. Many many months. Many places much worse than this. At the end of every day it's the same: find a safe place, find food. Sleep safe, be ready for the next day." She stands up: Per's coming back. "We know how to do it. At the beginning we make mistakes. Now, never. Tonight we'll be OK. Tomorrow we'll be OK. We go on. You're like Roma now, hmm? Traveling people."

He has a terrible vision of the rest of his life being like today, queasy, terrifying, trudging bewildered through wastelands carrying sacks for Silvia and Per and Lino.

She ducks close and whispers in his ear, "But we're close to the end now," she says, to him only. "Very, very close."

A sharp whistle comes from somewhere above. "Ah, Lino!" Silvia says, and just like that she's up and away, as if that's it, she's bored of trying to make him feel better. Per mutters something to her and the two of them head away among the buildings, stamping down nettles and sickly grass. No one gives him a second look. It's hard to be miserable when no one notices you doing it. He doesn't like being the last one left in sight of the tied-up dead man on the beach, so after a moment he decides he'd better follow them. A familiar smell stops him as he picks up one of the sacks. He pokes inside the top of it and finds a loaf of Libby's spelt bread.

After a lot of trudging around between abandoned cars and mounds of bramble the gang settle on a forlorn bungalow at the very edge of the village, the last house before it surrenders to the tangle of plant matter tumbling down the hill like a fetid green glacier. Inside it's thick with rat droppings and dust and pollen and leaves. There's a room with the remains of two chairs and a sofa. They look as if a goat's tried to eat them. A grey-white kitchen machine's lying on its side with cords trailing out of it like tails.

It's not even the ruin of a house. It bears the same relationship to a house as the crow-mangled flappy puff of flesh on top of the dead men on the beach bears to a human head. The back half of it has collapsed in a heap of brick and chunks of plaster. This is a good thing, apparently, because it means they can light a fire on the floor and let the smoke straight out. Rory can't believe they're really going to eat and sleep here but no one cares what he believes. They gather leaves and dry sticks and handfuls of flammable rubbish and collect their belongings and open bags and arrange themselves around the floor as if this is what they do every evening. Which, he supposes, it probably is.

In the comics the superheroes have secret lairs full of solemn machinery and grand lonely corners. In the comics they also don't smell. Rory didn't notice it on the boat but now they're crammed in together he can't miss it. Despite all their comings and goings none of the three of them has bothered to fetch a bucket of water, which even he knows is about the first thing you do in the evening, so it's not as if any of them is going to wash either. Though—this thought comes to him slowly, as if there must be something wrong with it—he doesn't actually know where you'd get water here, and, presumably, neither do they.

Silvia wasn't sure they should light a fire but Lino said the two people on horses rode away eastward and he's sure there's no one else nearby. "Look at this boy!" He hugged Rory theatrically. "Cold!" So they've made a pile at the back of the room, right on the floor. It's getting quite dark and uncomfortably chilly. Lino digs around in one of the duffel bags and comes out with a battered black box. He hunches over the tent of twigs in the middle of the pile and is about to open the box—matches, maybe—when Per says, "Let me."

"Not now," Silvia says.

Per unfolds the staff from his lap and gets stiffly to his feet. "Yes," he says. "They do it."

Lino shrugs and puts the box aside. Silvia sits up. She's a shadow in the room, darker around the edges than the rest of them. "Per," she says. "It's nearly night. Leave them alone." But Per's ignoring her, for once. He stands with his legs apart, as if he's on deck again, and thrusts the staff out towards the back of the room, shouting a strange angry word.

"Too long already today," Silvia says.

Per's only answer is to shout the word again. He jabs the staff into the gloom with a sharp motion, like he's fighting someone invisible.

A fleeting glimmer of uneasy light passes over the unlit fire, gone almost in the same instant it appears.

Per growls with effort and frustration and then shouts a third time.

"*Mamma mia,*" Lino whispers.

This time there's a kind of corkscrew of embers in the air, like the momentary trail of a spinning firework. It twists up with a weird sighing noise and vanishes.

"Per," Silvia warns.

The big man swings the staff up and grips it in both hands above his head. He strikes it violently down against the floor, once, twice, a third time, shouting the same word each time, and each time louder and angrier until the final blow makes even Silvia flinch. Not a flicker of light disturbs the room. He roars with rage and hurls the staff into the corner, where it thunks against one of the decaying chairs before rolling noisily to a stop. It's the first time Rory's ever seen him let go of it. Per stands there, breathing heavily. No one dares say a word.

Finally Lino picks up his box again and shuffles almost apologetically to the twigs. He unwraps some small smooth things from inside the box and starts striking them against each other, very rapidly, until sparks begin to trickle from his hands. It takes quite a long time for him to coax the sparks onto the dry leaves. While he's nurturing a frail twist of smoke, cradling, puffing, muttering, Per strides slowly across the room and picks up his staff again. He sits down without looking at Silvia.

She leans close to Rory.

"Men," she whispers, and winks at him.

They eat. Nothing's been washed properly so it all tastes of grit and sand. Rory's finally hungry, fiercely hungry as it turns out. There isn't enough food but he knows better than to complain. As well as Libby's bread there are other things from the Abbey cellars. It's hard to imagine how, but Lino's obviously stolen it. They'll have realized, back in the Abbey. Kate and Fi will be furious.

They'll all be there right now, he thinks, sitting in the big room as darkness falls. It'll be just like the evening Ol died, except now it's him who's dead. He's the missing face. He wonders whether his mother's sitting in the corner pale and wasted and not talking to anyone, like Molly was. He wonders whether someone's saying he was a beacon of good humor in dark times. He wonders whether they'll go over to the church on Briar one day to say good-bye to him.

He chews slowly, out of habit, and sneaks glances at his new companions, Per with his squinty eyes and huge shaggy beard looking like a squatting bear, Lino grimacing and picking his teeth, Silvia as dark as fate. They've got things like unzipped sleeping bags to wrap over themselves while they sit. There wasn't one for Rory but Lino found him a padded and hooded coat that's not too big and surprisingly warm. No one talks much until Silvia wipes her hands on her trousers and says, "Now, let's hear your story."

She means him. "What?"

"You know a little bit of my story now, a little bit of Lino's and Per's. It's your turn."

The others are all looking at him.

"I don't have a story," he says.

"Nobody," Per says. "Just a boy."

"This is England," Silvia says. Rory can't tell who she's talking to now. "This is where everything changed in the world. One day's walk from here, two days, is the end of our journey." She draws a wide circle in the air with her fingers. "The center. You think it's an accident when all of us are here together? Nothing here is a mistake." Per shrugs: he can't follow so much English, he doesn't understand and doesn't care. "You," she says, pointing at him: he blinks in the firelight. "You knew nothing, until Lino and me found you. Then the two of us became three." She mimes the addition, unfolding fingers on her raised hand. "Now we are four. It's the same road. All going together."

"With no Rory," Lino says, "nothing."

"That's right. Without him we would not be here."

Rory doesn't want to feel a shiver of pride when she says this, but he can't help it. In the silence that follows he stares at his hands. He doesn't want anyone to see that he's pleased.

"Is it so close?" Per says in a thick whisper.

Rory starts. It's as if someone else has spoken. He's never heard Per sound anything other than grumpy before, but suddenly there's longing in his voice, or hunger.

Silvia nods.

"Where?"

"East," she says. "Not far. Not more than two days. One, I think."

"For sure?"

She nods again.

Lino, who's been watching this exchange carefully, leaps up and starts dancing back and forth between her and Per and Rory, clapping all of them on the shoulder in turn, talking rapidly and with uncontrollable excitement, squatting down beside them and hugging them one after another. He ends up sticking close to Rory, evidently asking him something over and over again, turning aside only to implore Silvia to translate.

"He says what will you do when we find the ring." Lino's obviously not satisfied with this translation, and corrects her emphatically, but she smiles as if determined to ignore him and says, "If you could do anything. If you could choose. Lino, he's going to learn how to use his gift, and Per the same. What do you say? You won't tell us your story but maybe you can tell us this instead." Lino starts to berate her in Italian; she turns to him and with a quick *shh* cuts him off.

They're all looking at him again.

"What d'you mean?" he says.

"If you could wish for anything," she says, "and it would be true. What would you wish for?"

He stares between them. "So it's like a wishing ring?"

"Maybe like that," Silvia says. Per's about to grumble something but she silences him too.

"Seriously?"

"Seriously."

"Ring of biggest power," Lino declaims.

"*Shh!*"

What does he want? Silvia's waiting for him to say something. He thinks of extra chocolate and more TV time but it's like someone else has put those wishes into his head, Ol maybe. Then he thinks of wishing that What Happened could unhappen and everything could go back to how it was in The Old Days. He's heard the women wishing this all the time. Kate tells them not to but Missus Grouse especially goes on and on about it. A lot of them wish that the people they've lost weren't dead. He tries wishing that too, but it still feels like someone else is choosing, not actually him. He thinks about things nobody else can wish for, things which belong only to him, like reading comics or talking to Her, but he can't make them into one big wish. He knows he ought to wish he could go home. His mother, his bed. He can't say that to Silvia, though, it would make him sound like a baby. And anyway—he doesn't know where he gets this thought from: it's almost as if he's plucked it out of Silvia's face, her eyes glimmering as the fire takes hold—it wouldn't even be true.

* * *

They're going to take turns staying awake in case the people on horses come back. Rory doesn't have to take a turn. Silvia tells him to sleep while she watches. Per and Lino lie down and go to sleep just like that. He can't see how they've done it. It's incredibly uncomfortable. He's spread out a torn piece of carpet long enough and dry enough to curl up on but it's doing nothing to protect him from the hard floor, plus it's scratchy and smells of outside. He's got no pajamas so he's wearing the same clothes he had on all day, and the coat they found for him. They're salty and stiff, and he's cold anyway on the side that's away from the fire. It's noisy in the half-collapsed room too. The fire pops and hisses and there are things scuttling around in the brambles outside. Silvia goes out a couple of times and scrapes around for more things to burn.

It feels like half the night must have gone past and he's never going to get to sleep, when she looks at him and sees that his eyes are open.

"The first night is difficult always," she says, lowering her voice only a little. "The second, a bit better. The third better again. Always better, until it's OK."

He props himself up on an elbow.

"You never said what you were going to do."

"Hmm?"

He's been thinking as he lies awake, round and round. "When you were talking about when you find the ring. You said what Lino and Per want, and you asked me, but you didn't say what you want."

She's sitting with her knees drawn up. She leans her cheek on them, looking back at him thoughtfully.

"You didn't, also," she says.

"I dunno. Can't think of anything."

"And you still can't?"

"What about you?"

He's pretty sure he's got Per and Lino sorted out. He's been thinking about them and their quest and what Silvia said, that both of them want to learn to use their gift. That means Per wants to be able to control his magic staff all the time, because it's obvious he can't, and Lino wants to be able to turn himself into an owl at will, because it's obvious he can't do that either. It's that thing all the superheroes have where they need to learn to Use Their Power Wisely.

But he can't figure Silvia out. There's something different about her, something (he's decided this is by far the best word for her) *secret*.

She takes her time answering him.

"You ask me what I would do if I could wish for anything?"

He's not sure that's exactly what he's asking—what he really wants to know is what she's going to do when they find the Ring of Power, which feels like a slightly different question—but if she wants to talk about herself that's OK.

She closes her eyes. "You remember I told you about the morning when I wake up and I'm all alone in a strange country? I would find the person I lost that day. That's what I wish for."

"Who was he?"

Her eyes blink open and she smiles briefly. "Not he. She. It's the person who taught me English. I told you, remember? She took me away from the camp, away from the men who beat me, the women who pretend to be my grandmother or my aunt."

"What happened to her?"

She lifts her head up so she can shake it, slowly. "I don't know," she says, staring into the fire.

He's rolled over again and tried closing his eyes when she surprises him by speaking up again.

"Do you know this word, *Arcadia*?"

He twists around to check that she's talking to him. "What?"

She says it slowly. "Arcadia."

It sounds like a computer game. He doubts she's thinking about computer games.

"It means," she says, "good place, happy place. Where things are easy. Peaceful. Arcadia. But also, it's a real place. The name of a place in . . . Hellas. What do you call this country in English? Not Hellas. Greeks. Greece! You've never been to Arcadia?"

"Me? No."

She turns back to the fire, remembering. "Steep hills. Little trees, little dry leaves. Everything dusty. That's where we were."

"Who?" he says, after a while.

She shakes away some secret thought. "Me and the person I loved, the teacher. That's where we lost each other. In Arcadia."

He can't tell whether she's talking to him or not. It sounds like she's just remembering, but then she keeps glancing at him as if it matters that he's there.

"I thought it was the end, when that happened," she says. "Like my life was over, I'm finished. Although I was only nine, ten, little like you, I thought I would die from being so unhappy. But it was the beginning."

"Oh," he says, after another long pause.

"There is a light," she says. "Too bright to look at. Like the sun. That's how I see the road ahead of me, because of this light." Just when Rory thinks he must actually be dreaming, despite the ache he can feel in his back from trying to sleep on the floor, she turns to him again and he knows this is really happening. "I saw it first that day, in that place. Arcadia. I know then that everything I see is the truth. I know that all the time I'm going towards it, that at the end of my road I will see what makes this light. Just like I find you again. And her too. I know this will happen."

He wishes he knew what she wants him to say. He feels like she's handing him her secret, but when he opens it up there's just another secret inside it.

"And it will happen here," she says, leaning towards him. She's whispering now.

He doesn't doubt for a moment that she really can see the future. Her face is full of it, shadows and ghosts.

"Very soon," she says.

The night goes on inching by. He supposes he must have got to sleep eventually because he has a very peculiar dream.

He dreams that Per's sitting up by the fire in the middle of the night, his staff crosswise across his lap as usual. The fire's burned right down. Its last light has got into Per's face, as though he's sweating, or his skin's been silvered over like a mirror: everything's dark but he's shining dully. It's so strange seeing him like that, bolt upright, glowing, that Rory lifts his head to stare at him. That's when Per starts speaking not in his own voice (*oh,* Rory thinks, *it's a dream*).

"It belongs to me," he says. The voice coming from his mouth is a man's. It talks in normal proper English. "She gave it to me freely. I did no wrong." It all feels very clear and logical even though it's nonsense, as so often in dreams. "Knowledge is all I sought. What use is wisdom if it dies with you?" (Rory doesn't have to answer. It's the kind of dream where you're just watching.) "It ought to be mine. I have the right of it. I conversed with angels and beings under the earth. For my wisdom she chose me, me and no other. It was fated. Give it back to me." The voice is hungry. There's now something terrible about it, dark and urgent and yet horribly patient, as if it's got all the time in the world. "Put it in my hand. It is mine." An ember flares, and the light in Per's face burns harder for a moment. In the dream Rory can't see whether the man's eyes are open or closed. They're like embers themselves. "Mine," the voice repeats in a cruel whisper. Then the fire goes out.

15

The next thing he knows it's daylight. He aches all over and his mouth feels like he's been chewing dust. There's a mad riot of birdsong.

Silvia and Per are moving about, rearranging things in sacks. The damp light suggests it's early, painfully early for someone who's hardly slept. His hands and feet are almost numb.

"There you are," Silvia says. Per stops what he's doing and makes a disappointed grunt. Perhaps he's been hoping they were going to leave Rory behind.

Rory sits up, rubbing his neck. "Where's Lino?"

"Scouting."

Per loads himself up like a donkey. Silvia's got a little backpack but otherwise the big man carries everything. He slings sacks and bags over each end of his staff and then hefts the whole lot across his shoulders. No one questions this arrangement, even though Rory's not carrying anything at all. They leave the bungalow without a second glance and tramp through the detritus of the town until they come to a road rising away from it, inland. It's more like a canyon in the green morass than an actual road, but it's hard underfoot, and when Rory scuffs away a clump of rotting leaves he sees something which prompts another unlikely memory: a straight white line painted on the ground. He's suddenly remembering how all the roads on the Mainland had things painted on them, arrows and words and numbers, and his father explained: *It's so everyone doesn't crash into each other*. Everyone. There were lots of people. Just walking from where the helicopter landed to the place they got in the car, he saw more people than the entire population of Home. That's what he remembers, masses of people, driving and walking around. He thinks he does, anyway, but he can't have. There's no one here.

Lino appears, coming down the road ahead of them. "Everywhere quiet," he says, and then gives Silvia a longer report in Italian. They keep walking while he talks. It's steadily and quite steeply uphill. Per trudges rhythmically, he doesn't want to stop or slow down, not with the load he's carrying. Rory hangs back with the other two. Even though he can't understand a word of their conversation it's better than risking a look from Per.

"He says very few houses," she tells him, when Lino's finished. It's funny how much slower the words sound. Italian's like running compared to English walking. "He doesn't see anybody. But he sees the mark of horses, with the feet."

"Hoofprints," Rory says.

"*Ecco*." Rory's learned this word by now. It means one of *Look, There, OK,* or *I told you so,* or a combination of them. Lino's stopped. He points down by his feet. Rory would never have seen the mark on his own but now he's looking carefully there it is: a thick quarter-circle stamped into a patch of receptive mud. It's obviously part of a hoofprint.

Frowning, Silvia stops as well. Per glances back as best he can with the staff straddling his shoulders, but keeps on uphill.

"So they were watching," she says. "This is not old."

"I see no one." Lino explains himself to Rory in a noisy whisper. "This I don't like. I see them, they don't see me, that's OK. This, *psshh.* Not so good."

"Is it those people we saw?"

"I think so." Silvia's tapping her foot, thinking. "We think they go away but they must not go far. They come back, quietly, watching."

"Horse is big *animale.*" Lino trots with his hands and makes clopping sounds. "But I don't hear."

"They're careful, these people. Clever." Silvia leans close to Rory and grins. "Women."

Per shouts something which obviously means *Keep up,* though it's more snorts than words. The three others start following him again.

"Can we go a different way?" Rory says.

"Not us," Silvia says. "Lino says this is the only road. There are small roads, foot roads or horse, by the sea. But we can't go that way. You and me, yes. Them, no."

"*Le sirene*," Lino explains, seeing Rory's expression.

It sounds even better when Lino says it. He likes this word, searainy. It's much better than calling Them *Them*. It's glistening and misty, like Her skin.

Does She have a proper name too? He's never thought of it before.

"I thought it was OK with Per."

Silvia lowers her voice. "Sometimes, yes. Sometimes Per can keep the *sirene* away. But it's not good to trust those spirits too much." Rory's about to ask what she means when she goes on. "Anyway, look, the staff is busy." She grins, gesturing at Per's back. "Like a . . . What is it, male cow?"

"Ox?"

"That's right." She mimes walking under a yoke. "Like an ox, yes?"

Lino nudges Rory. "You know *le sirene*?"

"Er. Yes."

"You see?"

"You mean did I ever see Them?"

"*Si si*. Girls without clothings." He winks. "*Molta bella*. Very nice."

"No," Rory says, looking away. He's being teased.

"*Ma no*. For you is OK! Only a boy. You don't want to see this?"

"'Course not," he mutters.

Lino sighs. "After we find this ring, I take a *sirena*, I think. *Come sposa*. My woman, you know? I think this will be . . ." He smacks his fingers to his lips. "The most beautiful. You help, yes? You go them, you say, This Uccellino is good man, very good man. OK?"

Rory's saved from having to respond by the fact that Per's stopped in front of them. They've reached the top of the slope above the abandoned town. For the first time the road ahead dips instead of rising. The choking green mass they've been walking between has flattened down here, exposed to the sea wind, and all of a sudden there's a view inland. Disoriented, Rory looks around. He can't see the sea anywhere. It's gone.

The wind sounds different: narrower, farther away. Instead of the sea the horizons are all green and brown, with glints of yellow. There are distant trees whose leaves have gone the color of weak afternoon sunshine. There are open acres like fields, but twenty times the size of the fields on Home. The wind blows patterns like waves across their tall weeds and grass. A single heathy hill rises out of them, like one of Sansen's humps except the sea around it is green instead of grey. He has a picture of the Mainland in his head which shows a great mass of houses and shops and things going off in every direction, like a carpet of buildings unrolled over the ground. There's nothing like that in sight. He can see a few houses or barns but they're peeping out of the landscape, not the other way around. They're scattered in groups, little rocks in the grass ocean. Smoke's coming up from one of them. The black shapes moving slowly through the green around them aren't seals or birds but cows, real cows, like the ones there used to be on Home before they all died or were killed. There's so much solid ground everywhere it makes Rory feel slightly short of breath. So much of it, and so little of anything else. Birds drift around in ones and twos. There are no people, no women working or pausing in their work to chat. There's just a wide world lying utterly new in every direction, like a giant asleep.

Per sniffs. "Looks OK," he says. He shifts the staff with its dangling cargo and sets off again.

"I look," Lino says, meaning *I'll go and look,* and he's off past Per, disappearing quickly around the next bend.

The rest of them walk on quietly until Lino returns. He's in the middle of a whispered conversation with Silvia when a horrible loud ripping sound starts up out of nowhere. Per's dropped the sacks to the ground and swung the staff off his shoulders almost before Rory's stopped cowering at the noise. It's a throaty pulse of inarticulate fury, like the air shouting at him. *It's a dog barking,* he's telling himself: he used to know what that meant but he's forgotten. Silvia's pushing past Per, still talking to Lino. She beckons Rory forward.

"We go first," she says.

"Huh?"

The noise goes on and on. At least it's not getting any closer. "Lino says two or three houses, all closed, he sees no people. The dog is inside. If anyone's there and they see a woman and a child, they don't get scared, there's no trouble. Come."

She actually takes his hand, like his mother does when she's cross, and starts walking him towards the noise. There's a sharp right-hand bend in the road ahead. She motions Per and Lino to stay hidden behind it.

"What d'you mean, trouble?"

"*Shh.*" Her grip is unbreakably tight.

Around the corner lies a clutch of buildings wrapped to their waists in ivy. Their lower windows are nailed over with planks of wood. The road ahead runs straight between them, houses on either side. A charred and fallen pole lies across the road, spilling wires which disappear into the gorse. Beyond it, one small patch of ground in front of the buildings has been kept clear of weeds: a circle of grass around an old red phone box. The noise is locked up inside one of the houses, though it sounds like it's trying to get out. Something thumps against the inside of a door.

A crackle of bluish sparks shimmers over the fallen wires, there's a snatch of sound like the shaking of a tambourine, and the phone starts ringing.

The dog stops barking instantly. Silvia lets go of Rory's hand.

Rory hasn't heard a phone for at least as long as he hasn't heard a dog, but he remembers what the sound means at once. It's like it's hardwired into him. It's the lost sound of The Old Days. It was how you knew what was happening, where you were supposed to go, who you shared the world with. It was the first thing to go. He remembers his mother holding the mouthpiece to her chest and turning to the rest of them and saying *We're cut off,* and that's when they knew it wasn't a glitch or a hiccup or It'll Get Sorted Out Eventually. She said it like a death sentence. He remembers the adults going to each other's houses to see if anyone had a working phone. He remembers what his father looked like when he came back and said no one did.

Silvia's stopped, as dumbstruck as Rory. As the two of them stand there a man comes half-running, half-tumbling out of one of the buildings. He's wearing a kind of robe like a monk's, mud-colored, cinched at the waist with orange twine. He pauses only for a moment when he sees Rory and Silvia before picking up the skirts of his robe and hustling shakily across the road to the phone box. He's an old man, ragged as a pecked crow. He keeps glancing at the two of them and every time he does so he looks like he's going to lose his balance and trip over himself.

Silvia nudges Rory in the back. "Come."

The man cringes when he sees that she's started to walk towards him. As he tiptoes across the cleared grass towards the phone box he starts making frantic pushing motions with his arms which obviously mean *Stay back*.

"I don't think he wants us to—"

"*Shh*. Come on."

The man tries to open the door of the phone box with one hand, still waving at them with the other. It's too heavy. He whimpers, abandons his efforts to stop Silvia, heaves the door open, and vanishes inside. The windows of the phone box are all cracked and clouded but he must have answered it because the ringing stops.

Everything's suddenly quiet. Rory looks back and sees Lino peeking around the turn in the road. One of the wires in the road fizzes and there's a sudden smell of bitter smoke. A burst of music blows by like the echo of an invisible party, riotous and pulsing, gone as quickly as the closing of a door. Silvia whirls around but there's nothing to see.

They can hear the man inside the phone box. "Hello?" he says. He sounds like an ordinary man, speaking English: another forgotten noise from The Old Days. "Hello?"

Silvia levers herself over the pole. Rory follows. Now he can see that there are things in the grass around the phone box. They don't look like the usual scattered junk. They look like they've been put there. He sees a toy airplane, a violin, one of those lightbulbs made out of twisty spiral tubes, a notebook diary (the damp's made its edges curl up like a dead leaf), a tangled flattened mobile of colored animals, some little black statues which might be chess pieces, a computer keyboard, and four or five mobile phones.

The door half-opens and the man squeezes out. He's out of breath. His hands are splotchy and his face is almost grey. There's nearly as much hair in his nostrils and eyebrows as there is on top of his head. His eyes are wandering as if he can't see them properly.

"No one there," he says apologetically.

Behind the door of the house he emerged from the dog's scratching and whining. It sounds like a large dog. Silvia gives Rory a not very discreet prod in the back. The old man misinterprets their hesitation. "Don't mind Ralph," he says. "He always gets like that when the gods are about. Handy, actually. Like them canaries in the mines. Hush, you!" he shouts at the door.

Under her breath Silvia mutters, "Greet him."

"Er," Rory says. "Hello."

"Oh, yes. Hello, and all that." The man hitches up his robe, which appears to be made of brown curtains sewn together, and steps around the things lying in the grass. "I don't know you two, do I? You can leave whatever you like. Hair's good if you didn't bring anything else. Always gone by morning, the hair. I've got a little pair of scissors inside if you want." He sidles closer, peering. Only now does he appear to see them properly. "Is that a suntan? You're not with the Riders. Where have you come, oh, oh?" He interrupts his own question with a nervous stutter, stepping back and glancing at his door. "Oh, yes. Well, then."

"We just arrived," Rory says. "We came from—"

Silvia drops a hand on his shoulder, hard, and steps in front of him. "We are travelers," she says. "From far. I have nowhere else seen a telephone that's working."

"Just the two of you, then, is it?"

Silvia spreads her hands as if to say, *Can you see anyone else?* "Me and the boy. We are no trouble."

"Only they warned me someone had landed down that way. Men."

"Who told you this?"

"You're foreign," he says. It's an accusation.

"My name is Silvia," she says. "Silvia Ghinda." She puts her hand out. He stares at it like it's dirty. "We have our own food. We are only walking past."

"Yes, well, you'll have to leave something anyway. I don't know if foreign hair'll do. Ralph! Be quiet! That's Ralph," he says. He's backing towards the door all the time. "He's very fierce."

"How's that phone working?" Rory says.

"Eh? Gods, isn't it? At the crossroads. This is my crossroads, has been ever since . . . Ever since." There are side roads between the houses, and now that he's looking Rory can even see a signpost, its arms all but drowned in ivy.

"Do they speak to you," Silvia says, "these gods?"

The man droops shamefacedly, winding his fingers in the twine of his belt. "Not yet," he says.

"We should ask your blessing." The man blinks in surprise. "If you look after this road."

"That's an idea, isn't it?" He's stopped his nervous edging towards the door. The dog's still pawing at it. "Very good. Blessing, absolutely."

"And also," Silvia says, "you can say to other people that we make no trouble. You tell them, the gypsy and her friends, they do no harm. They respect the road."

"Oh, indeed. Respect, that's the thing."

"We pass quietly. The men too, who crossed the sea. All of us need only a day to go where we want, maybe two. You will tell these Riders this?"

"Should get there by the evening, I'd have thought," the man says, squinting at the sky. "No more than a day's walk for you young folk."

Silvia's face is blank. "Excuse me?" she says.

"Or don't you know the way, being foreign and all. You'll have to find it yourself, then. Just stay straight on, east, don't turn to the higher ground or the lower."

"The way to where?" Silvia says.

"Oh. Oh, now." The man waves a finger in an indecipherable gesture. If it's meant as a threat it's embarrassingly feeble. "Don't pretend I'm a fool. I may be old but I know what's what."

"Where is it you think we are going?"

"Used to be lots like you, back when, when . . . Back when. Tramping around all over the place. Take my advice, tramp back where you came from. No one ever came out again. Good luck to you. You can do your own hair, just put it in the grass anywhere." He takes a determined stride towards his house. The dog snuffles excitedly.

Silvia's between him and the door in a flash. The man almost jumps when he finds her in his way. His mouth begins trembling. "Now now," he says. "Mind out there, young lady." He makes the beginning of an effort to step around her. She barely has to sway aside to stop him.

"I think," Silvia says, raising her voice slightly, "you spend too long talking on the telephone to nobody, sir. You forget to answer when someone asks you a question. Where do you think we are going, please?" Rory's never heard anyone make the word *please* sound like a threat before.

"No funny business, now." The man's plainly worried, not to say frightened. The dog keens and thumps against the door. "The gods send you wrong if you mess with the crossroads. I'm telling you."

"Rory." How she can remain so icy with a thing which sounds like it's the size of a horse banging at the door just behind her back, Rory'll never know. "Maybe I'm not speaking English right. Or maybe this man doesn't like to talk to women. Or gypsies. You ask him, please."

"All right, all right. No need to be like that, is there? I'm not one of them racists. I said good luck to you, didn't I? Which you might have thanked me for, seeing as you'll be needing any luck you can get in the Valley. There, I said it. No point pretending I don't know, everyone knows what your sort want."

Lino and Per have come into view. They must have thought the situation was about to turn bad. Silvia glances back and waves them away with a swift impatient gesture. "The Valley?" she says, dropping her voice. She says it like that, the same way the old man did. Rory can hear the capital *V*. "What is this place?"

The old man's anxious look has fastened on his phone box. His madly sprouting eyebrows are bent in, as if he's remembering something.

"They say in the heart of the Valley there's a room with a phone," he says, "and if you use it you can speak to the dead."

Silvia steps forward and wraps her hands in the front of his robe. He gasps in alarm and makes as if to push her away but he might as well be a baby in her grip. The dog breaks into a frenzy of barking. "Tell me again," Silvia says, low and fast, "how to walk to this place."

"Hands off!" He's gone breathless and very shaky. "You can't do this."

"East from here," she says, "and neither high nor low. Is this right?" The old man nods, though Rory's pretty sure he'd agree to anything by now. He's almost dangling from her fists. Per and Lino are approaching fast. The door bounces in its frame as the dog flings itself against it. Silvia lets the man go. He sort of shrivels up where she drops him, cringing as Per strides over the fallen pole. Compared to the rest of them Per seems huge enough to block out the daylight.

"Silence your dog," Silvia says.

"Ralph," the man stammers. "Hush, boy."

Per's swinging his staff down in front of him as he approaches. He points it forward and shouts a command. Silvia's already holding her hands up to him—*Wait, don't*—but it all happens too quickly for her. An indistinct swish of blazing light arrows past Rory—though it's too faint and fast to see, he has the horrible impression that it's full of faces, smooth faces with empty eye sockets—and the door of the house is briefly outlined, as if a beacon has flared up behind it. The dog makes a dreadful strangled whining noise and goes silent. There's a muffled thump a moment later, and then nothing except the echo of Silvia's shout, "Stop!" Per turns the staff to point at the man, who's actually cowering, hands over his head and everything. Per's eyes are reflecting a fire no one else can see. "Stop," Silvia says again. Lino puts his hands on the staff to push it away. An angry whisper passes overhead, the sound of a sharp gust disturbing a pile of dead leaves. Per starts back with a snarl as if Lino's slapped him. Something strange and dreadful happens in his face which reminds Rory of his dream; then Lino skips in front of him and claps his hands in front of Per's eyes. The big man blinks and steps back, and Rory sees that there's nothing wrong with his eyes after all: just some weird trick of the light. "No," Silvia's saying. She repeats it more quietly as the danger drains out of the scene. "No." Per shakes his head, frowning, letting the staff rest on the ground. "No. This is a holy man. We make no trouble. All right?" The old man's peeking out between his arms. All of them can now hear him breathing, wheezing gasps like he's about to have a heart attack. "Look," Silvia says. She reaches into her hair and tugs out a few long strands. "OK? Like this?" She holds them out to the man. "Is this enough? I put it there, by the telephone?"

The man straightens, leaning against the wall. He can't take his eyes off Per.

"What do you lot want here?" he says. It takes him a while to get the question out. His teeth are chattering like he's just been dragged out of the sea.

"Only to pass," Silvia says. "With your . . ." She looks at Rory. "Allowing?"

"Permission."

"With your permission."

Now the man's staring between all of them.

Per loosens his grip on the staff and rolls his shoulders. "I bring the bags," he says. He sounds bored. "We go."

"You can jolly well find your own way," the man mutters. "Hey." Lino's begun to poke around among the objects around the phone box. "You shouldn't . . ." Lino looks up at him, quizzically, and the man's voice trails away.

"This is where I put the sacrifice?" Silvia says, stepping the same way. She means her hair. Per snorts and trudges away to fetch the bags. "Here?" She winds the strands into a curl around her fingers and puts them carefully down in the grass.

"He really shouldn't do that," the man says. Lino's opening the door of the phone box.

Silvia smiles a What-Can-You-Do smile at the man. "You too," she says to Rory. "Make sacrifice."

"Me?"

"Like our friend says, there are gods here." Inside the box Lino's picked up the phone and is talking to it in inquisitive Italian. "It's good to do. For your journey."

"You mean . . ." Silvia marches over to him and yanks out a couple of hairs before he can even think about trying to stop her. "Ow!" She puts them in his fist.

"Go on."

Rory feels pretty stupid laying his hair in the grass by Silvia's, but he's not going to argue with her. Lino reemerges, shaking his head. "*Niente*. This god, he is . . ." He shrugs, and mimes something like a feather blowing away.

"You'll have trouble," the old man mumbles, very nervously but trying to be defiant. "Don't say I didn't warn you."

Silvia only nods at him, peaceably. "This world is full of difficulty." Per's coming back, all saddled up with the luggage again. Lino asks Silvia something and they exchange a few words, rapid and purposeful.

"Knew you was all foreigners," the old man grumbles, though keeping his voice right down to make sure Per at least won't hear.

"So," Silvia says, when they're all gathered. "We go on. Thank you for your blessing."

"Eh? Oh." He looks like he's about to offer a grumpy retort, but a glance at Per makes him think better of it. "All right then."

"Remember this, please, if anyone asks. We go only one day, maybe two. We make no trouble if everyone leaves us alone."

He sniffs. "Won't have to worry," he says, half-swallowing his own words like Pink does when she's trying to be rude to Laurel but doesn't dare say it out loud. "No one ever comes back from the—"

"We wish you good day." Silvia interrupts him perfectly smoothly but very fast. "Let's go."

Per starts off without another word. She nods at Lino, who follows a moment later.

"What did he mean," Rory asks her, as the two of them set off as well, a few steps behind, "no one comes back from—"

She gives him a strange sharp look. "That's just a crazy old man," she says firmly. "I'm surprised you listen to anything he tells us."

Her manner's confusing. "You mean that's not where it's hidden?"

She stops him with a hand on his shoulder.

"What?" she says quietly, glancing to make sure Lino and Per are carrying on ahead.

Rory's said something wrong, he can tell by her eyes. When they go cold like this it's easy to imagine her telling that man who came to the gypsy camp he was going to die. "It sounded like that's where you wanted to go," he says, ashamed again. Sometimes she makes him feel like part of their gang, sometimes she makes him feel like a boy who doesn't know anything and shouldn't be here. "That Va—"

"Crazy man," she says. She bends over him, both hands on his shoulders. "I don't want you to repeat his crazy man words. OK?"

"OK," Rory says. Suppressed misery wells up in him. He wants to go home.

But there's no turning back. He tries picturing himself giving them the slip, running away. It turns out that the idea of taking a single step on his own in this weird unending wasteland is unimaginable. He drops back behind the others sometimes because his feet are getting tired and he hasn't had much to eat and it feels like they're just walking and walking, but whenever he gets too far behind he can feel the huge green overgrown strangeness like a monster at his back and he grits his teeth and scurries to catch up. He can't understand how Per can keep going carrying all that stuff, always at the same steady pace, whether the road's dipping or rising. Silvia walks behind him with her arms folded. She looks like she's thinking. Lino's gone ahead to scout. No one makes any suggestion of stopping for a rest or a snack.

Then, abruptly, Per's standing still, listening. Silvia turns back to Rory with her finger on her lips. He stops too.

There's a soft thumping sound in the distance. Slowly, Rory remembers it: hoofbeats.

Per puts his load down and frees his staff. For some reason this gesture makes Rory forget his aching feet and belly at once.

A few moments later and Lino appears. The hoofbeats are far off, somewhere on the higher ground to the left of the road. They're fading too, but Lino keeps his voice very low as he and Silvia have a long discussion. Then Silvia talks to Per. No one wants to tell Rory what's happening and he doesn't feel like asking, though he guesses from the way Silvia's giving quietly urgent instructions that it's not good news. He sits down in the road with his chin in his hands, thinking about the life he left behind. After a little bit Per and Lino turn around and start off back the way they came, back towards the crossroads and the phone booth, leaving Silvia and Rory and all the bags. The place where they've stopped feels high and lonely. Rory can't see anything over the billowing hedges except the sky. Silvia comes and sits next to him, pulling a flask from her pack. He turns his face away.

"Water?" she says. He's thirsty, but he shakes his head without looking.

She takes a careful drink. "It's not a good time to lose your voice," she says. "I think soon we will have company."

That gets his attention.

She puts the flask back without offering it to him again. "Lino sees people on horses, far ahead. He goes up a tree and watches. One of them goes alone and"—she draws a semicircle around the two of them with a finger—"goes behind, like this. I think it's to see where we are, while the others come along the road." She moves fist and finger in opposite directions until they meet each other. "I said before. These are careful people."

"Where did Per and Lino go?"

"These people don't know Lino sees them, I think. Per and Lino make a little surprise for the one who has gone behind."

"What do you and me do?"

"We wait." She smiles. "You want a rest, I think."

"But what if they come?"

She lies back, propping her head on a sack like it's a pillow. "They know we are here already. They have horses; they ride faster than we can walk. We can't always hide. Maybe it's time to show them why they should leave us alone."

"Are we going to fight them?"

"I hope not." She stretches her arms, entirely untroubled. "It's whatever they choose. We will see what kind of people they are." She prods the lumps in the sack under her head. "Some people will try to kill you for this." She means the food. "Some people would kill you for this." She pats between her legs. Rory doesn't know what she means but he knows it's embarrassing and to do with Sex, and looks away again. "Most people, they just want you to go away. Like your women on the island. They find a way of living in this world, they want to keep it, they don't want anyone to come and change anything. Ah." She opens her eyes wide and raises a finger: *Quiet. Listen.*

It's hoofbeats again, lots of them, scuffling and jingling rather than thumping: they must be on a hard road this time. Rory scrambles to his feet. They're far away and they don't sound like they're moving fast, but it's a thick sort of noise, a crowd.

"That sounds like a lot of them."

"Listen now," she says. "If they come before Lino and Per, I try to talk to them. All right? But I want you to stay quiet. You pretend you don't understand English, OK? You listen very carefully but don't speak."

His heart's thudding. He's one of the gang again but now he's not sure he wouldn't rather be the useless stowaway. He can't play tricks on an army; he's only ten. Silvia must be able to read his expression because she sits up and makes him look at her. "It's OK to be frightened," she says. "They will expect this. Just remember, don't speak. And don't worry." She grins at him. "Our road doesn't end here. I know this."

The riders are coming along the road from the east. The noise fades in and out as the road bends and dips but he's sure it's getting louder overall. In fact he thinks he can hear voices as well. Then, very suddenly, it's much louder. Silvia stands up, unhurriedly, and faces down the road, arms crossed. Rory glances back, hoping desperately to see Lino and (preferably) Per, but it's just the two of them, a child and a woman against an army. He's edging behind Silvia. He's aghast at his own cowardice. He sees something bobbing above the hedge by the turn in the road, hears a single laugh—a woman's laugh—as clear as if it's in the next room. "Remember," Silvia murmurs, "you don't know English." Then the riders appear.

Their chatter falls silent. They rein in, the horses shuffling to a stop, nudging against each other, blocking the road completely.

It's an army of four, all women. They shift in their saddles, staring. The stares aren't at all friendly. One of them, her face hidden by a pair of enormous sunglasses, reaches down into a bag by her stirrups and draws out a length of chain. The woman who'd been riding at the front of the group leans forward to pat her horse's neck, and as she does so says to the one next to her (who looks a bit like a horse herself), "Where are the men?" She says it softly but Rory hears it well enough. Her horse-faced neighbor shakes her head briefly: *I don't know.*

"Good morning," Silvia says, unfolding her arms. Rory can't stop himself glancing up at her in surprise. She's changed her accent, thickened it.

The women look at each other, all except the one in the lead, who keeps her eyes on Silvia. She has a weathered, freckly, serious face. She's wearing an overcoat with stripes on the shoulder like a general in a proper army, and a red scarf tying back her hair. She hesitates a moment and then eases the horse forwards with her heels. "Good morning to you," she says. Her voice is quite deep. She sounds suspicious, unwelcoming. The horses are astonishingly enormous. They're staring too, big dark blank eyes all fixed on Silvia and Rory.

"Is fine day," Silvia says, in her extra foreign voice.

"Not bad."

Silvia spreads her arms, palms open. "I am stranger," she says, "in your country."

"Where're the others?" This is the horse-faced one, who looks even more hostile than the first woman. She's older, probably the oldest of the four. She has the kind of face that looks like it would break into pieces if you tried to remove its scowl.

Silvia gestures vaguely behind her. "They get something."

"We should make a move," the one with the sunglasses says. She's talking quietly and quickly, as if she's assuming Silvia and Rory won't know what she's saying. "While it's just these two."

"Who's the boy?" says the general with the red scarf.

Silvia looks at Rory with an expression so unlike her normal face that he almost laughs. She's made herself wide-eyed, almost stupid-looking. "Friend," she says, and clasps him around the shoulders. On the spur of the moment Rory can't remember what he's supposed to pretend to understand and what he isn't, so he just stands there looking stupid, which come to think of it must be more or less what Silvia wants. "Only boy."

"Poor little bugger," mutters the fourth one, the woman at the back. She's stocky and tough-looking. Her voice reminds Rory of Missus Anderson, a proper local voice, but nothing else about her is remotely the same. Missus Anderson's dithery and wittery. This woman looks like she'd happily wrestle her own horse. She's dressed in a thick black jacket with skulls and lightning bolts and faded jaggedy writing on it.

"Hostage," says sunglasses woman. From her voice she's the youngest of the four. Her hands look slim and small, but she's winding the chain around them in a way Rory doesn't like at all. "Let's do it."

"We don't want fight," Silvia says. "Only walking through."

"Heading for the Valley, is it?" says the horse-faced one.

Silvia makes her face look like she doesn't understand. "We go east," she says. "One day. Then finish."

"Thought so," the same woman mutters.

"Where have you come from?" asks the general. As her coat suggests, she seems to be in charge.

"Sal," the one with the sunglasses says to her, "let's not negotiate. We had a plan, remember? If you want to talk to her you can do it at the Mount."

"Long distance," Silvia says, ignoring the interruption, or pretending to ignore it.

"Across the sea?" says horse-face. The general's questions sound reasonably polite. This other woman makes everything into an accusation.

"Yes," Silvia says.

The general, Sal, leans on her pommel. "We're quite interested in how you managed that, you see."

From somewhere behind Rory and Silvia comes a stifled shriek.

Silvia's hand goes tense on Rory's shoulder. The tough-looking woman starts and stares and says, "That sounded like Soph." Sal's expression loses its wary politeness at once. She's glaring, reining in her horse. Suddenly all the animals are moving, scuffling around each other. "Quick," sunglasses woman snaps. "At least grab the kid." She and the tough one are pushing their way to the front. Silvia folds her arms around Rory but doesn't move. She couldn't move anyway, there's horse everywhere. The atmosphere's turned dangerous in the blink of an eye. "I'll go and see," says the tough one, and spurs her mount into a noisy canter, disappearing down the road behind them. The general shouts after her: "Ace!" She's steered her horse behind Rory and Silvia. The two of them are now encircled by clumping hooves and angry stares. Rory feels like he's about to be crushed, and clutches at Silvia's hand. The woman in the sunglasses unwraps the length of chain from her hand and starts swinging it in circles over her head. "Hand over the boy!" she shouts. "Easy," Sal's saying, "easy," but now the horse-faced one's dismounted. She's wearing fingerless gloves with thick metal hoops over her knuckles; she holds them up, flexing her hands, and beckons at Rory. "Come on, you," she says.

Silvia stands her ground. A horse whinnies right by Rory's ear. He closes his eyes and burrows his head against Silvia. He can hear the chain whirring in the air. "For Christ's sake, be careful with that," Sal says, but the sunglasses woman's voice has a nasty edge now. "If that was Soph," she says, breathing hard, "God help you—"

"They've got Soph!" An angry shout from down the road behind them. "Get hold of them, quick!"

"Shit," says Sal, and "Here!" shouts horse-face, and the next thing Rory knows he's in the middle of a wordless scuffle, women tugging and pulling and grunting. Someone yanks him away from Silvia. "Don't touch me!" she snaps, in her own voice, and then there's more scuffling, and then a glint of metal, and everyone's suddenly standing still, breathing out clouds of steam like the horses.

Sal the general has taken out a knife. She's holding it almost apologetically, but firmly, showing it to everyone, her eyes on Silvia. The arm around Rory's neck belongs to the horse-faced woman. They all stand there, eyeing each other, not wanting things to get any worse, and in that pause the tough-looking woman in the black leather jacket comes back, riding hard around the curve of the road, pulling her horse to a skittery halt. "They've got Soph," she says. "The two men. One of them's a monster. Huge. Get that bitch wrapped up."

Sunglasses woman needs no second invitation. She steps quickly behind Silvia, pulls her arms behind her back, and wraps the chain around her wrists. Silvia hisses a curse and grimaces in pain, but she's stopped struggling. She glances at Rory and to his amazement gives him her briefest and most secretive smile.

"Are they with the Pack?" says the woman who's holding Rory, the horse-faced one. Her breath smells particularly foul. She's wedged her arm hard against his neck. He can't move at all if he wants to keep breathing.

"Don't think so." The tough woman has got a cricket bat from somewhere, and is hefting it purposefully in one hand while she steers her horse around with the other. "It's those two from the boat." The others are all on foot, horses milling around nervously behind them. Sal stands close in front of Silvia and slowly lowers the knife. "This will be OK," she says, speaking very clearly. "Do you understand me? No fight."

"Long as you behave," adds horse-face, giving Rory's neck a little tug: little, but enough to make his throat burn.

The next thing that happens is Lino comes haring down the road and around the corner, where he stops at once, taking in the scene, his enormous eyes round as saucers. He shouts something to Silvia, who answers.

"Sounds like Italian," Sal says. "*Italiano?*"

Ignoring her, Silvia exchanges something with Lino again. He trots back out of sight.

"He says your woman is not hurt," Silvia says to Sal, in her proper voice. "I tell my friend to make sure it stays the same. There is no need for this."

Sal stares at her in surprise.

"Well well well," says sunglasses woman. "This is a clever one."

"Be gentle with the boy," Silvia says. "He doesn't speak English. He is frightened."

Got it, Rory thinks. It's a weird feeling. He's being half throttled and Silvia's got her hands tied behind her back, but he can tell somehow that she's in control of the situation.

"Easy, Jody," Sal says to horse-face. "No need to strangle the kid. We can sort this out."

"Where's Soph?" says the one with the sunglasses.

"They're bringing her," says the tough one.

Lino returns, walking this time, soon followed by Per. Everyone goes very still when Per comes into view. He's holding his staff in one hand, as always, but with the other he's got a tall scrawny woman by the scruff of the neck and he's pushing her along like another of his sacks. They've gagged her with a band of red cloth, a long sock maybe, tied through her mouth and around the back of her head.

Sunglasses woman wrenches Silvia's arms. "Tell them to get that out of her mouth right away," she says in her ear. "And don't pretend you don't understand me."

"It's all right," Sal says. She raises her voice. "Everyone's a little tense. Let's calm it down." She turns to Silvia. "Can you ask them to take that gag off, please? Soph's a bit sweary but she doesn't bite."

"And you let go of the boy," Silvia says.

Sunglasses woman's about to say something angry but Sal stops her. "OK," she says. "Jody?"

With obvious reluctance, Jody removes her arm from Rory's throat. He rubs his neck, gulping air. Silvia says something to Lino, who unties the tall woman's mouth.

"Fucking arseholes," she says, as soon as she can speak. She's got an accent that's not from England: it comes out as *aahhsholes*. She has a narrow face, young but grown-up, pocked all around her cheeks and mouth with pimple scars. Her hair's longer and straighter than Silvia's and almost as black. She rubs her chin. "They were waiting for me at the crossroads." She says *waiting* like *whiting*. Per's holding her at arm's length, and even though she's very tall, taller even than Kate, she looks like a rag puppet in front of him.

"Let her go," the tough woman says to Per. She's still mounted and still gripping the cricket bat.

"Careful, Sal," shouts the woman called Soph. The two groups are separated by maybe twenty strides of road, littered with the gang's bags. "Fuckers knew I was coming. Must've seen me. This lot know what they're doing."

Lino calls a question. Before Silvia can answer sunglasses woman has twisted her arms again. "That's enough of that," she says. "They could be planning something. Only English now, all right?"

"Hold the woman." Silvia's answering Lino, in English, as she's been told. "If there is trouble, break her neck."

"Bitch," spits horse-face, and grabs Rory's shoulders. There's a lot of angry stirring, but Sal moves quickly, raising her arms and her voice together. "Everyone listen," she says. "Everyone!" She moves to calm her horse, then swings herself up onto its saddle and rides into the space in the middle of the standoff. "No one's going to get hurt. All right?" She glares at the rest of her army, and then at Lino and Per. "Do you understand me? No one gets hurt? Do they understand that much?"

"Yes," Silvia says.

"Good. Now. Let's talk. Just talk, OK? Let's find out what you want."

"To go on this road," Silvia says. "East. Left alone. We have food and everything we need."

"If they're so keen to commit suicide," the tough one says, "might as well let them go."

"No way, Ace," says the one with the sunglasses. "The Professor's going to want to talk to them."

"I don't like the idea of taking them to Dolphin," Jody says. "We could blindfold the men and march them to the Mount, like Haze said."

"It's on their way," sunglasses woman—presumably Haze—agrees. "Let's do that. Grab that kid."

"No," Sal says loudly. "I told you, we're just talking."

Haze mutters something Rory can't hear, though it doesn't sound complimentary.

"The giant's the one to watch," Soph shouts. "Benson wouldn't go near him. Bolted when he looked at him. I don't like that club of his either."

"Your friend is wise," Silvia says. "Per is not a man to make angry."

"You should try me," Ace says.

"Stop it," Sal says.

"Let us go." Silvia's still addressing only Sal, staying very calm. "Untie my hands, we will pick up our things, give you back your friend, go on to the east. We find what we are looking for and you will not see the four of us again."

"Well," Ace says, "that last bit's certainly right."

"What is it you're looking for?" Sal says.

"This I can't tell you."

"The Valley?"

"The room where your wishes come true," Ace says sarcastically.

"The well whose water cures every illness of body or soul," Haze says, as if she's reciting something.

"I have never heard this name, the Valley," Silvia says with a straight face. Rory gapes for a moment before remembering he's not supposed to understand anything.

"It's a long day's walk due east," Sal says. "That's what you said you were planning, isn't it? If that's where you think you're going, the Valley's where you'll end up. You're not the only ones who've gone looking in there."

"But we are the only ones who will find what we look for," Silvia says. Ace snorts a snort worthy of Per.

"They came in a boat, Ace," says Haze. "Think about it. Two men."

"Exactly," says Jody.

"This is serious shit," Soph says, apparently agreeing with the other two. "Listen, Sal. They did something to the old coot's dog. His dog, understand? Knocked it out cold. Good as killed it."

For some reason this makes a huge impression on the other women. Haze looks up at Sal.

"Christ," she says. "We've got to bring them with us." Jody and Ace are both muttering in agreement. "Might be our chance to finish off the Pack."

"All right," Sal says. She's speaking to Silvia. Rory has the feeling the two of them are eyeing each other up, conducting a kind of silent battle separate from all the others. "You've said what you want, here's what we want. We want you to come with us."

"No," Silvia says.

"You're going east, we'll take you east."

"Not Dolphin, Sal," says Jody, warning.

Sal ignores her. "It's on your way. You'll stay with us one night, that's all. We can talk properly. There are things we need to ask you. Then you can go, and I promise no one will interfere after that."

"No," Silvia says again. "We go alone."

Sal frowns, looks at her hands. "I'm sorry," she says. "Like I said, there are things we need to talk about."

"Get hold of the kid, Jody," Haze says quickly, and Jody does. "Don't!" Sal says, but she's not really a general. She may be keeping her head better than the rest of her army but she's not giving orders. Rory gasps as an arm squeezes his windpipe again.

It's hard to make sense of what happens next. For one thing he can't see very well with Jody twisting his head around and most of his attention focused on trying to breathe, and for another thing it's all over incredibly quickly, as collapses are. It's actually his gasp that sets it all off. Silvia twists around to see what they're doing to him, exerting herself for the first time, pulling away from Haze, who's not expecting it. Haze grabs at her with a "No you don't," and yanks her bound wrists too roughly, which makes Silvia yelp with pain. Rory doesn't exactly see what happens with Per but he hears the beginning of an angry growl and then gets a confused glimpse of Per and Soph tumbling together. It looks like she's kicked back with the heel of her riding boots and smacked him in the shins, making him let go of her collar. All at once everyone's shouting. Soph's rolling forward and running towards them and meanwhile Ace has spurred her horse and is charging the other way, towards Per, brandishing the cricket bat. Sal's yelling something no one's listening to. Rory's being pulled backwards while Jody tries to catch the reins of her panicky horse with her other hand. "Give me the knife!" Haze screams, and then, even louder, not screaming but commanding, Silvia shouts "Per, don't!" in a tone which sounds like it could stop tides and silence the wind, but Per does.

What he does, exactly, Rory doesn't see. He hears it instead. He hears a ferocious bellow in a language that isn't English or Italian or Danish, a language whose sounds don't come from anywhere in the human world. Then he hears a rush of wind, though there's no wind to go with it, and the sound's too hollow somehow, too parched and empty to be anything to do with the weather. Then he hears a lot of women and horses screaming. Jody drops him. His knees and palms sting as he falls but he looks up in time to see Ace's horse rear up and twist inside a miniature typhoon of evanescent flame. It's not the way horses are supposed to rear up. No animal's body is supposed to move like that: it's like it's being electrocuted, like it's trying to find a way out of its own skin. "Per!" Silvia shouts again, but he can't hear her. His eyes aren't his eyes anymore, they're something else, discs of brass. He's clutching the staff and holding it thrust out towards the tormented horse. Ace slides out of her saddle but her foot's tangled in the stirrup somehow and instead of falling she tips backward, screaming, and flips upside down. Her head hits the road with a crack so horrible it cuts through all the shouting and makes Rory seize up and double over and squeeze his eyes closed. The wind that isn't wind is roaring now: it sounds like voices, hundreds of them, each one a dead whisper but together an unbearable chorus. It forces Rory's eyes open again in time for him to see the maddened horse leap straight into the hedge, pulling Ace behind it like a sack. She's limp and leaking blood from her head. The horse's hind legs thump and clatter her as it scrambles for a footing in the thick bramble, plunging through thorns as if whatever's torturing it is ten times worse, heedless of the deadweight it's dragging against stones and roots and barbs. It tramples and claws its way over the hedge and vanishes from sight, galloping wildly across the abandoned field. There's more galloping, hooves beating on the road. Rory turns himself round to see the other riders disappearing, two of them doubled up on one of the horses. Somehow they must have got themselves mounted and away. Silvia's on her knees in the road, her hands still pinned behind her back, but all she cares about is Per. "Lino!" she screams, and then something in Italian. Lino's staring at Per in horror, but Silvia's order breaks his trance. He springs up and claps his hand in front of Per's face, four times, five times, yelling.

The staff drops from Per's hands. Something invisible, something that was never really there at all, whirls itself tight like a typhoon and vanishes up into the sky. Per clutches his face and staggers. "Don't," Silvia says again, her shout suddenly exhausted, despairing.

There's a little smear of very dark red on the road where Ace's head hit it. It's puddling, slowly; trickling into a crack in the wasted tarmac. Nothing else is moving. In the distance, the crackle of hoof-beats fades swiftly away.

Per takes his hands away from his face. He stares at the staff by his feet. Hidden by the shaggy mass of his beard and hair, his expression is unreadable. He picks up the staff, steps towards one of the sacks, and nudges it with his toe.

"OK," he says. "Let's go."

16

No one wants to talk. Well, perhaps Lino does, but he's not going to get anywhere. He and Per don't share enough English to converse, and anyway there's clearly nothing to be said to Per at the moment in any language. Silvia's expression is black and brooding. She looks like she might kill anyone who attempted to chat with her. And Rory's hanging behind the rest of them, staring at his aching feet as he walks, with just as little interest in exchanging a word with anyone. He's waiting for all of this to turn out to be a weird mistake. He's waiting for someone boring and normal to appear round the corner and say *All right, Rory, time for bed now,* and take him off to give him food and then tuck him in.

While he waits, he walks, and walks.

They come to a place where the tangle pressing in on the road has been hacked away, leaving a rough muddy rectangle of spongy grass where two ancient stones are standing upright, each about as tall as Rory. Someone's made necklaces or belts of feathers, white and grey and black, and hung one around each of them. There are words painted sideways on the stones, crude letters which might once have been white. Lino stops and bends his head over, trying to read them aloud.

" 'Curse . . . ' " he begins, hesitantly, his accent making the sounds comical. "Ah! *Maledizione.* 'Curse the black . . . ' "

Rory comes up beside him. " 'Curse the black pack,' " he reads, and moves to the second stone, where much smaller letters are squashed tight together. " 'Let them be drowned. Make them go to the shore and be took.' "

Per shifts his shoulders and makes an impatient sound. He doesn't like stopping. Lino shrugs, looks at Rory, then at Silvia.

"I go look," he says, and runs ahead. He seems glad of the chance to escape the others' company for a while.

The landscape's changing. On the horizon ahead are woods now. They're not the dull green spindly woods of Home; they're deep masses of autumn color, old green tinged with rust. The three of them walk through another set of buildings gathered close around the road. These are bleak and shattered like the village where they spent the night, all scabbing paint and empty windows sprouting weeds. They've started passing occasional cars in the road now. Not proper cars, any more than the houses are proper houses; they're the shells of cars, like the dry papery crab shells that wash up on the Beach sometimes. The road's more clogged underfoot, dotted with bits of brick and slate and broken glass. Curves of metal stick out from the undergrowth, and the last visible fragments of other buried things.

More walking, a dip and a rise in the road, and they come to a large sign, a white rectangle planted on poles high enough not yet to have succumbed to the bramble. It has proper writing on it, neat black capital letters. They say:

WELCOME TO PENZANCE
PENSANS A'GAS DYNERGH

Below them, in drippy, wobbly, painted black letters, it says

POPULATION: 0

The sign makes Rory's head spin. He remembers *Penzance*. It's the Mainland, the other Mainland, the one he's failed to arrive in, the one with cars driving around and people everywhere, ice cream and helicopters and Scarlet's big school and TV screens in shop windows all showing the same football match at the same time. He's been there—here—lots of times. It's where the helicopter and the ferry from the islands landed, and where the roads and trains start. It's the connection, the first port of call.

"*Vieni!*" Lino's reappeared on the next crest of the road. He's waving and shouting excitedly. "*Subito!*" He hops from foot to foot in impatience.

After a moment's hesitation Silvia hurries ahead, past Per. Rory jogs after her. When they catch up with Lino he beckons them over the road, his outsize eyes shining with enthusiasm.

"*Ecco,*" he says, as the view to the east opens before them.

Penzance. The land drops away below the crest to a scene of desolation. They can see for miles, across the breadth of a long curving bay, the sea glinting to the right and the green-brown land rising to the left. Between the two is a midden, a gigantic tide line of heaped and abandoned wreckage. In the near distance it's chimneys, rooftops, blocky concrete buildings, sticking up like misshapen tombstones out of a jungle of rampant weeds. Beyond the dead town is the edge of the bay, lined along its whole length with the beached hulks of massive washed-up ships, tankers as big as villages tipped uselessly on their sides, hanging gardens of barnacles and rust. Shipping containers are strewn at all angles in the sand. Some of them have spilled their contents onto the beach, bursts of congealed lava.

Beyond that, beyond the ruin and the graveyard at the edge of the sand, a fairy castle rises above the waste.

It's perched on a single steep cone of rock sticking out of the shallows at the far end of the bay. There's a faint mist over the sea, a midday haze going slightly gold where the sun breaks through to touch it, and the castle emerges above that mist as if it's floating on it, as if it's lighter than air. Its top is all towers and pinnacles, like it's part of the rock it sits on, the last delicate flourish of that soaring upthrust of stone. Slanting sunlight falls on those towers, turning them gold as well.

"*Ecco,*" Lino says again, in a wonder-struck whisper.

Rory's seen the fairy castle before. He's seen it with his own eyes and he's seen its picture on postcards. In fact he thinks he sent a postcard of it himself once, when they were coming back from the Mainland and the helicopter was delayed so his father made them all write to Grandpa George in Weston-super-Mare. If you were sitting on the right side of the helicopter you got a view of it as you landed, the old castle, which looked like a church (or maybe it was an old church which looked like a castle), almost balanced on the summit of its own private hill just offshore. You could see tourists like colored beetles crawling up and down its slopes. He remembers what it was called: Saint Michael's Mount. The name's trying to connect him to something that can't ever have been the same place, not *this* place. When they sent those postcards they went into town, into Penzance, to the post office. He remembers the post office, red and beige, people standing in line, a number flashing to tell you when it was your turn. If that memory's true that post office ought to be down there somewhere below him. He looks down and sees sickly purple spears of buddleia sprouting from flat roofs, fallen trees lying on top of houses, every window black. Population zero. If it was ever the place he remembers, it isn't anymore.

Nor's the castle, lifted up on its sea-moated spire. The Saint Michael's Mount he remembers was a picture on a card, a thing to look at out of the window, a place other people went. This one is a dream of fragile loveliness standing mournful guard over a wasteland.

"Yes," Silvia says. "That's it. That's the place."

The three of them have been standing there staring east for long enough that Per's come up to join them. He looks at Silvia, then shades his eyes and gazes east too.

"That's it?" he says. "The small island?"

"Yes."

"Where we go?"

"Yes."

"It's in there?"

"It is."

Per unslings the staff with its freight of sacks from his shoulders.

"You know? For sure?"

She just nods.

Per's breathing heavily. If you didn't know him you'd think it would be from the effort of hauling his load all morning, but it's not.

"So close," he says.

"*Certo,*" Lino says, or rather croaks. He might even be tearing up.

Per leans on the staff. His enormous fingers flex around it, almost like it's an instrument he's learning to play.

"Today," he says. He sounds throaty as well. All three of them seem almost dumbstruck. "How far?"

Lino makes a thinking noise with his tongue. "Three *kilometri?* Four?"

"Easy," Per says again.

"Yes," Silvia says. "We come there this afternoon. The end of our journey." She sighs and stretches. "We should rest here. Eat."

Per points over the bay with the staff. "By the sea," he says, in something like his more usual grumpy tone. The Mount's right next to the shore, but it's still a steep little island of its own, moated by the cursed ocean.

Lino slaps him on the back. "*Si si.* But you make safe, my friend. Eh? Your *spiriti,* no?" He flutters his hands around, making swooshing sounds, miming things darting through the air. "Is still day. Is four *kilometri,* one, two hour. Your *spiriti,* they come still."

Silvia's hardly moved at all. She's gazing over the lost town and the colossal flotsam, pinching thoughtfully at her lower lip.

"We will need a boat," she says.

Per grunts the beginning of a mirthless laugh and waves at the crescent of the bay. "Lots of boats."

"No," says Rory, "you don't."

All three of them turn to look at him. Lino stops hopping around.

"You don't," he says again. "You don't need a boat to get across to the Mount." He remembers this. It feels like what he's remembering was a thousand years ago, but the tides don't change. The tides are Law. "I know it looks like an island now but it's connected. When the tide goes out you can walk. They built a path. It's underwater now but it'll come out eventually." From the helicopter it looked like a thick black snake sleeping on the beach, the tourist beetles inching along its back. "It goes all the way across. And at really low tide there's just sand between, it's not even an island anymore."

"Oh," Lino says. "Oh! Oh!" He grabs Rory and lifts him off his feet. "*Questo ragazzo! É un genio!* I know, always!" He puts Rory down and kisses him on both cheeks. It's surprisingly like being attacked but he's so quick Rory can't react at all. "I tell you! I say, this boy, he is clever boy."

Per stares at Rory. His eyes are almost invisible under his fierce brow and his Viking straggle of hair. "You know this how?"

Rory swallows. "I remember. I've been here before. Lots of times." And it's famous anyway. Saint Michael's Mount is its own little island at high tide, but they built a causeway long ago so you can walk across when the sea goes out. Everyone knows that.

"*Si, certo.*" Lino waggles a finger at Per. "Clever boy."

"Where is the tide now?" Silvia says.

Rory's afraid she's asking him. He has no idea how he's supposed to know just by looking at the sea. But Per squints across the bay and says. "High. Going down."

"When tide is low, there is no sea at all between?"

"Yeah," Rory says. He's suddenly queasy with doubt. What if he's getting this wrong? But he's sure he remembers how it works, he remembers his father talking about it. "That's right."

Silvia doesn't appear to doubt him at all. "We wait for that, then."

Per frowns. "Hours," he says.

"We wait," she says again. "We must not see the *sirene.*"

Per snorts contemptuously and gestures with his staff.

"No," Silvia says. "Not like that."

All four of them know what she means. Per's staff can keep the sea-rainy away but she doesn't want him using it. None of them have spoken about what happened with the Riders but they're all thinking about it.

"We rest here," Silvia says. "Eat. Then, we go on, there." She points at the far end of the bay: not at the castle itself but towards the shore adjacent to it, where a few barren breaks in the scrub suggest the ruins of another, smaller town, beyond the wastes of what used to be Penzance. "Wait until the tide is down. It's only a little longer. We will still be there today."

Per doesn't like this, but it's always been obvious that this is Silvia's gang. Lino pats his back again, encouragingly. "Is more good," he says. "Is more safe."

The two men start picking around among the bags, finding food. While they're occupied, Rory sidles close to Silvia, who's still studying the long view eastwards, deep in some meditation of her own.

"So that's really where the magic ring is? On Saint Michael's Mount?"

"Is that the name?"

"Yeah. It's really famous."

"*Sfântul Mihail.* Who fights the dragon. The gypsy patron. That's good."

"Only," Rory says, "didn't those women say something about going to the Mount?"

Silvia blinks, looks down at him, then back at Per and Lino. She puts an arm around his shoulders and steers him a few steps along the road, away from them.

"Hmm?" she says quietly.

"I thought . . ." Rory finds himself almost whispering too. Silvia's hugging him close as if they're sharing a secret. "I thought they said something about it. Like it's their place."

"Oh," Silvia says. "Yes, I remember. It's a different place."

"What?"

"It's a different mount. The one they talk about. Not—" she indicates the island castle with her eyes—"this one."

Rory's very confused. "But that is the Mount. That's what it's called."

"There must be many hills in this country."

"I know, but that's not—"

"Rory." She bends very close. "Didn't I tell you I know the truth?"

You can't argue with her. He wouldn't dare even if he really thought she was wrong, and like she says, she can't be wrong, although it did seem awfully like the women with the horses were talking about Saint Michael's Mount.

"It's best if you don't say things like this to the others." They both glance back at Per and Lino. "Questions. It makes them nervous. I don't want Per nervous. OK?"

"OK," Rory says.

She smiles at him. It's a rather steely smile. "You were good to listen, though. You did well."

"That woman," Rory says. "The one who got dragged away by her horse. Was she all right?"

Silvia just looks at him for a while, then presses her lips tight and shakes her head.

"You must be hungry," she says. It's obvious she doesn't want to talk about it. "Come on."

As they rejoin the group Lino asks her something in Italian, glancing at Rory. It's pretty clearly something along the lines of, *What was all that about?* When Silvia answers, he nods sadly. "*Povero,*" he says, sympathetically. "But soon!" His look brightens. "Very soon! End of walking! Soon, 'obbits have ring of biggest power!" He laughs and tosses Rory a hunk of bread.

They sit and eat in silence. The bread's very tough and takes a lot of chewing. Lino starts up a couple of times, cocking his head, scanning the horizon, thinking he's heard something; once he scampers away and they hear him working his way to the top of a tree. But he comes back shaking his head, and mutters only a few words to Silvia.

Rory's very troubled. He's not sure why. He can't get his head around the idea that this adventure's about to finish. It only started yesterday! And he's even more baffled when he tries to imagine the ending that's coming up. Are they really, *really* going to find the Ring of Power this afternoon? He's not ready for it. And then what? The three of them keep talking about the end of their journey, but what happens after that? Where's he going to go next?

As if reading his thoughts, Per stretches out a leg and nudges Rory's back with the toe of his boot. "You," he says. "Boy. Time to go home."

At this Silvia looks up. "What?"

Per shrugs. "We don't want him now."

"*No no no no no,*" Lino says. He's in the middle of chewing a strip of some sort of dried meat. "Good boy."

"We decided," Per says. "Three, together. Not other people."

Silvia stands up. "You would leave him here? Alone?"

Per stares at her, as if he's thinking about it, then scrunches his mouth: *Why not?*

Rory's cheeks are burning. "I'll go if you don't want me," he says.

"No," Lino says. "Go with Lino."

"We decided this before," Per rumbles.

"We are not there yet," Silvia says. She steps between Per and Rory, decisively. "Until we have the ring, Rory is with us. After that we can talk about what we agreed."

"Agreed before," Per says. "Finish. No more talk."

Rory's gaping at Silvia. Is she really going to abandon him as soon as they find it? But she's filling her pack, suddenly brisk. "Let's go," she says. "We wait long enough. This is how we will do it. Rory comes with me"—she gestures over the sweep of the bay—"by the shore. You two—" she indicates the ruin of Penzance—"that way. Behind this town."

Now both men are frowning at her, slowly taking in what she's said. Lino begins something unhappy-sounding in Italian. She cuts him off impatiently.

"By the sea, it's safest. We don't know who's in that town. Look at it. There may be people in those houses. Hungry people, maybe. Or those women, who hate us now." She glares at Per. "I'm not going that way. On the beach, you can see there's no one there. It's the best way. You two, you can't go by the sea, but you will be OK in the town. You can protect yourself. I look after Rory. We meet again afterwards, there"—she's pointing across the long bay to the shore opposite the Mount—"and cross when the sea is low."

"No," Per says. "All go together." He swings the staff up, tapping it into his calloused palm.

"Listen to me," she says. There's no real argument. It's like a cat arguing with a bear, but it's obvious even to Rory that the cat's going to win. If you go by the water, if the *sirene* come, what then? You think your spirits will come when you call? You think they are your slaves? I don't think so. I think if you are by the sea and the *sirene* come you drown. You and Lino. You can see the end of our journey

ARCADIA 237

and you don't make it, you die. It's stupid. No. You men go the other way. You fight if you want to fight, hide if you want to hide, it's up to you. Rory and me want to walk in peace."

There's a long unhappy silence. Lino asks a question.

Silvia answers in English. "We meet there." She points. "See? On the shore, opposite the island. Wait there until the sea is low, and then we all walk across, like Rory tells us."

"Boy makes all the trouble," Per says. He's not sneering or threatening, just saying it like it's obvious. He starts arranging the bags over his staff.

There's a bit more arguing in Italian as they're getting ready. Lino sounds hesitant, Silvia determined. Rory can imagine what she's saying: *Don't argue with me. I can tell the future.* He's quietly happy with her Plan. He was beginning to worry about what Per might do. Perhaps they're going to end up fighting over the Ring like supervillains rather than heroes, but if they do he wants to be on Silvia's side.

They set off again. The road dips into a small steep valley which has almost filled itself in. There are fallen trees everywhere, plastered with stringy moss. Someone's trampled through the mess to keep the road more or less passable, though at the bottom of the valley there's no road at all; it's completely sunk under mud and matted willow branches and rotting leaves and general rubbish.

They climb away from that, round a corner, and find themselves at the outskirts of the town.

Another of the most important Rules on Home was that whenever you finished a job you always had to put everything you'd used back where it went. You did it even if you knew someone was about to do exactly the same job using the exact same things. If it was the end of the day you put things back and then went with a small bucket to wherever the nearest fresh water was and you cleaned everything with one of the cloths and dried it off again. It didn't matter how tired you were—everyone was always tired at the end of every day—you made sure the places where the little band of survivors lived and worked and ate and slept never got any worse.

The reason for this Rule was that everyone knew what would happen otherwise. It was there for all to see, in the abandoned houses smelling of sewage and mold, in the no-go zone of smashed glass and scrap metal around the Hotel, in the tendrils of bramble that had swallowed the island's untended gardens and fields over the course of two summers. Ruin and decay would grow as remorselessly as weeds if they weren't kept at bay by the endless, patient, boring work of tidying and cleaning and putting away.

And here's the proof. They walk down into it.

It's like a bomb combined with a typhoon. Everything's broken and everything in the wrong place. Inside things (a cooker, a toilet, a lampshade) are scattered around outside. A farm trailer's tipped up against the side of a house. There's a small pile of clothes heaped in a black puddle in a ditch between houses. Walls are sprouting weeds, and trees have plastic bags caught in their branches. Chimneys are sending up sheaves of grass or birds' nests. There are circles of charred ground on the verges, fringed with unburned rubbish. Rory can't list all the wrong things he sees. Everywhere he looks it's the same strewn chaos. As on Home, anything that might be useful has been taken away: anything that might burn, or hold water, or keep a body warm. The rest is left like stripped bones. Per and Lino and Silvia pick their way through it without a pause. They've seen it all before, Rory realizes. It must all be like this. All those times he stood on Briar Hill and looked out at the deadly sea and wondered about the world beyond it: here's his answer.

They come to a place where other streets branch off down the slope towards the harbor and the sea. Here Silvia stops. She and Lino confer for a while, pointing and looking around. Then she gestures for Rory to follow her downhill.

"This way."

It's where she's decided they're splitting up. She's already striding away. He doesn't look back. Lino shouts something after them. Whatever it is, she ignores it. You have to concentrate anyway: the roads are wide here in the town but they're full of obstacles, silted-up cars sticky with bird poo and pollen, and there are cracks and gouges and bare patches underfoot, as well as sharp scraps and dustings of the kind of shattered glass that looks like hundreds of tiny ice cubes. A pair of foxes startles Rory by trotting out of a gaping front door to watch them go past. The animals tread lightly and easily through the wreckage. It doesn't worry them. They live here now. When he looks back up the road Lino and Per are out of sight.

A fetid reek hangs around the bottom of the street. Gulls are swarming, diving at the ground and at each other. Rory and Silvia come down by what used to be the harbor; he can see the stone quay with the lighthouse at the end, across a span of slimy algae through which wrecks are studded like stepping-stones. The buildings are bigger here. Some still have words written on the sides, high enough that the creeping damp hasn't yet flaked them away. A single intact awning flaps above a window, waiting for another storm or two to tear it down. There are lampposts lining what was once a broad sea-side road and is now a dumping-ground of indistinguishable rubbish rattling occasionally in the fouled breeze. One of them catches Rory's eye as he trots along trying to keep up with Silvia. It's flickering on and off, the light just about visible though it's an increasingly bright afternoon. He points it out to her.

"Why's that one working?"

She stops, hands on hips. "I don't know."

"There's no electricity, is there?"

"There must be another thing instead. Another power."

He thinks about this for a little bit, then decides not to anymore.

"Did you mean that," he says, "about when we find the Ring? Leaving me behind afterwards?"

She looks at him for a long time, her face as indecipherable as the power that's making the broken lamp shine.

"When we get there," she says, "we will know what to do."

"I don't know anyone here." He hadn't meant to say this, it just sort of comes out. "I don't know where I'd go."

She appears to be thinking about it.

"But I told you," she says eventually. "Your road and mine. Like this." She puts her index fingers together, making the train tracks again. And off she sets while he's still trying to work out what her answer means. He never has the chance to finish working it out. He can't do anything but follow. There are disgusting soft patches in the mess, oozing squelching bits that tug at your feet when you step on them. Whatever he does he doesn't want to trip over. He keeps after Silvia's long steady strides as best he can.

It's almost worse when they finally pick their way across the seaside plain of rubbish and find a place to scramble down onto the sand. Now the whole length of the bay opens up, the ebbing sea leaving a blissfully unmarked sweep of beach below the heaps of scummy flotsam which mark the tide line. The problem here is the wrecks. They're terrifyingly huge. They're monsters of decaying steel lounging along the top of the beach. The mere height of them gives Rory sickening vertigo. Every time he looks at them he's convinced they're about to roll over, tip slowly with a grinding echoing sound, and crush him like an insect under a boulder. He makes himself concentrate on Silvia's footprints, following them along the wide curve of the bay.

At least the Mount looks a bit closer already. In fact . . .

"Look," he says, hurrying to bring himself alongside Silvia. "There. See?"

Between the Mount and the shore a thin line of waves is breaking, brilliant as a spill of broken glass in the sun. Above those sparkles a solid surface is showing. It's a bit like a mirage. It looks as if a phantom road has formed itself on the surface of the sea.

It's the causeway to the Mount. The tide's already come down far enough that the path has begun to emerge from the water. The waves are breaking against it.

"OK," Silvia says, quietly, to herself. "OK."

Rory's a little stung. He's pleased that he remembered about the causeway and he thought maybe she'd be pleased with him too. But she's unusually distracted.

They walk for a long while. It's slow going in sand. The softness underfoot is easier on his feet, which is good since they're aching badly now, but harder on his legs. They've come perhaps halfway around the long bay when in desperation he asks her whether they can stop for a bit.

He's expecting to be ignored, maybe even told off, but to his surprise she looks back and nods. "All right," she says. "Here." On their seaward side a pale blue shipping container is half-buried in the beach. She looks around and then motions him towards it. "Come."

Limpets and kelp have clustered around it, and the tides have filled its dark interior with swampy sand. Rory doesn't mind the containers so much. They drift into the Gap occasionally and bump ashore on the islands or the offshore rocks. Everyone always got excited when one beached itself on Home. One turned out to be full of toys, plastic rubbish, but sometimes the women found useful things. Once it was metal parts from a shipment of motorcycles, another time crates of flat-pack furniture, which kept the Abbey fires burning for weeks last winter. Best of all was the one that turned out to be full of bags of fertilizer. Fi says it'll last them years if she's careful with it. He's used to poking around inside them so he doesn't mind when Silvia settles down by the tilting mouth of this one. His legs throb as soon as he takes his weight off them.

"Here," she says, unslinging her pack and giving him water and a handful of spindly carrots.

She sits beside him and they stare at the sea while he eats. A bank of cloud is retreating behind them, its edge sliced off like a wall. The water's brilliant with white light and there's sun on his face. At the far end of the bay the windows of the castle on the Mount are shining too.

"How did it end up in there?"

"Hmm?" Silvia was thinking about something else, miles away.

"This ring. What's it doing in Saint Michael's Mount?"

"I don't know. I don't know the past."

"I mean, loads of people go there. Tourists. Used to go there. It must be hidden really well."

"Maybe."

"It might be guarded or something. Like with traps."

"It's possible."

"You don't know?"

She smiles at him. It's an oddly uncertain smile, like her thoughts are elsewhere and she's not really listening, like a normal adult. "I'm not the Internet," she says. "I don't know everything. I know only that where I want to go, I will go."

"You're definitely going to find it?"

She sighs. "Not so many questions," she says. "We'll see what happens."

Yeah, he thinks, *that's easy for you to say when you know the future.*

"Oh. I almost forget." She digs in her pack and brings out the plastic bag from Parson's with the comics in it. She hands it to him. "Per didn't want to carry these so I take them for you." She stands up. She hitches the pack back onto her shoulders.

"Wait," Rory says. "Are you going somewhere?"

"Yes. I go to find the others."

Rory stares at her in confusion. "Others?"

"Lino and Per. In the town."

"But." Rory's sitting with the pile of comics in his lap, feeling like he must have missed something. "I thought you said we were going to meet them there."

"We're quite close now. Faster than I expect. So I go back and see, maybe they need help."

"What do I do?"

"Rest," she says. She gestures at the plastic bag. "Read. Watch the tide. When it's as low as can go, come there." She points along the beach to the place where the causeway meets the shore. "We meet, we all go across."

This wasn't the Plan. Didn't she say she was going to look after him? "You want me to go by myself?"

"You're safe on the beach."

"Aren't you coming back?"

"We meet you there later. It's not far. You're hiding here." *Hidden,* she means: the container behind him blocks off the view of the land and the massive wrecks. "It's a good place to rest. You walk a long way today for a boy."

"I don't—"

Suddenly she's not distracted anymore. She turns her stare on him, the one that makes even Per do what she says. "Here's what you do. OK? Sit like this until the tide is at the bottom, there's no water there." She's pointing between the Mount and the shore, where the black causeway bars the sea. "I think maybe two hours. Maybe less. Then walk across the beach, we meet you. Easy."

"Two hours?" Alone?

"No one can see you here except the *sirene*. And they don't like boys."

"I want to go with you," he says. She just shakes her head. She doesn't do arguments.

"Now listen." She crouches in front of him. "This is important. If you meet those women again, tell them straightaway you are English boy."

What's she talking about? "The ones with the horses?"

"They look for us, I think. They will be angry. It's OK for you to talk to them. If it's necessary, tell them what happened, that you came with us by mistake. Do you understand?"

He's thoroughly bewildered now. A few moments ago he had the sun on his face, he'd had some food, everything felt like it was going to be all right.

"And one more thing," she says. "Listen very carefully. If anything turns wrong, there is a special word you can use. Italian. Do you know any Italian?"

"No."

"I teach you. If there is a problem, later, you say this word to Lino, tell him I told you to say it."

"But why—"

"Listen. *Arrivederci*." She says it slowly. "You try. Repeat it."

"Areevy . . ."

"*Arrivederci*." She makes him repeat it three times. "Say it while you sit here." She demonstrates, mumbling it over and over like a prayer. "Practice. It's like a magic word. And now." She straightens. "I must go."

"So you want me to—"

"Wait. At low tide, you come. Right there." She points again to where the end of the causeway heaps itself up at the top of the beach. "We wait for you, see you. Don't come before. And remember, *arrivederci, arrivederci*. Practice, practice." To his surprise she bends and gives him a quick kiss on the cheek. Her lips are very dry and her hair smells of salt. "Thank you," she says, and she's up and gone.

After a few horrible moments he crawls around the corner of

the container to look. She's striding up the beach very quickly. She doesn't look back. Already she looks tiny against the backdrop of the monstrous wrecks. He watches her go, thinking about grabbing the bag of comics and sprinting to catch up. He thinks about it until she walks under the angle of a vast overhanging bow and disappears.

Sand's surprisingly uncomfortable to sit on. You'd think it would be soft, but no. It's cold as well. Not properly cold, but beneath the sun-warmed surface it's damp enough to chill him through his trousers.

The sea scratches away at the beach.

He tries reading but he can't seem to get lost in the comics. He's read them all a million times before, of course. Normally that doesn't matter but this afternoon's different. The heroes and villains with their perfect skin and color-block costumes don't convince him today. If he let go of the comics the small breeze would tug them out of his fingers and they'd be little scraps of rubbish like so much else.

He looks across at the Mount. Its peak is actually lots of different buildings, not one castle. They're not really castlelike at all, in fact, more like normal houses, walls and windows and roofs; it's the way they're jumbled so tightly together which makes them look magical and mysterious and old. The steep slopes below them are thickly overgrown, though they don't look wild. Rory knows what ruin looks like, and that's not it.

The windows facing the bay are beginning to blaze golden as the sun angles lower. Suddenly Rory's imagining faces at those windows, invisible to him but watching. He backs a little farther into the mouth of his metal cave until all he can see is the tide, retreating from him, slowly, slowly.

What was she thanking him for?

The longer he sits there the worse it gets.

He's becoming increasingly agitated about his instructions. How's he supposed to know when it's low tide? It's not like you can ever see the point where the tide turns. He stands up, shaking stiffness out of his legs, and peeks around the corner of the container to check the causeway. The landward end of it is dry for a long way now and the rest is sticking high above the waves, but the sea still has a lot of retreating to do before the foot of the Mount emerges from the water.

Has it been an hour? It feels like it's been an hour. It's beginning to feel like it's been a lifetime.

He makes a Plan. The Plan is that he'll check the tide, then read one comic all the way through, then check again. That way he'll be able to see how much the tide's gone out, instead of looking all the time and not being able to see any difference.

He can't stop himself looking up every time he turns the page.

Indecision torments him like hunger. He shuts his eyes tight and whispers *arrivederci, arrivederci, arrivederci*. If it's magic it's not working. No one comes to rescue him.

The thing which finally makes up his mind for him is the descending sun. Time passes invisibly slowly, but there's a moment when he looks up from the doodle he's scraping in the sand and notices the ripe warm gold of late afternoon, and a feeling in the air too, a hint of coolness. This is the last straw. Whatever Silvia says he's not going to stay here all by himself while it starts getting dark.

Just like that, as soon as he's made the decision to stop waiting he feels a hundred times better. The tide's a long way out now, most of the way to the Mount. It has to be far enough. She won't mind if he gets there a bit early, and anyway it's her fault for leaving him on his own when he's only ten and she's already stolen him from his mother. He tucks the bag of comics under one arm and sets off. It even feels good to be walking again after hours of sitting on sand.

He keeps his eyes down to avoid looking at the beached tankers, steering himself around mounds of kelp and the humps of granite poking out of the beach. He's breathing very hard and trying not to run. The Mount rises as he approaches. He can hear the sea breaking on its seaward face. He angles his course towards the shore. Behind the last of the train of decaying ships he can now see another ghost town gathered behind a sea wall where the causeway meets the land, more buildings stamped with vacancy. Somewhere up there must be where he's supposed to meet them.

Something feels wrong.

Shells and shingle underfoot: he can't go fast. He's exhausted too. It's been a terrible day. The causeway's fairly close now, a rough-and-tumble wall slicing across the beach, high as a house. To his right, it attaches itself to the base of the Mount. To his left, on the landward side, it runs up over the sand and junk and stops by the sea wall at the back of the beach. He can see now that there's a gap in the wall there, opposite the start of the causeway. That's what he's heading for: the way up off the beach.

It's impossible to run but also impossible not to. He breaks into a stumbling jog. The tide's still not all the way out but never mind that.

At the back of the beach the fouled kelp's piled waist-high. In among it is a crust of that sickly residue of plastic froth, which is the farthest the sea can get towards annihilating the indestructible. The only way around it is to climb up the side of the causeway, scrambling over barnacles and massive lumps of eroded concrete and slimy rock. He makes it up eventually, at the cost of torn trousers and badly scratched hands. Catching his breath, he turns to face the Mount. It's a shadowed triangle cut out of the blue-gold sky.

For a moment he's convinced he sees something moving among the buildings on its peak.

He puts his back to it and runs properly, now that there's hard stone underfoot. The landward end of the causeway peters out into a rubbish-clogged ramp leading up through the break in the sea wall. At one edge of the ramp there's a clear slice through the flotsam and filth, like a path. Sides aching, Rory runs towards it. Nearly there. He's about to head up into what remains of the town above the beach when he notices a deep mark printed in a pocket of loose gravel in the concrete.

It's a horseshoe-shaped mark. A hoofprint.

It's neat, clear, deep. Its open end points up the ramp, which means the horse was going the other way, out to (he turns to look again, shielding his eyes)—

High up on the Mount there's a flash of metal. A sound drifts down: a drawn-out creak, like a gate opening.

He dashes up the slipway. At the top is an old beachfront road, cars without tires scattered all along it like roadkill, soft-edged dunes of sand heaped among them. He stares around but the buildings are all deserted. They've been thoroughly scoured by scavengers, or perhaps by the wind. Everything's barren and quiet. "Silvia!" he hisses, too frightened to shout. "Where are you?"

An owl hoots.

"Lino!"

There the little man is, appearing as suddenly as always, beckoning from an open doorway across the street. Rory doesn't think he's ever been so happy to see anyone in his life, not even Her. He bolts to Lino, who's bobbing his head around, peering up and down the road.

"*Eccola.* In." He motions Rory inside. Sand's blown in here, covering a moldering carpet; beyond is an empty grey space which smells of pee. Per's lifting himself sluggishly to his feet as Rory comes in, using his staff as a prop.

"*Bene,*" Lino says, ducking back in. "Silvia comes after?"

"What?"

"Silvia. After?"

Still catching his breath, Rory looks around. "Where'd she go?"

Lino frowns like he doesn't understand, goes back to the door, cups his hands to his mouth, and hoots. You'd never think it was a human mouth making the noise if you weren't watching him do it.

"What's this?" Per says. He rolls his neck, loosening cricks. He looks like he might have been asleep.

"Wait," Lino says. "For Silvia too."

Puzzled, Rory says, "Didn't she find you?"

Both the men go peculiarly still.

"She go with you," Lino says. He's stopped fidgeting around.

"Yeah," Rory says. "Then she said to wait while she went to meet you. She's not here?"

Lino says "*No no no no no*" in a completely Italian way even though the word's the same in English. "She with you."

"I told you," Rory says. "She and me went down along the beach. Then she said she was going to find you."

"Where is the woman?" Per says.

Rory's starting to feel a bit panicky. "I don't know! She said she'd be here."

"Here?" says Lino. "When here?"

"Now! With you, I mean!"

"You went with the woman," Per says. His voice has a dangerous rumble to it. "Meet here."

"She told me she was going to look for you. That's what she said. I swear!"

The three of them look at each other.

It's the stricken expression on Lino's face which reminds Rory. "Wait," he says. "Wait. She said to say . . ." In his rising panic he's forgotten it. "I was supposed to tell you something if anything was wrong."

"She say what?" Lino's eyes have gone even rounder than usual.

"She said tell you. It's an Italian word. Wait! *Arrivederci!*" Thank God he's remembered. All that practice has saved him. "That was it. *Arrivederci.*"

Rory's relief lasts no longer than the time it takes to draw one breath. Lino's reaction kills it. The round eyes fill with stunned shock, then pain, and then Lino gives an awful cry and sprints out into the street.

"Fuck," says Per. He shoves Rory out of the way and lumbers after Lino. Rory, without the slightest idea what's happening beyond the fact that something's gone horribly wrong, can't think of anything better to do than follow them outside. Lino's already far ahead. He's as light on his feet as a rabbit, sprinting for the slipway as if his life depends on it. Per roars, a bellow of pure frustrated rage, and then begins to shout in his own language as he runs after Lino. By the time Rory gets to the ramp he's way behind. There's a terrible drumming heaviness in his heart. He can hear it aloud. Lino's barreling down the causeway towards the Mount, shouting "Silvia! Silvia!" Per follows him, lurching heavily. The drumming gets louder. It's not Rory's heart at all, it's a sound in the air which rhymes with his gathering horror, accelerating, deepening.

Hoofbeats.

A little way down the causeway Per stops. He grips his staff in both hands and swings it over his head as if he's trying to bring down the sky, and he shouts with such concentrated fury that Rory skids to a halt, afraid to get any closer to him: "Bitch! Bitch! Bitch!"

The base of the Mount ripples.

Out of the shadows of its overgrown skirts a moving glittering mass appears, raising steady thunder from the causeway's stones. It's Riders, lots of them, too many to count. They're coming fast. The late sun gleams on the things they're carrying and the things they're wearing, flashing metallic glints. Lino stops, backs up, then begins running landwards again. He's shouting still but you can't hear him now; it's impossible to hear anything except the thrum of the oncoming army. The horses are rushing in like an unnatural tide. The Riders lean forward in the saddle, elbows wide. It feels like the ground's shaking. Per spins around as if to run, sees Rory standing at the top of the ramp, turns back again. Running's useless, you might as well try to outsail a hurricane. Per howls, braces his shoulders, and brings the staff cracking down on the causeway at his feet, once, twice, again, roaring a desperate summons with each blow. Ahead, Lino's about to be swamped. He swerves from one side of the causeway to the other but its sides are jagged and tumbled rock. The Riders are all screaming, swinging lengths of glittering chain up over their heads. Lino looks back in terror, misses his footing, falls forward, and then changes.

It happens as he's falling. He slumps forward, the wave of horses almost on top of him, and then as Rory watches in wide-eyed terror he keeps slumping, forward, in, folding himself inside his own clothes, and then there's a blurry eyeblink when there's no Lino left, only the clothes dropping towards the stone, soft and limp. Then there are wings. The horses swerve for an instant as a bird beats up over them, big, blunt-headed, ungainly in its rising but too swift and smooth to be caught. The wings reach out straight to grip the wind and he's gone.

The horses barely hesitate. They can't, their momentum is too full. A *crack* like the shattering of a bell snaps Rory's look back to earth: it's Per, driving the foot of his staff against the ground again with a force that must surely have either splintered the wood or cleaved the causeway in half. The air hums and crackles and for a moment seems alive with fire, but maybe Rory's imagined it, maybe it's just the gold of the evening and the whirring shimmer of the Riders' weapons. Per brandishes the staff one final time as the onrushing army closes in on him. The women are screaming war cries. One of the horses rears high, throwing its rider, causing skidding stumbling confusion behind it, but the others flow around it as effortlessly and irresistibly as the ocean. The first Rider to reach Per is a crop-haired woman who doesn't look much older than Laurel, standing up in her stirrups and yelling like a banshee. Her horse skids as Per swings his staff but another presses behind her, ridden by someone wearing a motorcycle helmet with the visor closed; she heaves a length of metal down on Per's back.

Then it's all chaos and noise. Rory can't follow it. Without knowing what he's doing he's facing the road again, running, and then he's surrounded by snorting and stamping and legs and shouting. At one stage he finds himself sitting on sand-scoured tarmac with one arm over his head, the other clutching the bag of comics to his chest like a lifebelt. Boots land in front of him and someone jerks him upright. The superheroes and soldiers spill out of the bag and across the road and are shredded under churning hooves. Rough hands haul Rory off his feet and throw him over the back of a horse like he's a sack. His eyes fill with streaks of pain. Someone grips the belt of his trousers to stop him sliding off again and they're away, hard muscle and bone jolting the wind out of him with every stride. Through his own breathless terror and the chaos of noise around him he still manages to hear Per somewhere behind, cursing and bellowing like he's being dragged to the gallows.

17

The one who grabbed him turns out to be Jody the horse-faced woman. She stops riding when she sees that Rory's having trouble breathing, and pulls him off the horse onto his feet, and that's when he sees it's her. She wipes his snotty nose. As well as dangling and bouncing with his head upside down he's been fighting back tears, so he's coughing and bubbling. While he's standing there trying to keep himself upright a few other women ride up and talk to Jody about whether they should tie him up.

"Please don't," he snivels.

"Eh?" Jody sticks her face close to his. She's yelling. "What's that?"

Rory starts crying properly.

"No need to get all Guantánamo," someone else says. "He's just a kid."

"Just a kid, is he?" Jody sounds out of breath too, pumped up on the adrenaline of battle. "You." She elbows him, almost knocking him off his feet. "Speak English, do you?"

"For God's sake." The other woman dismounts.

"Told us you didn't speak English, didn't they? Any more lies? Eh?"

In the abysm of his misery Rory remembers what Silvia told him to do. "I'm not with them," he says, between sobs. "It was an accident."

Jody snorts—*pah!*—but the other woman interrupts.

"What's your name?" she says.

He tells her.

"So where's home for you, Rory?"

A distant roar stops him answering. It's Per, far behind, but shouting loud enough for them to hear even though they've ridden up out of the town.

"What are you doing to him?" Rory says.

"He'll get what he deserves," says someone else, still mounted.

"Leaving him for the man-eaters," Jody says, with grim pleasure.

"Better than he deserves," the mounted woman says. "If they take him before he dies of thirst at least he'll die happy."

"Bet they will too," another woman says. "Big bastard like that." Rory thinks he recognizes her accent and looks up to check. It's Soph, the skinny black-haired one with the pockmarked cheeks, the one Per and Lino ambushed on the road. "Reckon we should have kept him for ourselves." *Kept* comes out as *kipt*. "The fish get all the fun."

"We'll get him gagged soon, don't you worry," Jody says. "Won't hear him no more after that."

The one who dismounted looks at Rory closely. She's the one he saw at the head of the charging Riders, standing in the stirrups and yelling. Now she's calm she looks incapable of that sort of fury. "Is he your dad?" she says.

"No."

"Were any of those people your family?"

He shakes his head.

"Not too many questions, Ellie." *Quistions:* this is Soph again. "Better save them till everyone's listening. This little bugger's going to have a fair bit of explaining to do."

"I want his arms tied at least," Jody says. "Till we know what we're dealing with."

"Really?" The one called Ellie gives Jody a sarcastic look. " 'What we're dealing with.' "

"You didn't see what happened to Ace. And that other one turned himself into a bird and flew off." Jody's already unwrapping some twine from a pocket. "Turn round, you," she says, prodding Rory with the toe of her boot.

"At least let him have his arms in front," Ellie says.

Jody glares, but lets Rory face her as she begins wrapping the twine around his wrists. "Where's that woman?" she asks him, while she's tying it.

Silvia. She knew all this was going to happen. She knew the Riders were in the Mount. When she gave Rory that quick kiss it was because she was saying good-bye.

"Never mind, then," Jody says, when his only answer is more sniveling. "We'll find her. Or something else will. Strangers don't last too long around here, specially not at night." She's about to yank Rory back to her horse when Ellie steps between them.

"He can ride with me," she says, and before Jody can answer, "All right, Rory?" she adds, in a gentler voice, and steers him away.

She lets him sit straight, squeezed on the saddle in front of her. With his hands tied she has to pull him up but she does it carefully, never forcing. She's a short well-built woman with a button nose and a rather faraway expression. She has an extraordinary collection of rings, mismatched and lurid: some are shaped like flowers, one's like a miniature ball of twine in silver, one's a winged skull. Every finger has at least one. "Sorry about tying you up," she says in his ear once they're both mounted. She's reaching around him to take the reins. "Ridiculous." The rest of the women come riding up from the beach soon afterwards. There must be twenty or thirty of them in all. One's cradling her left arm and grimacing and catching her breath in pain. The one with the motorcycle helmet turns out to be Sal, the general. He sees the helmet propped on her pommel. She gives Rory a long hard-eyed look but doesn't say anything to him. The one called Haze is there as well, still wearing her sunglasses although the shadows are long by now. From their discussion it's clear they've left Per tied up on the beach. Rory thinks of the dead man who greeted them on their arrival, bleached and bloated and pecked by birds, and goes faint for a moment. "Careful," Ellie says, holding him upright. When they set off in a slow convoy she tells him how to keep his back straight and grip with his knees. Rory can barely keep his head straight, let alone his back, but he does his best. He can't see any option but to do as he's told. He's a prisoner. A Rider comes past them, exchanging a curt comment with Ellie while giving Rory a black resentful look, and as she passes Rory sees a length of sturdy wood sticking out from her saddlebag: the wizard's staff.

The journey's a torment. He thought they might be taking him back to the Mount, but from things the Riders say to each other he gathers it's not their home, it's just some kind of base, safe for the women because it's in the sea. They're heading somewhere else. It's not close by. He's aching up and down before they've ridden away from the gorse and scrub near the coast, and by the time they're in among dark tree-shaded lanes he's so sore he thinks he might die of the pain, though at least it helps him not think about how utterly miserable he is. No one speaks to him. They don't even speak to each other much. They stop at a village of boarded-up houses where children come running out of an alley. An exhausted-looking man leans out of an upper window to talk to a couple of the Riders, and Rory hears them saying something about Ace being dead. Someone gives the children a bag of food.

They stop a couple more times, at a road junction under wind-stunted trees and then by a washed-out bridge where they have to ford a stream. The stop at the ford is longer. Some women at the front dismount and do something before the rest cross, scattering things in the water and speaking in unison. Ellie says something under her breath as she steers her horse across. Rory's head is bowed as they go, and for a moment he thinks he sees a shy and shadowy face among the eddies, breaking the surface like a fish except it's a human face. No one else notices, and he's too bound up in his battle with the agony in his bum to care.

On and on they go, under taller trees, the shadows twilight-deep. Single leaves drop slowly. Rory bites his lip and squeezes the pommel with his bound hands and keeps going as long as he can but eventually he can't hold it back anymore and he's making swallowed whimpering noises and shaking like he's in fever.

Ellie reins in. "The kid needs a break," she calls out.

"Now?" someone replies from behind. "We're nearly back." No

one else stops. Horses plod past in the gloom. They're in a wide lane under a high canopy of slender branches.

"Just five minutes," Ellie says. "You go on ahead." She leans close to Rory's ear and whispers, "Keep your wrists together." She's got a knife from somewhere. She starts sawing through the twine around his wrists, surreptitiously, stopping whenever anyone passes them.

Two others insist on waiting with Ellie. One's Haze, though it takes Rory a while to recognize her now that she's pushed her sunglasses up. The other's a grey-haired woman with a faintly mad expression. She was one of the three who got off to pray when they crossed the river. Ellie gets Rory out of the saddle and sets him on his feet, sending shooting pains all up the back of his legs. He hobbles a few steps.

"Hang on." Haze jumps down in front of him and grabs. "He's got his hands free."

Ellie twirls the knife in her fingers.

Haze glares at her. "We lost a good friend today. You didn't see what these people can do."

"He's just a kid," Ellie says.

"I doubt that."

"Keep moving," Ellie tells him. "It'll help. He doesn't really look like he's about to run away, does he?"

"Let me look," says the older woman, dismounting slowly. She turns out to have an absurdly posh voice, even more so than Missus Grouse, though it's soft and quavery. She peers into Rory's face like it's an inspection. "I see no mark on him," she says.

"To be fair, Margery," Ellie says drily, "it is getting a bit dark."

"Speaking of which," Haze says, "let's not waste time."

"A bit longer." Ellie nudges him. "Keep walking. It'll be murder when you get back on but it's not that far now."

"The question is," the older woman says, "what we're going to do with him when we get there."

"No need to make it sound so alarming."

"Doesn't matter," Haze says. "He doesn't understand anyway."

"Yes he does. Don't you, Rory?"

"Rory?" Haze steps in front of him again. "Is that your name?"

Trying very hard not to well up again, Rory nods.

"That woman said he didn't speak English."

"It was a mistake," Rory says.

"What?"

"An accident," he says. "I wasn't supposed to be with them. I got kidnapped."

"Where are you from?"

"Here," Rory says. "England."

"Here?" Haze has a sharp face and a sharp manner and she's turned them on him like a threat. "What do you mean, here? I've never seen you before."

"Not here. I'm from," he remembers the name from The Old Days, "the Isles of Scilly. Tresco."

There's a long pause. He's stopped hobbling around. He's intensely aware of being stared at.

"There are people living on the Scillies?" Haze says, in a completely different tone.

"Did you say Tresco?" says the old woman, Margery.

"Yeah."

"Do you know any of the Le Rieus?"

That's Kate's family's name. They were the important family on the island, for ages. "You mean Kate," he says.

"Katherine Le Rieu? The daughter? Is she alive?"

"Yeah."

Margery closes her eyes, clasps her hands, and whispers something.

"This could be a trick," Haze says.

"Could be," Ellie says. She's got the kind of voice that conceals its sarcasm well enough to be polite but not so well that you could miss it. "I think Rory's going to have a date with the Professor."

As she predicted, it's torture sitting in the saddle again, but the brief respite was worth it, and with his wrists untied and only three of them riding together he doesn't feel quite so much like a captive. He's clinging to the fact that Ellie's being Nice to him. He can't imagine what's going to happen to him when they get where they're going, whether he's going to be punished or tortured or interrogated, so any slight hint of kindness is a straw to clutch at.

"Who's the Professor?" he asks her, as they plod along.

"You'll see," she says. "Nothing to worry about."

"I'm sorry about the one who died," he says. He wouldn't dare say this to any of the others but maybe if he tells Ellie she'll believe him. "It wasn't supposed to happen. We told him to stop."

"I heard that bloke drove the horse mad."

"Yeah."

"He did it to Charlie as well, back there. She's lucky she only broke her arm."

"Sorry," he says.

"Do you know how he did it?"

"No. It's to do with his staff. I think it didn't work properly the second time."

"You'll have to tell the Professor all this later on."

"What's going to happen to him?"

"Who? That big bloke?"

"Yeah."

"Why? Friend of yours?"

He doesn't know what to say.

"There's an easy way to dispose of annoying men around here," she says, and leaves it at that.

Aching and exhausted and benighted, in the midst of strangers, Rory's beginning to feel like he's not himself anymore, like he's no one and nothing, a brittle, empty, washed-up carcass, when from nowhere he catches the smell of wood smoke, and suddenly it's just like coming up the tree-lined Abbey road in the evening, knowing there's a fire and food and a warm room waiting, a reminder of Home so sweet and pure it forces tears into his eyes. "Here we are," Ellie says, pretending not to notice him crying, or perhaps she's tired of it. A chorus of barking starts up, and soon he hears other voices as well. The sun's long down by now. A strong glimmer of firelight seen through a screen of trees makes everything near it seem entirely dark.

They come to a gap in the tall hedge. There's a gate here, wrapped up and down in barbed wire. From branches overhanging the gate many objects are suspended on long strings, hundreds of them and all different it looks like, though it's getting too dark to see what most

of them are except for one or two of the bigger or shinier ones: a
bicycle wheel, a spanner, a frosty bauble like a Christmas decoration.
Someone on the inside pulls the gate open and they ride in. Four
big dogs come racing up a wide avenue and start frisking around the
horses' legs. No one seems to mind. There are suddenly more people
milling around, talking with each other, men as well as women. They
talk quietly and most of them stop to look at Rory as Ellie rides him
down the avenue. "Doesn't look like much," one bearded man says
to her. She ignores him.

The avenue runs dead straight between two neat lines of enormous trees. Ahead Rory can see the outline of a single bare hill. To
the left are lots of buildings, firelight and movement and chatter
all around them. Some of the Riders have dismounted by a stone
trough ahead and are talking while they let their horses drink. It's a
camp, the enemy camp. It feels startlingly alive and busy. There are
even children, running around in and out of the trees, chasing dogs.
A woman in a puffy jacket and a woolly bobble hat comes over and
takes the reins of Ellie's horse. She's the first woman Rory's seen for
more than a year who looks like she might have more than enough
to eat. She glances at Rory in a bored, businesslike fashion and says,
"So this is the prisoner, is it?"

"Yup," Ellie says, swinging herself down and offering Rory a
hand. Neither of them seems to be joking, not even slightly.

"Let me, I'll look after the nag. What are you going to do with
him?"

"Feed him, I think, first up," Ellie says. She plants him on his feet
again. He wobbles and nearly falls.

"Your lucky night," the other woman says to him, without
warmth. "Was he with the lot that killed Ace?"

"I don't know the whole story," Ellie says.

"Not the Pack, though?"

"Doesn't look like it."

Another person comes marching over. It's Sal, still in her general's
coat. "Who untied his hands?" she says. "Was that you, El?"

"He didn't give me any trouble."

"Yet," Sal says. She takes off the red scarf tied around her head, unknots it, and bends in front of Rory without even looking at him. "Hands out," she says. "I hear you speak English perfectly well after all? Is that right?" Rory's abject with humiliation, standing there with legs so stiff he can barely keep himself upright while this woman trusses his wrists as indifferently as if he's a piece of meat, and can't muster any kind of answer.

"Says he's from Tresco," Ellie says.

That makes Sal stop and look. "Scilly?"

Biting his lip, Rory nods.

Sal checks her knot, tugs it a little tighter. "Let's leave him like that," she says to Ellie, "all right? Will your posse keep an eye on him?"

"As long as we can eat while we do it."

"In the barn, then. We'd better keep him inside. They're talking to Hester now. I imagine she'll want to see him tonight."

"All right."

"El, seriously. Don't leave him on his own. Those people weren't like anything we've come across before. I'll tell Soph as well."

"It was a mistake," Rory says.

Sal looks at him like he's interrupted something important.

"They kidnapped me," he says. "I was never supposed to go with them. They didn't even want me. I'm nothing to do with it." He's started to snivel again.

Sal looks at him. She's got a rather hard, rather handsome face. "What's your name?" she says.

"Rory."

"You want everything to be all right, don't you, Rory?"

He mumbles that he does.

She props her hands on her knees and stares him in the face like an angry teacher. "Later on this evening someone's going to ask you some questions. There's one simple thing you have to do if you want everything to be all right. Do you know what it is, Rory?"

No, he doesn't. He wishes she'd go away. He should never have opened his mouth.

"Tell the truth." She straightens. "There. That's easy to remember, isn't it? Make sure you do it." She turns on her heels and stalks away.

Ellie's behind him. She leans close to his ear again. She doesn't have to lean far. Her cropped fringe tickles his face. "Oh well," she says. "I tried."

After more talking a small group gathers around them. It's a different sort of talking from the kind he's used to, the hesitant and tired back-and-forth which takes up so much time at the Abbey. It doesn't have that undertow of perpetual anxiety. It doesn't feel like it might turn at any moment into complaining. There's no sense that at any moment someone might mention The Future. It's so different he can't help noticing it. These people feel like they know what they're doing even when they're arguing about what to do. They take him through a group of low buildings rank with the smell of horse and then through an arched gap in a holly hedge, and all at once he's at the heart of it.

The heart's a fire. A wide gravel circle rings it, noisy with people going back and forth, men and women and some children too, amazing numbers of people. In the center of the circle there's a lawn, and on the lawn a bonfire's burning, as wide as a man is tall, tossing fistfuls of sparks up into the dark. It's as hot as the summer sun. Beyond it Rory sees the front of an old house, a very old house, long and squat and grey, the upper floor resting on a row of fat columns, all its windows alive with reflections of dancing flame. The space around the columns makes a kind of long porch, and there are lots of people sitting there, a crowd, so many that it takes Rory some effort to remember that there were once such things as crowds like this. But they don't look like the people he remembers from The Old Days, squashed onto the island ferries or pressed close together around the tables in the garden of the Pub. They're *messier*. Their clothes are gaudy and mixed-up, with lots of odd decorations, belts and bangles and patches. They're not even standing and sitting around the way Rory remembers people standing and sitting around. They're not divided up. They don't look as if some of them are pretending others aren't there. They don't look as if they're on the way between one place and another, or taking a few moments off between work and home. They look *planted*. Rory can see it at a glance. They look

like they're supposed to be there, all of them, equally. They look like
they're at home.

He's led around the side of the house to a much newer set of
buildings arranged around a courtyard. It's getting quite dark now,
and candles and fires are appearing all around him. Rory can't imagine what these people's Stash must be like to be able to burn so much
wax and wood, and to be wearing so many things they don't need,
like Ellie's collection of rings. Perhaps they don't even need a Stash.
There's no cursed sea closing them in. This land, wherever it is (he's
long since stopped thinking of it as the Mainland, or England, or
anywhere he ever imagined he knew), seems to go on forever. Maybe
they use as many things as they want and then just go out the next
day and get more, the way everyone used to.

They take him inside, into a low-ceilinged smudgy room with
shuttered windows and lots of unmatched chairs and a smell of old
clothes. There are rugs and sleeping bags scattered around the floor.
A couple of fat candles in alcoves give enough light for him to see
that the walls are decorated with shells and bits of sea-glass lined
up on narrow strips of wood. Five people have come in with him,
Ellie and Soph and Haze and another woman he doesn't recognize,
and a man with a shaved head and a multicolored scarf so long it's
wrapped four or five times around his neck. They shut the door and
sit him down in a chair. He's trying his best not to snivel but there's
something about sitting down in a strange room with people he
doesn't know which makes him feel so desperately small and lost that
he can't stop himself. They all go a bit quiet when he starts crying.

Then they feed him.

It's almost worth being kidnapped (twice), seasick, terrified,
footsore, saddle sore, all of it, just for the plate of food Soph hands
him. There's meat, charred at the edges but juicy when he bites it,
smoky and peppery, and there's other charred stuff which isn't meat
and tastes sweetly earthy in the places where it's almost burned, and
there are leaves which are as peppery as the meat juice, and a dollop
of some sauce thing with so many flavors it's like eating five meals
at once. There's absolutely no fish. Its absence makes him notice for

the first time that nothing in the camp smells of fish, not the people, not the cooking fires, not the evening breeze. He has to maneuver the food around with his hands lashed together, which slows him down, and once he's got it to his mouth he eats slowly and carefully from long habit, so each mouthful becomes a little act of pilgrimage, a concentrated effort followed by a blissful reward. He forgets he's miserable while he's doing it. He forgets everything else, in fact. He forgets where he is so completely that he doesn't notice the room's gone quiet and everyone's looking at him until he glances up between mouthfuls.

"I guess" (*giss*) "that other lot didn't feed you much, eh?" Soph says, and though no one actually smiles he's aware of a subtle transition, as if he's taken the first step from being an enemy to becoming a friend.

When they're watching him struggle to mop up the last few spots of juice and sauce they decide to untie his hands. Haze thinks they shouldn't, but instead of arguing about it or discussing it Soph just laughs at her. "What are you afraid he is, some kind of fucking vampire? Hey." She means Rory. "Show us your teeth, Tiger. Go on." She bares her own in a grimace. They're the dirtiest teeth he's ever seen, so stained they look almost as black as her hair. He sees that she's making a joke, and copies the gesture. "See? No pointy ones in there." She kneels by his chair and unknots the scarf. "There you go. Don't go getting any funny ideas now. I know there're only five of us against the one of you, but we're tougher than we look. Especially Haze, she's fucking hardcore."

Haze stands up without a word and goes outside, banging the door behind her.

"Shit," Soph says. "Sorry."

"She'll be angry about Ace for a while," Ellie says. "She wanted to kill that guy on the beach herself."

"I reckon it's not the guy we need to worry about," Soph says, settling on the floor. "It's that fucking great piece of wood. Who's got it, anyway?"

"Sal."

"Took it to the Prof?"

"I assume so."

"There was something whacked about the way he held it. I swear I heard him talking to it."

"Why don't you just ask the kid," the man says. "He must know better than anyone else."

They all look at him. He stares at the plate in his lap, scraping with his fingertip for nonexistent specks of food.

"The one in charge was the woman," Soph says. "She was the brains of the operation. Hey." She pokes Rory gently with her toe. "Tiger. Whatever happened to her? Is she still wandering around out there? That'd make me nervous." She sits up suddenly. "Fuck. What if she goes and unties the big bastard?"

Now the others all look at each other. The woman Rory doesn't know stands up. "Haze was right, we should have finished him off. I'll go tell Sal."

She's got her hand on the door when Rory says, "She won't."

Once again they all go quiet.

"What do you mean?" says Ellie.

"Silvia won't rescue Per if you left him tied up. She's gone off by herself."

"Who won't do what?" says the woman by the door.

"Silvia's the woman who was there before," Rory tells Soph. "She's a gypsy, she can tell the future. Per's the man with the staff. They were all supposed to be going together but Silvia tricked them and went on her own."

It feels better saying it aloud. He's been turning this over as he jiggled and jolted along on the horse, tasting the misery of the thought. Now he's said it aloud it's like confirming it. It's obvious, really.

"Where did she go?" Ellie asks.

"To that place the Valley, I bet. She was the one who knew where it was hidden. That thing they were looking for. She pretended it wasn't in the Valley but she knew it was, she split the rest of them up and deliberately sent them to the wrong place."

Soph runs her fingers through her long black hair. "That makes a lot of sense," she says.

"It does?" says the man.

"It does, actually. You'd know what I mean if you'd been there. She was just the type who'd try her luck in there."

"What's the Valley?" Rory says.

"Yeah, well, that's a good question," the man says.

"Mainly because no one's ever come back to tell us," Ellie says.

"The Valley's the place where it all began," says the other woman, still with her hand on the door, though she no longer looks like she's going to run outside. "Where they first saw the angel. Where all the pilgrims went that first winter. It's only a few miles east of here."

"The valley of the Helford River," Soph says. "Used to be a couple of pretty decent pubs down there."

"What's wrong with it now?"

They look at each other. Soph shrugs.

"They say the roads move behind you so you can't get back out," the man says.

"They say a lot of stuff," Ellie says. "Makes me wonder how they know. Or who 'they' are, in fact."

"The priest was the last person in there," the man says, "wasn't he? I've heard him say there's a well in the heart of the Valley whose water cures every illness of body or soul."

"The priest's off his fucking rocker," Soph says.

"Sanity's probably not that useful when it comes to the Valley," Ellie says.

"Are you sure about this?" the woman at the door says to Rory.

"There's nothing we can do until tomorrow anyway," says Ellie. "It's too dark to go back out. Someone can check in the morning."

"Haze," says the man. "If he's still there she'll be more than happy to do for him, by the sound of it."

"Baker," says Ellie to the man, warning, glancing at Rory.

"Sorry," mutters the man. *Baker* is apparently his name.

"How the hell did you get mixed up with that lot?" Soph says to him, stretching herself out on the floor again, arms over her head, so she seems to take up most of the floor. "Don't answer that. Save it for the Prof. We'd better find you some more water, actually. You've got a lot of talking to do."

18

"They're ready for him," Haze says, putting her head around the door.

He thought he was too tired to move, but the words jolt him like sea spray. The five of them walk him back out around the big house to where the fire is. A lot of people are sitting closer to it now, leaning on each other back to back, or kissing, or just watching the flames. There's a man with a guitar, singing. One group is passing a pipe around. A peculiar animal is browsing the grass at the edge of the gravel. *Sheep,* says some part of Rory's mind left over from The Old Days, and he thinks of fluffy dots in flat even fields: ridiculous memories, impossible. He's taken under the porch and in through an ancient-looking pair of doors. A few others get up from whatever they've been doing and follow. They cross a courtyard contained by the four sides of the house, empty apart from big drums at the corners to catch rainwater from the gutters, and a single tree in the center. Lots of people touch the tree's trunk and whisper as they pass it. Under an arch on the far side a door opens into the house, allowing a hum of mingled conversation to leak out into the night. It dies away almost at once. Soph motions at the door.

"After you," she says.

He doesn't know how many people there are in there. Too many. Seeing a crowd outside is one thing, but being indoors with them is another, especially since every single one of them stops talking to look at him when he goes in. It's a long room, as long as a church, though the ceiling's low and the walls are hung with what look like rugs covering any windows. All the people are sitting on the floor, on cushions or folded clothes or just straight on the wood. It's almost oppressively warm from all the bodies, and from a low fire in a stone hearth on one side. It's dim too, full of restless shadows. A few people are holding lanterns, and there are a couple more hung on the walls. They've left a space clear down the middle of the room, leading from the door to the far end, where five thick candles in glass jars are burning on a big table, bright enough for Rory to see that the other thing on the table is Per's staff.

Beside the table a woman sits in a wheelchair. The wheelchair's metal, so it catches flickers of candlelight. He can't see much of the woman except that she looks older, and she's clearly watching him, like everyone else.

Next to her is an empty chair.

Something quite unexpected happens inside Rory. He's got no one left: that's not news, he's horribly familiar with that feeling by now, the feeling that he's utterly by himself, no family, no friends, no landmarks, nothing familiar, no one he's ever known. What's new is a funny little rush of resistance, a tentative clutch of determination like a hardness in his heart. He's got to be brave, he thinks to himself. He's got to be strong.

No one has to tell him what he's supposed to do. The empty chair is obviously waiting for him. He walks up the cleared space on the floor between all the people. He's thinking of what Silvia told him: *You have a gift.*

The woman in the wheelchair speaks as he approaches.

"Welcome to Dolphin House, Rory."

She's quite old. There's a big tartan blanket over her knees and another one around her shoulders. Her hands are folded in her lap. They're trembling a little all the time though the rest of her looks calm. She has a quiet, sad-eyed face and a rather tired but clever-sounding voice. "Come and sit down, please. Have you had enough to eat?"

"Yes," he says, and (remembering his manners—she seems like that sort of person), "thank you."

"Speak up!" yells someone from the floor. Nearby people shush her.

"I'm Hester," the woman in the wheelchair says. He feels like he ought to offer to shake hands, but hers remain in her lap. He's relieved he won't have to touch them. They're very wrinkly, and then there's the tremor. "I hope you don't mind the audience. A lot of us want to hear what you have to say." He sits in the chair. He's aware that the room's gone intensely quiet. The chair's turned so he's facing all the people sitting on the floor. He sees Sal near the front, among some of the other Riders who attacked them at the Mount. "You'll probably find it easier," Hester says, "if you pretend it's just you and me talking. As it will be, I hope." A grouchy murmur ripples around the floor, subsiding under a burst of *shh*s. "First of all, Rory: do you know where you are?"

"No," he whispers. He doesn't mean to whisper but his voice sort of stops in his throat.

"Excuse me?" Hester says. "I'm a little deaf, sorry."

"No," he says.

"I'm not talking about this house. I wouldn't expect you to know that. I mean this place, this country. Where you arrived on your boat yesterday."

"Is it England?" he says nervously.

Hester keeps her eyes on him. She's got the saggy lined skin of an old person, but not the eyes. They're not at all vague or wandery. "That's right," she says. "It is."

"Or it was," mutters a man near the front.

"*Shh!*"

"Now," Hester says. "You got off that boat, didn't you, yesterday afternoon?" He's so anxious now he's not even sure if that's right, but he nods. "Where were you when you got on it?"

He blinks. The question seems too easy. He wonders if it's a trick. Nothing in her face suggests any kind of trap.

"When I got on the boat?"

"Yes."

"Home," he says, and realizes at once how stupid that sounds. "On the island, I mean. The harbor. My mother . . ." He looks down. "It was a mistake," he mumbles.

"The island?" Hester says.

"Yeah. Tresco. We all called it Home after . . ." But the room has already filled with agitated chatter. A man near the back stands up and says, "For God's sake keep quiet or no one'll hear anything!" An older woman at the front gets up on her knees. She's staring at Rory with a kind of desperate anger. "Gareth Newlyn!" she says. "Is he alive?"

"Not now," a man next to her says. An uproar is rising behind her. She shakes the man off. "Do you know Gareth?" she says, shouting now to make herself heard. Sal's standing up too, trying to get everyone to be quiet. The woman who's shouting at Rory pushes herself forward through the crowd.

"All the men died," he says. No one hears him, it's too noisy, but maybe the woman can read his lips or something because she stops. Everyone's shushing again now.

"Please," Hester says. "Let him speak." She's not loud but there's obviously some kind of power in her because silence spreads as fast as the hubbub did. "I'm sorry, Rory," she says. "What did you say?"

"The men." It's so quiet again that he can hear his own fingers scratching nervously against the side of the chair. "They all died. I'm the last one. I was going to be."

And now the silence is like every single person in the room has stopped breathing.

"But instead you got on that boat," Hester says.

"I wasn't supposed to. It was by accident."

"You never meant to sail here with those people."

"No."

"You didn't know it was their boat."

"No."

"And you'd never seen them before until you got on their boat by mistake."

"No. I mean yes. But I didn't mean . . . I wasn't going to . . ."

It takes a very long while to explain. All the time he's thinking he shouldn't be telling these people all this, it's nothing to do with them, it's not what he thought they were going to ask about, but there's something about the way Hester asks her questions, patiently, going back and forth, sometimes going right back to the beginning so he feels like he's telling her everything twice, which makes it all come out. In fact it's like her questions are actually putting everything that's happened to him in the proper order, as if he didn't actually know what was going on himself until she asked him about it, even though he was there and she wasn't. Bit by bit, without him ever meaning it to happen, the whole story comes out. No one interrupts. The audience is so still he almost forgets they're in the room. Rory's afraid at one stage he's going to end up talking about Her, but whether by good fortune or because he's managing to be clever Hester's questions never quite lead him in that direction. She doesn't want to know about his life on Home. What she's really interested in is Silvia and Lino and Per. Especially Per, it turns out.

"So you never saw Silvia or Lino holding the staff."

"No."

"He wouldn't let anyone else touch it?"

"No."

"Did he say what would happen if they did?"

Rory shakes his head.

"And he held on to it all the time you were on the boat, even though he was sailing the boat as well."

"And that was because it made the fiery ghosts come." *Fiery ghosts* is how he described them to Hester when she first got him to explain about the staff. It's not right at all, it sounds thin and flat like something from the comics, but Hester's adopted the phrase as if it's perfectly normal.

"Yeah."

"And they protected the boat from the sirens." Hester took a while earlier on to untangle what he meant when he told her about the sea-rainy. It turns out it's an Italian word which means *sirens,* which is another way of saying mermaids. Hester seems to know all about Italy, and Romania, and gypsies. Nothing surprises her.

"Yes."

"Do you think Silvia or Lino could have made the staff work like that?"

He doesn't understand.

"Imagine"—she's very quick to realize when he doesn't understand—"a wave had come and knocked Per overboard, and he'd dropped the staff. I know it's not very likely, but just imagine for a second. So now it's you and Lino and Silvia on the boat, with the staff, in the middle of the sea. You'd have been all right, wouldn't you, and Silvia too, because the sirens don't take women or children, but Lino would have been in great danger, wouldn't he? Do you think one of them could have taken the staff and made the fiery ghosts come to keep him safe?"

He thinks about it.

"No. I don't think so."

"What about you?"

"Me?"

"Could you have done that?" She nods towards the staff, lying there on the table in front of the candles in their glass jars. The marks on it are strange and beautiful but also sinister. It's because they obviously mean something but you can't begin to imagine what it is. "Picked it up and used it to save Lino?"

"Me? No way."

"You look like you don't even like the idea of trying."

He shakes his head.

"Do you think she or Lino would have liked to try holding it?"

"She didn't like it." Had he properly understood this until Hester made him say it? It's obvious now.

"Didn't she?"

"She didn't like him doing things with it. She tried to stop him when, when . . ."

The other trick Hester has is *not* asking another question. Sometimes, like now, she just leaves him dangling, and the silence goes on and on, and she just watches him with her mild, clever eyes until he has to speak.

"When he drove that horse mad and . . ."

Eventually, she takes pity on him. "And our friend Ace died."

How did that happen? Just a moment ago they were talking about being on the boat, they were nowhere near the high place in the road where the Riders first appeared. Rory can feel the pressure of every single person in the room watching him.

"Sorry," he says. "It was . . . No one meant to."

"You say Silvia tried to stop him?"

"She never liked it when the fiery ghosts came. She told him he thought he was in charge of them but he wasn't. He wasn't really one of them anyway, not like her and Lino. Her and Lino had come all the way together but they only just met Per, when they got to the sea. They just needed him to get across. 'Cos of the sirens."

Hester checks that he's finished and then says, "She didn't think he was really in charge of them? 'Them' being the fiery ghosts?"

"He tried to make them come once to light a fire but they didn't. He got really angry. And, yeah, actually, the first time, in the Hotel, I remember he said 'They're going' and it started getting dark so I had to leave. And on the boat too. When we were sailing across. He kept saying it was nearly time, near the end. They were all really worried."

"Worried that the fiery ghosts would leave them before they reached land?"

"Yeah. That's it."

"And of course when Sal and Ellie and Charlie and the others came out of the Mount when they saw you there. That's the time you'd think he'd really want the fiery ghosts to come and protect him. Wouldn't you? But they didn't. Not enough, at least."

"He was trying."

"Was he?"

Rory nods. "I bet he was. He was whacking the staff up and down like this"—he mimes a feeble imitation of Per's furious gestures—"and shouting."

"Do you know why it didn't work?"

"No. Maybe . . ."

"Maybe what?" she says after a long pause.

"Maybe you can't ask them too many times." He hadn't thought about this properly before, but when he thinks about some of the things Silvia said, or even just the way they looked when they talked about it, it feels right. "Maybe they don't like being ordered around."

"That's an interesting way of putting it," she says. If Ol had said those words they'd have been oozing sarcasm. Hester's entirely, gravely serious. "Tell me, Rory, did you ever see the fiery ghosts come on their own? Without Per doing something to bring them?"

He shudders a little and looks away from the staff. "No."

"You don't like that idea?"

He shakes his head vigorously.

"You make it sound as if you're like Silvia, you didn't much like the fiery ghosts."

"I don't. Didn't." He corrects himself quickly. He can feel that it's much better if he puts distance between himself and Silvia's gang. He can feel that's what the room wants to hear.

"So let's see. Per used the staff to light an underground room, and to keep the sirens away from his boat, and he tried to use it to light a fire, is that right? And to attack our horses."

"Yeah."

"Is there anything else you saw him do with it?"

He's about to say *No* when he remembers, yet again as if Hester knows everything better than he does himself. "And that dog."

For the first time in a very long time, a whisper blows through the room, quickly stilled. Everyone's suddenly paying attention, he can feel it. Rory thinks back to when they first met the Riders on the road, and how the mood changed when they started talking about the old man's dog.

"The dog," Hester says, "yes. Sorry. I forgot." He's quite sure she didn't. "What happened to it, exactly?"

"I don't know. It was inside. Behind the door."

"But you—"

"I heard it go *thud*. Like it fell over."

"And you didn't hear it after that."

"No."

"Can you remember if Per did or said anything special that time?"

"What d'you mean?"

"When he made the fiery ghosts attack Old Edgar's dog. Or was it just the same as all the other times he did something with the staff?"

"Silvia asked the old ma—" He swallows. He doesn't want to sound like he's being rude about old people. "The man, to keep the dog quiet. Then Per just came up and pointed the staff and . . ."

Hester waits.

"And whatever, and the fire sort of went through the door, and I heard it go *thud*."

There's quite a long silence. Rory fidgets in his chair.

Hester leans back a little. "All right. I don't know about you but I'm very tired." A sighing murmur rises around the room. "You've been very helpful, Rory. Remarkably helpful. You're a very brave young man."

He has no idea what to say.

"Just one more thing." People at the back have started to whisper to each other, and some of them are stretching and getting up. Hester unclasps her hands for the first time since he's been sitting there and directs them carefully to the wheels of her chair. Seeing what she's doing, a couple of people—Sal's one of them—get up quickly to help. They push her close to Rory. "You don't know anything that could help us find Silvia, do you?"

He shakes his head.

"Are you sure? Because I'm very much afraid that you're right, she is trying to enter the Valley, and it would be so much better if we could stop her before she does that."

"Too late by now," Sal says. "It's hours past. If she knew where she was going she'll have got there easily by now."

"I've no doubt she knew exactly where she was going, unfortunately," Hester says. "It's a shame."

"She'd never heard of the Valley before until that old m—That man at the crossroads said it," Rory says. "You could tell she hadn't."

"She wouldn't have known the name, perhaps," Hester says. "It's just our name for it anyway. But from everything you've told me about her, I'm certain she had the destination in mind all along. She came all that way to get here. Extraordinary thought. She found two other remarkable people and used them to help her travel safely. Three other remarkable people, perhaps I should say." She smiles at Rory. "She's transparently a person to be reckoned with."

"We're better off with her out of the picture, if you ask me," Sal says.

"Well." Hester tugs the blanket higher on her lap. "Perhaps."

"She'll make it," Rory says, surprising himself.

"You think so?" Sal and the man behind Hester's chair are smiling slightly, but Hester herself is taking Rory seriously.

"You'd know if you'd met her. She'll find the ring."

"Ah, I very much doubt there's any such thing."

Rory stares.

Hester chuckles. He wouldn't have thought her capable of it until now. "A magic ring of power? Goodness me. It's almost too much. I'm a bit surprised the other two believed her, to be honest. Perhaps Tolkien hasn't penetrated quite so deeply on the Continent. Still, it obviously worked. She must be very convincing." Seeing Rory's expression, she makes herself serious again. "We've all heard the stories about the Valley. None of them are like that. Magic's not about rings of power. Even that thing"—she motions towards the staff—"you've told me yourself that Per couldn't actually *use* it, could he? No. Your friend Silvia told you the truth, I think, though I fear she was deceiving her other companions. It's all about where she was going, not what she was trying to find there. She's aiming herself into the heart of magic. She was always going to the Valley, I'd stake my head on it. All that talk about a ring, that was all *pour encourager les autres*." She reaches a shaky hand across to pat Rory sympathetically. "You're right, I'm sure. She'll get where she wanted. She sounds like an impressively determined woman. But, alas."

Sal, standing behind the wheelchair, says what Hester won't say. "She won't come out again. No one does. Plenty have tried. Not so much recently, but there used to be quite a few. Plenty of them were probably pretty determined too."

"I'm sorry," Hester says. "Sal's right. Powers that care nothing for us have forbidden the Valley to people." She gives his knee a weak squeeze. "You liked her, didn't you?"

He's remembering the way she said thank you and gave him a kiss. A last thought occurs to him. "Can you speak Italian?"

Hester looks startled, though only for a moment. "Not really. A little. Why?"

"Do you know a word that goes . . . A-veevy . . . Areevy . . ."

"*Arrivederci?*"

"Yeah." He was sure she'd know.

"That's an easy one. It means *good-bye.*"

He sits there. Something rather horrible happens somewhere inside him, his stomach maybe, or his heart.

"Ah," Hester says, quietly, as if she understands.

"Screwed the poor lad over pretty good, didn't she," the man who got up with Sal says. "Who'd chuck away a ten-year-old like that?"

"Hey," Sal says, her look softening a fraction. "He hasn't done too badly. At least he's ended up here with us."

They get him out of the big room. Only then does he remember how exhausted he is. Suddenly he can hardly walk, he's got nothing left to go on at all. He ends up being half carried to the loft of another building. It's more bare even than the most thoroughly looted houses on Home, just stone walls and wooden beams, and it smells of horse and straw, but Baker the man with the scarf brings foam mats and piles of blankets. There are no windows and the only way in and out is up a ladder which comes through a square hole in the floor. Soph brings a lantern up, and then a shallow dish of water, a towel, and some proper soap. The last time she comes back, while Rory's in the middle of washing himself, she brings the staff.

"Not letting that out of my sight," she says, good-humoredly. "We don't want it getting into the wrong hands."

It turns out she's going to sleep up in the loft as well, along with the other woman who was with their group before. She's called Sandra, she says, acting friendlier than she did before, though she's still a bit awkward with Rory. She and Soph change into big T-shirts. They've got one for him too. It's old and very soft, and though he's cold while he's getting his own clothes off as soon as he burrows himself down under blankets he's incredibly comfortable, so comfortable nothing else matters anymore except the fact that he'll soon be asleep. Soph snuffs out the lantern and he hears the women settling themselves down. There are others in the room below, talking quietly. It's white noise, like surf.

"So what were you and the Prof having your little chin-wag about at the end there?" It's completely dark but there's no mistaking Soph's voice.

"Let the poor kid sleep," Sandra says.

"Just wondering."

"Who's the proff?" Rory likes the way Soph talks to him. She's one of those adults who can talk to children without looking like it's hurting them to try.

"The Prof! Professor Aitch Lightfoot. That's the old biddy you've been talking to for the past hour."

"Is she your ruler?"

Sandra giggles. She's a broad-shouldered, strong-looking woman with a husky voice but her giggle makes her sound like Pink.

"We don't have a ruler," Soph says. "Who'd want one of those?"

"She is a billion times cleverer than everyone else, though," Sandra says.

"Two billion times cleverer than you."

"So," Sandra goes on, unruffled, "I can see how you'd think so."

"You did great," Soph says. "Pretty intimidating setup for a kid."

"What's going to happen now?" Rory says.

There's an awkward silence. He hears Soph rustling like she's sat up.

"I wouldn't worry too much," she says. "Get some sleep now and we'll get you sorted out in the morning."

"Can I go home?"

The awkwardness thickens.

"Back to the Scillies?" Sandra says. "That's unlikely, I'm afraid."

"The thing is, Tiger," Soph says—*toiger*—"nobody goes out of sight of land. That's the problem."

"No satellites," Sandra says. "I don't even know how you'd find the Scillies. Even if someone was prepared to risk the sea."

"Which they aren't. Don't set your heart on it, OK? But maybe someday, who knows."

He pulls the blankets tighter around himself. He's so tired everything feels like it's happening at a remove, even his own thoughts. He's experimenting with the thought: *I'm never going to see my mother or Parson's or Laurel or Viola or Kate again. I'm going to live the rest of my life here.* He can feel the terrible bleak misery of it, but it's so wrapped up in tiredness and sheer strangeness it's like the misery doesn't quite touch him.

"Look on the bright side," Soph says. "That gypsy chick could have dragged you into the Valley. At least you're alive. And if you've got to be anywhere in what's left of Cornwall, Dolphin's as good as it gets."

"They might all be alive in there," Sandra says. She sounds sleepy too. "Just because no one comes back doesn't have to mean they're all dead."

"Yeah, yeah," says Soph.

Sandra rolls over. The boards squeak under her. "They say there's a place in the middle of the Valley where all your wishes come true."

"Is there really?" Rory says.

Now it's Soph who laughs, a low gentle laugh. "Might be," she says. "I'm happy not knowing, thanks all the same."

"Hester said you're not allowed in."

"Where? The Valley? Oh, don't tell me . . . What's that thing of hers? 'There are powers which care nothing for us'? Did she give you that one?" She chuckles again. "Swallowed a whole fucking shelf of dictionaries, the Prof."

"Language, Soph."

"Hey, I'm sure the kid's heard worse. Haven't you, Tiger?"

Silence. He thinks he hears rain outside. More white noise.

"To be fair," Soph goes on, "she did actually live there once, didn't she?"

"Don't you ever get tired, Soph?"

"Still a little wound up, I reckon."

"There'll be a ride tomorrow, I bet. You could volunteer for that."

"What, you think we'll go over to Goonhilly?"

"That's what I heard."

"Makes sense. It's what I'd do. If the Prof can't help, poor little Amber's the next best bet."

"Yeah. That's what Sal was saying."

"Ellie'll go, won't she? Might as well take the whole posse."

"More than one, if you ask me. The Pack's been sniffing around Truro."

"Fuckers."

"Wouldn't it be amazing if we could use this staff thing to get rid of them."

"Declare a national holiday, I reckon."

"Do you think there's a chance?"

"I don't know. This whole business is pretty fucked-up. On the other hand"—a long sigh—"I've never seen anything like what I saw today, and that includes some seriously weird shit. And the old coot's dog looked like it had had forty thousand volts."

"Was it really like that? Fiery ghosts?"

"I don't know what it was really like. It was fucking whacked. Poor Ace."

A very long silence.

"Christ," Soph says, to herself, later. "I need nicotine. Hey. Kid. Kid. Do they have tobacco out on the Scilly Isles? I'd try sailing you there myself. Well, I'd think about it."

Someone squirms their blankets around.

"Kid? You asleep?"

He is.

Or perhaps he isn't. The sounds go on for a while around him, the white noises, the mumbles and rustles. Sounds from the room below. He dreams of his mother and father arguing downstairs, their despair whispering up through the floorboards. *You can't stay here. . . . I don't care, I'm not letting Rory go. . . . What do you think you're going to do when the food runs out?* He thinks he's in the Abbey, bedded down in the big room where the women snuffle and snore. He wonders why he's there instead of in his bed at Parson's and then remembers it's because Ol's dead. The white noises bleed together and become Her voice, the voice of the sea in a girl's mouth, telling him her secrets. *I loved a boy once but he left me and never came back.* "I'd stay with you," he says, bravely, and She smiles and answers *Yes, you will, one day.* Her voice unwinds into separate strands until the dark loft's full of whispers like tiny waves over shingle. Together they say his name. *Rory. Rory. Awaken.* Has he gone to sleep, then?

He sits up. The loft's not dark anymore. It's glimmering with a
strange soft light. It's cold. He reaches around to pull the blankets
over his shoulders and sees there's a man in the room, a naked man
the color of a dying fire. *Rory,* the man says. He might not even be
a man because he doesn't have a willy, but he's not a woman either.
He can't be anything. He's a phantom made of congealed light. His
voice blends weirdly with the deep breathing of the two sleeping
women. *Rory. Do you hear us? Do you see us?* There's only one phantom, though its edges swim and shimmer. *Answer us, lost child. We too
are lost.* It's in the corner of the room beyond where Sandra's sleeping,
by the staff. It reaches out beseeching arms. Its substance ripples like
water. *Are you awake?* It seems unlikely, but he nods nevertheless.
He's not frightened. Nothing's real enough for fear. It's dream rather
than nightmare, all detached and obscure. *Speak to us. Without your
welcome we cannot stay.*

"Who are you?" he says. He hears his own voice say it, very quietly. He mustn't wake the women.

The phantom's face is smooth and sculpted like a face from the
comics. It has shapes for eyes but no eyes in them. It smiles. The
smile makes the room feel colder.

We are friendless as yourself. We are forsaken.

"Is this a dream?"

*It is not. Two mortals lie here asleep. It is you only we came to sup-
plicate.*

"What do you want?"

A master.

As always in dreams, there's a feeling that it makes sense, even
though it makes no sense.

"Why do you keep saying 'we'?"

We are legion. We will do as you bid us. We will guide you home.

"Where am I?"

*Among strangers and old spirits. Be our master and we will teach
you all their names.*

"I don't know what you're talking about."

Wisdom. Power.

"Are you the fiery ghosts?"

Stand, the phantom says, with a little hiss. *Cross the room and take the staff. We will teach you the words of command.*

He doesn't get up. As long as he's in bed with blankets around him it's close enough to dreaming.

The phantom wavers and appears to grow bigger, or perhaps come closer, which he doesn't like.

We would kneel before you, it says. Its voice (or voices) is (are?) totally passionless, in the same way that there's no doubt or dread in his heart despite his feeling that something's very much not right. *Rise. Accept our homage.*

He shakes his head.

If you do not desire us, the phantom whispers, *then pity us. We too are far from home.* Now it's definitely gliding towards him, slithering snakewise through the air.

"Go away," he says.

The phantom shivers and diminishes. More of the room's natural dark seeps into its texture. *We are obedient,* it whispers. It's retreated. *Would you not command us so? Take the staff and speak the words and we will serve you. You might leave this house tonight. We fear no night-walking spirits. We can guide you home.*

Home. He's got a strong feeling he mustn't let this thing come home. It's important. Someone told him.

"I don't want to," he says.

How will you recross the sea without us? The nymphs will not suffer your passage.

"Leave me alone."

It gets darker. The manlike shape has blurred until it's little more than a molten haze. It's his dream, after all: he can decide what happens. "Don't come back," he adds.

You are no man. The voices are as faint as blowing sand. *A coward boy, sleeping among women. You are ignorant as empty air. We will seek a better master.*

"Yeah, well," Rory says, "I don't care." It's a rubbish comeback. He's always been terrible at it. Ol said he couldn't be bothered to tease Rory because it wasn't even fun.

You will wish you had been braver, it whispers, *when we meet again.*

"Shut up. Go away." He thinks of the way they'd say it in the comics. "Begone."

It's perfectly dark. He can feel the coarse warmth of the blankets clenched in his fists. He's definitely awake. He said that last word too loudly and heard himself saying it. It's like pinching yourself.

Someone shuffles.

"Rory?"

It's Sandra. She's got a nice ordinary voice. She sounds like someone from The Old Days.

"Are you all right?"

"Fine," he whispers.

"Bad dream?"

He lies back down, pulling the covers to his nose. "Yeah," he says. From somewhere outside comes the ghostly call of an owl.

19

If this was the comics there'd be a king. Or maybe a queen, with Lustrous Raven Hair and the downward turn in the corners of her mouth which means Serious Lady instead of Nice Lady. There'd be someone, anyway, in a big room with splendid decorations, and everyone else would be slightly afraid of them and stand respectfully waiting to be told what to do.

There's no king or queen at Dolphin House. In all sorts of other ways—the horses, the food turning over a fire, the ragged children running around (though they're chasing a football), the blacksmith banging away at his forge—it's just like something out of the comics, the Knights in Armor stories from the old hardback comics, which Rory liked best (Ol said they were girly except for the war stories. *Britischer Schwein!*) But no one's in charge. People are constantly gathering in little clumps and chatting about what to do, and splitting up and joining other little clumps and changing their mind. It's strangely like Home that way, except they seem to get it all done more quickly. Also, he has to go off and poo in a bucket and then carry the bucket around the side of the big hill to a place where there's a trench for emptying it; afterwards he has to throw a spadeful of earth in. That never happens in the comics.

Rory doesn't even realize that some sort of Plan's been settled on until he comes across Ellie and a man sitting on a log together wrapping what appear to be strips of old sheets around their arms and legs, and Ellie asks if he's going to ride with her again.

"Where?"

"Aren't you coming?"

"Coming where?"

"Hey," she calls to another man, who's leading a shaggy horse out from a nearby gate. "Is the kid coming?"

"Up to him, I suppose," the man calls back.

"There you go then," Ellie says to Rory. "If you are, you're probably riding with me again. I'm quite little and I've got a big horse."

"And she's the best rider," the man sitting beside her on the log says.

"And that, yes."

"Where are we going?"

"Up to Goonhilly." She holds a layer of sheets in place over one arm while the man starts winding twine around them, tying them on. It's like she's putting on a layer of padding. "To visit our local oracle."

"Know what that means?" the man says.

Rory's shy about getting things wrong in front of these people, so he shakes his head.

"Means she knows stuff," the man says.

"Sometimes," Ellie says, like she's not at all convinced.

"More often than not," the man says. Ellie cocks her eyebrows.

"What for?"

"The idea's to see what we can do with that staff of yours," Ellie says.

"It's not mine," Rory says quickly. He's been bothered all morning by his dream-which-wasn't-a-dream, the kind of bothered you can't tell anyone about.

"Well, whoever's it was, it's ours now, and it might come in useful."

"Sal's hoping the kid'll come," the man says, exposing himself as the normal kind of adult, the kind that's happier talking about children than to them. "Knows more about it than the rest of us do. Might recognize something Amber says."

"Fluent in gibberish at all?" Ellie asks him. Even the man chuckles at that.

"What's Amber?"

"Amber's the oracle."

"A person?"

"Oh yes. Actually, she's probably about your age."

"They might get on," the man says, winking at Ellie. He holds his arm out and she starts wrapping it the same way he did for her. She's changed some of her rings since yesterday. There's a new one with a gargoyle face, and one studded with purple and black cubes.

"So what do you think?" Ellie says to Rory. "We've got a double saddle, it'll be a lot more comfortable. And I certainly won't let any of Sal's posse tie you up."

"Less uncomfortable at least," the man says.

"All right," Rory says, mostly, if he's honest, because he likes the idea of going with Ellie, though it's also true that he'd rather not have to hang around the camp with the other children, who haven't been particularly friendly so far that morning.

"All right?" the man says, grinning. He's shaved his head almost bald and has a hard, pitted face; the grin exposes hard, pitted teeth. "See oracles every day over on Scilly, do you? Got hundreds of them, have you?"

"Stop it, Rog," Ellie says, not crossly.

"What are you doing that for?" Rory asks her. Ellie's tugging the twine as tight as it'll go. She and Rog exchange a different kind of look, more serious, before she answers.

"It's normal," she says. "We always prepare before we ride out from Dolphin."

"Sensible precautions," Rog says, as if reciting something.

"We'll be fine. It's not all that long a ride, you'll be glad to hear."

Draped on the log beside her is a black leather jacket. Rory didn't recognize it as clothes at first because it's sewn all over with pieces of metal: chain links, rings, rivets, eyelets. Now that he's looking properly he sees that quite a lot of the people he thought were just standing around fiddling with things are, in fact, arming themselves. As he scans them, a skinny man with a straggly beard moves apart from the people standing nearby and unfolds a long leather satchel on the ground. Out of it he takes a sword. An actual sword.

Ellie sees what's caught his eye. "Ah," she says. "Perse. He does love his big weapon."

Rog giggles. "What's his real name? Brian?"

"Quiet," Ellie says. The man with the sword hefts it in his hands and waves it around a few times as if pretend fighting. "God help us. Where did he get that thing?"

"Off that loony up by St. Ives."

Ellie shrugs. "I don't remember that one."

"Called himself the Pendragon."

"That doesn't narrow the field much."

"Some kind of hobbyist. He had bits of chain mail too. Shame we lost that."

"I wish he wasn't coming," Ellie says, watching the man with the sword out of the corner of her eye. "He's going to take his own arm off one of these days."

Rog grimaces. "You know what he's like. Missed a fight yesterday, he'll be desperate for something to come along today."

"Rog," Ellie warns.

"Eh." Rog looks at Rory as if only just noticing him. "Just kidding. There won't be any fighting or anything."

But when all the groups finally assemble by the gate at the end of the long avenue of trees, there's an unmistakable sense of an armed expedition. There are about twelve or fifteen of them (it's hard to count with them all milling around), mostly but not all women, and every one of them is padded or cloaked or helmeted in a ragtag assortment of homespun armor. He sees Sal carrying her motorbike helmet under her arm, and Jody looking more than a bit silly with lumpy stuffing under her trousers and coat, and Soph wearing a tunic of mismatched metal sheets overlapping like scales. Soph sticks out because hers is actually quite striking: some of the scales are tinged with rust or oil maybe, so she's glistening almost-colors, like a fish. Haze is there too. Among the men is a long-haired, muscled young bloke who came up to Rory earlier that morning and asked him in a low embarrassed voice whether he knew anything about Tiffany Someone-or-Other from Maries; he didn't. A lot of the Riders have things which look like weapons sticking out of saddlebags or slung over their backs, not just Perse and his sword but lengths of wood and bicycle chains (the women seem to prefer the bicycle chains). One of the clubs has nails sticking out all over its top.

Sal's got the staff. He sees it poking out by her leg as they ride under the strange assortment of things (a teddy bear, a belt, a mobile phone, a framed photo, a plastic milk bottle) suspended from the trees at the gate. He has a sudden feeling that he ought to go up to Sal and tell her they should ride to wherever the nearest cliffs are and throw the staff into the sea, or maybe take it somewhere far away, dig it a grave, and bury it. But he doesn't. Who'd listen to him anyway? Hester might, he thinks, but he hasn't seen her today. He's overheard someone saying her legs were bad, and talking about poppy juice. (There's a scene in one of the old comics where the hero's fallen down a mountain in Tibet and gets rescued by a Villager with funny-shaped eyes and a big glossy curly beard who takes him to his humble goat-shed and gives him a bowl to drink, saying *Here, stranger . . . Milk of the poppy*: he never understood but always liked the idea of a place where flowers have milk.)

It's a cool grey day, of a kind he recognizes from the islands, blowy and hinting at scattered rain. If he could see the sea there'd be ghost curtains moving over it, distant showers. They've found him a warm hooded coat and a black-and-yellow shirt with a logo that says CORNISH PIRATES. He didn't want to give up his own shirt but Soph said it stank and they have soap. It's very alarming being so high off the ground, perched across the back of this huge swaying horse, and his legs and bum start to get achy quite quickly, but it's not so bad with a saddle to sit on and Ellie showing him how to hold himself. And being high up means he can see over the hedges sometimes, across the folds and rises of the green-brown land, studded with dull-windowed ruins and barns swamped in ivy and little dots of color which must be late wildflowers. The breeze rolls stripes across tall grass.

Ellie's in a chatty mood, which is OK because she's just chatting, not trying too hard to be friendly, and she doesn't mind if he just listens. She tells him about the things hanging over the entrance gate. Everyone living in the camp at Dolphin has to put one up, so they know they belong there (what she actually says is "so the house knows they belong there" but that's more like the kind of thing Esme would say, and small sturdy sarcastic Ellie's about as unlike Esme as anyone could be, so Rory wonders if he heard wrong). She won't tell him what her thing is. She tells him a story about one woman whose token kept falling down no matter how carefully they tied it: one day she hurt a child and they expelled her. She tells him that Dolphin House is very old, and so has stronger attachments, which makes it safer. (She doesn't say what this means.) It's true that there's no king or queen. Thinking of Kate and Fi, he asks who organizes their jobs, and she says they just work it out, and if people don't like it they go and live elsewhere. He looks around as they ride and wonders where those other places might be. The land's so devastated, so empty. It's like a world before people. Or after, maybe, he thinks, as they pass a double decker bus leaning into a stand of trees, branches nosing through its long-broken windows, its green paintwork scoured and peeling so it's dappled like the autumn woods.

They go at a steady walk, jangling and clanking and talking. It's a louder ride than yesterday's. Rory wonders whether that's because there are men with them (Rog has come, and the man with the scarf who's called Baker, though he's not wearing the scarf today). One man in particular, an older-looking man whose neck is black with tattoos, rides up and down the group a lot making loud comments and laughing noisily. He tries to chat with Rory, stuff about how Rory's one of them now, but he's definitely one of those grown-ups who sounds like he's faking it when he talks to children, so he gives up after a while. Ellie doesn't seem to like him much either. He asks her why there are men riding today when there weren't any yesterday.

"Don't you have the man-eaters in the Scillies, then?" she asks, surprised. "Yes you do, I heard you talk about them. The sirens."

"Oh," he says. "Yeah."

"We're not going in sight of the coast today," she says. "Up at Goonhilly you can see the sea in the distance but it's so far off it's safe for the men."

Rog is riding nearby. He spurs his horse alongside. "We're an endangered species," he says to Rory, winking again. "We blokes.

Need lots of looking after, hey El? Wouldn't want you girls to run out of men."

"Goodness no," Ellie says very drily. "Imagine that."

"Used to like a bit of the old surfing," Rog goes on. "But I've had to give that up. Remember Simon, El? Smiley Simon? Thought he'd be all right 'cos he was gay. Turns out the man-eaters don't care about your sexual preferences." He rolls his eyes at the last two words, making them into some sort of joke which Rory doesn't get. "They just want us all dead."

"Rog."

"What?"

"You weren't in the audience last night, were you?"

"Better things to do," he says roguishly.

Ellie's not interested in sharing his joke. "Rory told us that every man in the Scillies is gone. He was the last boy."

"Oh," Rog says, not quite abashed, but getting there. "I see. That can't be much fun for the . . ." He sniffs, wipes his mouth, thinks better of whatever he was going to say.

"Did you have brothers and sisters?" Ellie says.

"A brother and a sister. They left with my dad."

"Left?"

"Sailed. They went to find out What Happened."

"Oh."

"Me and Mum stayed behind."

"You never found out what happened to them?"

"No. They were supposed to go to the Mainland."

"Let's hope they didn't," Ellie says. He wasn't expecting that answer and has to think about it.

"Do you miss your mum?" she says, while he's still thinking.

"Dunno." He's embarrassed now.

"I miss mine." Ellie has an even voice. She says everything as if she's very slightly bored, or perhaps very slightly annoyed.

"Where is she?"

"No idea. She was at home with my younger brother and sister when it all started. In Hertfordshire. I tried to get back there after the blizzards but it was chaos."

"Is that far? Couldn't you look for her?"

"Look for her? Up country?"

He's said the wrong thing. "Sorry."

"Maybe one day," she says. "If we can get rid of the Pack. And if I can raise an army to go with me."

Rog chips in, trying to be encouraging. "If your mum was tough like you she'll have been all right."

"She wasn't," Ellie says.

"Oh."

Jody drops back to join them, relieving an uncomfortable pause. "Hear about the big bastard?" she says.

"I heard they took him already," Rog says.

"Looks like it," Jody says. "Just been talking to Haze about it. She said bits of the twine had gone black."

"She went down to check this morning?"

"Her and Stella. He was gone when they got there so they didn't bother looking close. But she's wondering now why the ties'd be charred."

"How does she know they're charred if she wasn't looking closely?" Ellie says.

Jody gives Ellie a cross look. "Just saying what she told me." She turns the look on Rory. "Made me wonder if the boy might have any ideas."

"About what?" says Rog.

"Whether something funny happened down there in the night."

"Rory was asleep in the top of our barn in the night," Ellie says.

"I know that," Jody says. "Whether he knows what that big bloke might have got up to, is what I'm talking about."

"Can't see there's much point worrying about it now the man-eaters got him," Rog says.

"Man-eaters don't set things on fire," Jody says. It's obvious she's not that friendly with Rog and Ellie.

"Who said anything about a fire?"

"Does any of this mean anything to you, Rory?" Ellie says, in a way which invites him to say no.

"No."

"Get Haze to tell you," Jody says, spurring her horse ahead again.

"Maybe later," Rog calls after her. But now the slow parade is halting in front of them.

They've reached a rise where the road widens. The front group of Riders has stopped. Ellie leans against Rory's back to make the reins tighter and pulls their horse up too, letting it scrunch at the hedge while they wait.

"Here we go then," Rog mutters.

At the head of the procession Sal's wheeled around to face the rest of them. She stands up in the saddle.

"Usual rules from here on," she calls. "Let's be extra careful, we don't know if our cargo's going to make a difference. Minimal talking and even less looking, all right? El, you'll look after the kid?"

Ellie raises an arm in acknowledgment.

"What's going on?" Rory says, alarmed. Ellie's doing something with a strap around his waist.

"Think of this," she says, tugging the strap through a buckle and pulling it tight, so he's suddenly fastened to the saddle, "as your safety belt. There's nothing to worry about as long as you don't get off."

"Helston up ahead," Rog says. "Right close to the Valley."

"You might see or hear some weird things," Ellie says, nudging the horse forward as the line starts moving again.

"Or smell," adds Rog.

"Ignore everything," Ellie says. "The best thing is not to even look."

"Like what?"

"*Shh* now. Talking's a bad idea too. It seems to get them excited."

"Who?"

"*Shh.*"

They're descending now, and it's not just the chatter that's gone quiet. The whole noise of their passage seems suddenly muffled. Very soon Rory sees why. The horses are no longer trampling on a hard road. Under the scattering of debris there are still patches of decaying tarmac but it's now mostly grass, moss, ferns, breaking through the road like craters from green bombs. The line of riders squeezes to one side ahead and slows down, as if negotiating an obstacle. When it's their turn to reach it Rory looks down and sees a neat ring of mushrooms in the middle of the road, sprouting from a swathe of flattened grass.

Then they're on the outskirts of a town.

It's not like Penzance at all. Penzance was a jumble of rubbish and decay. Nothing's broken here, though the feeling of emptiness is even deeper. The paint on the walls of the houses is streaked and bulging with damp, but no worse. The doors still have numbers on them. There are cars sitting by the sides of the road, sticky with dried sap and dusted in cobwebby old leaves but not dismembered or rusting open. They pass a shop which could almost be a shop from The Old Days. Its sign is tatty but legible: R & P NEWSAGENTS. Its awning advertises *Sandwiches Off License Hot & Cold Drinks*. In an upstairs window of the neighboring house a pair of straw dolls look out from the sill, as if someone still lives there.

But no one does. The town's been invaded, not by ruin but by the not-town, the country. Its streets and pavements have turned into paths and fields, their edges are like gardens, and the old gardens behind them have turned into secret jeweled jungles, unfathomable thickets of bushes and climbers where flowers hide in deep shadow. The roofs are half moss. One terraced house has tipped back from its neighbors like a dislodged tooth, lifted by the massive root of a chestnut tree in the middle of the road. Saw-toothed yellow leaves float down as they ride under the tree. A door creaks and slams behind them. Rory twitches around, only for Ellie to straighten him at once. She puts her fingers to her lips.

The side streets are dark mouths. Up one of them he glimpses colored lights near the ground, flicking around each other like dragonflies. Ellie nudges him in the back: *don't look*. He doesn't really see why he shouldn't. He can feel the other Riders' anxiety all around him but as far as he's concerned he'd much rather this than Penzance. Streetlamps bend over the road on either side, wound to half their height in some plant with flowers like tiny spotted bells. For a moment he thinks he can hear them ringing. The sound makes him think of silver and rain. Between three of the posts hangs an enormous veil of spiderwebs, threads delicate as dew.

The sloping road begins to descend more steeply, and he hears running water. A little farther and they come to a river, running left to right. It's cut through the town like a cleaver. Upstream it tumbles through buildings, and where its course meets them their walls and corners have simply vanished, sliced away into nothing. It spills across the green road and drops over a lip on the downstream side into dense woods, in the middle of which Rory can just about see a long pond with a bandstand and a playground beside it. Five or six swans are paddling around in the shade.

The horses don't want to go into the river. The riders at the front urge them towards the ford at a canter but the animals shy away each time. One woman's thrown off. She remounts hurriedly, looking around in fear as if the ground might swallow her for standing on it, but eventually all of them have to dismount and lead the horses, pulling their reins and smacking their rumps, dragging them across. This leaves Rory the only one mounted, so he sees Silvia before anyone else does.

She's running down the way they've just come, close under the dripping stone walls of the old part of the town. She's running fast, stumbling, looking over her shoulder. Rory's so amazed to see her that at first he can barely draw a breath, let alone cry out. Her face is full of terror. She looks like she hasn't even seen the knot of Riders wrestling with their horses. "Hey!" he manages to blurt, but the wrestling's making quite a lot of noise now, and no one notices. Silvia staggers to a halt as she comes in sight of the river. She stares ahead, breathing hard, totally oblivious to everyone else. Rory tries to turn himself round in the saddle so he can see her properly, forgetting he's strapped in. The moment he starts twisting against the strap Ellie stops pulling the horse, splashes close, and grabs his leg. "That's—" Rory begins, but Ellie hisses at him to be quiet. Why hasn't Silvia noticed them at all? She looks dazed, rapt. She glances over her shoulder and then starts towards the river with a visible spasm of dread. Some of the others have noticed her by now but they look only for a second before turning away without a word or making any attempt to help, though Silvia stumbles in the current, falling to her knees before pushing herself back up, her hands muddy. Rory squirms; Ellie grips him tighter.

"Don't!" she says, as sharply as she dares. "Whatever you think you're seeing, it's not really there."

Something's not right. He's suddenly not even sure it's Silvia at all, though she's a gypsy woman with a messy tangle of black hair and Silvia's clothes. She looks like someone younger, smaller. She wades on through the current. "Rory," Ellie snaps at him, "stop looking!"

How can he stop? It *is* Silvia, but she's changing before his eyes. It's as if the river's whittling her down. The water's up to her thighs where it was only running over her shins before. Her face is turning bright-eyed and smooth. She hitches up her jacket to stop the current tearing the hem away. It's suddenly loose on her, much too loose. She shakes drops out of her hair and lets it go. She takes the last few steps across to the far bank. A girl of perhaps Rory's age clambers out onto the pale flat grass, a curly-haired gypsy girl. She's smiling triumphantly. She stretches her arms to the sky, hands open. Invisible sunlight falls on her face. Then she vanishes into thin air.

"Rory!" Ellie's shaking his leg. He blinks. "Look at me! What's my name?"

"Ellie?" he says uncertainly. Is this another trick question?

"Eyes down," she says. She's cross. "Now." He complies. She sounds surprisingly fierce when she's cross. He sneaks glances when she's not looking but there's no sign of the Silvia girl anywhere. All the horses get safely across and Ellie mounts up behind him again.

"Whatever you saw," she whispers in his ear, "forget it. Shut your eyes. Keep them shut."

He doesn't want to make her any angrier so he keeps his head half-bowed and scrunches up his eyelids, pretending they're closed though he can still see out through a slit. They're riding up now between grey little houses and tatty workshops and sheds, every cranny in the concrete bursting with stalks or saplings. Rory can hear fairground music but he knows better than to ask about it. He's turbulent inside. Even if it wasn't really Silvia at all it was a reminder of her. She may have fooled him and abandoned all of them but all he has to do is think of her and straightaway it's obvious she knows something none of these other people know, she's seen things no one else he's ever met has seen. Even when he closes his eyes properly he can feel the Riders' fear all around him. Silvia wouldn't have been afraid of this place. Or of anything.

And she told him he had a gift too.

He keeps a surreptitious watch in case she appears again, girl or woman. He sees a couple of faces in the windows of houses, brief and ghostly, but they're older, maybe not even people's faces at all, and Ellie snaps at him when she catches him looking. Farther on there's a row of starlings on a flat garage roof. Their heads all turn slowly together as the Riders pass. They're almost out of the town now, wide fields spreading out around them again. The forlorn rectangles of road signs mark the horizon like the standing stones of a lost civilization.

A sudden mutter runs through the procession. Ellie draws the horse to a halt. Rory looks up and sees that everyone's stopped again, this time because a man's come out of a dingy shack beside the road.

"Well, well," Ellie says.

Apparently it's OK to talk now because Rog, still riding next to them, leans over and says, "Good sign?"

"I wouldn't go that far," she says.

Up ahead Sal's talking to the man. He has wispy brown hair and spectacles. He's wearing extraordinarily tattered black robes, not a makeshift patchwork robe like the old man at the crossroads had but actual robes, though full of tears and holes. He has a walking stick in one hand, one of those fancy lightweight extendable ones. He looks terribly thin, almost starved, that sunken-cheeked, stringy-necked look Rory remembers from last winter on Home. Nevertheless he's presumably a real person because Sal gives him something from her saddlebag; food, judging by the way he sniffs it before bowing his thanks to her. A few of the others have dismounted now, joining the conversation. Ellie unstraps the safety belt, letting Rory squiggle around in the saddle to ease the soreness.

"See him?" Rog says. "That's the priest. That's what everyone calls him, anyway. Don't know if he was ever a real priest."

"He was," Ellie says.

"If you say so. Maybe that's how he survives up here. Someone upstairs looking after him."

"I doubt that."

"Used to live in the Valley," Rog goes on. "Before, I mean. That's what they say."

"He was the parish priest at Manaccan," Ellie says.

"Oh, you're the expert now, are you?"

"The Brownes knew him. They're churchy."

"Well," Rog says, "whatever. Got to be some reason why it doesn't bother him so close to the Valley. No one else lasts long up here. Way I heard it is, he keeps trying to go in but it won't let him. They say the man-eaters won't touch him either. Story is, something bad happened to him that first winter and he went to the sea to be drowned, they wouldn't take him. Typical bloody fish. The one poor sod who actually wants to die and they won't kill him. Hello. Don't like the look of that." The group of people in conversation with the man ahead have obviously been told something they didn't want to hear. A number of them look agitated. A nervous mutter works its way back through the group.

"The Pack," the woman in front says.

Rog swings off his horse at once and jogs to the front.

"We should turn back," the same woman says. A man next to her, the older-looking man with the tattoos who was being so noisy when they started out from Dolphin, snorts. The woman rounds on him angrily. "Oh, and you're so brave, is it? If you ever ran across the Black Pack you'd hardly have time to piss yourself before you'd be off fast as those four legs can take you."

The man scowls but doesn't answer. He rides off towards the front as well.

"They have no idea," the woman says to Ellie. "Idiots."

"What's going on?" Rory says, but by now everyone's heard whatever the news is and they're all beginning to argue, until someone shouts "Shut the fuck up, the lot of you!"

It's Soph. Everyone shuts up, maybe because she's unexpectedly loud or because she looks quite impressive sitting tall in her scaly tunic. She's shown no signs of bossiness before but everyone's listening to her now. "This is a stupid place for a fucking powwow," she says. "Sal and I are going to carry on. If there's any trouble we can outride it. Anyone who wants to go back, go back. That's it. Keep quiet and get moving." She bends down to say something to the priest and then kicks her horse into a walk.

"Not me," says the woman who's been talking to Ellie. "I'm heading back to Dolphin."

A few people have already started off in Soph's wake. Those who haven't are hanging back, looking slightly ashamed of themselves. Rog trots back to Ellie and remounts, giving her an inquiring look as he steers his horse around.

Rory twists around to look at Ellie too.

"I should take you back," she says, clearly displeased by the thought.

"I don't mind," he says, mostly because he doesn't want to annoy her anymore.

"He's OK, El," Rog says. He catches Rory's eye. "Look, all you have to do if anything happens is hang on. Ellie rides like a champion."

"It's probably nothing anyway," Ellie says. "Where did he say he'd seen them? Penryn? They wouldn't pass this close to the Valley."

"Someone needs to let them know at Dolphin," the anxious woman says.

"I've had the odd run-in with the Pack before," Ellie goes on. "Even if we do bump into them they're just men, they can't catch up with a horse."

"And dogs," Rog says.

"I'm not bothered about the dogs."

"Who are they?" says Rory.

Ellie sighs. "Wastes of space. People too lazy to work out how to live like we do, so they dress themselves up to look tough and go around stealing."

"Don't they worship their dogs or something? Got that leader wears a dog mask."

"They're a pain in the arse is all they are."

Sal's riding back to them, the staff poking out of a bag behind her leg. "Ellie?" she says.

"Rory says he's all right with going on."

Sal frowns. "I'd rather you took him back."

"He's safer with her than anyone," Rog says. "Safest place in the whole of Cornwall is in the front of that saddle."

"At the first sign of anything funny I'll ride straight for the sea," Ellie says. "It's just a few miles in either direction."

Sal looks at Rory. She's not convinced, but there's no king or queen here, everyone does what they want. "Up to you," she says, and wheels around.

"Are you sure about this?" Ellie says to Rory.

He is. Far more people are going on than turning back, anyway, and he feels instinctively that the bigger group is better.

The so-called priest is standing at the edge of the road watching them all go past. As Ellie's horse approaches him he stares at Rory frowning.

"Excuse me," he says. His voice isn't at all what Rory would have expected. It's thoughtful and sad. "Who's this?"

"Does it matter?" Ellie says.

The priest appears unoffended, though Rory's surprised she answered so rudely. "Probably not," he says. "Hello, young man."

"Hi," Rory says. The horse is walking past.

"May I ask you a question?"

"I've got to keep up with the others," Ellie says, not at all apologetically.

"I've never seen you before, I think," the priest says, talking now to Rory's shoulder. "Can you tell me if you've ever come across a girl called Marina? She'd be a little older than you."

"Uh," Rory says. He has to twist uncomfortably to face the priest. "What?"

The priest blinks behind his round spectacles. "Never mind."

"Good luck to you," Rog says to him, trying to be polite.

"And you."

"*Shh,*" says Ellie.

"Blimey," Rog mutters, as they leave the man standing alone. They go on in silence, listening only to the dull pulse of hooves on the green road. There are faces in the windows of the last couple of houses, but this time it really is better not to look at them.

20

Thunder trembles to the east. The sky's peculiarly thick that way, or maybe not thick but shiny, as if it's made of something denser than air and clouds. It's hard to see properly. Distances look funny. The remaining Riders are completely out of the town now and traveling on a very wide mostly tarmac road along the edge of an open heath. Between road and heath are the remains of a tall wire fence. Beyond, on the heath, the barren expanse is dotted with burned-out buildings and machines, big ones. Some look like they were once helicopters, if Rory's remembering helicopters correctly. The expedition has turned southwards. The wind smells of ocean and has started blowing spits of rain into their faces. On the horizon ahead are strange huge shapes like giant concrete eggs, four or five of them tilting this way and that.

"What you got against the priest, then?" Rog says. It's the first thing anyone's said since they left the town. Five people turned back, all women. The rest of them are spread out in a long line along the road. The atmosphere's gloomy. The thunder doesn't sound right. It's almost like there's a voice in it.

"Nothing," Ellie says.

"Could have fooled me."

"It wasn't a good place to stop for a chat."

"You could have been civil to him. More to him than meets the eye, isn't there."

"I can't stand people like that." Rory looks around in surprise. "Obsessed with their own grief. Like we haven't all had our problems?"

"Well," Rog says, after a moment. "That's him sorted."

"Who's that he asked me about?" says Rory.

"No idea. It's not a good idea to spend too much time thinking about things that happen in Helston."

"Living that close to the Valley's got to have its effects," Rog says.

"Exactly."

He eyes the uncanny sky to the east. "Makes you wonder what it's really like in there."

"Not me, it doesn't," Ellie says.

"Is that the Valley?" Rory asks.

"Yep," Rog says. "Just the other side of the old airfield. Feel it, can't you? They say somewhere in the middle there's a crystal tree with silver fruit. Live forever if you eat it."

"They can say whatever nonsense they like," Ellie says, "since no one's ever going to confirm it one way or the other."

"What's got into you?"

"Nothing."

"Time of the month, is it?"

Ellie kicks the horse into a brief canter. Rory grabs the pommel, the saddle suddenly bucking and swaying. It only takes a few seconds for them to be riding apart from everyone else; she slows again, leaving him gasping. The rider in front, who's the big tattooed man, gives them a curious look before turning back to the road. Ellie zips Rory's coat and pulls his hood up. The rain's spitting harder.

"I hate that place," she says.

"The Valley?" Rory says, cautiously, not sure if she really wants to talk about it.

"Helston. Everywhere around here. There's just too much of . . ."

"Of what?"

"Whatever it is. Whatever they are. They're not like us. People pray to them and make them offerings but they don't care. They're nothing to do with us at all."

Rory remembers the old man at the crossroads. "Do you mean gods?"

"If only they'd just go back where they came from," Ellie says. "Let everything go back to how it was."

He's heard this complaint, or versions of it, too many times to count. He's always associated it with the older ones. It's funny hearing it come from a young woman.

"What do you miss most?" she says, a bit later.

"From The Old Days?"

"Yes."

Kate always told them not to talk like this. No good looking back, she said, it just makes you miserable. But they always did anyway, when she wasn't listening. Rory knows what you're supposed to say because he's heard the answers so many times. *The children. The news. Orange juice. Clean toilets, oh please God.*

"Nothing, really," he says.

There's a long pause, just the horse clip-clopping along, and then Ellie says "Really?" in her dry disbelieving voice: he can almost hear her eyebrows going up.

"Yeah."

"It's better than school, I suppose."

This too is something they always said. Ol and Laurel used to say it all the time. *Never have to go to math lessons again.* Rory remembers math lessons in a patchy, greyed-out way.

"It's not that," he says.

"Isn't it?"

He's overheard this conversation a zillion times and never once said what he really thinks, because it's so different from what everyone else says that he can't even imagine mentioning it, it would be like breaking a Rule. He's thought about it, though.

"I wouldn't like it if I looked at the sea and it was just water," he says.

Clop clop clop clop.

"What's wrong with water?" Ellie says.

He's blushing. He doesn't know how to say it properly, and also he's thinking now about Her.

"I quite liked it," Ellie goes on. "I quite liked it when it came out of a tap whenever you wanted it to. I quite liked going for swims.

Then drying off with a big clean towel and lying on the beach with my headphones on. Then driving back to the cottage and opening a bottle of wine."

He can't answer her, any more than he could answer the old women or Laurel and Ol. He wonders if there's something wrong with him, some problem or difference which means he doesn't have those memories everyone else does, as if everything was happy and comfortable before What Happened.

"Ah, well," Ellie says. "It's all what you grow up with, isn't it."

The Riders at the front have come to a junction where a road turns off to the left, eastwards, dipping down into wooded country. There's a big road sign at the junction. It's been painted over, a dirty drippy white background and then a huge black image of a bird.

"Supposed to be the angel," Ellie says as they approach. The first Riders have already passed it, keeping to the straight road which rises gently towards a brown waste of heathland. "This is where it first appeared. Over the Valley. I wouldn't look left as we go past if I were you. This is as close as we come to it. Ten steps down that road and you might not be able to get back."

In among all the scratchy greyed-out memories the angel's as solid as night. Everyone remembers the pictures, the photo, and the videos. Jake said he knew how they did it, it was all just computers. That was in those first few weeks, when it still seemed like the whole thing might be some kind of joke.

"The Professor's supposed to have spoken to it," Ellie says.

"Really?"

"That's what I hear. She was there the day it appeared. When the snow started. She was caught out in the snow. That's why she has the problem with her legs. She was about to die when she saw it. Just down there somewhere. Careful, don't look."

The left turn is almost entirely overgrown. It looks as though it's been a very long time since anyone went that way. As the tattooed man in front rides past the junction he stops and stares.

"Hey," he says.

"So much for not looking," Ellie mutters.

"Come and see this," the man says, turning back. He's grinning a gap-toothed grin.

"Is that a good idea?"

"Look," he says, pointing as Ellie and Rory ride up. Ellie's unwilling to follow the gesture but Rory can't see what's wrong with looking down a road, even if it is forbiddingly overgrown.

A small face is peeking out of the tangle, staring back at them.

"Cheeky little sod," the man says.

The face looks like a cross between a dog and a person. It's sharp-nosed and bright-eyed, furry, the muted earthy color of the most wintry leaves.

"Wolf," Ellie warns, still without looking. Rory's confused for a moment, since the animal doesn't look big or scary enough to be a wolf. Then he realizes it's the man's name.

"It's just a fox," Wolf says. "Looks like a baby one. Look at him. Sitting there watching. Hey. What are you looking at?"

Ellie steers her horse around him and starts riding past.

"Don't you stare at me like that," Wolf says, amused. He reaches into his saddlebag and brings out a stone. "Cheeky bastard."

Ellie doesn't see what he's doing until he's let go of the stone.

"Don't be a—"

There's a thump and a yelp.

"Ha! Got it!" Wolf sounds delighted with himself.

"For fuck's sake, Wolf!" This is Rog, riding up behind. "Leave it alone."

"Quality shot," Wolf says, "if you ask me."

Ellie makes an infuriated noise and eases the horse into a trot, leaving Rory unable to think of anything beyond his largely hopeless effort to protect his bum from punishment.

Beyond the junction the road crumbles. It looks like there's been an earthquake, though Ellie says it was floods. The heath soaked up so much water it turned into a giant sponge, she says, and with nothing solid under it the tarmac broke up under its own weight. They ride onto a track instead, a bare brown line scratched through the heather. It's a lot like the north end of Home, except everything's on a bigger scale. The heather's taller and bushier and the horizons are much farther away. There are flowers dusting the heather even though it's late in the year, scrubby pinky-red pods clustering tight to their stems like they're in hiding.

The massive concrete egg things reappear on the horizon. They're monstrously huge, completely alien to this place, though it's obvious now that the Riders are heading towards them. Their enormous scalloped profiles suddenly fall into place as Rory stares—it's like getting the answer to a puzzle—and he remembers what they are, or at least the name, though it's like remembering a word in a foreign language. They're satellite dishes. They're vast blind concrete eyes pointed at the heavens to send invisible messages at the speed of light. Rory's reminded of the rusting tankers tipped around the bay by Saint Michael's Mount: huge things turned useless. Beached whales. The dishes are stranded at the very highest point of the wide heath. The Riders plod slowly up towards them, single file, ducking against salvos of steely rain.

Underneath the satellite array there's a handful of low windswept buildings. While the Riders are still a fair way off someone appears on the roof of one of these, looking their way. Ellie notices the silhouette as well.

"They'll be happy enough to see us as long as we've brought food," she says. "That's the trick to staying popular."

Soon they're all gathered in a grimy, puddly, more-or-less paved clearing in front of a long building with a curving glass front. The horses are misting with sweat and the Riders are beginning to drip. Everything reeks of damp. The dishes loom bleak and gigantic above, extracting moans from the breeze. There are littler ones and bigger ones, all of them stark and motionless and peeling. It's like a family turned to stone, or to streaked concrete. The building doesn't look anything like a stable but they tie the horses up outside it anyway, under a projecting roof. Rory's incredibly relieved to be on his feet again, though he needs Ellie's help to get down and his legs feel like they might be permanently bent. He and the remaining Riders, twelve of them—Sal, Soph, Haze, Sandra, Ellie, Rog, Perse, Wolf, the muscular young man who asked Rory about Tiffany Whatser-name on Maries, another man and two women he doesn't know—go in the building. It's a cavernous echoey space with baffling posters and patterns and maps on the walls. The people who've invited them in are a man and a woman who don't look anything like each other and yet are equally and identically crabbed and dirty and suspicious and old. Not old in years, maybe—they're certainly not as old as Esme—but in some other way, as though too much has happened to them and they're visibly fed up with it all.

"That was easy." The man Rory doesn't know comes strolling over to where Ellie and Sandra are standing with Rory. He cracks his shoulders and flexes his fingers. "Bit of a shame, really. I'd like to have given the Pack a taste of ol' Headsmasher here." He taps the handle of a smooth round club stuck in his belt.

"Would you," Ellie says, her sarcasm plainly audible to Rory but apparently not to the man.

"We'll do it one day," he says. "Get a few of the lads together, find wherever they're holed up, break a few skulls." He rocks on his heels. "Long overdue, if you ask me."

Soph joins them. "Hey, tiger. How're we doing?"

"I'm OK."

"Hungry?"

His expression must make it obvious, because everyone laughs.

"We'll break out the picnic in a minute. Looks like we're here for the night; have to deal with the nags first."

"Oh?" says Ellie.

"Wonder-girl's asleep, apparently. The old codgers won't wake her up. Maybe it disturbs her oracular bits. Going to be too late to start back by the time they let us see her."

"I'd better look after Drum, then," Ellie says, and heads outside. Rory's about to follow but Soph stops him.

"Manage all right on the ride?"

"Fine," he says. He's rubbing his back, so he adds, "A bit sore."

Soph grins. "I meant in the town. It can be a bit unnerving your first time."

"Why?"

"Why, he says. You're a bit of an odd one, aren't you?"

"Bet he's too young," Mister Headsmasher says. "Didn't see anything yet. Same with the man-eaters. They got no interest in kids."

The dismissive tone annoys Rory. "I did see—" he begins, and stops himself. He doesn't want to tell these people about Silvia.

Mister Headsmasher smirks. "Never mind, son," he says. "Once you start seeing the little people and the ghosties you'll wish you hadn't. Gives even me the creeps sometimes. Not anymore, but they used to."

"Good on you," Soph says to Rory, as if the man hadn't spoken. "Why don't you hook up with Sal there, she'll get you sorted out."

Rory's introduced to the old couple who apparently live here. They look at him with squinty suspicion. Sal's obviously trying to placate them as much as possible, acting polite and offering them as much food as the whole population of Home would have shared on an average evening, and that's before anyone else even gets to think about eating. Eventually the Riders finish looking after their horses and break up into smaller groups and go out to the smaller buildings spread around the site. Some of the buildings are right under the satellite dishes, including the one Rory ends up in. Its tiny windows are blackened by dirt and moss and it stinks the distinctively unhappy stench of moldering concrete and stale indoor air. It's all narrow corridors and tiny rooms and defunct banks of mysteriously clunky machinery. Everything drips with chilly gloom. Rory finds a swiveling chair and sits out of the way while a lot of disarming and unwrapping and eating goes on. Sal gives him food, bread and cold salty meat and two tiny hard tomatoes. He spins himself around slowly as he chews.

Quite a bit later the old woman comes and bangs on the door of the building. A lot of the Riders are dozing. Sal sits up and prods Rory.

"Ready to go?"

"Me?"

"I'd like you there. You've seen this thing in action." She's kept the staff close to her all the time.

"Where are we going?"

"To the oracle. She must have woken up."

The old woman isn't pleased to see Rory. "I'm not having two of you in there," she says. Her lips suck when she stops between sentences. "One at a time. She gets upset."

Sal's holding the staff. It's far too big for her. She plants it on the ground in front of the old woman.

"Rory won't be any trouble," she says. "He won't say anything. He's just coming to watch."

"Trouble. Everyone's trouble. No. Rules are rules."

Sal sighs. She leans over the old woman. She stops pretending to be nice.

"He's coming with me," she says. "All right?"

The woman fidgets and sucks until she makes the mistake of meeting Sal's look. "Suit yourself," she mumbles. "Won't be answerable." She turns and heads away along a battered path. "Hurry up, then," she says, though even Rory has to slow to a saunter to stay behind her.

Sal sticks out her tongue at the woman behind her back.

They're heading towards the biggest of the satellite dishes. As well as being bigger than the others it's clumsier, much heavier-looking, braced on gantries of rusting steel; it's like some prehistoric stone monument compared to its sleeker companions. It sits atop a squat grey building in an area cordoned off by a chain-link fence. The grumpy old man's waiting for them at a gate in the fence, bundled in thick waterproofs. The patchy rain has stopped but it's a dismal late afternoon. The wind up here is already thinking about winter.

The man tries to make a fuss about Rory coming. Rory doesn't hear what Sal says to him—he can't help staring upwards: it's like looking over the edge of a cliff, but upside down, as if the monstrous weight is going to suck him up to be crushed against it—but the argument doesn't last long. The man unlocks the gate with the worst possible grace, banging the padlock open and leaving Sal to slide the metal slats herself. They screech in their clogged tracks.

From inside the building a high-pitched whimper answers the screech.

"There," the old woman says, with enormous satisfaction. "You've upset her."

The four of them cross scattered gravel and dead heather to a door. The dish is like a second sky above them, solid, threatening, the wind humming in the gantries. The woman bumps the man out of the way, unlocks the door, and calls into the dimness, "Amber lovey?" Or rather croons: it makes Rory think of the way Missus Grouse used to talk to her dog. "It's your auntie come to see you again. And some," she scowls at Rory and Sal, "nice visitors too. We've got some milk for you. Lovely lovely milk." She motions them all in with one arm, into a dark corridor with corkboards on the walls. With her other hand she's fumbling in the pockets of her coat. "Lovely lovely . . ."

A horrible scream rings out from deeper within. The woman's half managed to extract a stoppered glass bottle of milk from her pocket; she flinches and drops it. It thuds onto linoleum. There's a smell, a new smell, sudden and drenching, spicy smoke. It billows down the corridor like a solid thing. The scream trails away. In its wake the old woman's mumbling frantically, something like *oh now oh dear oh dear*. The man's busy trying to grab hold of Sal when the bottle of milk rolls to a stop by his feet, cracks, and pops neatly apart. Milk pools around their feet. "No, Amber, dearie," the old woman says, hurrying forward into the dark. A moan begins where the scream was. It's a drunken wail of pain. The man's trying to pull Sal away but she shrugs him off and goes after the woman.

There's an instantaneous blinding glare. A strip of old fluorescent lighting has blinked on, showing the corridor and the door at the far end in a single searing glimpse before they all have to shield their eyes. The man quails and cringes. Rory scurries after Sal. The lights go off again and the moan stops. An afterimage of the corridor is imprinted on his eyes in black phantom light. "Hush now, hush," the old woman's saying. A grey dimness unfurls ahead; she's opened the door and there's the ghost of daylight in the room beyond. The smoky smell is even stronger, as if opening the inner door has unsealed it. Someone in there is keening and whimpering like a terrified dog.

It's a clean bare room with a thin strip of windows high up. A single thick column of concrete fills its center. There's a bucket of water, a camp bed and sleeping bag, and an unplugged electric heater. And a girl, a doughy-faced girl with straggly gingery hair, curled up on the floor at the base of the column, wrapped to her shoulders in a yellow sheet. She's trembling and pushing herself along the floor in a ball, like an insect with its legs pulled off. The old woman's knelt beside her and is cooing into her face. The girl twists in revulsion and screams again. Rory's never heard a sound like it. It's not pain, it's not even normal fear, it's like some limit of perfect terror, as if she can see the ceiling cracking and the thousand-ton false sky above them about to fall. The old woman's cooing rises to a panicky *no, no* and she cradles the girl almost violently, like she's pinning her down. Squeezing his hands over his ears, Rory sees another afterimage, impossible but perfectly clear, as if imprinted over the room: the dark negative of a forest, wide gnarled trees widely spaced, something unnamable moving among them like a dancer.

The scream stops.

The old man stumbles into the room behind Rory. He tries to kneel beside the girl as well but the woman pushes him away. "There there," she's saying. "No need for all this fuss." The girl twists herself upright and backs against the column. It's covered in tiny pencil marks, Rory now sees, little scribbles all around it and from top to bottom. The girl sees Sal and Rory for the first time. Her eyes go shocked and dull-witted and she whispers, "Dad?"

"It's not your daddy, is it, Amber lovey? Silly girl. It's your auntie, isn't it? Auntie Sibyl. Here we are. Just Auntie Sibyl. Everything's all right, see?"

"Dad?" The girl's looking around. She sounds like a normal ordinary girl. "I got it. I still got it, ain't I?"

"'Course you do, dearie." The old woman's hoarse with empty reassurance. "'Course you do. This is all your fault." Rory can't tell which of them she's spat the aside towards. "'Course you got your special. Holding it now, aren't you? Silly old Amber."

"Where is it?"

"In your own hands, silly." The woman's unwrapping the yellow sheet. Her hands are quivering as if the girl's an unexploded bomb.

"Shall we look? Shall we let Auntie find it for you? Here we are, see?" She's pushed the sheet apart. Amber's arms are folded tight over her chest and she's clutching something in her hands, pressing it against herself. "Look, there's your special. Had it all along. Didn't Auntie tell you?"

Amber looks down at her hands. She opens them a little. The thing is a little silver statue, a crucifix. "Stop pawing all over her." The woman bats away the old man, who's trying to help. While they're whispering crossly at each other Amber stares up at Sal.

"Hello again, Amber," Sal says.

"Don't—" the old couple begin, in the same breath.

Amber interrupts them. "All right?" she says shyly.

"I'm fine," Sal says, "thanks for asking. How are you?"

The room seems very quiet. The smell has gone. The dumpy girl smiles, rather stupidly.

"These are the nice visitors I told—"

Amber's look slides to Rory. "Hello," she says.

Rory's suddenly intensely conscious of not knowing what to do with his hands.

"Hi," he says, swallowing.

The man and woman try to silence him with simultaneous angry stage whispers. Amber stops them.

"Shush," she says. She holds the little statue out towards Rory. "Would you like to see?"

"Oh no, Amber lovey. Don't show anyone your special."

"OK," Rory says. "Thanks." He steps closer to the girl.

"It's special," Amber says, holding it up. It's about the size of one of her hands.

"Nice," Rory says.

"It's Jesus."

"Right."

"Me and Dad found it."

"Oh."

"Actually me. Dad couldn't fit through the door. So it was just me."

"Cool."

"Dad's dead now, and I'm mad."

The old woman pats the girl nervously. "What a thing to say," she says. She's half trying to be reassuring to Amber and half trying to make a cross face at Sal, with the result that neither effort comes off. "We're perfectly all right, aren't we? Shall Auntie get you some of that lovely lovely—"

"Cracked," Amber says. "Spilt. Gone."

"—lovely lovely." The woman's patting her pockets, mumbling vacantly. She shuffles around on her knees and hisses at the man. "What have you done with the milk?"

"Amber," Sal says. "May I show you something else special?" She sounds sane, grown-up. She's like fresh air blowing into the room.

"It was in a box." Amber hasn't taken her eyes off Rory. "A green box. Daddy knocked the lock off. It was where the nutters lived. The Christians. With their holy acorn."

"Now now, let's not tell the nice visitors all—"

"Acorn," Amber says, sharply, to shut the old woman up. Her expression is still earnest, friendly, dim. "Acorn, acorn, acorn. *Velanidi zhulud ghianda eichel*. It came from Arcadia. She brought it all the way. With her talisman." Amber lifts the crucifix higher, inviting Rory to look. "She thought it would save her because it's God." She waggles it at him. "See? God."

Rory's feeling trapped. "I think Sal wants to show you something," he says.

"It's OK," Sal says. "Let her speak."

"I can't help it," Amber says. A trace of worry comes over her. She hugs the crucifix to her neck. "I can't stop speaking."

"Hush now, lovey. You mustn't upset yourself."

Amber turns to the woman in petulant little girl fury. "I can't hush!"

"She's upset now," the old man says. "You've got her all worked up."

"Things happen," she tells Rory. It's like she's apologizing to him. "And I say them. I have to. Even when no one's here."

Rory glances at Sal, desperately hoping for some sign that they can go now, but Sal's watching the girl.

"It feels like being sick," Amber says. The old woman tuts and clucks. Amber nudges her out of the way impatiently. "You understand. Don't you?"

"Yeah." Rory can't guess what might happen if he disagreed with anything she said. Maybe she'd attack him. Or scream again, that would be the worst. "Know what you mean."

Amber's fixed her attention on him now as if he alone in the whole world can save her. "She'll follow you," she says. He feels a pulse of sudden shame in his heart. "Across the water. She thinks you belong to her and she doesn't want you to get away. She's afraid of what went with you. She hasn't been afraid for ages. She gave it up with her *hymen*." On the last word her voice changes, abruptly, impossibly: it becomes someone else's, a deep, resonant, man's voice. The whole room seems to waver. A dry scented wind rustles through phantom trees. The old couple whimper and Sal flinches in shock, as if something huge has swooped overhead. Amber clutches the old woman. "What am I talking about, Auntie?" Her own voice has returned. "What's that word?"

"It's nothing," the woman says. "You're having one of your funny turns, that's all." She hisses over her shoulder at the man, "Get them away!"

"All right now," the man says, getting to his feet and plucking Sal's coat. "That's enough."

Sal stares at Rory. "Who's following you?"

"Never mind that," the man says. "Out, you two."

"Everyone out," the woman says.

"He's coming," Amber says. She grabs the woman's arm so hard it makes her gasp in pain. "He's coming."

"No one's coming, lovely. Hush."

"Out!" says the man, but he's having no effect on Sal at all. Amber's fastened herself to the old woman like a frightened toddler, but she's looking only at Rory.

"Don't go," she says.

"Auntie won't go, lovely. Auntie won't leave you."

Sal brushes the man's hand away. "She wants us here," she says.

"Don't you tell me what—"

Amber cuts him off with a shriek. "Don't go! You have to listen!"

Sal snaps at the man. "Get your hands off me." She elbows him away and crouches in front of Amber, propping herself up with the staff. "We're listening, Amber," she says.

"Ah!" Amber's increasingly wild look switches from Rory to the staff. She jerks herself back against the column. Her fingers scratch against the floor. "Unlife! Unlife!" She kicks the old woman away with a ferocious spasm. "They should have left it drowned! He went down in the storm but he wouldn't stay down. They're coming. They're all coming!" She flings herself forward on her knees and grabs Rory around the waist. "He's nearly here! Don't leave me!"

The stench of invisible smoke is suddenly overpowering. The woman's on the floor, groaning, while the man bends over her. Sal drops the staff. It falls with a hollow thump. Rory tries to squirm out of the girl's grip but he can't, he's trapped. The thump echoes, and goes on echoing, as if the room's ten times bigger and carved of stone, until it becomes the dying beat of some massive drum.

A golden light touches the windows.

"He's coming," Amber whispers, in terrified surrender.

The light's like sunrise. Around the ceiling the thin rectangles of filthy spotted glass flood with molten warmth. It leaks into the air. Gold wreaths everything.

"What the fuck," Sal whispers.

"He's—" Amber begins. Then her arms are flung apart and her head jerks back. Rory shies away, completely terrified, and falls to the floor. All of them are crouching now as though the light's forcing them down, all except Amber, who kneels straighter, stretching her fingers to the ceiling.

"—here," she says, and now the man's voice has taken over her mouth again. It's far too big for her, for the room. It's huge and slow as a planet. "Here. I walk this place. I am I am I am invoked and I answer. By my light all things are seen as they are. Boy." Rory's cowering, bent over, head pressed to the floor, hands jammed over his ears. He's probably screaming but there's no way anyone could tell, not with that voice invading every atom of the room. "Answer me. Would you see God?" Someone's got hold of him. It's Sal. She's crawled to his side and is tugging him towards the door. "Answer me," the voice thunders. Amber looks like she's choking on it. Its every syllable makes her shake. "Would. You. See. God." Sal's got to her feet. She's very strong; she yanks Rory upright too and hurls him towards the door. "Answer me," the voice peals behind them as they bolt down the corridor. The two of them barrel out into miserable twilight, the bulk of the great dish looming, its face turned up to the infinity above. They run for the gate. Sal wrenches it open and they collapse onto the weed-cracked path beyond, clutching each other, recovering breath.

"OK," Sal says. A couple of the other Riders have spotted them and are running over. Sal gives Rory a weak smile. "That went well."

21

He can't sleep.

They don't even have the foam mats they used at Dolphin House. The floor tiles feel damp and sticky. Every corner's patched with mold. He can smell it in the dark, even over the reek of people sleeping in their clothes. The little rooms only fit one or two people but the doors must be open all along the corridor because the sweaty stench of people is stifling, and he can hear snoring. Earlier on there was a bit of muffled talking. *Earlier,* he thinks, but even then it was late, everyone except him and the muttering people was asleep. He feels like he's been awake for days. He gave up on the floor a while ago and has come to the room with the swivelly chair. It swivels without squeaking so there's no chance of waking Haze, who's on the floor somewhere. He reaches out for the wall of machinery with his foot and pushes himself around. Spinning in the dark.

The wind's noisy too. It surges and sighs. It's like trying to sleep with someone standing next to your head. He's not going to manage to drop off, he can tell.

They have to leave as soon as it's light. The old couple are furious and Sal doesn't dare make them any angrier. She and the others talked for a while about whether they should force the man to hand over the keys, but in the end they decided they have to go on being polite. Sal wouldn't say very much about what happened inside Amber's room, but Rory could tell she wasn't keen on going back in there either. The only thing is that the staff's still in there. Sal says she'll make them bring it out tomorrow or she'll refuse to leave.

Tomorrow. It feels unlikely.

Even though it's pitch black his eyes are open. This is because the voice starts up every time he tries to close them. Not actually speaking again, it's just that he starts remembering it, and when he does it's like sticking his head inside a bell. It doesn't even sound like words. It's just exploding bombs of sound. *Would. You. See. God.* Round and round he spins. He's not sure he's on the earth anymore. When he tries to think of Home, his mother, the stub of candle beside his bed, the handles of buckets of icy water biting into his palms, it feels like he's floated out of his own body, out of Rory, and he's swimming around in interstellar nothing.

There's a distant noise, more solid than the wind. A dog somewhere.

His attention drifts that way. It's weird in the dark, it's like he's porous. The barking is pinpricks in the texture of the night. They disappear. He folds back into the dark room. Spin, spin.

More dogs. They probably run wild, he thinks. There were dogs on Home, in The Old Days, and even a few afterwards, until they had to eat them. Missus Grouse and Missus Anderson and Laurel and Pink (and Viola, in sympathy) said they'd rather starve than eat the dogs, though they all did in the end. Starvation was worse than they thought it was going to be.

Rory wonders about that dog behind the door at the crossroads. Ralph. Stupid name for a dog. Even Lino and Silvia and Per don't feel real anymore. They've spun away like Home. Superheroes, gods. *That stuff's for kids,* Ol says, though he'll ask to read the comics anyway if he's bored and Laurel's not around.

The barking's a bit louder. There must be a few of them out there.

There's a shuffle in one of the other rooms. Someone else must be awake.

More barking.

"Shit," a voice says. Lots of rustling. Louder: "Shit."

Rory stops spinning.

"Dogs!" someone shouts.

Haze snorts herself awake. Judging by the sound of it she's just sat up. She's very still for a moment, listening.

"Oh Christ," she says. She gets up, banging something. Everyone's waking up now.

"Dogs!" the first voice shouts. "Wake up!"

"Fuck," Haze says. She drops something. "Who was watching?" she shouts. Doors start banging. "Where are my fucking boots?"

"Get the horses!" shouts the first voice. A glimmer of light flickers in. Someone's opened the front door, and it must be so late it's early, a little of tomorrow's light has appeared outside. Silhouettes bump into each other in the corridor. Outside someone—a man—yells "Wake up! Wake up!"

The barking's quite loud now. There're a lot of them. A big group of dogs, which, Rory thinks, would be a pack.

He starts feeling around on the floor for his coat and shoes. Haze has left the room. There's an abrupt and overwhelming atmosphere of panic. Lots of people are shouting outside now. He can't find his shoes; it's still black as the bottom of the sea in his tiny room. His hands keep whacking against the spider legs of the chair. "Everyone!" That sounds like Sal shouting. "Horses! Now!" Everyone else must be outside. He tries to think. Should he go outside in his socks?

No one's remembered him. No one's here to help him get his shoes on. He tries to think and discovers a wall of terror in his head. His hands brush accidentally against a shoe. He starts putting it on, though it's hard when you can't see and your hands are shaking. Now there's the sound of horses too, whinnying and stamping. Hoofbeats batter a rapid approach and fade: someone riding away. They're leaving. They're leaving already. Rory stands up, realizes he's only got one shoe on. He lopes into the corridor.

A silhouette appears at the front door. "Rory?"

"I'm here," he squeals, so tight with relief he can barely speak.

"Rory!" It's Ellie. "Out here, quick."

"I can't find my other shoe."

"Come on." She turns her head and stares at something outside. "Come on!"

The barking's continuous now, a wave of savagery. It's really close.

In the dim blue light behind Ellie someone rides past at a gallop. "Stand and fight!" someone shouts, a man. "Stay together!" Rory limps to the door. Ellie grabs his wrist. She's wearing a big loose white T-shirt which makes her look like a ghost. She yanks him outside.

There's torchlight across the heather barrens, and black shapes advancing. He hears howls which aren't dogs. A horse clatters close. The big tattooed man called Wolf is standing outside one of the other buildings, waving a club. He tries to grab a horse as it rides by. "Fight them!" he snarls, but the rider swerves to avoid him. Ellie's running. He tries to run too but he can't do it in one shoe, he keeps tripping. He stumbles and drags her down. Another horse thuds up out of the dark.

"Got the kid?" It's Soph.

"Can you take him?" Ellie says, getting to her feet.

"What about you?"

"Go." The wave of horrible noise has changed. It's breaking into small pieces and they're very close, coming very fast. The dogs are off the leash. "Now! Grab him!"

An arm comes down and heaves Rory up. He thumps against the flank of Soph's horse. It skitters and rears but she hangs on. Rory scrabbles for anything to cling on to and gets a fistful of mane. The horse whines and twists, and then suddenly the ground's alive with snapping black bodies. "Ellie!" Soph yells. The horse bucks and kicks, flipping Rory into the air. He comes down across the saddle, the pommel smashing into his ribs. "Hang on!" Soph shouts, and everything starts bouncing wildly. They're riding. Trying to pull his head straight, Rory sees Wolf go down, a black shape knocking into the man's chest and laying him out flat. A dog yelps right under him; he hears the crack of a hoof against its body. Soph's clinging on to him and swearing nonstop under her breath, *fuckingbastardsfuckingbastards*. They're riding hard out onto the dark heath. He's being pummeled. He's clinging on, sick with terror and crazy motion. There's a terrible lurch. Soph's litany stops in a single sharp gasp, the world inverts itself, and he's flung down into bristles and mud. The horse screams, staggers, falls beside him, rolling. Soph

screams too. The force of his fall has stunned and winded him and
he can't move or breathe. "Fuck!" Soph shouts, and makes an ago-
nized yelping noise. The turmoil of barking is behind them, mixed
with men's shouts. The sky's an indigo blanket. "Rory?" He sucks
in a breath. It hurts all over. "Rory! Can you get up?" Can he? He's
got to try. He drags his arms and legs into motion. The horse tries
to heave itself up on its forelegs but collapses, making a sound like
it's being strangled. "Run!" Soph tells him. "Get the fuck away!" He
can see her sitting nearby. Her mailed tunic is glimmering softly in
the shadow of dawn. "Listen to me," she says. Her voice is crackly.
"Stand up straight. Can you do that? Good on you." Her face is glimmering softly too: it must be wet. "Now go. Fast as you can. Always
downhill, understand me? Get to the sea. That's all you have to do."
She twists to look over her shoulder. Leaping torchlight scars the
horizon above. "Off you go. They'll send the dogs soon." He stares
stupidly. "Now, Rory. Now."

"What about you?"

"Shut up," she says. "Go."

"Are you—"

"I can't move." He looks at her feet. One of them's turned at a
funny-looking angle. "Don't just fucking stand there, kid. Run!" She
sounds so desperate that he takes a few steps away. It's like wading
through a dry and thorny pond. The horse makes another helpless
effort to right itself. He sees Soph dragging herself closer to it, whispering to it, flinching away as it throws its head in a frenzy of pain.
Up on the crest of the slope above a man's shape appears against
the torchlight. The outline of his head is horribly deformed. "Don't
stop!" Soph hisses at him. Tears fill his eyes and then his heart. He
blunders away alone.

Dawn finds him crammed in a muddy hole under an elder bush.
He tried to keep going downhill but he got stuck and can't go any
farther, it's impossible without his other shoe, and anyway he's exhausted and heartsick. He came to a road at the edge of the heath
but it ran out and left him in a morass of green. He squirmed in as

far as he could and hid. From time to time he can still hear distant barking. There's no one to tell him what's happening. His face and hands are filthy but there's no one to show him where the water is. He doesn't know which way is north or south or east or west or which way he's going to go next.

The people with the dogs are like villains in the comics. He imagines cruel men with mad-eyed leering grimaces who shout boasts and order destruction. *Kill them all!* If they find him he's dead. Ellie and Wolf are probably already dead, and Soph too. He's used to people dying but this is different. When They take people it's quiet, they just disappear, like Ol, walking down the hill with a vaguely puzzled look, never to be seen again. Slipping into the water with a white hand guiding them down. Not torchlight and teeth and howling. He can't stop thinking about Soph sitting on the heather, angry, afraid, all by herself. He should have got her away. In the comics the hero would have helped her up—*Lean on me*—and they'd have limped off to hide together, battered but defiant.

In the comics Ellie would have gotten away too. She had her boots on. She'd have kicked her way through the dogs to her horse, Drum, and ridden off into the night, leaving the villains cursing and waving their fists. *The princess, she rides like the wind!*

It's not like that. He's dirty and empty and hiding in a ditch.

No one's going to come and rescue him.

He cries for a while, feeling horribly small.

When he starts getting shivery and stiff he makes himself wriggle out from under the elder bush and back through the mess of branches onto the road. It's barely a road at all, just a crumbling lane which vanishes under a turbulent lake of bramble. He's supposed to keep going downhill but it's all blocked that way.

He can't be on his own. It's not possible.

It's a drier morning, the clouds higher and thinner, streaked with blue holes like torn clothes. The curve of the high heath above hides all but the tops of the satellite dishes. It's very quiet where he is, his little patch of solitary ground. No one knows where he is.

He stands for a while, waiting, but there's nothing to wait for. No one's coming.

He knows what he'd do next if this was the comics.

It's completely stupid. It's the stupidest idea ever. He's not in the comics. He's Rory, aged ten.

Nevertheless, oddly, every other idea sort of fades away beside it. He can imagine standing there for a very long time waiting to discover something else to do, and nothing changing in all that time, just small birds occasionally darting in and out of the bushes. It's the stupid idea or nothing, then.

Perhaps he is in the comics after all, he thinks as he starts limping painfully back up towards the heath. Where else would someone ask him if he wanted to see God?

22

*B*e can't go the wrong way. The big dishes dominate the horizon above. There must still be people there too, because he can see smoke rising. The smoke's thick and very dark. They must have made a big fire. Every so often there's a snatch of noise which might be a shout or an argument or the dogs again. It's not even that far away. He didn't make much of an escape in his one shoe.

The only things growing here are gorse and heather. It's too exposed for anything to survive that isn't scrubby and prickly. The gorse gathers in squat clumps, tilted by the prevailing winds. There are places where he can use it as cover.

Narrow trails wriggle through the heather. Animal tracks, probably. He's little enough to tuck himself down in them if he has to. He finds one that zigzags up the slope, towards the dishes and the smoke and the noises.

He's incredibly frightened. It's a crisp, buzzing, excited sort of fear. He whispers to himself as he sneaks up the slope, trying to make random words turn into a Plan. *See what's going on. Do that first. Do some recon. See what we can do after that.* Even if he could just find a left shoe that would help.

When he first sees people it gives him such a squeeze of fear he nearly pees. He's crouching by a thicket of gorse, pretty well hidden, and he's smeared in mud and bits of leaves and twigs by now, and it's just two people—men—walking around the corner of one building in the distance, not even looking his way, but still, it's enough to make him think about what he's doing. Going closer instead of getting away. The men look shaggy and bulky, like they're wearing furs instead of clothes. Wild men. *Barbarians.*

He can hear Soph pleading with him. *Go. Get to the sea. Now.*

It's the fact that he can hear her voice so clearly that's the problem.

He waits crouched by that gorse bush for a long time. No one else appears. He hears the dogs a lot now. Often someone shouts angrily when they start up, telling them to be quiet. He thinks about turning back down the hill. He contemplates the idea with frantic eagerness.

He stays where he is, though.

He's on the broad flat top of the heath. There are nut-brown pools dotted around, and bits of fencing wire, and a couple of concrete huts too tiny to house anything but equipment, though they're not connected to anything, they're just plonked down in the waste. One of them's between him and the camp under the satellite dishes. He can see how he could hide behind it if he could get that far.

He ducks low and scurries across the heath. Every step he takes with his left foot is an unpleasant adventure. That sock's a murky brown mess now, saturated with squelchy water. He goes as fast as he can and gets himself tucked tight behind the concrete hut without seeing anyone else. He leans against it, gasping.

There's a soft rattle and a blur of brown movement. He flinches.

A bird's landed on the roof of the hut. It fluffs itself and peers over the edge at Rory with huge round black-ringed eyes. It's an owl, a stocky mottled owl with a nasty hooked beak and an expression of concentrated ferocity. It's not much bigger than Rory's head but it looks like it's thinking about eating him. It's entirely unafraid of him.

It glares. It shows no sign of going away.

"Hello," Rory says. A muffled grumble of male laughter comes across the heath. Rory ignores it. He's safely out of sight of anything but the bird.

It twitches its domed head. Something about the movement reminds Rory of someone, of—

His heart plays a fast little dance.

"Lino?" he says.

It just sits there. Or stands there, whichever birds do. It nibbles in its feathers.

"Is that you?" Rory says.

It blinks. Its eyes are brilliant orange stones. It manages to look simultaneously furious and bored. Rory realizes his question wasn't very helpful.

"If you're Lino," he says, "er . . . Hoot."

It looks at him like he's a complete idiot.

"Well, I don't know, do I?" Rory says.

It swivels its head halfway around and then drops almost noiselessly off the roof, unfurling striped wings. It flaps and glides over the matching tawny brown of the heather, then drops out of sight behind a little furrow.

"Just a bird," Rory says, cross with himself.

A barrage of shouting comes from the camp, and some metallic banging. He sneaks a look around the corner of the hut. The nearest of the buildings around the dishes is about as far away as Briar is from Home, across the Channel. There are two much smaller dishes sitting directly on the ground nearby, not much bigger than the ones people put on their houses, angled almost flat to the horizon instead of pointing at the sky. If he could get up behind them, he thinks, he'd still be hidden from the buildings. It sounds like most of the people and dogs are on the other side of the camp, near the fire, which he still can't see.

It's a horrible feeling going out into the open beyond the hut. He's too frightened now to worry about his soaked scratched foot, his bruises, his tiredness. His heart's pumping some kind of tingling ice all through his body. He feels electric. He passes a web of fence trailing lifelessly from a metal pole, one of a row of them. He can hear snatches of distant chatter now, and lots of barking. A bout of woofing is answered by a rough shout: "Shut up!" He keeps himself bent double. The backs of buildings are facing him but won't the dogs sniff him out soon? He can't stop in the open, though. He'll get as close as he can, and then he'll . . . and then he'll—

The owl swoops in front of his face. It gives him such a fright he can't help squeaking even though he's got to be as quiet as he can. It beats its wings jerkily, soaring and dipping, and then spins round and drops to the heather nearby, on his right.

It stares at him. He stares at it.

He can't stop. He presses on, closer. Then the bird's there again, right in his path, making the faintest whisper as it passes, swerving away, flapping up—it's a beautiful soarer but an ugly flier—and twisting to one side before coming back to earth off to his right. It settles, and stares.

Rory stares back. It probably isn't for a long time, actually, but every moment crouching still and exposed feels fearfully long. He's got to make up his own mind what to do. No one's going to tell him whether he's right.

He turns aside and battles across the heath towards the owl.

Now he's moving parallel with the broken fence, completely in the open. The only cover would be if he got all the way to the nearest buildings, a particularly grim pair of rain-streaked one-story outposts squatting beside a medium-sized dish with a faded logo in its bowl. He's just thinking about how far away they look when the owl lifts itself up and flits over to one of them in one ground-hugging guide, then drops onto its roof and sits there, a bit like a squat chimney.

It stares at him.

He steers towards it. What else can he do? An outburst of terrifyingly close barking sends his heart leaping into his mouth. He throws himself down in the heather but there's nowhere to hide, he can't stick his face in a carpet of gnarled twigs. Angry men yell at the dogs, but they don't stop barking. The men are coming closer. They sound like they're just on the other side of the pair of grimy buildings. He knots up with dread.

The owl drops lazily, swings around the corner of the building, and goes out of sight. The barking gets even more frenetic, and the shouts even angrier. "Stop it! Shut it!" A dog yelps like it's been hit. "Quiet!"

"Only a flippin' bird," a second voice says, quite clearly. Both voices belong to men.

"You hear that?" The first voice is enraged. There's a thump and another pained yelp. "Only a bird. Stupid"—yelp—"animal."

Dogs and voices recede, grumbling. Perfectly silent, the owl reap-

pears over the roof of the building, circles neatly, and plops back to
its perch on the roof. It looks at Rory.

"Lino," he says to himself, and stands up. For the first time all
day he feels a little spark of something like courage. He pulls himself upright and hurries forward. A little farther on and suddenly
there's firmer ground underfoot, chunks of tarmac under the litter
of the moor. The weeds are soft nettles and grass. A few moments
later and he's under the cracked guttering of the nearer of the two
buildings. He stands there for a long time with his back against the
wall, breathing hard. When he looks up the owl's still there, watching him.

There's a letterbox-shaped window above him, its frame warped
and splintering. Some desperately tenacious weed has got a foothold
there and sprouted a few mangy purple flowers.

From inside the window comes a little moan of pain. Not a man.

Rory goes numb all over. He stares at the owl. It gazes back,
completely unsympathetically. *Go on then.*

As quietly as he can, he edges around the corner. Now he's looking in towards the main group of buildings. The column of dark
smoke is rising on the far side, by the building with the curved glass
wall. The smell's much stronger, not just smoke but a thick cloying
roasting smell as well. He catches his breath and ducks away as a man
strolls into sight, coming past the fence around the building where
Amber was. He was close enough that Rory could have seen his face
if he'd turned to look. He had a dog on a leash, a big square-headed
brown brute of a dog, and he was wearing a hood which looked like
a dog's head too. The dog starts barking as if it saw him, but there's
barking and yapping all around and the man didn't turn his way.
Rory takes a few good deep breaths and then starts around the back
of the building.

He's safely around the next corner and halfway to the door when
it occurs to him: what if one of them's in there? But it's too late for
that. A burst of raucous shouting comes from somewhere not far
enough away. He charges to the door—it's half-open—and all but
jumps inside the building, into stinking moldering darkness. His
sock squelches on the floor.

Someone inside has heard him, and goes quiet. He can feel it: the sound of someone holding their breath.

He waits. No one moves. The smell's revolting, like going into one of the abandoned houses on Home and finding the toilet dirty.

It's another narrow corridor. His eyes adjust gradually. The room with the broken window where he thought he heard someone would be at the far end. If anyone's here, they're as scared of him as he is of them. He tries to creep along carefully but he can't help splatching on the floor. He pulls the collar of the shirt the Riders gave him up over his nose. The door at the end of the corridor is slightly open. He stops to listen and hears tight shaky breathing. Someone in there is absolutely terrified. He opens the door.

"Oh my God," Soph says.

She's backed up against the far wall, under the window, where a cold grey light drizzles down on her. She's sitting on the floor with her hands behind her back, leaning against a metal filing cabinet with no drawers. There's a rope tied around the cabinet; the other end of it's behind her. She's smeared with dirt and bruising. Her top lip is puffy. She looks terrible and smells worse.

"What are you doing here?"

He hurries across to her, holding his elbow over his mouth to take a breath. "Lean forward," he says.

"I told you to get away. These people are fucking crazy."

They've tied her hands behind her back. "I can't reach," he says.

She sits up and shuffles herself away from the wall, wincing and swearing under her breath. The rope's quite thick and the knot's tight but crude. He starts pushing the loose end in. There are raw marks on her skin where the rope's been rubbing.

"Rory—"

"Keep still."

"Listen to me, Rory. I want you away from here. Right now."

"I'm rescuing you." He gets the knot loose. She shudders and sighs as her hands come free.

"Oh, God." Everything she says comes out in a wet whisper, like she's fighting tears. "Oh, shit. Worth it just for that."

"Come on," he says. "Let's go."

"Bless you." Her eyes are wet too. "It's good to see you. One last friendly face. I'm not going anywhere."

"Why not?"

"My ankle's broken, Rory."

"I'll help you."

She's shaking her head. She puts a hand on his arm. "I can't walk. I can hardly crawl. It hurts like fuck. Leave me here, all right? You can't let them find you."

In his head there's the idea of escape, of rescue. He can't make it into an actual Plan, it refuses to get itself organized like that, but he knows how it basically works. You go in, you find them, you run away. That's what they're going to do.

"I'm not leaving you," he says.

"Look at me." He does. Her long hair's gone as wild as bramble. There are puffy purple bits around her eyes as well as on her lip. She looks only half human. "I don't know what these crazies have planned for me, but I'm not having you around to watch it." She clutches his hand in hers. "I mean it. I swear, I've never been as happy to see anyone in my whole life, but now you're going to run as far away from here as you can, and you're not going to stop running until your feet are in the sea."

He's thinking of things like bandages and splints. Or a horse, he could put her on a horse like she did to him. "There's got to be something—"

"Listen!" She drags him close. He's almost sick with the stench. "They made Perse and Wolf fight their dogs. OK? They even gave Perse his sword. They could see the stupid fucker didn't know one end of it from the other. They set the really bad dogs on them. Really bad, really big. Understand me, Rory? Do you understand what happened?" He doesn't need to try working it out, he can see it in her face. "They made sure me and El were watching—"

"Is Ellie here?"

"Fuck, Rory, I don't know. They trussed her up same as me, dragged her off somewhere. Whatever they did to her it won't have been good. I took the precaution of shitting myself. Desperate times, eh?" (*Dispurut toimes.*) She makes a weak quivery grin and for a moment she's almost herself again. "No one wants a girl smelling of shit, you know? Someone comes in here with a bucket and sponge and I'll get really worried. Ah!" She lets him go and clutches her leg. "Fuck, it hurts!"

He's trying to think. Wheelchairs, stretchers. Creating diversions. Tie a message to the owl. Get disguises. It's hard to think through the horror and the smell but he has a weird certainty that he can't just run off again. In fact he now has to rescue Ellie too. When all the other Riders panicked and ran for their horses in the dark, she was the one who came to find him first, and that's why she didn't have time to get away. There are things you can do and things you can't, and leaving her and Soph here is one of those things you can't do.

"What if I get some of their clothes and—"

"Rory, Rory!" She shakes him again. She's shouting and whimpering together. "Those dogs ate the boys alive. You know what these crazies said? They said since we give them to the man-eaters they'd give us to their gods. Like they worship the fucking dogs. They're not sane. If you don't get out of here I'm going to scream. I swear I am."

"I'll find Ellie," he says. If she's tied up somewhere he could free her too, then there'd be an adult to figure out how to get Soph away. He stands up. She's watching him, her cheeks stained with filthy tears. "You stay here."

Soph almost laughs. "Yeah. Yeah, I reckon I'll stay here."

"We'll come back," he says. "We'll save you."

"You're the most obstinate little toerag on the planet."

"We'll put you on her horse."

"They killed her horse. They hung it upside down last night to drain the blood and now they're fucking roasting it."

"We'll . . ." Do something else. Ellie will know.

"Rory," Soph begins.

"Stop trying to get me to run away. I'm not going to."

"I hate you," she says, her voice cracking. "Do you know that?"

A sudden explosion of barking makes them both freeze. A moment later and they hear a voice, very clear, very close, calling to someone else, something about *getting her*. Another moment and they hear feet scuffing.

In that moment Rory feels terror like nothing he thought possible. It's like someone's shoved a wedge of ice right into his stomach.

"Over there!" Soph whispers. She's shifting herself back against the wall. Rory's so dumbstruck he doesn't even understand what she's talking about. She's nodding towards the shadows in the opposite corner of the room. "Rory!"

He gets it just in time. There's another filing cabinet lying on its side there. He dashes across and drops to the floor behind it, squirming into a dusty niche. Someone shoves open the outside door and starts down the corridor. He wiggles and writhes and curls his legs up, thinking, *the dogs'll know I'm here, the dogs—*

Heavy steps come in the room and stop. No barking. "Ah, fuck's sake," a man's voice says, disgusted. "Like a sewer in here. Up you get."

"I've broken my ankle," Soph says. She doesn't sound brave or defiant. She sounds like someone who thinks they're about to be eaten alive by dogs.

"Hop, then."

"I can't stand up."

"God." The man's voice is bored, grumpy. "Don't tell me I'm going to have to touch you."

"Where am I going?"

"Time to see the boss," he says. "Meet the big dogs."

"You've got a knife there, haven't you?"

"Hmm?"

"I don't know who you are." She's very quiet, entirely desperate. "But you were just an ordinary person like me. Before all this started. I'm begging you. Please kill me now."

The man makes a short surprised laugh.

"Please," she says. "Or use the rope. You can say I did it myself."

The man chuckles. "Don't think that's an option, love. Come on then, let's get you on your—eh?" Scuffling noises, and Soph bites back a gasp of pain. Rory's legs are beginning to sting. He can't move a single muscle. "Got your arms free, did you? What were you going to do, start crawling?—Oi!" A slap and a wince. "Hands off that! Fuck me. Got to keep an eye on this one." A metallic clatter.

Rory understands: she's made a grab for a knife the man's carrying, and he's tossed it out of reach. "Shit, look at you. Disgusting. Right. Up."

He must have pulled her to her feet because she screeches in agony, deafeningly loud in the miserable little prison. The man swears. There's a thump, and a long moan. He's dropped her. They go silent, if you can call it silent when he's breathing hard and she's whimpering.

"Going to need another pair of hands," he grumbles. "And gloves, if I'm going to have to touch your filthy arse. I hate Australians."

Rory hears a kind of choked hiccup, which might almost be a laugh. "Me too," Soph whispers, as the man stomps back down the corridor.

He waits only until the footsteps are outside before unpacking himself from his hidey-hole. Soph's staring at him.

"Get the knife," she whispers. It's on the floor near the corner where he is. It's a thick kitchen knife with a scratched and rusty blade. He picks it up, then realizes what she's thinking, and drops it in horror.

"You don't have to do it," she whispers. "Just give it to me and then go."

"No."

"Give me the knife. Give me the fucking knife." He picks it up. The look on her face might qualify as the worst thing he's ever seen, which given how the last couple of days have gone is saying something. She bares her teeth at him and begins shuffling his way. "Give me that fucking knife right now, you stubborn little sack of shit."

"I'm going to rescue you," he says, and runs out the door, stopping his ears against her moan of despair. He's going to save her. He's got a knife, he's armed, he can do it. There'll be a Plan any moment now. He'll attack them with the knife when they come back for her, something like that, but first he has to—

Hide. A dog goes wild. Men shout, at the dogs, at each other. He sees them, right out there, in plain sight, two men now approaching the door. They can't see him because he's in the dimness of the corridor. He looks around in panic, sees a tiny side door, throws it open, pushes himself into a completely dark cupboard, and shuts himself in.

The two men come by, coughing, muttering. They go to where Soph is and pick her up between them. They come back down the corridor, bumping, panting, cursing. Now, he's thinking, as they pass his door. Now. Jump out while their backs are turned, stab them both, now now now. They kick open the front door and go back outside, leaving him in his cupboard, clutching the handle of the knife in a death-grip. Whatever was supposed to happen hasn't happened. He doesn't know how to jump out of a cupboard like a ninja and kill someone. He doesn't even know where to start. There's no Plan, there never was. Soph and Ellie are going to be eaten alive and he's just a useless boy.

23

He goes back into the corridor and peeks outside.

People are gathering. They're coming out from the various different buildings under the satellite dishes, heading away from him, towards the fire. They're all men, all dressed in layers of shaggy torn clothes and strips of fur, though some are younger and some older, some swaggering and some scurrying. A lot of them are pulling dogs, big dogs which snap at each other and strain at their collars. They're a vicious army and he's one ten-year-old with a kitchen knife and an empty head. He can see the two men carrying Soph, they're just going out of sight beyond one of the buildings now. He can't think of a single thing he can do. He can't even see the owl. He looks up at the sky but no help's coming from there. Only the vast empty dishes face it, eyeless monuments from a lost civilization, looking up to dead gods. It's completely obvious that if he goes running over there with his knife to try to rescue Soph he'll be grabbed by the first men to see him and then maybe they'll feed him to their dogs as well. He understands now, properly understands, why Soph was telling him to run away.

But still he can't.

No one's coming his way now. Everyone's walking in the other direction. Soon they're all out of sight, though he can hear a rumble of mixed voices now, a crowd. People are cheering and shouting by the fire. No one cares about him. He could walk out the door and behind the building and down the heath and no one would notice.

Instead, he jogs across the weeds and rubble to the shelter of the next building. He's breathing so hard it's like he's lifting himself off the ground and dropping himself back every time. He doesn't know what he's doing. He just knows there'll be another Plan eventually, because there has to be, and anyway, if he runs away now and leaves Soph and maybe Ellie too, then when he got to the sea he'd have to drown himself in it, or use the knife to stab himself on the shore. He waits a long time behind the next building, then scampers over a dead parking lot to the next one around, and goes on like that, working his way along the outer edge of the camp, until he can see the long building with the curvy glass front and the flames of the huge bonfire burning in front of it. The crowd's assembling there. He's keeping his distance still but even from here he thinks there must be thirty or forty of them. He can see two men standing on the ramp in front of the glass wall where he and the Riders tied up their horses the day before. They're addressing the crowd. He can almost hear them sometimes, though there's a lot of mingled talking, and the dogs are yapping and growling at each other all the time, winding in and out around the gathered men.

He kicks against something hidden in the weeds, sending it rolling across the scarred pavement. It's his other shoe.

He looks at it in confusion. A flutter of motion distracts him. For an instant he's afraid someone's spotted him. Someone has spotted him, but it's the owl. It's come to rest on a corner of the sloping roof of the long building.

He picks up the shoe and steers his way behind the cover of a pair of abandoned trucks with telephone company logos until he's around the back of that building, completely hidden now from the Black Pack and their fire. He squats down, wrings out his sock as best he can, and ties on the shoe. It feels like the beginning of a Plan. He's not sure yet how one shoe plus an owl, which may or may not actually be an Italian man in disguise, add up to a rescue, but it's better than nothing. He works his way through the debris behind the building—it's like the Hotel here, nettles and broken glass and rusting service doors—until he reaches its far corner, where a straggling thicket of gorse has grown in its shelter. Now he's as close as he can get to whatever's happening out there. He ducks low and eases himself as close to the gorse as its thorns will let him, peeping through gaps between bare stems.

He can feel the heat of the fire from here. It's not a huge bonfire but it must have been burning for a while because its heart is deep red. A hideous silhouette is staked in the middle of it, a blackened and distorted mockery of muscle and hide; flames lick all around it, making it spit and pop, stripping oily sparks from it and sending them up to twist in foul smoke. The men are mostly on the far side of the fire from where he is now. They're facing his way but he's well hidden, and the air between is swimming, melting. They're listening to the two men standing up the ramp to Rory's left. He wiggles around until he can see them very clearly through a slit between the wall of the building and the gorse. There are five other people he didn't see before because they're huddled on the ground below the ramp. One's Soph, sitting with her hands tied up again. Next to her is someone he can't see because she's bowed over, but she's a small woman wearing a long baggy T-shirt which was once more or less white: it's got to be Ellie. At the base of the ramp on the side beyond the two men are the miserable old couple, huddled close to each other. Between them and the men, a bit farther up the ramp, white as a cloud and plainly terrified, is Amber.

Unseen by anyone but Rory, the owl squats at the end of the roof, watching too.

The two men are still speaking. Not together, nor taking it in turns, just interrupting each other and finishing each other's sentences. Rory has to hold himself still to hear the words over the noise of the fire and the fretting of the dogs. There's a lot of umming and errring, and one of the men speaks English with a strong foreign accent, making the words slidy and pointy like he's permanently sneering. He's the shorter and slighter of the two. Rory doesn't like the look of him at all. He has a dangerous face, sharp, weirdly pale, with a fringe of hair so blond it's virtually white. He's wearing a cape made of the skins of dead dogs. There's a flaccid dead-eyed dog's head staring out from each of his shoulders, and small black claws in a string around his neck. He doesn't umm and errr as much as the other man, who's bigger, heavier—almost fat; it's been so long since Rory's seen an overweight person he takes a while to remember the word—and messier, with untamed curly reddish hair over most of his face as well as his head. The bigger man has glasses, which he keeps taking off to wipe on the sleeve of his long black leather coat.

He's also holding Per's staff.

"So," he shouts, "anyway. OK. Now, I know you thought we had some entertainment last night." He pauses as if waiting for a laugh or a cheer. "Ha. Er. But actually we've got a bit of a treat for you. Pav and me."

"Not what you are thinking," the other man chips in, the blond foreign one. He's also addressing the crowd by the fire but he doesn't have to bellow like the big man does. He's got a clear sharp voice, the kind that makes itself heard without an effort. The listening men seem to have gone a bit quieter already, as if they're expecting something.

"Oh yeah," the big man says. "Yeah. We'll get to the bitches later."

"All of us?" someone yells from the crowd, and a few people cheer. Some of the dogs join in excitedly. They're quickly beaten down. The foreign man holds his hands up for quiet.

"You wonder why we brought you to this place," he says. "It's not just to break the horse people. Jon, give me that."

The big man gives him a resentful look, but it's obvious already that the foreigner's the more important of the two. He hands over the staff. The foreigner takes it gently, balancing it across his palms. Then he grips it hard in both hands and holds it up over his head. Men and dogs together go very quiet.

"This is an old thing," he says.

"Yeah," Jon adds. "Ancient."

"And full of power." The foreigner lets go with one hand and draws a wide arc over the heads of the crowd with the other. "This place is full of power. Here, where we used to send messages into space. The gods are close here."

"That's right," Jon says, not wanting to be upstaged.

"There is a god in here." The foreigner swings the staff in front of him and brandishes it at the crowd.

"In the staff," Jon says.

"I have called this god to join us. We make him a sacrifice." With his free hand he gestures at the ground below the ramp, where Soph and Ellie are tied up.

"So if you're wondering why no one gets to touch the bitches, that's why, OK? Yeah? All makes sense now, doesn't it?"

"But you know, we have our own god. Our first and greatest. Yes?"

A roar answers him. It's not like a cheer. There's not the slightest trace of joy in it. It's like massed hunger. Rory shrinks himself tighter into the cover of the gorse.

The foreigner waits for the crowd to go quiet again. Then when they're silent he waits a bit longer, staring out at them, forcing them to hang on his words.

"Which of you," he cries at last, "wants to hear our god speak?" As he says this he reaches behind his shoulders and lifts something he's been carrying there high over his head. At first Rory thinks it's another shriveled dog's head, but it's not. It's solid, black, hard, and the sockets of its eyes are completely empty. It's a dog's face carved in wood.

There's no cheer. The crowd is completely still, all of them, men and animals. It's as if he's cast a spell on them. Even the wind feels like it's gone quieter.

"Yeah," Jon the bigger man shouts. "Because we can do that. Like, right here. In front of everyone. You all get to see."

"Sometimes," the foreigner says, "perhaps you all ask yourself, Jon and Pav, do they really speak to our god? Today we will show you. In this place." He's still holding the dog mask high in the air, turning it slowly from side to side so it looks like it's watching them. Rory's very glad he doesn't turn it around far enough to point towards where he's hiding, because he's convinced its empty eyes would be able to see him.

"The thing is, though," Jon says, "you've got to have a special ingredient."

"Blood," says the other man, Pav.

"Yeah." Jon grins. "And not just any old blood. It's got to be special." He takes two steps down the ramp and grabs Amber by the wrist. She shuts her eyes and gives a little screech. The old couple start towards her but one look from Jon makes them cringe and retreat. Amber looks pathetically tiny in the big man's grip.

Some murmuring has started up among the Pack. Pav raises his voice. "Just a cut," he says. "We don't hurt her. We are not stupid."

"Hear that?" Jon's turned to Amber, but he's still shouting, so everyone's obviously supposed to hear. "We're not going to hurt you."

"We respect everyone touched by the gods."

Ellie raises her head for the first time, coughs noisily, and spits. There's a horribly tense silence.

"Unlike," Jon says, bubbling up with clumsy anger, "unlike some people. Who should probably shut their mouths. Yeah? Got something to say?"

"They will hear too," Pav says. "After that they will show more respect."

"Not going to be much of an 'after' for you bitches anyway. Not once you start burning with your fucking horse."

"Jon," Pav says, aside. "Now now."

Rory's had a glimpse of Soph's face. She's so pale under her bruises it's like she's already dead. He clutches the knife convulsively. He's going to have to do something soon, whatever it is. Run out there and cut them free. Something. Anything.

Pav gives the staff back to Jon so he can hold the dog mask up with both hands. "Now," he says. "These old people here, they tell me this girl is special. That she looks up to the sky and speaks to powers above." Amber's shaking in Jon's grip, her chin tucked down on her chest. "I hope for their sake they are not boasting."

"Right," Jon says. "'Cos if they're lying they go straight to the dogs."

"Not much meat on 'em," someone shouts from the crowd. Nobody laughs or cheers. The air's thick with hateful anticipation. Pav glares at the men as if daring anyone else to interrupt him.

"All of you," he says, "on your knees."

A brief chorus of rustling. Rory can't look. He's fixated on Pav and his mask.

"I think they are not lying," Pav says, when everyone's quiet again. "I have heard stories about this girl, about this place. I think she has the special blood. A god talks in her mouth."

"And the god speaks the truth," says a voice in Rory's ear. Right in his ear. He jumps—actually leaves the ground—and squeaks in fright, spinning around, a fist closing around his heart: *caught*, he's thinking. *They got me.* A man's appeared behind him without the slightest sound. Rory's legs give out, but at the very moment he's falling on his face he knows it's not the Pack who've found his hiding place, because the man couldn't look less like one of them if he was the mirror image of Rory himself. He's a tall clean smiling man in a long coat the color of the flowers on the gorse, of late-afternoon sun in autumn. He's not making any effort to hide himself, though he's tall enough to overlook the bushes. He's standing straight and strong, like his brown boots couldn't actually be attached to something as messy as the ground. There's something about his face which is impossible to look at, and yet Rory still knows he's smiling, which is almost the weirdest thing of all: how could anyone possibly smile at this? Rory cowers in front of him on the broken earth.

"Do you know," the man says, in a brilliant, beautiful voice, "what God is?"

Something's still going on beyond the gorse, on the ramp, where the torture and the horror are. Rory can hear it, dimly: the two men talking, a girl's voice rising to a breathless shriek. None of it matters anymore. The man with the yellow coat has banished everything else to an irrelevant distance.

"Necessity," he says, "and death, and disease, and love. Famine and fear. The ocean and the winds. Fire is a god. Hunger is a god. Joy is a god, and madness. The power by which things grow, and its twin by which things waste. Music. Silence. The sun. The sun is a god."

The girl screams once, and stops; they've cut her. Everything else goes still. The air feels heavy. The man keeps talking as if nothing else matters or will ever matter.

"All these things," he says, "are gods. Have you understood? God is everything in the face of which man is no more than animal."

Someone shouts *Look!*

There's a collective gasp. Rory, groveling in the mud, is thinking (with whatever defiant fraction of himself remains available for thought) *They've seen him. That's it. We're done for.* He twists around and looks up.

A shadow falls over the camp. Falls, and stays there, drifting slowly, turning in the air.

It's winged and taloned but it's no bird. It's a hundred times too big for any bird. If it plunged and clutched it would be like death itself descending. A huge black creature is wheeling silently over the kneeling crowd. It dips a wing and circles again, watching.

The first person to speak is the old woman, Amber's auntie. She's on her knees. She gibbers hoarsely but everyone else is so still they can hear what she says perfectly clearly.

"The angel!" she says.

She's right. Rory knows she's right. Everyone knows this shape, everyone in the world. It was, when you look back, the dividing line. It marked the moment when Before turned into After. No one in the world knows What Happened. No one can say, though millions of people tried. But everyone knows what it looked like. It looked like *this*: this gigantic black thing halfway between a crow and a man, seen in that one photo everyone saw, and in all those wobbly videos, described in dreadful detail in that BBC report they tried to stop everyone from hearing. This was the sign. This was the messenger. *Everything's changed,* it said. *You no longer know anything you thought you knew.* Its arc in the air sliced The Old Days away from the new.

"Everything returns," the man says, and steps around the thicket of gorse.

Something's happened on the ramp while the man was busy terrifying Rory. Jon is holding Amber in front of him. There's a cut on her hand, dribbling blood. The other man, the foreigner, has put the dog mask over his face and crouched down on his hands. He's pushing his head under the dribble so the blood splashes down on him. They're all frozen like that, staring at the black apparition overhead. Soph and Ellie are gaping up at the sky as well. So are all the kneeling men beyond the fire. The dogs have flattened themselves against the ground. Nothing moves except the angel above and the man in the yellow coat, striding out towards the fire, one step, two, three.

Then things begin to happen with bewildering speed. It's as if the moment of silence was a tipping point, a teetering on the edge, and suddenly the whole scene's falling headlong and screaming.

A man in the crowd shouts "The black angel! It's back!" The dogs spring up, howling, tearing at their leads. A few men are up and running too, scattering for the cover of the buildings. Other men get slowly to their feet. Quite a lot of them have noticed the yellow-coat man now. They stare at him with expressions of surprise turning to slow bullying anger, pack rage. Ellie and Soph have squirmed against each other. They're both staring at the angel with open mouths. Ellie's face is horribly scratched and scarred. Amber screams again, a long mad scream, which makes lots of people turn that way even though there's a mass of stumbling and shouting now. Rory looks towards the ramp as well. The masked man is still crouching by her feet. There's something odd about the way he's doing it, like he's ill. He's hunched, shaking. His hard black face appears to be twitching. The big hairy man shoves Amber away. He lifts the staff and is about to try shouting over the hubbub when he too notices the yellow-coat man, who's now walking straight towards him.

"Who's this joker?" he says, squaring his shoulders but stepping back a little, like he's pretending he's not afraid. The yellow-coat man doesn't break his stride. He tilts his head back a little and answers in a golden voice.

"The joker in the pack," he says, and points his arm at where the masked man is crouched.

The man howls. It's a sound so savage it makes Rory want to dig himself into the mud to hide. It's utterly inhuman. The crouching man isn't a man anymore. He's down on his hands and knees but his hands and knees have become legs, covered in ragged grey fur. The black mask has become his face. Its muzzle writhes and opens, baring vicious teeth. Where the foreign man was, a huge dog is prowling the ramp. It snarls at Amber, who collapses in a dead faint. The big man is staring at the beast with a stupidly dazed expression. Per's staff drops out of his hand, clatters, and rolls away. The dog springs up at him and tears a spraying red chunk out of his throat.

Rory's stomach goes liquid, turns. He throws up. Everyone's

screaming—men, women, dogs, monsters. The angel's screaming
too as it wheels above, a guttural black scream, *wrraaaakk*. Loudest
of all screams the yellow-coat man, but his scream is like thunder.
"I." Each word is louder than the last. "Am." The third is a peal
which shakes the earth. "Inviolate!" Rory's trying to stand up, spitting bile from his mouth. A maddened dog thrashes into the gorse
bush, howling as the thorns scratch bloody furrows in its hide. Men
and dogs are running everywhere, in every direction. Rory breaks his
cover to run as well, so witless with terror he doesn't even know what
he's trying to run from. A dog crashes into his legs and sends him
sprawling into another man, who trips and falls. In the next instant
there's a growl like concrete shredding and the beast which used to be
the foreign man leaps over Rory and lands on the fallen man's back,
swiping down with open jaws; in the next instant its muzzle comes
up oozing red and Rory's hands are flecked with warm dark spots.
Someone shouts his name. It's Ellie. She's on her knees, bending over
Soph who's flailing around on the ground. A man runs past them,
knocking her over. Lots of men are running up the ramp, trying to
get inside the building. Rory crawls forward through the carnage
towards the only faces he knows. There's a blistering eruption of
breaking glass: the beast has jumped straight through the glass wall.
"Rory!" Ellie yells again. He realizes he's still got the knife in his
hand. He's clutching it so hard he can't feel his hand. He starts sawing through the ropes around Ellie's wrists. The body of a big man
crunches onto the ramp above them, flung out from the building
through a halo of splintering glass. His slack head lolls over them,
seeing nothing. Ellie's saying something and so is Soph but he can't
hear what it is, his eyes are misting up and all he can hear is things
being killed. A dog runs straight into the fire, arching in hideous
pain as it becomes smoke. He loses his grip and drops the knife. He
scrabbles in the mud and picks up something else instead, a small
shining thing: the crucifix, Amber's talisman. Ellie's got her arms free
now and has picked up the knife instead. Someone leaps over their
heads. Soph's screeching in pain and Ellie's trying to hold her still,
cutting her free. A man lands beside them, stares for a strange breathless instant in sad confusion, and then crumples like empty clothes

as the beast springs at his face. There's a wet gurgle and a ripping noise. The beast flings back its blood-matted head and howls again, a sound which obliterates every single thought and feeling beyond the last-ditch instinct to run.

Clutching the crucifix, Rory runs.

He can't stop. It's like his legs have a mind of their own, with only one idea in it, which is *go faster or die.* He'd never known before what it actually means to run for your life, but it turns out his legs do. No matter how often he stumbles, no matter how the rough ground of the heath tries to slow him down, they won't stop. His laces come undone: they keep running. His lungs burn and his eyes water so badly he can't really see: they keep running. There are people running past him sometimes, big men clothed in the skins of dogs with knives in their belts and boots: he takes no more notice of them than they do of him. Each time one of them drops in despairing silence under a grey-black snarling blur and doesn't get up again his legs just make him go even faster. Once a man tries to grab him as their paths converge, not in rage but with the frantic helpless clutch of a toddler seeking its last comfort. Rory ducks away from the desperate hand. The man trips in the treacherous heather, falls, and there's a tearing crunching sound, and maybe the faintest ghost of a moan.

His legs keep running.

The ground under them turns from heather to tussocky yellow grass pocked with soft snagging holes. He tumbles down, pushes himself up, runs. There's a ditch shin-deep in foul icy water. He sprints into it and scrabbles up the far side and keeps running. He crosses a road and runs into a waste of ivy and nettle, each step a struggle with snarling undergrowth. His heart feels big as a balloon and heavy as water and it's going to burst soon: his legs won't stop. He's running on and down, whichever way allows him to keep going, over or through a stony hedge into a field of dry bracken and tall weeds, stumbling now with nothing but slaughter behind him and no one beside him except the rasping pounding echo of his breath, but still his feet forbid him to slow down. At the far end of the field is a line of trees. Everything's blurry and spotted with phantom stars of pain but the trees look like shelter. His legs are about to shake themselves into pieces and he's got the worst stitch in history but still he keeps going across the field towards that promise of an end, until he senses a black shadow at his back and the conviction that he's going to die *now* locks his legs at last: he drops.

The shadow passes over his head, perfectly silent, and glides away out of sight beyond the line of trees. It's the angel.

Fighting for breath, Rory looks over his shoulder. No one. On the horizon behind him the satellite dishes are veiled in a pall of smoke.

It turns out he can't stand up. He grits his teeth and crawls through the shoulder-high weeds. The hedge at the far end of the field is submerged in bramble but he finds an old gate wreathed in bindweed, trumpet flowers all turned south to the sun. Beyond it there are woods, a long domain of silence. Its floor is all undisturbed leaves. He can't manage to get over the gate but he forces himself between its bars. He drags himself as far as he can under the canopy of autumn branches. There at last he has to stop.

III

***

Fairy Tale

24

e's prodded out of a reverie of exhaustion by a scampering noise among the leaves. The thin undergrowth parts nearby and a little russet animal scoots out, sees him, and stops on the spot, pointy ears twitching. A matching one runs out behind the first, snapping at its bottlebrush tail until it too catches sight of Rory slumped between the roots of an old tree and skids to a halt. Foxes, he thinks, slowly. (Slowly's the best he can do.) Baby ones. Identical, except that the second one has a torn ear and a small but nasty wound in its fur below it. They look at him. He looks at them. He's been doing nothing for a while except waiting for his heart and lungs to feel like they fit in his chest again, so he's not thinking about danger, in fact about anything at all, but he does (slowly) remember that baby animals are fine but you have to be careful because whenever you see babies that usually means somewhere close by there's—

The straggly saplings twitch again and a tall fox prances into view. The first little one twists around.

"Mum!" it says. "Look!"

The adult lunges forward and nips its tail. "What have I told you two about running ahead?" it says. It lifts a forepaw and cuffs one of the babies, knocking it over. Both small ones slink behind their mother, keeping their keen little eyes fixed on Rory.

He'd been starting to think about getting to his feet and moving slowly away. Now he's just sitting there. His mouth might have dropped open.

A fourth fox steps lazily into the clearing around Rory's tree. It's bigger than the female, lean, high-shouldered. It pauses when it sees Rory, then steps around the other foxes and sits down in front of him. It licks its nose, exposing for a moment a muzzleful of nasty teeth.

"Sometimes, Sharon," it says, "I despair of these children."

"It's only a little one, Dad!" squeaks one of the babies.

"It still might be dangerous," the female says. "You've got to be more careful. How many times do I have to tell you?"

The words are all quite clear. They've even got a foxy sort of accent.

"But Mum—"

"And don't answer back."

"Hello there, young fellow," the big fox says. He says "fellow" *fella* and "hello" *'ello*.

"Why's Dad talking to it?"

"Hush!"

"But we're hungry, Mum!"

The big fox glances round at the babies. "Would you remove that child, Shaz, if she can't keep quiet while I'm trying to have a conversation?"

"I've told you a hundred times never to interrupt your father," the mother whispers, cuffing the baby with the torn ear again.

"Sorry about that," the big fox says to Rory. "Kids. You try your best."

Rory's not at all sure what would happen if he tried to use his throat and mouth to make a sound, so he just stares.

"You'll be too young for all of that, of course," the fox goes on. It scratches its chin with a hind leg. "My mistake. We don't see a lot of juveniles around here, as a rule, that's what threw me off. Can't think of any, in fact. Shaz? Have we ever had a juvenile in here before?"

"What about that one with the thing on its head?"

The big fox's ears twitch. " 'Thing on its head'?"

"You remember. Tasted of clover."

"Oh, that one. No. No, that one was fully grown. Just naturally small. They vary quite a bit."

"Is it OK to eat the joo-viles?"

"Juveniles." The fox stretches its neck towards Rory. "Do excuse the missus. Yes, perfectly all right. Though they can be a bit bland."

"I'm hungry," one of the little ones whines.

"Cyrus!" The mother nips at its neck.

"Don't eat me," Rory says. It's the first—in fact, the only—thing he can think of to say. Habit compels him to add, "Please."

All the foxes stare at him.

"Why on earth not?" says the father.

Rory's having vague thoughts about getting to his feet and running away, but even in his current state he can see there's no point. The fox is surprisingly big up close, and it's planted itself near enough to him that they'd be in the same room if this was a house. "I haven't done anything to you," he says.

"What?"

"I haven't done anything. I'll just go and leave you alone. I swear."

"What's that got to do with anything?" It doesn't sound at all angry. If anything, it has an air of being rather pleased with itself. "It's just food, isn't it? What do you eat, normally?"

"Er," Rory says. "Fish."

"There you are, then. None of them fish ever did anything to you, did they? There they are, swimming around minding their own business, and you just up and snap them out of the water and bang, munch away. It's nothing personal, is it? Just how we all get on."

"I hope you're listening to your father," the mother says, in a foxy stage whisper.

"Nature," the big fox goes on. "Nothing sentimental about it. That's the problem with your poetry and all that."

"How come you can talk?" Rory blurts.

The fox angles its head and then answers, "How come *you* can?"

"But normally—" Rory can't tell whether he's more frightened, tired, or just plain confused. "I thought it was just people."

"I wouldn't like to say what's normal from where you're sitting.

Though they do say there's different conditions as obtains here-abouts. Different from what, now, I couldn't tell you. All relative, isn't it, when you think about it."

A thought drops on Rory like it's grown on the branch above and now wants to demonstrate gravity. "Is this the Valley?"

"Sharon?"

"Yes, dear?" The female's been nosing the cubs, who are getting fidgety.

"The Valley? Sound familiar at all?"

"Some of them call it that, don't they?"

"I think you'll find I was asking you."

"Sorry, Phil."

"Never mind."

"Are you going to be much longer? The kids are getting—"

The big fox silences her with a glare, before turning back to Rory after a suitably dignified pause.

"It's certainly *a* valley, if that helps. Characterful little spot. Not too many of your sort crashing around these days either, which I must say counts for something. Used to dribble in in ones and twos but not so much anymore. They never seemed to last long anyway. Much like yourself in that respect."

"Phil?"

"Now what?"

"You've upset it."

"Please," Rory says. "Can't you just let me go?"

"Well," the big fox says, doubtfully, "I *could*. But it wouldn't be very sensible."

"It's not fair to spin it out, Phil."

The big fox whirls around and snaps its jaws. "Excuse me! I'd actually prefer to be allowed to speak, thanks very much."

"Do get on with it then, there's a love. It's only a little one."

"Sharon, I'm disappointed in you. What do you think little Per-simmon's thinking, listening to you twitter on about whether her lunch is getting upset? Did that big oaf yesterday give anyone else a moment's thought when he pegged our cub with a bloody great stone? Might have knocked her brains clean out."

"I'm hungry, Dad!" wails the one with the torn ear, but the father has already turned back to Rory.

"I ask you," he says. "All the poor little nipper wanted to do was watch. Lucky to be alive, is Persimmon, after the clout that stone fetched her. An inch or two the other way and . . ." The fox shivers. "I don't like to think. My fault, really. I shouldn't have let them get that close. But we were quite enjoying it, until that lummox started flinging missiles. Weren't we, kids? Wasn't that fun, yesterday? Watching all the people go by, sitting on them horses?"

"'Simmon got pranged in her ear'ole!" squeaks one of the cubs.

"Phil," the mother says. "You're going on again."

"Am I? I suppose I am. Sorry, young fellow. Sharon's always telling me I'm a bit too fond of the sound of my own voice, aren't you, Shaz?"

The female coughs a short bark.

"Right, then." The big fox stands up, arches its back, stretches. "Let's get on with it."

"Wait," says Rory.

"Best not to, in all honesty."

"No. Wait. Wait!" The fox has taken a couple of loping steps towards him. He pushes himself to his feet, his back against the tree trunk. "I saw that! Yesterday. I was there. Wolf, he was called. He chucked that stone." The fox has paused, ears twitching. "I can . . ." Rory stammers, "I can tell you what happened to him. After. He's dead. Wolf is. The man who did it."

"Dad?" says the fox with the damaged ear. The father is standing still. He smells of the woods, very pungently.

"He got killed by the Pack. By their dogs. He got torn apart."

"I'm not a hundred percent sure," the big fox begins, "what the point—"

"The guy who, who hit your—" Rory points shakily at the injured cub. He almost says *that* but corrects himself in time. "Her. With the stone. He got killed that night."

The fox's tail twitches.

"Horribly," Rory adds.

There's a longish pause.

"And?" the big fox says.

A branch overhead dips heavily, rustling. Both Rory and the fox look up. The owl's appeared there. It settles, opens its hooked beak, and makes its cry, not a hoot at all but a sort of repeated cough, worryingly close to laughter.

"And," Rory says, feeling a surge of deranged confidence, "and, God talked to me. Just now. This morning."

The fox sits again.

"Dad!" yelp the cubs together.

"This is all a bit deep," the father says, ignoring them, and ignoring his mate as well, who's slumped to the soft floor of decaying leaves in an attitude of resignation. "You're not . . ." It cranes its neck very, very close to Rory's chest, and sniffs. "*Lying,* are you?"

"No. I swear."

"I can't understand the trick of it, but they say you lot are born knowing how to. Like those thumb jobbies you've got."

"I'm not. I promise. It's all true."

"Are you telling me that chap who nearly took Persimmon's ear off has just been eaten?"

"Torn to bits," Rory says, nodding overenthusiastically.

"Hang on." The fox pauses to lick a foreleg. "Would this be an example of . . ." It shifts around as if embarrassed. "That poetic thing. Poetic whatsit. What is it, what is it, poetic . . ."

"Justice!" Rory almost yelps himself. "Yes. That's it. Exactly."

"I see," the fox says, very unconvincingly.

"Phil? What's going on?"

"Put a sock in it, Shaz," it snaps. "I'm trying to think."

"About what?"

"You wouldn't understand."

"'Course I wouldn't. 'Cause it's bollocks. Either kill it or don't kill it, just do us all a favor and don't stand there waffling like you know what justits is."

"Justice!" the big fox barks, losing its temper. "And I do know perfectly well what it is, which is not something every fox in the world can say."

"Well, what is it, then?"

"It's not a simple thing to explain. Quite tricky to put into words, in fact. It's, how shall I put it. It's . . ."

"It means you have to let me go," Rory says quickly.

"Exactly! Wait!" The fox snaps its head back towards him. "Does it?"

"Yes," Rory says. "That's how it works."

"Mum! You kill it!"

The female lays its long snout on the ground. "If only," she sighs.

"You have to," Rory says. "Because I told you about it. So it all evens out. And don't forget." His mouth is running away with him. "God."

"Right," the fox says.

"That's the most important bit."

The fox eyes his family. "As you lot would know," he says, "if any of you ever took the time to give it a bit of thought, instead of running around in the woods not looking where you're going."

Rory backs around the tree. His legs feel tight and stringy but they're doing the job still, somehow. "OK then," he says. The owl flits down behind him and glides to a perch deeper in the woods. "Bye."

"It's not as complicated as it sounds," the big fox is saying, as Rory turns his back.

"Dad! It's running away!"

Which is overstating it, since the best he can do is a cramped and plodding jog, but they're not coming after him, so he pushes on, following the owl because there's nothing else to follow. "Look," he hears the fox say, "why don't we all try some fish instead?" Rory stumbles away into the shadows under the trees, and dives for a hole in the trunk, escaping just in time.

25

The wood grows thicker and darker the farther in he goes, which seems right. It's full of whispers and half-glimpsed things. He's quite sure at one point that he passes a big-nosed man no taller than his shins who's hacking away at a rhododendron bush with a tiny golden axe and stops to mop his brow as Rory looks on. But Rory doesn't look for long. He has to keep a careful eye on the owl. It's very easy to lose sight of it in the tawny autumn trees.

They come to a tiny stream, really just a trickle in the mud. He lies flat to drink and discovers he's too exhausted to get up again. At least the water gets the taste of sick out of his throat. Throwing up's stopped him feeling hungry, which is something too.

The owl watches him from a bough while he lies there in the leaf mold. It looks annoyed with him but it doesn't say anything. Perhaps if it did start talking it would be in Italian anyway. He'd like to get moving but it's actually strangely peaceful here, wherever he is. "Sorry," he says to the owl.

He tries to decide whether it really is Lino or not, and discovers something quite interesting. The difficulty turns out not to be about trying to figure out which of the alternatives (is Lino, isn't Lino) is correct; it's more that he doesn't know what *really* means.

It reminds him of a conversation he had with Her once. He'd been trying to explain to her that she didn't exist, not properly, not the way his mother and Laurel and Pink and Kate and all the others did. (He must have grown up a lot since then, he thinks. He'd never talk like that now.)

—But you weren't there *before.*

—Where?

—Anywhere. You weren't . . . There wasn't any such thing.

—That's a funny thing to say.

—There wasn't. I remember. Everyone knows. You could sail around wherever you liked. There were lots of boats in The Old Days. All over the place.

—I remember that too. I remember watching them.

—No one ever saw anything like you. You weren't . . . You just weren't. Things like that didn't happen.

(She waits for him to finish, curious.)

—They're not real. You're not. Not, like, really real.

(He thinks she's going to get cross. He'd quite like her to get cross, actually, because then maybe she'd tell him why he was wrong, and explain What Happened. But—)

—Still. (She smiles her funny lopsided smile.) Here I am.

And here Rory is, in the Valley. He wonders how big it is. It feels like somewhere you'd measure in a way that wasn't to do with distances.

He's heard many times by now that no one ever comes back, but it's not frightening. It's very beautiful. There's none of the debris from The Old Days at all, not even the cap of a plastic bottle or a scrap of a soggy label sticking out among the dead leaves. It feels untouched. He's alone and completely lost but as he lies there listening to the trickle of water beside his head he doesn't feel like he's going to wander around hopelessly until he dies of starvation and exposure. It doesn't feel like that sort of place. It feels more organized. Like it knows what it's doing, even if it's not telling you. He can well believe that no one ever comes back from it, because it doesn't seem like the kind of place you'd go in and out of, like it was just sitting there waiting for you to decide what to do. He supposes he'll never get out of it either but at the moment that doesn't seem to matter so much. He doesn't feel so much lost as *found.*

When he's had his rest he gets to his feet. The owl swoops away at once and he limps after it. It's leading him down a slope. Every direction is just trees. He comes to a patch of evergreen shrubs and loses sight of the owl there, but he can see clearer ground beyond so he keeps going anyway, squeezing through the dead-looking twiggy bits inside the shrubs. He wriggles out onto a grassy path just in time to see the bird flit out of sight over its far end, where the roof of a house is poking out between yellowing trees.

There's a skeleton lying on the path. It has boots on its feet, trousers on its legs, and a coat on its back, but thin bones stick out of the cuffs of the coat and the head's just a skull. A few spears of grass have grown up through the eye sockets. Stopping to look, Rory notices bits of more skeletons in the hedge beside the path, mostly hidden in the tangle. The toes of a pair of running shoes poke out from the bottom of the hedge.

A small thing neither animal nor person scurries out from a bunch of leathery leaves. "Travelers!" it says. It has arms and legs and a stumpy top bit like a miniature man but it's all woody and gnarly, wound around with cobwebby scraps. It's carrying something rattly in a tiny cup like the cap of an acorn. It races out onto the path in front of Rory and addresses itself to him. "Game of chance, sir?" The voice is crabbed and wheezy-croaky. It shakes the tiny cup. "Throw of the dice? Cast your fate in fortune's lap?"

"No, thank you," Rory says, looking for the owl.

"A question if you win. Any question you like. Answer guaranteed as honest as language allows. Go on, sir." It rattles the cup in a manner which is probably supposed to be enticing. "You know you want to."

He'd like to walk past but he's having difficulty doing so. The owl's disappeared, and the grotesque miniature thing keeps positioning itself so he feels like he'll step on it unless he stays still. "I'm all right," he says. "Thanks."

" 'All right,' says he. That's a good one. Me oh my. All right, are you? Don't you want to ask how to get out of here? Most do." It jiggles in a way which might be intended to indicate the skeleton in the grass. "All of them, actually. Tell you what, sir. I'll double my offer, how's that? Two questions if you win. You get all the time you want to decide what to ask. I'd suggest along the lines of *How do I escape the Valley* and *Will I make it out alive*, but up to you, of course, up to you."

"I'd rather not."

The thing growls in frustration. "Three, then! Three questions. And no more haggling, three's my limit."

"Really," Rory says, wondering if he can just kick the thing out of the way, though he doesn't like the idea of touching it at all. "I'm fine."

"Do you doubt me? Is that it? Here." It holds up the cup as high as it can, about the level of Rory's knee. "Inspect the dice. Roll them a few times if you like, you'll find they land fairly and without favor. One throw each, highest total wins. What's not to like?"

"What happens if I lose?"

"Oh! Well." Its voice drops to a sort of gargling mumble. "The usual penalty."

"The what?"

"Standard sort of thing. You know, your soul, or something of the— Now hold on, sir! Don't be hasty!" Rory's jumped around the skeleton to the edge of the path and is already hurrying past. "It's nothing to worry about, surely?" It's making no attempt to pursue him, just cawing at his back. "Mainstream opinion these days holds that you probably don't even have a soul! One game? Please?" Against the most strenuous protest from his legs, he forces himself to break into a run again. When he looks over his shoulder nothing's there but old bones in the grass.

The path brings him to a broken wooden gate and then on to the back of a broken house. It's a big grey low-slung old-looking house traced with moss and ivy all the way to its roof. Every one of its ground-floor windows is broken; they make a gallery of abstract pictures composed of glinting glass and darkness. The gutters hang like half-snapped branches. There's no junk around, nevertheless. A meadow of wild grass has grown up around the house. Best of all, there's a huge patch of bramble bursting out of the woods, and it's thick with blackberries. He sets to work on them hungrily. They're unbelievably sour-sweet and ripe. He works his way along the bramble until he finds himself around the other side of the house, the front. There are big hedges of box and yew here, once carefully sculpted but now bulging and sagging. A flight of stone steps leads down between them to some other buildings. There's a signpost covered in bindweed. Curious, Rory pulls the tendrils away to read the signs. Down the steps they point to TOILETS CAFÉ SHOP COMMUNITY CENTER. In the other direction, TRELOW HOUSE MAIN GATE CAR PARK. *Café?* he thinks, peering down the steps, and sees Silvia.

26

The owl chooses that moment to reappear. It sails over Rory's head, making its *whuk whuk whuk* call, and lands on top of the barn she's just stepped out from.

Rory watches, waiting for her to vanish like she did when the Riders were fording the stream in the haunted town. She doesn't. She's staring back at him. Her arms are fidgeting in a nervous, very un-Silvia-like way. She doesn't look pleased to see him. She looks almost alarmed. It's like she's never seen him before.

She starts towards him. It's very cluttered and overgrown where she is, a sort of courtyard in the middle of a group of beaten-up barns. She picks her away around the bowl of a broken fountain and stops, her route blocked by a barrier of upended picnic tables and a tangle of wires trailing loose from a solitary pole. The owl rasps again.

It's definitely Silvia, but at the same time it isn't. The difference is in her manner. She's got the same face and everything but she seems completely different on the inside. She looks like she's lost her way.

She stops on a buckled paving stone at the base of the steps.

"Hello?" she says. She appears not to know who Rory is. Something's been erased from her. She looks (he gets it suddenly) *younger*, not in her face but in every other way. "English? Hello?"

"Um," Rory says. This is frightening. It's like looking at someone he knows but with a different person inside them. "What d'you mean, English?"

She lights up with mingled relief and surprise. "You speak Romani!"

"Silvia?"

The light vanishes. She flinches as if he's aimed a punch at her. "Who told you my name?"

"Silvia, it's—"

As suddenly as her relief turned to suspicion, the suspicion now turns into eager excitement. "Was it her? You must have seen her! Where is she?"

"Where's who?"

"The English lady! She came up here somewhere but I can't find her." Clearly exasperated by Rory's bewilderment, she stamps her foot. "The tall English lady! Didn't she tell you to look for me? Where did you see her?"

Rory stands with his mouth open. It's definitely Silvia, but it's like she's pretending to be a little girl.

"Please," she says. "She's my friend. She's going to take me to England and adopt me. I can't find her anywhere. She was going to visit the temple in the night. She said she'd be back before I woke up but I've been awake for ages. You must have seen her. A woman by herself. She's tall; she's got black hair. Not an old woman. Why won't you talk to me? What's wrong with you?"

"I . . ." He has to say something. "I don't know what you're talking about."

Her lip trembles. Her hands make fists. "Did something happen to her? Where's the temple? Can you show me how to get there?"

Rory looks back at the big house. It's quite grand and old but no one would describe it as a temple. "Where's what?"

"The temple of Apollo. It's famous, you must know it. It's in these hills somewhere. It must be along this road but I can't read the signs, I don't know all the Greek letters."

"Who are you?" Rory whispers, wondering whether he ought to start getting properly frightened.

"I'm Silvia Ghinda. I'm going to be Silvia Ghinda Clifton when Ygraine adopts me. Clifton's her name. It's English. Who are you? You don't look like a Roma boy."

"Rory," he says. He wants this to stop, now. "I'm Rory. Don't you remember?"

"Rory? That's not a Roma name."

"It's Scottish. I told you."

She frowns in childlike confusion. "I don't understand you," she says. "Do you live here?"

"Here?" It strikes him that he can't even begin to say where *here* is.

"Can you read the signs for me?" She's too anxiously impatient to wait for an answer. "If we keep going up the road we're bound to see one."

There's something about her eyes. It's like she's not taking things in. She doesn't look or sound mad, but she must be mad. She's turning this way and that, peering as if waiting for someone else to appear.

"Which road do you mean?" he says cautiously.

"This one, obviously. Or are there others? Is there another way?" She comes up one step and examines him carefully, as if he's the mad one. "Are you all right?"

Perhaps he isn't. He's just been talking to a bunch of foxes, after all.

"Silvia," he says. "It's me. I want to help you but I don't know what you're talking about."

Her eyes moisten. "Why is everyone so stupid?" she shouts, but it's a sad anger, feeble, defeated, not like Silvia's fiery contempt at all. She cups her hands around her mouth and calls, "Ygraine! Ygraine!"

"Don't you remember any of it?" Rory says. "Lino? Per? We came on the boat together. I wasn't supposed to be with you but I came by mistake. The beach? Any of that?" All he's doing is frightening her. "You really can't remember?"

"Something's wrong with you," she whispers, after a long pause.

Why is he pressing on? It must be because he so badly wants this to be Silvia, someone who'll look after him and show him what to do. He won't be lost if he's with her because the real Silvia can't get lost, she told him so herself. "All those things you told me on the boat? You told me all about yourself, remember? The orphanage? And that camp with the old woman, where you lived." She makes a squeaky gasping noise and puts her hand to her mouth in shock. She does remember, then. "Where they made you tell people's fortunes or whatever? And then that teacher rescued you—"

She springs up the steps and grabs him. Ordinarily it would be scary but her hands feel weak and her face is full of desperation. "Please tell me where she is," she says. "I'll do anything. I'll give you the car. It's down in that village. Look, I've got the keys." She pats the pockets of her coat distractedly. "We've got some money too, I'll give you all of it."

She looks so terribly sad that Rory surprises himself by putting a hand on her cheek, like he's seen Viola do with Pink; like Kate's done to him sometimes when no one else would. "Silvia," he says. "It's me. Rory. I haven't seen anyone else. I don't know what you mean."

She stares at him, wide-eyed. She folds her coat over herself as if she's cold.

"Sorry," he adds.

"How did you know my name?"

"We met. You don't remember. Something's happened to you. We're friends." She's shaking her head. "I wish you could remember. I was so happy to see you."

"Are you from the orphanage?"

"I'm not."

She backs away. "You must be. You're lying. You must have followed us all the way here."

"Where?"

"How could you have done that? You're not old enough to drive." She stares around wildly. Whenever she's looking away from him her eyes don't seem to focus properly. "You're with someone! Is it the police?"

Rory's beginning to understand, if *understand*'s the right word. "I'm not with anyone, I promise. Silvia?"

"Did the police catch her?"

"Where do you think we are?"

"What?"

"Tell me." He tries to keep his voice gentle. "Where is this?"

She peers at him again, keeping her distance this time. "What do you mean? Arcadia? Do you mean this road? I don't know where it goes."

Rory points back at the big house. "What's that?" he says.

She looks over his shoulder, shielding her eyes from an absent sun. "What? Where?"

"Behind me. What can you see?"

"There's nothing there. Just more mountains. Is that where the temple is?" She puts her hand to her mouth and shouts again, "Ygraine!" There's no echo. Everything's soft, shrouded in rampant growth.

"You're looking for someone, aren't you."

"Ygraine!" She twists around and shouts louder. "Ygraine! Can you hear me?"

"Is it the English teacher you told me about? The one who took you from the camp?"

She backs away from him again, all the way down the steps. He hates seeing her so frightened.

"I don't like you," she says. "You're scaring me."

"It's all right. Don't worry."

"Do you want her to adopt you instead? Is that why you followed us? She won't. She chose me. I'm special; I have a gift. We've already arranged it all. We're going to Kyparissa tomorrow to get on a boat."

"I'm not trying to do anything like that. Something's happened to you, Silvia. I just want to help."

"Leave me alone." She's edging back towards the courtyard with the broken fountain. The owl's still perched on a roof beyond, watching. "Go away."

He puts his hands out to show he's not going to do anything bad. "How old are you?" he says.

"I can look after myself," she says. "You better not try anything."

"I'm not going to, I swear," he says. "How old are you? Please?"

She draws herself up. "I'm twelve," she says. "And I can fight. Don't think I won't because I'm a girl."

"Silvia," Rory says sadly. "You're not twelve."

"I am!"

"Look at yourself."

She looks at her hands. "All right!" She's beginning to get angry now as well as frightened. "I'm only ten. But I've fought lots of boys like you." He's walking carefully down the steps towards her. He's afraid she's going to start running and he can't bear the thought of losing sight of her even if she is mad. "Stop following me!" she says. She backs away faster, trips over the leg of a green plastic chair and falls with a clatter among the upended picnic tables. "Ow!"

He's got to stop talking to her like she's Silvia, he realizes. He's got to imagine she's Pink, except not annoying. "Careful," he says. "It's OK, I don't want to fight."

"Who are you?" She sits up, rubbing her knee. "How did you get here?"

"You've forgotten," he says. "You don't realize but I promise you have. Why don't you tell me what you remember, all right? That might help. How did you get here?"

She's jutting her chin out at him. "I remember you now," she says, quite obviously lying. "I remember all the orphanage kids. I remember all about you. I know what you're after."

He goes around the tumbled picnic tables, giving her a wide berth so he won't scare her worse. He's near the fountain now. It's a big dirty stone bowl under loops of twirly metal, which are where the water would have come down when it was working. It's full to the brim with rainwater. Yellowing leaves mottle the surface.

"I'm not from the orphanage," he says. "I'm not following you. I never thought I'd see you here. Please don't be scared."

"I'm not scared!"

"Something weird's happened to both of us. What's . . . What's the last thing you remember?"

She stands up carefully, dusting herself off (though there's no dust).

"Swear you're not with the police?" she says.

"I swear. I bet we're the only two people for miles."

"Where's your family?" She looks around. She's hemmed in by the pile of tables.

"Nowhere near," he says. "I'm a bit lost too. That's why I was so happy to see you."

"I just want to find Ygraine," she says.

"Maybe we can look together."

She seems a bit less nervous. "Could I have gone the wrong way out of the village? Is there really a temple around here? It's so empty. It looks like the middle of nowhere."

He makes a face like he's thinking about it. "I think there is, actually," he says. "Far as I know."

"She said it's a temple to Apollo. He's the god of prophecy. I bet you didn't know that."

"Wow," Rory says. "Is he?"

"That's my gift. So she was going to walk to his temple, just to see it. She left in the night; she wanted to be back before I woke up. I wonder if she got lost."

It's almost funny, Rory thinks. She's an abandoned child, just like me.

"That's probably it," he says. "Bet I can help you." Saying that, he glances down at the leaves floating in the bowl of the fountain and has an idea. "Hey," he says. "Can you come here? I want to show you something."

She plants her feet and glares. "What?"

"It might help you remember."

"You keep saying that. I think you're crazy."

"No, please. How old did you say you were? Twelve? Look, I'll show you something's happened to you." He gently sweeps the leaves to the edge of the bowl. "Here. Don't worry, it's nothing bad."

"What are you doing?" She comes towards him. "What's that? There's nothing there, is there?"

Although she obviously thinks she's somewhere else she still steps around the plastic chair, so, Rory thinks, there must be some bit of her that's still here, wherever *here* is. He fishes a few of the leaves out of the fountain. They're lobed, oak leaves. A few acorns are bobbing around in the water too, blown down with them. He scoops them out too, trying to disturb the surface as little as possible. "What have you got there?" she says.

Maybe if he gives her something from *here* she'll understand that she can't really be *there*? "Acorns," he says. "See? I just picked them

up." He reaches out and puts them in her hand, one two three four
five smooth nuts in nubbled caps.

She frowns at them. "Where did you get those?"

"From the fountain. Look." The water's smooth again, a dark
mirror. He takes her hand and leads her gently to the edge of the
bowl. "Look at yourself," he says. "Look, Silvia. You're not twelve.
You're grown up. You left the orphanage and all that ages ago. You
met Lino and Per. You were all coming to England. You always know
where you're going, you told me. You've got to remember." She's staring down into the water, her eyes wide and clear. "It's your gift," he
says, leaning over beside her.

There's a third face reflected in the water.

Rory's had a complicated sort of day, by any standards, but this
is the most intimately uncanny thing that's happened to him yet.

First, he sees the face: a man's face—a tall man, it must be, because he's behind Rory, leaning over him—reflected quite clearly.
That's OK. But second, he's aware that there's no man standing
behind him, where his reflection says he ought to be; that's less OK.
But third, he's quite sure that the man *is* in fact standing at his back
even though he appears not to be. And that's not the end of it, because fourth and strangest of all, he knows that the reflection man
is also the man with the yellow coat who appeared out of nowhere
by the gorse bush where Rory was hiding from the Black Pack and
said things about God, and he knows this even though the reflection
man has a different face. As to *how* he knows that it's the same man,
even though the reflection man's face is younger, smoother, perfect
in some way there's no word for (*perfect* isn't quite good enough),
Rory couldn't say, not even if someone put a gun to his head and
threatened to shoot him if he didn't explain. He can't explain. He
just knows. It's completely obvious, plain as day.

Silvia's transfixed. She's stopped talking. She's staring at herself
in rapt silence. As Rory gawps, she reaches her hand to her collar
and pulls out the little pouch thing she's got tied there like a secret
necklace. She looses the top of the pouch and drops the acorns in,
one two three four five.

Something too big and dark to be a thought revolves wordlessly and mightily in Rory's mind, like the whole universe turning itself upside down around him.

"I have walked at her shoulder all her life," the reflection man says. His voice comes from the place over Rory's shoulder where he ought to be standing. Although (on reflection) Rory's not sure about that either: maybe it's coming from everywhere and everything. "But she can't see me, or hear me."

"What's happened to her?"

Rory's pretty sure he's talking to God. This would be extraordinarily cool if it was in any way believable.

"Her gift," the man says—you can see his mouth moving, reflected on the surface of the water, framed by the faded leaves of oaks—"is also a curse."

"Can you fix it?"

The man laughs. It's like a bundled sheaf of sunlight. "No," he says.

"Is she going to be all right?"

"She has come," the man says, "where she was going. This is the end of the road. I am the light she sought. I am here."

"You mean she's going to die here?"

"To you"—Rory feels the reflection man's attention turn to him; it's like a mountain moving—"I do not prophesy."

"What's that mean?"

"To you." The shadow of the mountain falls on him. "I do not prophesy."

"You should cure her. If you've been with her all your life." Rory swallows. "It's not fair to leave her like this."

"Among my many names is the name *Destroyer*."

"So you're a bad god."

"And I am the *Youth*. And *He of the White Hands*. I am *Far-Aiming* and *Shining* and *The One Who Compels the Muses*. And I am *Helper*."

Rory interrupts to save himself. The names feel like they're piling up on him like an avalanche. "Why don't you help her, then?" Silvia's staring at her reflection as though she's a reflection too, they both are, neither able to move first and so both stuck forever.

"I have told you the truth. Have you forgotten? So my gift goes. It is the truth that will always be denied."

"I haven't, actually," he says, annoyed. "I do remember." And, saying so, he does. The trick is to concentrate on the fact that the reflection man is the same as the yellow-coat man who spoke to him before. "You said you . . . You said God's everything which people can't . . ." He can't remember the exact words. It was right before the foreigner turned into a dog-beast and ripped the big hairy man's throat out: there was a lot going on. "You said God doesn't care."

The reflected face smiles, and in doing so becomes so beautiful Rory can feel the image of it burning itself into the back of his eyes.

"Shall I tell you why you have lived to reach this place, when so many before you have died?" It's not a proper question—God doesn't care—so Rory just listens. "It is because you are unsurprised. You do not doubt yourself. I am the Helper. Make me your offering and I will help."

"What d'you mean, offering?"

"Make me your offering and I will help."

"No, thanks," Rory says. He's not doing deals with a bad god.

The god's smile becomes, if anything, brighter. If it wasn't reflected in dark water he thinks it would actually turn him to ash.

"You," the voice says, "are wiser than many. Here," it finishes. Or it could be *Hear*, or perhaps both words at the same time, because as soon as the god finishes speaking a telephone begins to ring.

It's very loud, startlingly loud in that empty soft waste space, and it makes Rory's head jerk away. As soon as he moves the god's gone. Silvia steps back from the fountain with a vaguely puzzled expression. The phone keeps ringing. She turns her hands in front of her eyes as if wondering who they belong to.

"Are you all right?" Rory says. The phone's horribly insistent.

Silvia opens her mouth, shuts it, then slumps to her knees. She doesn't look like a child anymore. She doesn't look like anything. Something inside her has been completely switched off.

"Silvia?"

She mouths the word back at him without looking—*Silvia*—but makes no sound. The shrill ringing nags.

"I'll just get that," Rory says. "OK? Wait here."

She doesn't seem to understand but since she's kneeling in the junk looking blank he thinks she's probably not going anywhere now. He hurries around bushes of woody lavender and scraps of broken pottery into what used to be the café, where the noise is coming from. The phone's in a whitewashed side corridor, in a niche by a window. It's a dusty yellow pay phone. In the corridor between him and the phone someone's hung a length of knotted tablecloths from a beam in the ceiling and put a plastic table under them, like they were trying to escape through solid wood from an invisible prison. The phone rings and rings, daring him to answer.

Just as he's putting his hand on the receiver he remembers something the old man at the crossroads told Silvia: *They say in the heart of the Valley there's a room with a phone, and if you use it you can speak to the dead.*

He picks it up anyway. He's grateful for the silence.

27

ho's there?

"Hello?"

Rory! Oh, thank God!

"Mum?"

I'm so glad you called. I've been worried about you.

"Is that you, Mum?"

Is everything all right?

"Yeah. Everything's fine."

Oh, good. Good. I don't know why I'd got so worried.

"Where are you, Mum?"

I'm . . . Never mind that. Where on earth have you been?

"I'm sorry, Mum. It was an accident."

Well, as long as you're OK now.

"Yeah. I'm OK."

You should have called before.

"I know. Sorry. I couldn't, I got caught up in stuff."

Anyway, you're here now. That's the main thing. Isn't it?

"Yeah. Yeah, it is."

I was worried . . .

"What, Mum?"

For some reason I was worried I wouldn't be able to talk to you again.

"Really?"

Yes. Stupid of me to worry like that.

"That's OK."

You'll understand if you ever have children of your own. One day.
"I suppose."
Well. At least it all worked out.
"Yeah."
And you're sure you're all right?
"Yeah. Are you . . ."
What did you say?
"I was wondering if you're at home."
Home? Where else would I be?
"Just wondering."
Where do you think I am?
"It's nothing, Mum. Just wondering. Don't worry."
I'm not . . . I'm not sure . . .
"So how are you? How's everything been?"
Oh, you know, Rory. Same as usual. It's so nice we can talk like this!
"Yeah."
I've missed you.
"Me too. Missed you, I mean."
For some reason I thought you were . . .
"Don't think about that."
About what? No. You're quite right. Sensible Rory.
"Yeah."
Funny, the things you start imagining.
"I know."
So. It's late, isn't it? Is it? You must be tired. After . . . Everything.
"Not too bad."
Do you have everything you need?
"Yeah. Think so."
Glass of water? You should have one by the bed.
"OK."
Got your comics? For the morning?
"I think I lost them, actually."
Lost your comics?
"I think so."
Oh no! Where?

"I'm . . . I'm not sure exactly. Don't worry. Actually, you know what, I'm sure I've got some left."

Are you sure?

"Yeah. Yeah, it's fine."

You and your comics. Perhaps we can look for some new ones for you, when we . . . In the morning.

"That'd be nice."

I'm so glad you're here! I thought . . . For some reason I thought . . .

"Don't worry. It's all OK now."

Don't you go off like that again. I was worried sick.

"I won't, I promise. I never meant to. It was an accident."

Well. Never mind. You're back, that's the main thing. You'd better go to sleep now. It's been a long day.

"All right."

I'd give you a hug if . . . It's very dark tonight, isn't it? I can't . . .

"Doesn't matter, Mum. Don't worry about it, remember?"

As long as you're here.

"Yeah."

That's the main thing.

"Yeah."

Sure you've got everything?

"Think so. Yeah."

All right then. Well. It's such a relief! Good night.

"Mum?"

What?

"Love you."

Rory!

"What?"

You don't usually say that!

". . . Sorry."

No, it's nice. It's like tucking you in when you were little. I love you too. Night night now. See you in the morning.

"Night night."

Night.

"Night."

* * *

Later on he goes back out to the fountain. Silvia hasn't moved. He's
been watching her through the window by the phone.

"Silvia?"

She doesn't answer.

"Can you stand up?"

She doesn't answer, let alone stand up. Rory looks up at the owl.
It doesn't fly off anywhere to show him where to go next.

He waits awhile. No one comes along to tell him what to do.
There's no god now, good, bad, or indifferent. There are no talkative
foxes. There don't even seem to be any insects.

His mother is dead.

It's the end of the road.

He wonders whether he's actually dead now too. There were some
apple trees back by the big house but you can't live off apples and
blackberries forever. If nothing goes on happening it doesn't matter
about food anyway, you can't just keep eating and doing nothing else
and say that's the same as being alive.

Or he wonders whether he's like Silvia. She's not dead, as far as he
can see, but she's not alive anymore either. When he speaks to her or
pokes her she either ignores it or frowns a little and looks aside with that
look of someone who's trying to remember what they were just doing.

He wonders how his mother died.

At some stage he gets an idea.

He's been thinking about his mother, and the phone which lets
you talk to dead people, and thinking of that must in turn have made
him think of what the old man said about the Valley, which then
made him think of all the other things "they" say about the Valley,
and he remembers the one about the well which cures every illness of
body or soul, and that sets him wondering whether Silvia would go
back to being herself if she was cured, which makes him think about
whether he could find the well, and that's when he gets the idea.

The last time he remembers coming up with an idea, it ended up with his getting accidentally kidnapped. If he hadn't had that idea, he thinks, he'd still be on Home, with (probably) his mother, waking up in Parson's every morning and going to bed there every night, working day after day with the women so they could all stay alive another week, another season, boring, tiring nonstop work, until they got too old or too few in number.

He stands up.

"I'll be right back," he tells Silvia.

The owl coughs, *whuk whuk whuk*. It doesn't follow him.

28

It's not clear what time of day it is. Fitful sunlight washes over the grassy path. It might be afternoon light but he can't be sure. He stops by the clothed skeleton. He's extremely nervous now. This often happens when you have an idea, he's noticed. You don't actually grasp what's involved until it's right in front of you, and then it suddenly all looks very different.

"Hello?" he says.

The grotesque thing—halfway between an extremely ugly miniature man and a chunk of a rotting branch, with a bit of toad thrown in—pops up from the ground as if from a concealed hole. "Travelers!" it cackles. "Game of ch—Hold on. Weren't you just here?"

"Yeah," Rory says.

It limps closer on warty leg-things. "Not dead yet?"

"Apparently."

"Or mad? A lot of them go stark raving bedlam first."

"I'm OK."

The creature swivels around, making a sniffing noise. "Something funny must be going on."

"Do you still want that game?"

"Say what?"

"That game. With the dice. Do you still want it?"

It goes motionless.

"What are you saying?" it says, very suspiciously.

"I'm up for it now." Rory's feeling a bit sick. This is now feeling like the worst idea in the universe. "If you are."

"Really?"

"Yeah. Long as it's fair. No cheating or anything."

"Cheat? Me? At the game of chance? What would be the point of that? I always win anywaghhagghh." The last word becomes an extended cough. "*Aghkk aghkkk.* Excuse me. That is to say. I always winnow out any possibility of, ahem. Foul play. Yes."

Rory shoves his hands deep in his pockets and closes his eyes for a moment. *Bad god,* he thinks. *Help me out now and I'll give you* . . . His left hand bumps into something. It's Amber's little silver crucifix. He'd forgotten he still had it. *That,* he thinks. *OK?*

"Are you really the irritating little squirt who wouldn't play before?" Rory doesn't feel this deserves an answer. The thing hops closer and appears to study him from below Rory's knee height. "It seems unlikely."

"Well, I want to play now."

"Why the change of heart?"

"You said you'd answer three questions."

"Three? Three? No, no. What on earth do you take me for?"

"Yes you did. You said three."

"That's absurd."

"Well, you did. I'm not playing otherwise." He makes as if to walk away.

"Two," the thing says hurriedly.

"Three questions, or I'm going."

"Oh all right, curse you! It hardly matters anyway, since you won't—" It does a thing like clearing its throat. "Anyway, never mind that. So, on your way back, are you? Did you find what you were after?"

"What would I have been after?"

"How should I know? The fountain of youth. The philosopher's stone. The golden apples of the Hesperides. The secret of perpetual motion. The healing waters. The room where all your wishes come true. The perfect cocktail. Whatever you people"—it kicks the skeleton's foot, loosening a small toe bone—"come in here to find. Was it as remarkable as advertised?"

"Can you find anything you want in the Valley?"

"In a manner of sp— Wait! Ah ah ah! Aren't you the slyboots! Trying to slip a question in without"—it extrudes a kind of arm, holding the tiny cup, and rattles whatever's inside it—"playing."

Rory takes a deep breath and grips the crucifix in his pocket. "I'll play," he says, "but I have to know it's fair. No cheating."

"Of course it's fair! We each roll the same pair of dice, in plain view, we count the pips together. How could anyone possibly cheat?"

"Then how come you said you always win?"

"I said no such thing."

"Yes you did. You nearly did. It's what you were going to say, it's obvious."

"That's a cruel aspersion. Do you really mean to impugn my honesty? I'm not like you lot. None of your lies from me. I'm incapable of them."

"What, lying?" He remembers the fox saying the same thing; at least, he thinks it was the same thing.

"Precisely."

"OK, then. If you can't lie. Do you always win?"

There's a rather stunned silence.

"Go on. Answer. I'm not playing unless you answer. Do you always win this game?"

"Yes," it admits, as sheepishly as a thing with no resemblance at all to a sheep can manage. "I always win."

His hand feels sweaty. "How come?"

"I don't know! And that's enough free questions!"

"You must be cheating. It can't be fair if you never lose."

"Sir. Look." It hops onto the skeleton's skull, making bones in the neck click softly. "Watch. Come down so you can see. I entreat you." It pats out a smooth area on the coat covering the skeleton's back, arranges itself in a crouching down sort of way, and motions with its bulbous version of a hand. Two tiny white dice spill out over the coat and come to rest. Each one's smaller than a cuff button but the black pips are clear and Rory can read them easily enough: a two and a six. The creature scoops them up and casts them again: two twos. It keeps throwing them as it talks. "See? Random! Entirely random! Stay and watch as long as you like. I'd defy the most warped of mathematical prodigies to discover any trace of a pattern in the throws. Two dice, one total. Add the pips up and look. Higher sometimes, lower sometimes, more usually towards the middle, which is as you'd expect, so the science of statistics tells us, not to mention plain common sense. See? See? Try them yourself. Go on. Pick them up. Roll the bones." It hops down and backs away as if to encourage him. Rory sits beside the skeleton and picks up the dice between his fingertips. "As many times as you like." He drops them. Six and four. "If you can discern any power other than mere blind chance directing the fall of the dice, you're welcome to accuse me of whatever fraud you please." It's almost like playing with grains of sand, but they roll and stop just like any other dice he's ever used. Six and three, three and five, double ones, three and four. "There! Look at those last four throws. Imagine that had been the game. The first thrower would have won the first, the second the second. Luck, I'm telling you. Luck!"

"Who goes first when you play the game?"

"It doesn't matter, does it? That's precisely my point!"

"But you always win."

It sniffs.

"I must just be very lucky," it says.

Rory's remembering what it said when he arrived: *something funny must be going on.*

"Tell you what," he says. "I'll play, but I get to roll both times."

"What? That's hardly fair."

"You just said it doesn't make any difference. If it's just luck, who cares who's rolling?"

"But where's the fun in that?"

"Technically, I suppose, but—"

"Yeah, well, that's the deal. I throw both times. I'll do it for you first, then for me. We do it again if it's a draw. Highest or lowest wins?"

"Highest, of course, but—"

"Highest wins, OK. That's the deal. Otherwise." He drops the dice again. Two and three. He makes himself glare at it, as assertively as he can. It's a bit more like a person close up, though it would be a miniature person made out of splinters, pus, flaps of snakeskin or fish scales, and the rind of rotting fruit. "No game."

"It's a poor deal," the thing mutters.

"You'd better take it if you want a game. I don't think anyone else is coming by here anytime soon."

"All right all right all right! Have it your way. Satan's skunks. I fully expect your soul to be as bitter and shriveled as an old pea. All right, then. If you're going to take all the fun out of it you might as well get on with it." It clumps back on top of the skull to get a better view. "Go on."

Rory's been concentrating so hard on arguing with it that he somehow missed the fact that he now has to play. "OK," he says.

"Not really. But, whatever."

"Ready?"

"Of course I'm ready."

"First throw's for you."

"Yes, yes."

"Highest total wins."

"Yes yes yes yes! I've already agreed to your blasted deal, haven't I? This is poor sport."

"Right."

He closes his eyes, thinking again of the bad god, and rolls.

"See? Just lucky."

He opens his eyes. He bends close to the dice and peers at them in case he's somehow reading the pips wrong. Five and six.

He wonders what it's like having your soul eaten. Will it be quick?

"Normally at this point I'm capering with delightful anticipation. But watching my good fortune fall from someone else's hand takes all the fun out of it, I don't mind telling you. I'm not sure I wouldn't rather have not played at all. Well, hurry up."

His fingers are clammy and won't grip properly. He fumbles the tiny dice as he gathers them up again.

"And don't try running away, or any nonsense of that sort. I've seen it all before, believe me. You won't be able to avoid your turn. Which is particularly satisfying in this case, I must say, since we're playing by your blasted rules."

"Destroyer," Rory whispers. "Accept my offering."

"Excuse me?"

He rolls.

"Right. That's that. Lie down, please, and open your mouth."

Rory opens his eyes. He rubs them. He blinks. He counts the spots again.

"I won," he says.

"You may also want to keep your eyes sh— What?"

"I won." He hunches right down and looks at the dice very, very carefully, to make sure they really are showing double sixes. The thing wasn't even paying attention. It crooks over the dice too.

"Twelve," Rory says. "You only got eleven. I win."

The thing doesn't move.

Helper, Rory thinks. *Thank you.* He feels like if he stood up he'd take off and fly like Lino.

"You can't have," the thing croaks.

"But I did."

"It's . . . It's . . . ." The thing springs down off the skull and begins hopping around in the grass, shrieking. "I lost! I lost the game! Unprecedented! Intolerable! I demand an inquiry!"

"So," Rory says. "That's three questions."

"Play again?" it wheedles. "Rematch?"

"No."

"Double or quits?"

"No."

"Six questions if you win again. Go on."

"Deal's a deal. You agreed."

"Ten questions."

"No."

"Twenty! A hundred! As many as you like!" It's choking on its own rage. "You won't win anyway. You can't possibly. A thousand! Ask whatever you want and I'll stake your soul against it. Anything you want!"

"When you've quite finished," Rory says.

"*Raaahh!*" it squeaks, and smashes a limb down on the skeleton's head, which shatters. It chases fragments of bone around the path, kicking them. "*Raaah raaah raaah!*"

"First question," Rory says.

"One! No, there's no way out of the Valley. Two! Yes, you will die here. Three! No, there's nothing you can do about it. There! Done! And I hope you're happy! Now be off with you and never ever come this way again!"

He waits until it's stopped hopping and kicking and shrieking.

"First question," he says. "Is there really a well in the Valley where the water cures every illness of body or soul?"

"Ha!" It dances with angry delight. "Ha! Ha ha ha! Yes there is, but you've already been told that, obviously, so that's a total waste of a question. Idiot! Bumpkin! Fathead! Epic, epic f—"

"Second question," Rory says loudly, feeling stupid. "OK, so where is this well?"

"It's in the deepest darkest part of the woods at Pendurra, of course, but oh dear, oh dear oh dear, you don't have the foggiest where that is, do you? Oh dearie me, could that possibly be another wasted question? I suspect it might be. You know, I never thought losing the game would turn out to be such fun. I should almost thank you for the experience. Although I can't imagine anyone else would have been as stupid as—"

"Last question." He nearly shouts. He can't let the taunting get to him; he's got to be careful. He's got to think. He's so ashamed and cross he nearly says *Are you listening?*, but by some miracle he just manages to bite his tongue in time, because that of course would have been a question. He takes a few deep breaths. "OK," he says. "OK. Tell me exactly—*exactly*—how I get there from here. Along roads. Proper roads. Which I can use. Safe ones." It's not answering. "Turn by turn. Tell me each turn."

It stands still.

"I'm waiting," it says.

"For—" He so nearly says *For what?* And then even as he chokes off that question he nearly says *Why aren't you answering?* and then he's so frightened by how close he's come to messing up that he can't say anything at all, he just scrunches his eyes shut and tries to make himself concentrate. It's his last chance. Why won't it tell him?

"Still waiting."

Is it that there aren't any safe roads? Is that it? What's the best way of rephrasing it? He knows it'll trick him if it can.

"Sometime before Christmas would be convenient."

Take your time, he tells himself. *Be careful. Think.*

"You're not very clever, are you?"

"Shut up."

Of course. He never actually asked a question.

"If you can't think of a third one, that's fine with me. I'll let you off."

"I said shut up," he says. "Right. Here goes. What would you say, exactly, if you had to—like, absolutely *had* to—say the very best and most helpful description you possibly could say of how I can get to the place I just asked you about?"

It's quiet for a long time, so long that he starts thinking he must have messed up. He's going over his question in his head again wondering where he went wrong when it kicks the ground, raising a little spray of earth.

"All right. That was quite good, I'll admit."

He thinks he'd better not do anything at all except shut his eyes and concentrate very hard on what it's about to say.

It does the throat clearing thing again. "Very well, then. I would say: 'Leave Trelow by its main gate, turn left, then immediately left again, follow that lane to the first village you reach, there turn right and then the next left, where that lane ends go left, and then ignore all turnings right or left until you reach the gate of Pendurra on your left, and if you are able to gain access there you may ask Holly the way to the well.' That's what I'd say. And I won't repeat a single word of it if you fall on your knees and beg me. *And* it gives me particular pleasure to inform you that you won't be able to enter Pendurra should you try from now until Doomsday, and indeed you'll almost certainly die impaled on a thousand thorns if you do try. That's no small comfort to me." It snatches up the dice. "It's my earnest hope that we never meet again. You've ruined my whole day." It's burrowing into the ground, or just sinking as if the earth were thick water, grumbling as it goes. "Keep your nasty little soul. I never wanted it anyway. Yuck."

Rory pays it no attention. He's repeating the directions to himself. He sits there, saying them over and over again until he's made them into a little song.

29

ilvia's where he left her. The owl's come down to perch on top of the fountain. It's very big when you see it close up, especially its enormous round face with the odd inside-out cheeks and stony eyes. Rory's still humming his song to himself, but he takes a moment to say "Hi, Lino." The bird blinks.

He's decided to drop the crucifix in the fountain, since that's where the god appeared. After that he'll worry about how to get Silvia to follow him. First things first. He's pretty sure you've got to keep promises you make to gods.

"Helper," he says aloud, feeling silly. "Thanks. For, um. Helping. So here's what I said I'd give you. OK?" He takes the silver statuette out of his pocket and holds it over the water.

Silvia moves so fast he doesn't even see her get to her feet. She almost takes Rory's fingers off in her eagerness to snatch the crucifix out of his hands. She grabs it and stares at it as if it's the answer to some problem she's been trying to solve her whole life.

"What are you doing?"

Her mouth works, but nothing comes out.

"I need that back," Rory says. "I've got to give it to that god." She doesn't resist when he tries to tug it out of her grasp, but nor does she let go, and she's a lot stronger than him.

"Please, Silvia," he says. He peels her fingers back one by one. "I really have to. I promised." He has to wrestle her fingers away, but there's no fight in her, and eventually he manages to get the crucifix back. He drops it in the fountain quickly.

"There," he says. "Now we've got to go, OK? Out the main gate, left, immediately left again." He sings the whole song to himself again to make sure he hasn't forgotten it. "Come on." He pulls at her arm, rather shyly. "Understand? Go." He makes a walking motion with his fingers.

It's easier now she's standing up. He tugs her off balance. To his surprise she makes a hesitant motion to follow him. "Yeah, that's right. Off we go." It's like he's taking a dog for a walk but it seems to be working. "This way. I saw a sign for the main gate, it's up past that big house. Keep going."

She's about to follow him out of the courtyard when she stops and looks back, for all the world as if she's forgotten something. She goes back to the fountain and sticks her arm in without rolling up the sleeve. She fishes around for a bit and comes back out with the crucifix. Satisfied, she trots back after Rory and stands beside him. Her wet sleeve drips onto her shoes. The owl coughs raucously.

Rory turns his eyes heavenward. "I tried, OK?" he says. He can't stop to worry about it now. The day must be getting older, and for a nasty moment while Silvia was messing around he thought he'd lost a line of his directions.

He feels a bit like the Pied Piper in the story, though without the flute. He never understood why a piper would have a flute anyway, though no one in their right mind would follow someone with a bagpipe so maybe that's why. (Also he never understood where the pies came in.) Silvia plods along at his heels, not saying anything, stopping when he stops and following when he starts again, never letting go of the silver crucifix. Lino—he knows it's Lino now, because how could it not be? The Valley's just like that—swoops along behind. It's a peculiar procession, though no more peculiar than the things he glimpses, or thinks he glimpses, among the trees or across fields or out of the corner of his eye. Really the weirdest thing about it is that he's the one at the front. He's not used to being the leader.

For the first little while his biggest worry is whether he's remembering his song right. And what if he gets to one of those junctions where it could be straight on or could be left, depending on how you look at it? But it turns out that each time he gets to a place where he might have to make a decision, the way he's supposed to go is the only way he *can* go. At the main gate of Trelow he has to go left because the way to the right is blocked by a hill of rubble where one of the stone houses guarding the entrance has collapsed into the road. After that he remembers he has to take a quick left, and when they get to the turn there's something squatting between the hedges straight ahead, a hooded thing with its back to him, scraping a scythe against a big rough stone between its knees; he's quite sure that he doesn't want to go that way. Then he's supposed to keep going along the lane to a village, and all the side roads turn out to be closed. One's been washed away by a frothing stream. The next has been swept clear of weeds and gravel and chalked with unspeakably horrible pictures. There's only one way to go after all, it seems, and that way is farther in.

They walk past a lot of quietly abandoned things. They get to the village and it's quietly abandoned too. It's not all smashed up like most places from The Old Days. It's just deserted and overgrown. It's on a little ridge, so as they pass between its peacefully empty houses he can see for miles in different directions. Not a single thing is moving apart from the three of them. The horizons are hazy with autumnal mist.

The angel appears again, in the distance, wheeling lazily over wooded ground before gliding down over the horizon. He points it out to Silvia but he's not sure she even knows what he's saying. She might be listening or not: it's impossible to tell. He hums the song to himself. He's leg-weary and hungry but for some reason it's not as hard to keep going as you'd think. The turns pass quite quickly. Wherever he's going, it doesn't seem to be all that far.

They reach a crossroads near the top of another ridge. To Rory's left the land drops away quite steeply into a long concealed valley. Looking back along its length he can see fragmentary stretches of a wide river. There's a crashed car in a hedge at the crossroads, almost entirely buried in very tall grasses and the black sprigs of fruiting ivy. He stops, because for the first time there's more than one way to go.

He remembers he's supposed to ignore every turn to the right and
left but he hasn't had to think about it until now. Here, though, every
direction seems open. It's like the Valley's daring him to go wrong
now, at the last moment.

He can hear music.

He might not have noticed it if he hadn't stopped. It's very quiet,
and it's sort of wreathed into the air, almost like it's only the noise
of the breeze, but with a bit of a tune. He can also now smell something, in the same subtle, not-quite-there-at-all way, a mild sweeten-
ing. Both the music and the smell are as lovely as they are elusive.

"Nearly there," he tells Silvia. The look she gives him in answer
is no more expressive than the owl's.

He goes straight on, as he was told to. He's walking along a gently curving road with a field to the right and a hedge to the left; beyond the hedge are tall trees. A little way beyond the crossroads the
hedge on the left starts to get taller. The farther they go, the higher
it becomes, until it meets the place where the woods come right up
to the edge of the road. By that stage it's so high it reaches halfway
up the trunks. It's not even a hedge anymore, it's a huge green wall.
Up close you can see that it's made of plants, boughs knotted tightly
together all over and round each other, covered with small deep
green leaves, but when you step back from it and look up it's more
like a solid barrier. The boughs are finger thick and barbed with
thorns hooked as viciously as the owl's beak. In among them a few
limp flowers are clinging on still, scattering more or less shriveled
petals through the hedge and down onto the road. The farther he
goes, the more flowers there are, and the fresher they look. They're
a warm pink color. The smell's getting stronger all the time. It's the
scent of the flowers, he realizes, turning aside to sniff one. Looking
around a curve ahead he sees that so many petals have fallen it's like
a pink carpet.

The music stops. He was just getting to the point where he was
pretty sure it was someone humming. He rounds the curve and sees
a girl in a green dress sitting on a heap of bones.

"Good evening," the girl says.

According to Rory's directions the gate's supposed to be on the left. He goes a bit farther, carefully, hoping he'll get to it before he reaches the girl, but there's no break in the wall of thorns, which is now at least five times higher than his head.

"Welcome to Pendurra," the girl says in a pretty voice. "I'm Rose."

So he's in the right place, at least. He examines the impenetrable hedge more carefully and sees what might be a pair of stone gateposts wedged in among the woven boughs, exactly adjacent to where the pile of bones is in the road. The space between the gateposts is just more hedge.

"Aren't you going to introduce yourself?"

The pile Rose is sitting on is almost as wide as the lane at its base, and nearly as tall as Rory. It's a little bone-colored mountain, rising like a volcano from a pink sea. There must be thousands of bones. There are big ones and little ones, straight ones like clubs and curvy plate ones. There are skulls too, heaped in with all the rest. The girl's sitting with her legs curled up on the flattened top of the volcano. Her dress is the exact deep soft-looking green of the leaves in the hedge. She has pink-blushed cheeks and her hair's as black as night. She's more a woman than a girl but her skin's so smooth and her voice is so pretty she seems younger.

"Don't be shy," she says. "I won't eat you." She adjusts herself a little, tucking her hair behind her ear. The bones whisper and sigh beneath her.

"Hi," Rory says, keeping his distance. Maybe there's another way in somewhere.

"That's a start," the girl says. "I suppose."

"Is this the gate?" says Rory.

She gestures towards the pair of stone posts in the massive hedge. "It is." Her arm moves to wave at the pile she's sitting on. "And these are all the people who tried to get in. I pick the bones from my branches and pile them up here. Even the fiddly little ones. Look." She plucks up something too small for Rory to see and holds it between thumb and forefinger. "Inner ear."

"How do I get in then?"

"You don't, silly. You want to, but you don't. Well"—she pouts— "he does."

The owl's come feathering along the lane behind. Rory turns in time to see it sweep up into the trees over the barricade of thorns and drop down out of sight on the other side.

"But he doesn't really count, because he's turned into a bird and can't turn back again. So that makes him actually just a bird, doesn't it. Birds come and go as they please. They don't *want* to get in it. They don't really want anything, not properly. Isn't your other friend going to say hello?"

Silvia's sat down in the road, as if she's guessed they're not going anywhere for a while. "She can't," Rory says. "I think she's forgotten how to speak. I'm taking her to the well."

"The well whose water cures every illness of body or soul?"

"Yeah."

"But that's inside."

"I know."

"You're not allowed inside."

"Why not?"

"Because it's what you want. Never mind, you won't understand, no one does. I'm just the barrier anyway. Why won't you tell me your name?"

"Rory," he says. "It's Scottish."

"You're Scottish?"

"No. The name is. Rory."

"Your name's Scottish but you aren't? How does that work?"

There's something funny about Rose's teeth. He sees it in glimpses while she's talking, between her very red, very pretty lips. "Dunno," he says. "Why shouldn't I be? You can be called anything, can't you."

"*Can* you?" she says, delighted.

"Obviously. Like my sister Scarlet, that's not Scottish."

"Is she red?"

"What d'you mean, red?"

"Scarlet. You said your sister was Scarlet."

"'Course not. It's just her name. She's dead anyway."

"Oh. I'm sorry."

"It's all right," Rory says, rather embarrassed.

"Is it? I suppose it must be if it happens to everyone."

Rory's head is starting to feel thick with frustration. He remembers the nasty warty root-thing telling him he'd never be able to get in but he assumed it was just being bad-tempered. There must be a way in. What would be the point of coming all this way if he was stuck now?

"It's nice to talk," Rose says. "No one's come for a long time." She picks up a big bone and turns it over in her hands thoughtfully. "Even when they did they didn't usually talk much. Most of them had gone mad."

Rory makes the mistake of looking at the pile. A pair of huge eye sockets looks back at him. *I was a person once,* the skull tells him, silently. *I got this far, and no farther.*

"Did you really kill all these people?"

"My petals are oh so soft," Rose says. "But my thorns are oh so hard." She gives Rory a quick grin, letting him see her teeth properly. Each one of them comes to a sharp point. Her mouth is full of little white fangs. He can't help himself. He shies back a step, horrified. She laughs.

"People usually only want to think about the pretty parts," she says. She sits taller in a way which makes the hem of her dress come up over her knees. It's only a little wriggle but for some reason it makes Rory feel acutely uncomfortable. " 'Oh, a rose,' they say. 'How lovely. I want to put my face in it and sniff sniff sniff.' Then they get all tangled up."

"You're actually a rose?"

She sighs and slumps, disappointed.

"How come you look like a girl, then?"

"It's always got to be one thing or the other with you people."

He thought it was a perfectly reasonable question but he's made her cross now. "Sorry," he says quickly, thinking about her teeth.

"Is it or isn't it. This or that, yes or no. I'm sure that's why most of them"—she flips the bone she's holding up, lets it spin once in the air, and catches it again—"were mad by the time they got this far. Asking all the wrong questions until their brains went *pop*. 'Where am I? What's going on? Why can't I go back the way I came? What does it all mean?' " The bone's thicker than her arm but she braces it in her hands and snaps it in half with no effort at all, *crack*. "Is that what happened to your friend? I bet it is."

Rory looks back at Silvia. She's still sitting in the road, hands in her pockets, looking at nothing in particular, like one of the Riders' horses after they'd been tied up.

"No, actually."

"Really?"

"No. She always knew what she was doing. Where she was going."

"So what's wrong with her?"

"I think the problem is she got there."

Rose puts the broken halves of the bone gently back down on the pile between her knees.

"You're not stupid, are you?"

"Everyone says I'm stupid." Well, Ol always did.

"Shall I explain about this place? Maybe you will understand after all, a little bit."

"The Valley?"

She nods towards the clogged gateway. "This place. Pendurra. Where magic lives. You see, for a long time it was secret because nobody knew about it. They didn't need a barrier then. Anyone could have come in, because no one wanted to. I just lived quietly in a back garden. We all did. We all lived inside, and no one knew anything about it, and no one cared. Everyone was happy. Happy enough, anyway."

When Rose doesn't add anything, Rory says: "What then?"

She smooths her dress. "Then someone from outside came to live here, and got curious. A person, a woman. She started wondering how it worked. She wanted to know more. She wanted to find the secret." Her voice is still pretty but it's gone solemn. It's like the difference between pretty Kate in the portrait in the big room in the Abbey and the real Kate, the same face but serious and capable. "And so they Fell."

There's a long pause. Rose is watching him, so he finds himself looking around. He can't see a cliff or anything.

"Fell where?"

"Not where, silly. They Fell. They just Fell. You know. Dropped from the zenith like a falling star. Earth felt the wound. That sort of Fall." Baffled, Rory looks up at the misty evening sky. "And that's what made it a different kind of secret, you see. Because now everyone knows. Pendurra's just the same, but now everyone wants to find it. So instead of just sitting here forgotten, it's closed. It's forbidden. Do you see? It's just like what you said about your friend. It's once people know what they want that they're doomed."

"I don't know what you're on about."

"Exactly. I bet that's why you've made it so far. You don't have the faintest idea what you're doing in the Valley, do you?"

"But I'm taking Silvia to the well—"

"—whose water cures every illness of body or soul, yes. And since that's the one thing you do want, it's the thing you're not going to find, because I won't let you in. But I'll bet you anything that's not why you entered the Valley. Is it? You probably didn't even know about Pendurra, did you?"

He has to admit he didn't.

"In fact," Rose says, and she's gone back to being girly-pretty now, "I expect you didn't even mean to enter the Valley at all. Am I right? You can tell me, I won't laugh."

He tries to remember how he got here. All he can remember is running in witless terror until his lungs were on the edge of bursting. He can't remember crossing any border.

"Do you know," she says softly, ruffling the bones by her knees as if stroking sand, "you're the first person who's ever got here by accident. It's a kind of innocence."

He's no closer to understanding what Rose is talking about but he seizes on the wistful tone in her voice. It's almost as if she likes him.

"Maybe you could let me in, then," he says. "As a special thing."

She shakes her head. "No. I've told you now. I've spoiled it."

"Told me what? You haven't told me anything. I don't get what you're saying at all."

"That you're here. Pendurra. This is it. The heart of everything. Where all the magic in the world was locked up for five hundred years, all quiet and forgotten. Where you can be a girl and a rose at the same time. Where the house never rots and the springs never fail and everything is properly itself. Even grief."

Rory stares.

"But . . ." He struggles to get the thought straight. He's got to get her back to whatever it was that made her talk sweetly to him. "I don't care about any of that. I don't want magic wishes or anything. I'm only trying to take Silvia to that well. I'll leave as soon as she's better, I swear."

Rose breaks into a delicious peal of laughter.

"I swear," Rory mutters, humiliated. "I will."

"Oh dear." She's wiping her eyes, trying to stifle giggles. "I'm sorry. Poor you."

"What."

"Do excuse me . . . That's the only thing you want? To find the well?"

"Yeah. I swear."

"The thing you want more than anything else in the whole world?"

"Y—"

Her shoulders stop jiggling. Her mouth settles straight.

"You see?" she says, not cruelly.

"What," he says again, though he thinks he does get it, after all.

"You're not innocent anymore," she says. "You want something. You've Fallen too. That's why the gate's closed to you, and always will be."

"But—"

"I'm sorry," she says. "You can stay if you want, though. We can go on talking."

Rory's mouth is open but he can't think of any more answers. He slumps down next to Silvia, dejection and exhaustion taking their toll.

"But what about her?" he says.

"There's no way in," Rose says. "It's forbidden. I really am sorry. I can see you care about your friend, it's sweet. Wait." She sits straighter, causing a clattering tremor in the pile. Some vertebrae jiggle loose and bounce down the side of the heap. "What's that?"

"What?"

"That. That she's holding."

Silvia's pulled the crucifix out of her pocket and is looking at it again as if it might start talking to her.

"That?" Rory looks up at Rose and sees a change. The girl's gone tense. Something's different. He hasn't a clue what it is but in his desperation it feels like a tiny advantage, a possibility. He seizes it as best he can and tries the same trick that seemed to work on Phil the fox. "That thing? It's from a god, actually."

"Let me see." Rose is straining her neck forward, hands on her knees. "Bring it here."

"You can come and look if you want. It's special."

Rose uncurls herself and slides down the pile onto the road, bones slipping noisily after her. At ground level (and with her mouth closed) she looks less alarming. She's hardly taller than Rory, and very slight. She nudges a skull aside with her bare toes and approaches.

"I want to see it properly."

Rory swallows. He remembers the moment the fox hesitated. If there's any sort of opportunity here, he's got to sound like he knows what he's talking about.

"You can't just say it like that," he says, standing up. "You've got to have respect. It's from a god, like I said. One of his names is Destroyer. I spoke to him. Earlier on. He said he was . . ." Rory's winging it. He can't stop now. He tries to remember what the terrible god said, when he was at his most terrible. "He was In Violet."

Rose gives him a surprisingly withering look for such a young-looking woman. "What are you talking about?" But it's all right, she's not really listening to him. All she cares about is the crucifix. "Show me."

Silvia snatches it away, frowning. Rose bares her teeth and hisses.

"All right." Rory hurriedly gets between them. He takes Silvia's hands and does what he did before, unpeeling the fingers one by one, saying "All right, all right" all the time, like he's soothing a dog, and at the same time trying to think of the right thing to say to Rose. Silvia lets him take the statuette, though when her hands are empty she stares at the space where it used to be as if wondering

what just happened. He turns and shows it to Rose. He's got to try
something, right now.

"It came from—"

"His mother," Rose says, almost whispering. She touches the crucifix with a finger. She's standing almost on top of Rory. She smells
amazing, like a mixture of the human body with the sweetest food
ever invented. "His mother, and their sister." She looks up at Rory.
Her eyes are full of wonder. "This is hers."

Anything he says is just going to break the spell. Not daring to
breathe yet, he just nods, as if he knew that already, obviously.

"Where did that woman get it?"

"From a god. I told you."

"It's another sign," Rose says. She looks like she might be about
to cry. Cry with joy, that is. "First Corbo and now this. And look
at my blossoms. I flowered for him when he first came here, to welcome him to his proper place. He must be coming back. He must
be. He's coming home." She smiles. It's horrible, with her fangs, and
yet somehow lovely too. "At last."

"Who is?"

"The white hawk." Her brown eyes are definitely moistening.
"The hawk of May. The boy who belongs here and nowhere else. He
promised he'd come back. Six hundred and thirteen days ago." She
scoops a handful of petals from the road, reaches up, and dribbles
them over herself like pink snow. "As soon as I saw Corbo I thought
it might be today."

Rory's not quite sure what comes over him. By the time the words
are out of his mouth it's done, it's too late to think about it.

"Oh yeah," he says. "Actually that's me."

The loveliness vanishes in an instant from Rose's face.

"Hi," he says. "Sorry. I should have said before. I'm back."

She stares at him like he's mad.

"So how's everything been?" he says.

She laughs, loud and long. While he's waiting for her to finish
Rory feels the red heat rising in his cheeks and thinks, *Don't back
down now, whatever you do*, and, *Oh, shit*. He grips the crucifix tight
and sends an inarticulate prayer in the direction of the bad god.

The laugh peters out. Is he imagining it, or is there something a teeny bit hesitant about the way it trickles into silence?

"I'm not surprised you didn't recognize me," he says. "A lot of weird stuff has happened. Still."

She's very, very close to him, staring at his face, smelling like heaven.

"It's nice to be back," he says. "After, you know. Six hundred and whatever. All those days."

He thinks: *If the next thing she does is anything other than kissing me dead with those teeth of hers, I've got a chance.*

"You're barely a boy," she says. "He was almost a man."

And that's when he knows it really might work. He remembers what Phil the fox said about lying. Well, not exactly what it said, because he doesn't have time to remember anything exactly: everything's got a sort of downward momentum now, carrying itself along without time to stop, like Ol trotting down Briar Hill to his death. But he remembers the feel of it, the way the big fox became hesitant and confused. *They don't understand lying,* he thinks to himself. *They don't know what it's like.*

"Like I said," he says. "Weird stuff. Going back in time and things. It changed me."

Rose leans closer, which is tricky since she's almost standing on his toes anyway, and inspects his face as if checking for specks of dirt.

"You're nothing like," she says. "You're a completely different boy."

"Yeah, but you said, didn't you, about how you can be different things at once. Like you being a girl and a flower."

"Plant."

"Plant, whatever. It's the same thing. I'm me now, as well as that . . ." Has he remembered this wrong? "White hawk."

"You said you were Scottish."

"No, I said my name's Scottish. Remember? Totally different thing." What's he doing? He's babbling. He can feel his face going purple as a bruise and his breath coming short. Anyone with half a brain could tell he's lying. He might as well have a big red light on top of his head flashing the word *false*. But Rose still hasn't bitten his mouth off. "I should have explained right when I got here, shouldn't I? Sorry. It's just I'm a bit tired; it's been a really long day. And, um." He tries to do a casual-looking survey of the road, the hedge, the bones, the girl. "Everything's so different," he guesses.

"Yes," she says. Lucky guess. He fingers the crucifix gratefully. "It's all changed since then."

"Me too." *Bad god, don't give up on me now.* "That's why I look totally different, see. And younger. That explains it."

She doesn't breathe like a normal person because if she did he'd be feeling it on his face, but he gets the impression she's sniffing him.

"There's no magic on you," she says. "Not a trace. You're just a lost boy leading a dumb woman."

"The god took it all away." He's seeing pages from the comics flipping through his head. Curses, trials, origins, antidotes, powers lost and found. It's as good a story as any. Well, maybe not, but it's the first one that pops into his mouth and he doesn't have time to pick and choose. "And made me look different. But I got this." The crucifix was what started her off. He's got to try to get her to pay attention to it instead of him. "So I could bring it back here. It was like a sort of quest. It was, actually. A quest. That's what I was doing. Getting it. So I could, you know. Bring it. Back." He swallows. "Inside." She's just staring again. "So you should. Um." What he wanted to say was *You should let me in now* but his nerve's finally failed.

Very slowly, she raises a finger and touches his cheek. Her skin's softer and colder than proper flesh.

She jumps back.

"Marina!" she says. "You found her!"

You?

"Yeah." Rose is looking at him in obvious amazement, like he's someone else entirely. *Keep going, keep going.* "I did." Who the hell's Marina? Where has he heard that name before? It doesn't matter; he can't stop now. "Just about," he says, because Rose's mouth is hanging half-open and he needs to make her start talking again. "It took a long time."

"Isn't she coming back as well?"

He shrugs airily. "Maybe. One day. It's up to her. Probably. She might have changed too, you know. So you'd better let her in too." He puts as much emphasis as he dares on the word *too*.

"You're not the white hawk," Rose says. "Why would you say you are when you aren't?"

"I knew you wouldn't believe it, Rose." He ought to sound like he's known her for ages. "That's why I didn't say at first, actually. Didn't want to give you a shock."

"But you're not mad. You won your way to the gate fairly."

He's trying to think of her like Pink: a younger girl, not too bright. She is pink, he tells himself. She's a rose with pink flowers, petals soft as water. "I know it's all a bit weird," he says. "But it's me. It really is."

He's lying so hard he almost believes himself. How bizarre words are, he thinks. He's just said *really* when it's nothing of the sort, and yet saying it makes it sound a little bit more true.

"Gawain," Rose says.

His heart leaps because what he hears her say is *Go in*. She said it a bit funny, but what else could she have been saying?

"Thanks," he says. No, that's wrong, what would he be thanking her for if he owns this place anyway? "For waiting," he adds. That's stupid too, she's a flower (plant!), what else was she going to do, stroll off to see the world? "For so long," he finishes. "It must have been . . ." *Lonely? Boring?* Shut up, he tells himself. He turns to Silvia. "Come on," he says to her. "In we go."

Silvia doesn't answer, of course, so he takes her arms and starts tugging her to her feet.

"I thought this day would be so joyful," Rose says behind his back. "I thought we'd all be happy again. But it feels dry."

Silvia's standing now. She makes a move to take the crucifix back but he dodges and steers her towards the gate instead. It's not a gate at all, just a solid mass of thorny wood between two stone posts, and he has no idea how he's supposed to get through, but he starts walking towards the hedge as confidently as he can.

"It'll be better soon," he says to Rose. He doesn't like seeing her so downcast.

"Who'll rejoice at your return if they don't even know you? Maybe I ought to kill you after all."

"You can't do that," he says, tugging Silvia faster. There isn't even a glimmer of light coming through the dark weave of clawed boughs. "Everything would go wrong if you did that. You'd be stuck waiting forever."

There's a rattle behind him. Rose is reascending on top of her little mountain of the dead. She lays herself on her back over its summit, back and back until she's lying with her arms and legs spread and her hips higher than everything else. Her dress has ridden right up and there's a sort of pink flower between her legs, which makes Rory look away very fast, though not before he's seen her arch herself with a weird gasping effort. As she moans the knotted branches at the base of the hedge between the gateposts begin to arch up too, as if an invisible hook's tugging them away from the ground. A dark cavity opens beneath them. Rory doesn't wait. He drops flat to his stomach. "Follow me," he tells Silvia, and forces himself to crawl into the narrow space. It's dusty and scratchy and thick with the smell of earth and the musty sugar of faded blooms. The thorns above him are quivering as if they might snap down at any second, but when he wriggles his head right in he can see that there's light beyond. "We have to crawl," he says. "Just do what I do. OK?" He presses himself flat to the ground, arms by his sides, and squirms his way through into the forbidden garden.

IV

Eden

30

usic.

A summer night. It could even have been midsummer night, when the twilight feels like it goes on forever. Long past his bedtime anyway. The dusk was infinitely slow. He might have been trying to stay awake to see but it never got dark, just quieter and quieter, as if there was a single dimmer switch turning light and sound down together. Dad had taken Jake and Scarlet out for an evening sail. He was too young, they all agreed, but he didn't mind. He didn't wish he was anywhere else. No school next day, or next week, or even next month. Just enough breeze to move the edge of the curtains, and the stars in their holiday brilliance. The night made tiny noises outside, muffled crickets and finger-high waves.

Downstairs, Mum put on a CD.

He remembers it so clearly. He remembers what it was like to be warm, dry, clean, idle, at peace. All of that's there in the memory of the music. He doesn't know what it was. Something classical. It came up through the floorboards and around the partly open door of his bedroom. It was in the air. It *was* the air, the summer night air, endlessly tranquil, suspended forever on the edge of perfect stillness. He must have fallen asleep before it stopped playing but he doesn't remember that. Can you remember falling asleep?

The air here has that kind of music in it.

He's standing in waist-high grass. The grass is a little dry and just faintly yellow: thinking about the end of autumn. There's a cottage nearby. It's in two halves. The top floor's all neat and quaint, thatched roof and lattice windows and a rambling plant with small fading leaves. The ground-floor windows are charred and shattered, there are bulges and cracks in the brickwork around them, and instead of a front door there's a ruin of smashed wood. But the two halves go together even though they're opposites, like the sad and happy parts of a story.

Down the slope from the cottage are golden woods. To the side is a simple iron fence with a meadow beyond. There's a car, a normal one, not pillaged or rusting. It's parked beside the cottage as if someone lives there.

The music's all around. It's a hum, almost soft enough for him to think he's imagining it. It's a tune he's sure he remembers but can't name. He feels like if he sat down in the grass and listened to it for the rest of his life he'd never be unhappy again.

In front of the cottage there's an odd statue. He can't tell whether it's actually carved out of a tree or just made to look like that. It's a tree trunk which turns into a green woman with bright red eyes. At the end of her raised arms it turns back into a tree, long twisty branches. The woman bits are incredibly lifelike. Its green face is turned right towards where he and Silvia are standing. The eyes are blank, just red ovals.

The wall of thorns has closed behind them.

Rory brushes himself off. Silvia looks a bit bedraggled with earth and leaves all over her so he brushes her off too, shyly at first.

All that business with Rose has driven his directions out of his head. He was supposed to ask someone what to do next, as far as he remembers, but he's forgotten who. There's no one here anyway.

He has an overwhelming feeling that it doesn't matter.

He's not hungry or tired anymore. Or rather he is but he doesn't care. Hunger and tiredness are there inside him alongside relief and tranquility, peaceful neighbors, like the upstairs and downstairs halves of the cottage.

He does remember the first thing the warty creature told him about the well: *It's in the deepest darkest part of the woods at Pendurra.* Silvia's staring blankly as ever down the slope towards the line of trees. A mossy track leads that way, past the cottage.

"All right, then," he says to her. "We might as well have a look."

The music stops. It's as if he's broken the spell by talking. He takes Silvia's hand to show her she's supposed to follow him. Out of nowhere a beautiful clear woman's voice says:

"Welcome, liar."

He looks around. There's still no one there. For a weird moment he almost persuades himself that it was the statue which spoke.

If someone's watching him they're as invisible as the music. It's probably God again, Rory thinks, as he leads Silvia down the track into the woods. This is the kind of place God would live in. Everything's perfect. Not perfect like in tidied-up: there's grass sprouting in the middle of the path, and drooping nettles and leathery dock and the big candelabra of dried-out hogweed at the edge of the wood, and the undergrowth is messy with rotting boughs. But still, everywhere he looks, it's perfect. It's like the difference between the photos in fancy calendars and the photos you take yourself. Even if they're exactly the same place the calendar makes everything look gleaming and beautiful where your own picture ends up washed-out and sort of boring. There's nothing about these woods that aren't ordinary autumn woods, and yet it's the most beautiful place he's ever seen. It makes him go on tiptoes, like it'll vanish if it realizes he's there.

Everything that's happened to him in his life before now feels like a dream.

It's funny, because he can suddenly remember all of it. In fact it's almost like he can't stop remembering. He looks at the caked layers of fallen leaves and thinks of a time when his wellies got stuck in deep mud when he was little, and of foraging for mushrooms with Ol who bragged on and on about kissing Laurel, and of his mother turning a stick over and saying *Look, a beetle!* He looks at the curve of a bough and thinks of rough seas, and of the handle of a knife in his hand, and of Soph terrified and wanting him to kill her. He glances back to make sure Silvia's still following and thinks of how far she's walked across Europe, and then he's thinking of maps in Geography, and then school, little humiliations, pointless triumphs. The smell of school lunch. The smell of when the toilets stopped working. The smell of Missus Stephenson dying. The whole world beyond this place buzzes around in the back of his head, a gargantuan anthill of biting crawling distresses.

It occurs to him that he's found what all those people were looking for. Everyone who came to the Valley, people like Silvia and Lino and Per, looking for the heart of magic. This is where they were trying to get. All left behind.

He thinks it's probably heaven.

Beyond the woods is a garden. Actually the woods feel like a garden too, but this is a proper one, with borders of different flowers laid out with grass spaces between them, and small trees dotted around. On the far side of the garden is a house. It's a big old higgledy-piggledy grey mansion, as big as the Abbey but heavier and wilder somehow, and all built of stone.

He stops. "Look," he tells Silvia, pointing. "Smoke, see? Someone must live here."

It's as though his words have magic power, because as soon as he says that he sees someone, though it's only a cat. It appears from somewhere, the way cats do, skipping up to the steps at the front of the house and then disappearing inside the big double doors.

Which means they must be open, Rory thinks.

They walk through the garden and across to the doors. There's a crack between them. He pushes and they swing in without a sound. Beyond is a warm brown dimness. He can smell the fire.

He can imagine a god living here, in a grand old country house with fruit trees in the garden and a cat for company. If he was a god it's what he'd do.

He goes inside.

He's in a corridor lined with panels of wood. It's more like a museum than a house, but comfortable. It's incredibly quiet. It feels like nothing here's moved for a very long time. There are paintings on the walls, unmoving old faces. It's like stumbling upon a secret, an incredibly ancient secret no one's thought about for centuries. He's glad he's not by himself. If it weren't for Silvia shuffling along behind him he'd feel very small and irrelevant.

There's just the faintest crackle of sound: burning logs muttering to themselves. Halfway down the corridor on the right a door is open. That's where the sound's coming from, and a hint of warmth as well.

He doesn't shout *Hello,* or knock, or clear his throat. It's not that sort of place. You don't just show up like a random visitor. A god would know anyway. He looks around the open door on the right, into a hallway with a high ceiling and a stone arch at the far end. Beyond the arch fluid shadows shimmer in a big room.

He looks back at Silvia on the off chance that she's woken up now and can tell him whether or not this is a bad idea. In the dimness her dark head is almost invisible.

He goes down the hallway into the big room.

It's like a church. It's taller inside than the church next to Parson's, its vaulted roof crisscrossed with massive wooden beams. The three tall windows on the left wall are cased in pointed stone. A gallery runs along the right wall, way above head height. The fireplace beneath the gallery is as big as double doors. Light flicks out from it across the top of an enormously long table of smooth wood, so there's a dusky aurora spilling like water down the whole length of the room, from where Rory and Silvia are standing at one end of the table to where the god's sitting at the other.

The god is dressed all in faded black. He's facing them, but his head's bowed and shrouded in some kind of cloaking hood. He doesn't move. Perhaps he's dead, a dead god. He's sitting in a high-backed wooden chair, his arms on its arms. In the firelight his hands look small and old.

Rory goes a little farther into the room.

What he took for a hood or a cloak is in fact hair, masses of it, black hair that's grown down to touch the floor. The god's a she, not a he.

She raises her head.

She pushes her hair out of her face and looks down the length of the room at Rory. He can't really see her face very well in all the shadows but he can tell at once she's a sorrowful god, a god of old and forgotten things.

Her hands grip the arms of the chair. She stands up.

For the first time since the fountain Silvia speaks. She says a single word, which doesn't sound like a word at all, at first.

"Ygraine."

She walks past Rory, then jogs, then runs. Her scuffing steps echo in the cavernous room as if someone's turned on a tap. She runs the length of the table, falls to her knees in front of the sorrowful god, and hugs her around the waist, like a lost child come home.

31

ight's come at last. They've drawn chairs closer to the fireplace. Rory's is a puffy old one with bandy legs; it smells of cat. The lady's has a low wooden back. She's sitting very straight. Silvia stands behind her chair, cocking her head thoughtfully. She snicks scissors in the air.

"Light is not so good," she announces.

This isn't the huge churchlike room where they first saw the lady. It's a warmer shabbier place altogether, full of heavy-looking old-fashioned things. There are fat weeping candles in sticks taller than Rory, but the lady—whose name turns out to be Iz, short for something he didn't hear properly—hasn't lit them: only the fire. It's burning sort of bright and dark at the same time, in that way fires do when they're the only light. Three sash windows show nothing but black. Full night. It took them quite a long time to get Silvia back to the house, especially without the lantern.

She takes a thick handful of Iz's hair. "But, good enough," she says, and slices through it. A black mess slithers onto the rug, making the cat twitch in brief surprise.

She's talking in her own voice. She's Silvia again. She's even in a good mood, Rory thinks, which is amazing, given that she's just lost something he imagines most people would give their right arms to have.

They took her to the well, Rory and Iz. It turned out to be more like a pool. Rory'd been imagining a cylinder of bricks with a pointy wooden roof and a bucket on a handle. Instead, the lady led him to a tiny ancient stone building deep in the woods beyond the house. On the way she explained why she's not Ygraine. Ygraine turns out to be the name of someone who died a long time ago. The lady is her twin sister. It took her and Rory quite a long time to get even that much from each other but they managed eventually, though the only thing that was really clear to either of them was that just one person knew the whole story, and that was Silvia.

So they nudged and cajoled her to the well, which cures every illness of body and soul, and got her to kneel beside the pool, and made her drink.

"Your sister used to let me do like this for her." Silvia snicks away at Iz's hair. She's already ankle deep in it. "In the car. She sat in the front, I'm in the back. With too big scissors for my little hands. I must have made her look like . . ." She raises an eyebrow at Rory. "*Gorgona?*"

"A gorgon?"

"Gorgon, yes. Like Medusa. But she always said I made her look pretty. It makes me so proud. I feel like an adult." She stops slicing, distracted. "All the time she speaks to me that way. Never like I'm just a little girl. Everyone else I know, they shout at me, hit me, tell me what to do, don't listen. Like adults normally do to children. I'm right, yes, Rory?" She winks at him.

She's teasing him now. He hates being teased, usually, but tonight it makes him feel better. It was much worse after she drank the water. She was screaming then, raving, flat on her back in the ancient stone building, thrashing her arms around so wildly she knocked their lantern into the pool and plunged them all into the pitch dark. Some of the screaming was in English. The sun's in my eyes! I can't see, I'm blind, help me. My eyes are burning! Even after she stopped raving and flailing, and they got her outside into the twilight, she clung on to Rory and wouldn't let go. She kept whispering *Am I blind? Where am I? Is this place real?* They got her back to the house eventually and wrapped her in a blanket and made her eat and drink, but it was like she was shell-shocked and Rory was the only thing in the world she could hang on to. While Iz lit the fire and got water and whatever they needed he kept on trying to explain to Silvia that she was safe, everything was OK, he's cured her.

Cured?

Gradually, she understood. She'd drunk from the well whose water cures every illness of body or soul, and it turned out her gift had been an illness too. She doesn't know where she's going anymore. Her future's gone dark. The god's been washed out of her for good.

Perhaps that's why she's a bit more cheerful now. Rory's met that god, and he'd be quite happy never to go anywhere near him ever again.

Silvia nods to herself and resumes cutting Iz's hair.

"The one thing your sister won't let me do is drive. I begged her, let me try, let me try! She said she needs me to use the map. To help me learn reading, see."

"She'd have made a good mother," Iz says.

Iz is very shivery. Of the two of them, she's the one who looks like she was screaming her head off in madness a while ago and has had something terrible happen to them. She's been getting worse as Silvia's been getting better. It's because she wants to know about her dead sister, but at the same time sort of doesn't want to know. She was getting so worked up, starting to ask questions and then stopping herself, telling Silvia to say things and then telling her not to, that eventually Silvia asked for a pair of scissors and told her just to sit quietly.

"Do you have children?" Silvia asks.

Iz is very pale. It's easy to imagine that she's been sitting in that high-backed chair in the big room for years, her hair growing to the floor, never going out into sunlight and fresh air. Silvia's question seems to make her go even paler.

"No," she whispers, eventually. "I found out I couldn't."

Silvia crouches to inspect her handiwork so far. "Maybe that's good. This isn't a good world for children anymore."

Iz winces. "You're right," she says.

"And your sister," Silvia goes on, getting back to work. "She was wonderful, she was clever, she taught me everything, yes. But then she left me. So not such a good mother, maybe. Still, it's lucky for you. After she left me I had to learn to cut hair properly." Silvia smiles at her own joke. The contrast with Iz's face—stiff with suppressed pain—is awful.

Perhaps it's a relief not seeing the future, Rory thinks. He can imagine that. If he'd known even parts of what was going to end up happening to him, he might have asked Her to drown him like Ol.

"You have the same hair as her," Silvia says. "Same ears. Same everything."

Iz turns around, making Silvia tut. "What happened to Iggy?" she says. "Where did she go?" She's hoarse, like it hurts to speak.

Silvia gently takes hold of her head and pushes it straight.

"*Shh*," she says.

"I tell you everything. Just listen. Be patient."

She's in charge again. It's like she can't help it. Other people go weak next to her. So that's not part of her lost superpower, then, Rory thinks. That's just Silvia's nature.

"She sent postcards to you, yes? You received them?"

"Yes," Iz whispers.

"Do you remember from where the last one came?"

"She was going south, wasn't she. Greece. The last one might have been from Delphi."

"I help her post them. I go with her to buy . . ." She looks at Rory, miming licking.

"Stamps." It's taken him a while to figure it out, but he understands now that Ygraine, Iz's dead sister, the one she's so desperate to know about, was also the English teacher Silvia told him about before, the one who rescued Silvia from the gypsy camp.

"Yes. I know a few words in Bulgarian, I can help in that country." She's shorn Iz to her shoulders now. It looks ridiculous, like half a black cooking pot on the back of her head. She begins to snip more carefully, talking all the time. "That's how we traveled. Helping each other. It was a long journey. Small roads always. Never through the big towns. Sleeping in the car. We find a place to stop each night and lie in the car and she teaches me English words. She talks to me in English all the time, whether I understand or don't. But always soft, you see. Kind. For me she's like an angel. In the orphanage we used to say, In the West, America, Germany, England, the people have so much money they piss gold. One day they come to Romania and take us to live in their houses big like castles, that's what we tell each other. We will have all the clothes we want and when the rich people die they will give us all their money. When Ygraine takes me away, at first I think she's one of those. I think, All the other kids pushed my face on the floor and bit me and told me the rich Americans won't choose me because I have dark hair and dark skin, and now it's me who's going to be rich and grow up pissing gold. And instead we drive along in this terrible old car, just driving, no airplane to England, no house like a castle. She makes me lie down in the back sometimes, down where the feet go, covers me with suitcases. After two, three days I understand, the English lady is not rich. She is not turning me into a princess. But I don't care, because by then I know she's better than rich. She's kind."

The scissors click in silence for a while.

"I remember," Iz says. "She found some sort of job working with children in Romania. After the Wall came down. I remember her ringing up to tell me she was going. That was the last time I spoke to her until . . ."

Iz is very out of practice at speaking. She keeps stalling like this, as if she doesn't have enough air to make words out of.

Silvia waits patiently until Iz holds still again and then goes on snipping.

"Of course I understand now what she did. She stole me. She went to the camp one day to take me to her lessons like normal but instead of going to the orphanage where she teaches she hides me in her shitty car and drives away. That's why we go only on little roads. When we get to the border, out of Romania into Bulgaria, we pay a man to put the car on his truck, we hide in the back. I don't understand what's happening. I think I fell asleep. I don't worry, because I know, you see. I know she's taking me the right way. So even when I get angry with her, because I'm just a small stupid child and sometimes I get angry, I don't run away. I don't care that she doesn't take me to a castle in England with servants. She says, Silvia, you are special, I'm going to look after you. That's enough for me.

All my life until then, everyone else, the old women, the old men, everyone, they say, You are special, make us money. You have a gift, make us rich. Otherwise we'll beat you. Your sister taught me what this means, to have a gift. Before she appears everything is bad in my life, after she comes and takes me everything is good. I thought maybe she's a real angel. From heaven."

Iz almost smiles. "You'd have been the first person ever to think that about Iggy."

"She was a difficult woman?"

"Impossible."

"Yes. I can imagine this. But to me—"

"Of course. How far did she take you?"

"Bulgaria, Greece. Through the mountains. Once we arrive in the south of Greece she tells me there is a plan. There's going to be a boat, sailing from Kyparissia. It's a little town by the sea on the west. In Arcadia."

"Is that really a place? I didn't know."

"Far from anywhere. It's a quiet town, very small. A good place to get on a boat and no one notices. Of course I don't think any of those things then, I just think, OK, this is how we're going to get to England, where I will be Ygraine's daughter."

Rory's been feeling dozy. The mention of the boat wakes him up a bit, that and the name of the little town. Where's he heard this before?

"She was going to adopt you?" Iz says.

"Yes."

"How could she do that? Without paperwork?"

"Your sister wasn't interested in the right papers."

"No," Iz agrees. "She wasn't."

"I said to her, Yes, take me to England, it's the right place."

"She asked you?"

"Of course. She knows my gift."

Iz absorbs this for a while.

"That's why she took you," she says. "Stole you."

"Of course."

"How did she know?"

"She came to my grandmother one day."

"Your grandmother?"

"In the gypsy camp," Rory says. He's quite glad of the chance to show he knows part of the story. "Not her real grandmother, she just made Silvia pretend she was. She said she could do fortune-telling but actually it was Silvia."

Silvia nods at him. "One day an English woman comes in, in a shawl. The old women are very excited because the English have lots of money. My grandmother puts red on her cheeks, makes tea with too much sugar. She tells me to stand like this"—Silvia puts her arms straight at her side and bows her head—"and say nothing, only pour tea. But I have to be there, to listen, because of course my grandmother knows nothing without me. So the English lady comes in and bows to my grandmother, very polite, and looks at me, and says, 'Who's this?' And as soon as I look at her I see the god in her face."

She's stopped snipping. The fire spits and murmurs unaccompanied.

"God?" says Iz.

"I see it like a shadow. It's like she stands in front of the sun. I see the shadow of the light all around her. I know this light, I recognize it, it's what shows me everything I see. But I've never felt it bright like that before. My grandmother gives me a little cup to hold. For tea, for the leaves, you know? She pretends to see the future in the leaves. When I look at the English lady I drop the cup, I can't help myself. I say to my grandmother, This lady walks in light. My grandmother is so angry with me for breaking the cup, for speaking, she beats me in front of the English lady. Ygraine stops her like this." Silvia snatches Iz's wrist and holds it up dramatically. "I think she's even angrier than my grandmother. She speaks very slowly, she doesn't know Romanian so well, but she says she's going to teach me with the other children, at the orphanage where I used to be. There's no argument. She says she will come to pick me up every second day, and every time she will look to see if I'm hurt. She says if she sees they have hit me she will call the police. Then she takes me outside, by myself, and she asks me, What did you say? I'm too frightened to tell her anything. But she knows. She can tell it's me who is the famous gypsy fortune-teller, not this horrible old woman. Later she told me she knew as soon as she looked at me. She said it's like love at first sight."

"Iggy always thought that was the only kind."

"The only kind of love?"

"Yes. She used to say you knew straightaway. Otherwise you were just trying to persuade yourself."

"And you don't think so?"

"No." Iz rubs her wrist where Silvia was holding it. Not because it hurt her, Rory thinks. It's more like she'd forgotten what it was like to be touched. "The opposite. You don't really know you love someone until after they're gone."

Silvia smiles. "I don't agree."

"Did you know her fortune? Did you ever tell her?"

"Of course. I told you, I know it's the same as mine." She makes the roads-going-together gesture with her fingers like she did with Rory. "I told her we travel the same road. Towards the truth."

"That's what you said? To Iggy? No wonder she stole you away."

"I told her what I see," Silvia says sharply. "I don't lie."

"No. Of course."

What I tell her is the truth. You want to know what happened to your sister? That's what happened. She came to the end of the road and the truth was waiting for her."

There's a rather unhappy silence, so Rory says, "That god."

They both look at him.

"He said so. At that other place, where I found you. He said"—he closes his eyes and finds the words branded on his memory like a permanent scar—"'This is the end of her road. I'm the light she sought.'"

He'd forgotten how alarming it is when Silvia stares at you full-bore.

"You spoke to him? You saw him?"

He can't explain about the reflection so he just says, "Yeah."

"God," Iz says.

"Yeah. Well, not *God* god. Not like . . ." What's he talking about? "He said there were lots, not just, you know, like, one big one. And he said . . ." The words may be burned on his brain but that doesn't make them any easier to grasp. They're still livid and strange. "He had lots of names and they're all different but still him.

Iz exchanges a look with Silvia over her shoulder. Silvia arches her impressive eyebrows.

"Wasn't it frightening?" Iz asks him.

"Not really."

Iz turns around in her chair. "Where did you find this boy?"

"Ah," Silvia says. "Now this is an interesting question."

Instead of answering, she comes around to the front of the chair, squats down, looks at Iz from the left and the right.

"I'm making you look like her," she says.

Iz reaches forward and grabs at her arm. "Tell me what happened to her," she says.

Silvia sighs. She puts the scissors down and sits on the rug next to the cat. She scratches its head. She's facing the fire, her back turned to the others.

"All I can tell you is what happened to me," she says. "Maybe Rory can say more."

He'd just been starting to feel properly sleepy again. He sits up. "What?"

"Maybe."

"How would I know?"

She turns around. Her face is transfigured by firelight.

"Because you were there," she says.

32

e came past Korinthos. There were many boats there but all too big, too many people, too many papers. She has to find somewhere small. Quiet. So we go south, west, into empty country. We end up in Arcadia. She talks to men, pays them more money, I guess. I don't know. I remember she tells me one day that we're not going to sleep in the car, we're going to have a room in a taverna. Like a tiny hotel. It's just a village in the hills, small, very poor, a village taverna with three white rooms, but I remember I'm so excited to sleep in a bed, I think it's like a palace. She's very excited too, very happy. She says next day we're getting on a boat, on the way to England. It's a beautiful warm evening, we eat outside, by a mountain river. She's smiling all the time. She's not always happy but that evening she looks like maybe she'll come off the ground. She says to me, Silvia, do you know, in the mountains here there is an old temple which belongs to the god Apollo. She says he's the god of oracles; he's the one who shows people the future. She's laughing. She says, That must be your god, Silvia.

"We're talking in English, I remember. I remember the funny way she says his name, *Apollo*, with the English *o*. She tells me she wants to go and say thank you to this god. She's going to leave me in the white room in the taverna and walk to the temple in the night. I want to go with her but she says no, I need to sleep, the next days will be tiring and maybe it's hard to sleep on the boat. So when we're finished eating she takes me to the little room, puts me in bed. She says she will wait to go until I am asleep and come back before I'm awake, so I won't even know she isn't there all the time. I remember her sitting in a little wooden chair by the bed, saying that, and I look at her and think, Yes, that's perfect, I won't even know. I trust her so much. She can say anything to me and I believe it here, you know? In my heart. I close my eyes and I never see her again. It's the last thing she ever said to me.

"I woke up early. Maybe even when I'm sleeping I can feel she isn't there. The room is locked and she's taken the key. I wait a long time but I know something's wrong. I climb out of the window and down to the street and go looking for her. Walking. I'm very frightened but I'm more frightened of being by myself without Ygraine so I walk up into the hills alone, the way I think she went. All the time I'm calling, Ygraine, where are you, Ygraine, unless a car comes by, then I hide in the trees. It's a steep road. I keep walking like that until it's just coming light."

"Getting light," Rory says.

"Then I meet this boy."

She stops for a long time.

"What boy did you meet?" Iz eventually asks.

"This boy," Silvia says, without turning away from the fire. "Rory."

Iz looks at him.

"How old are you?" she says.

"Ten."

"And this was . . ."

"Twenty years ago," Silvia says. "Nineteen ninety-three, ninety-four, I'm not sure. I told you, it's impossible. But it's the truth."

Iz shuts her eyes for a moment. "I didn't say I don't believe you," she says. "I spent too long saying that to someone."

Rory's sitting bolt upright now. Something inconceivably strange is expanding inside him, impermeable to thought, like a black hole.

"I think because he's a boy, alone, younger than me, it's safe to talk to him. I don't know enough Greek so I talk to him in English.

He doesn't look like a Greek boy anyway. He answers me in Romani. My own language."

Rory knots his fingers together. They feel solid. They're picking up the warmth of the fire. He can hear the cat purring. Everything's steady and straightforward. Everything feels normal.

"He knows my name. He calls me Silvia. I think, He must be a spy, from the orphanage maybe, he wants to take me back there. Or he's from the police. But he knows things about me and Ygraine so I don't knock him down or run away. I think he must know where she is. He says he wants to show me something." Silvia's reaching to the back of her neck. She unties a knot under her hair and takes off her necklace, the little pouch on its cord. She loosens the pouch and tips its contents into her hand. "He gives me," she says, swiveling around, "these."

They have a dull gleam in the light of the fire. They're so smooth and dark they look wet. Rory falls into the black hole and feels the whole universe turn itself inside out.

Iz leans forward to look. She glides a fingertip over them.

"Acorns," she whispers, as if they're exactly what she was expecting.

"I don't understand what the boy is doing but I take them anyway. Then . . ." She rubs her face, drawing a slow breath. "The sun came over the hills. Suddenly there's light everywhere. I feel like I'm swimming in it. Everything's too bright to look at. The next thing I remember, I'm standing alone again. No boy. But I'm holding these, which he gave me."

Rory remembers too. How could he not? It was only this morning, or afternoon perhaps. He scooped the acorns out of the fountain and put them in her hand himself.

"Ever since then I carry them. Day and night, all the time. I never take this off except to change the string. Not until now."

"May I?" Iz says. She's completely fascinated by the acorns. They're just random acorns. Rory could have picked up twigs or leaves, there was all sorts of other stuff in the pool. But Silvia lets Iz take them and turn them over between her fingers, one by one.

"It was you, Rory," Silvia says. "When I saw you on the island, in those ruins, I recognize you straightaway. Even before you tell me your name. Same face, same age, same size, everything. Even your voice is the same though you spoke to me in Romani then and now in English. Why do you think I told Lino to bring you to us, told you everything about us? Do you think I would say who we are, where we're going, if you are just any English boy on that island?"

Rory's got no answer.

"That first time I meet you, on that road, in Arcadia, I think afterwards you must be like a god."

Even though he's floating around in the middle of his black hole at the center of an unmoored inside-out universe, that gets through to him.

"Me?" he says.

"You know these things about me. You're just a boy alone but you speak Romani, you say you want to help me. Then the sun rises and"—she raises a hand and flicks the fingers open—"you disappear."

"But—"

"Then twenty years later I see you on that island where the storm blows me, and you're still a boy, not older, not younger. Was I right, Rory? Are you the god?"

He's blushing madly. She's totally serious. He's never met anyone who does serious like Silvia. You can't possibly miss it.

"She had an acorn with her," Iz says. "Iggy did." To his relief, Iz is concentrating equally seriously on something different. She's staring at the little brown pellets as if they might be God too. Perhaps everything is. Perhaps the sodding cat's actually a god. Rory's so far out of his depth he's thinking about standing up and announcing he'll go to bed now, thanks very much, though he suspects that if he tried getting out of his chair he'd fall over. "On my way here from London I met a man who'd known Iggy," Iz goes on. "He ended up giving it to me, the acorn. He told me it was hers. He told me it was the only thing she cared about." She looks at Silvia. "You don't know why she'd have carried an acorn with her?"

"She used to call me Little Acorn. Like that, in English. Little Acorn. It's my name, Silvia Ghinda. In Romanian *ghinda* is acorn. I thought that's why the boy gives them to me that day. It's like he's giving me myself."

"She fled," Iz says. "That's all I know. She was terrified of something. And of the sun, terrified of the sun. That same man I met, he told me she never went outdoors except at night. She did get back to England somehow. That was ninety-four, it must have been quite soon after she left you. She wouldn't see any of us. She sent us all a letter. The same letter for everyone, I mean, all her family, everyone she knew. I'll never forget the day I read it. She said she'd discovered she was a sinner and her only hope was Jesus's forgiveness. She said she was going into hiding and none of us should look for her or expect to hear from her ever again."

"Jesus's forgiveness?" Silvia says, incredulous. She takes the acorns back from Iz.

"Yes. She wrote about giving herself into God's protection. I found out later she joined one of those communities. A Christian retreat. Very near here, actually."

Silvia looks up sharply. "She lived near here?"

"Very near. Just a few miles away, in the days when that meant anything. I can show you on the map if you like."

"What's it called?" Rory says, though he knows. He's definitely not God, but he does have the strange feeling that the whole of the universe has somehow ended up inside him, instead of the other way around.

"What? The place?"

"That community you were talking about."

"It was in the grounds of an estate called Trelow."

"Thought so," he says, which makes both women look at him with widened eyes. "That's where I found you," he tells Silvia.

"I don't understand," Iz says.

"Just now. Earlier on today, I mean. When I came into the Valley and was wandering around. I got to that place. Trelow. I saw the name on the signs. That's where Silvia was when she didn't know who she was. I mean *when*, when she was. She didn't know how old she was; she thought she was a child. She thought she was somewhere else. Then that god showed up and emptied her out completely." If he knew how to do it he'd explain about giving her the acorns, about how everything she remembers happening ages ago in that place called Arcadia actually happened earlier on today, but there are things words just won't do, apparently. "It was definitely that place," he goes on, because they both look like they're having a hard time believing him. "There were signs for a community center."

"She lived here?" Silvia says. "So close to where we are?"

"I didn't find out myself until I was nearly here," Iz says. "I wasn't looking for her, I was looking for . . . Someone else." She's kneading her hands against each other. "I even found some things that belonged to her. Something she wrote, though you couldn't read it anymore."

Silvia has that look on her face which makes Rory suspect she's forgotten there's anyone else in the room. "I found her then," she whispers.

"She must have been with the community two years or so. I never heard from her. She promised we wouldn't and she meant it. As always."

"Two years?" Silvia says. "Then what?"

"She got pregnant. I can tell you exactly when that was. It would have been January of 'ninety-six. The Christians obviously didn't approve. She wasn't married or anything. So they made her leave. She . . ." Iz is hunched over herself in her chair now. The mess that's left of her hair hides her face. "She had the baby alone. That's what killed her. In the end, I mean. She had the baby, a boy, and she brought it to . . ."

Rory watches her squeeze her hands between her thighs.

"She died quite soon afterwards, I think," Iz goes on. "She suffered terribly from the birth."

"The child?" Silvia says.

"The boy survived," Iz whispers, with a minute shake of her head, which means something like *I can't say anything more about this or I'll die myself.*

"My brother," Silvia says, with a smile.

Startled, Iz looks up.

"She always called me her daughter. I think she means after we come to England and she adopts me, but she says, No, Silvia, as soon as I took you away we become mother and child." Silvia turns to Rory. "I didn't tell you the truth. Or Lino, or Per. I don't come all this way to find a magic ring." Just like the Professor said, Rory thinks. He should have known, really. "I said this because I need men to help me, the world's too dangerous to travel on my own. But always I was only looking for her. For Ygraine. Always, all those years, the only thing I want, it's to find her again. That's why I make a way to leave you and Per and Lino when I know I'm close."

She stares at him, calmly unapologetic. She's not the sort of person you can imagine being sorry for anything they've done.

"You went all that way looking for someone who's been dead for years?"

"I don't think so."

"You don't think she's dead?" Iz says. Her voice has gone scratchy with distress.

"Maybe it's that. Or maybe she left something behind that's here still." She pushes herself across the rug to crouch in front of Iz, arms resting on her knees. "All my life until today," she says, "I know what lies ahead of me. I know that I find what I am looking for. I can't remember what happened to me after I came in the Valley and now my gift is gone but listen, listen." She shakes Iz gently but insistently. "I found your sister. Or I found part of her, or what remains from her, whatever she leaves behind. It's true. Maybe I'll never remember now but I know it's the truth. Always, always."

Iz is shaking her head in despair. "Don't," she says. "Please don't. She's dead, and her boy's lost. It's all finished. Nothing happens here. Nothing more can happen."

"Look!" Rory says.

The night sky has filled with stars. Behind the muted reflection of firelight in the three sash windows there's a great chorus of faraway light, like moonlight scattered across the sea except permanent, motionless, and hard, and spread from horizon to horizon. "Look!" he says again, and as the three of them turn to see they hear a sound. It might be falling from the stars themselves it's so beautiful, though it's just one voice, a single pristine carol singing on behalf of the innumerable pinpricks of silence.

The two women stand up. They all go to the window. You can't not go to the window, that's how amazing the stars are. It's like the sky's disappeared entirely and there's absolutely nothing, not a bubble of air, not a mote, not a molecule between the earth they're standing on (if it is even still the earth) and the billion suns in the unthinkable distance.

"Holly," Iz whispers. "I've never heard her sing like that before."

A deep scraping noise echoes down the hallway, making them all jump. The old front doors of the house have just been pushed open. As if in confirmation, a trickle of cold air washes in around their ankles. They all look at each other. Only Silvia has the presence of mind to move: she goes out into the corridor. The doors scrape and creak again, opening wider. Iz clutches at Rory's shoulder.

"Oh yeah," he says, slightly ashamed. He should have mentioned this before. "Rose said something about someone coming. Back. Someone coming back."

Iz turns a slow look on Rory, the kind of look which feels like it might abolish speech altogether. Silvia calls from the hallway.

"There are people at the door," she says.

33

Rory's never liked watching adults get emotional. His mother cried a lot after Dad and Jake and Scarlet left, and it made him feel terrible, like she expected comfort from him which he didn't know how to give. So as soon as someone notices him again he says he's very tired and is there somewhere he can go to bed?

It's not true, though. He's not tired. That's why he's still awake. The bed feels lumpy and crusty and smells of maybe sawdust or straw, something clean and dry but uncared for. It's enormous. It's high off the floor and so wide he can't reach both sides with his arms out. It's one of those four-poster beds, with curtains to make it into a little room of its own, though he asked Silvia to make sure they wouldn't close. He can still hear noises from downstairs. It sounds like they've calmed down a bit. He's propped up on a big doughy pillow, eyes wide open. Starlight picks out details of a bare wooden room: carved leaves and berries in the mantelpiece, a bowl on the floor, the drooping tail of a rocking horse.

Silvia sounds much louder than the others, or clearer at least. He can't quite hear the words, though. Perhaps she's telling her story all over again.

After a while—a long while, perhaps—he hears footsteps on the gravel in front of the house, outside the window of his room. He climbs across the bed and looks out. The panes of the window are diamonds of cloudy glass in a frame of iron, so it's hard to see, but it looks like the man and Iz are going around the house towards the garden and the woods. They're walking pressed right up against each other, arm in arm. Sometime later (he's still sitting in the window seat, caught in the starlight like a moth) they come back. The man's carrying a big jug, cradling it to his chest in a way which suggests it's heavy. Full of water, perhaps, from the well which cures every illness of body or soul. For the burned woman, then, who could obviously use it. They're about to reach the steps at the front of the house when the angel appears, blotting out a swathe of the sky like an animated hole. It falls to earth beside them and says something to the man. Rory can hear the sound of its voice through the window, though not the words, if they even are words. It's like a saw struggling through a tough branch. The man looks up at the window where Rory's watching.

So Rory goes back to bed.

Another while later the cat appears, hopping onto the bed and prodding its way around the covers until it finds a comfortable niche on top of his legs. By this time the voices downstairs are beginning to go quiet. Some of the others come up the stairs past the open door of his room, candlelight accompanying them. He hears the unmistakable shuffle of the burned woman, and Silvia's confident stride. He wishes Silvia would come in to check on him but she doesn't. He thinks of nights at the Abbey, those times when his mother couldn't or wouldn't look after him at Parson's. *She just needs to be on her own for a bit,* Viola would tell him. *It'll all be all right in the morning.* He doesn't know if he's even in the same world as the Abbey anymore. To them he's probably just another lost person now, gone like everyone else who's not a girl or a woman. They'll have gritted their teeth and told each other, All we can do is carry on, keep working, survive another winter.

They don't quite feel real to him. There was something wrong with the way they looked at the world, clinging on to whatever fragments of The Old Days they could dig out of the ruins. Drops of diesel, scraps of solar power, specks of toothpaste. Hating and fearing Them. He can't imagine his mother or Laurel or Pink or even Kate following him into this world of magic gypsies and talking foxes and God and everything.

The only person he properly misses is Her.

Someone is coming into his room after all. Maybe he dozed off, he can't tell. There's no candlelight but he can hear the steps.

He sits up. "Silvia?"

"She's asleep." It's the man. "Everyone's asleep except us."

The man goes to sit in the ledge by the window. He's changed his clothes, not surprisingly since the ones he arrived in were in tatters like a castaway's. He's wearing an old man's dressing gown. Oddly, this makes him look younger. He's hardly a man at all anyway. When he pulls his legs up on the window seat and rests his chin on his knees he could almost be younger than Laurel.

He's washed his feet off a bit but they still look like they belong to a bird, scrawny and leathery and knobbly. White hawk. He wiggles his toes.

"Aren't you tired?"

"Dunno."

Rory's not sure what he thinks about the man, whose name is Gawain, though Iz and the burned woman both call him Gav. He has a lurking sense that he ought to apologize for pretending to be him when he was tricking Rose. Plus he liked it better when it was just Iz and Silvia and himself, before the others arrived and it all got emotional.

"What made you choose this room?" Gawain says. Like Iz (who both is and isn't his mother, in some way Rory still doesn't properly understand) he's got an odd stuttering way of talking, as if he's not used to it and it takes a lot of effort, or at least a lot of thought.

"Dunno. I didn't. Silvia chose it. Said it looked OK."

Gawain sees something on the floor and bends to fetch it. A pencil. He examines it in the soft white light.

"I can go somewhere else if this is your room," Rory says.

"No need, it's fine."

Gawain taps the pencil against his lips. Rory waits for him to say something else. After all, the man's the one who invited himself in.

"Is this your house?"

Gawain stops tapping to think about it.

"Yes," he says, a little doubtfully.

"So you're the white hawk." It sounds like a superhero. The man could just about work as a superhero, one of the moody troubled ones.

Rory feels foolish as soon as he's said it.

"Who told you that?"

"Rose," he mumbles. "At the gate."

"It's just my name. Gawain. One of the things it might mean. *Gwalch gwin* is 'white hawk' in Welsh. They have trouble with names."

"The Welsh?"

"Spirits. Beings like Rose. Names turn out to be complicated things. They're true in an unusual way."

"Spirits? Like . . . ghosts?"

Gawain leans back. Again like his mother (or whatever Iz is) he has a way of starting a smile without ever getting there. "One of the things I found out," he says, "is that you don't get very far trying to say what something actually is. I learned that lesson early on. When I was your age, probably. How old are you?"

"Ten. And a half."

"That's good," Gawain says, as if Rory's confirmed something he already knew. "No wonder the rose let you in."

"I tricked her." He mumbles it, head down.

"That's all right."

"Is it?"

"Yup. Doesn't it sound weird to you? Saying you tricked a rose?"

Rory hasn't thought of it that way. "She looked like a girl and everything. Almost," he adds, remembering the teeth. "She talked. Anyway, it's different here, isn't it. Earlier on I ran into some foxes and they could talk."

"You've come a very long way from home," Gawain says, or maybe he says *from Home*. "For a ten-year-old."

Rory's faintly annoyed by the man's tone. "Yeah," he says. "That god said it's because I'm not surprised."

Gawain looks at him very steadily. He's got a rather pointy face, meaning there are deep shadows in it whenever he turns side-on to the window.

"You met a god?"

"Twice, actually."

"And you're not surprised?"

Gawain's not at all like Ol, but Rory still can't help wondering whether he's being mocked. "Should I be?"

Gawain's not offended. "I'd like to give you something, Rory," he says. He puts the pencil into a fraying pocket of the dressing gown and takes something else out, hidden in his fist. He climbs onto the bed, startling Rory. "To look after." He sits cross-legged and opens his hand to reveal a plain dark ring threaded on a metal chain. The chain glistens, a tiny snake coiled on the man's palm. He finds the clasp, unhooks it, draws the chain out of the ring and puts it away. "Here," he says, holding out his hand.

Rory hesitates.

"So there really is a ring," he says.

"Yes," Gawain says. "There really is."

"A magic ring."

"Yes."

"Silvia told me she'd made that up."

"She might well have. Perhaps she couldn't help telling the truth anyway."

"So is it what she was actually looking for?"

"No. I'd have offered it to her if it was."

It's not shiny or carved with mystic runes, at least not that he can see. It looks like it's made of plain wood. "What does it do?"

"It doesn't do anything. It *is* something."

"Is what?"

"Magic. As you said."

Rory puts his fingers out and then stops.

"Is it safe to touch it?"

"I'm not trying to play some kind of trick on you, Rory. No harm can come to you here."

"What's magic about it? If it doesn't do anything?"

"That's one of the other things I've found out. Magic isn't about doing things. I have a feeling people just don't get that. Probably because doing stuff's like air to people, it's what they live on, without even noticing. If a person was stuck like Holly is they'd go mad in a couple of days. Like taking away their air."

"Who is this Holly everyone keeps talking about?"

"I'll take you to meet her in the morning if you like." He pushes his hand a bit closer. "Will you take this?"

Rory picks up the ring. It's completely smooth in a soft, almost grainy way. It feels light and ordinary and a bit boring. He can tell just by the feel of it that it's not going to summon armies of the dead or let him turn invisible.

"Where's it from?" he asks.

Gawain's fiddling with the chain, looping it back around his own neck and reattaching the clasp. "I could tell you," he says, "that at the beginning of time, when people began to write things down and so created the past and future, a god gave this to a woman as a pledge of love, and then made her keep it when she broke her promise and refused to love him back. And that it was lost under the sea when people decided to forget about magic, and came back when they remembered again. But that probably wouldn't help much. I walked a very long way to fetch it, and then Auntie Gwen and I sailed even farther to bring it back here. This is where it belongs. If it belongs anywhere."

"So why are you giving it to me?"

"To look after. And because I'm not sure I want it anymore. And because you're not surprised."

"Are you going somewhere?"

"I might be."

"You only just got here!"

"I know. And I promised I'd never leave again when I did. I can't break a promise if I'm carrying that ring. I'm a bit like Silvia, I have to tell the truth even when I don't want to."

So is it really a magic ring or not? Rory's very confused. Silvia and the Professor were both quite certain there was no such thing, that it was just a hoax. "Does it matter if I put it on?"

Gawain thinks for a while before answering. "Nothing matters in this place. I think that's what being here means."

Rory repeats that to himself a couple of times and decides it's an unnecessarily complicated way of answering *No*. He puts the ring on the index finger of his right hand. Nothing happens. What can happen in Paradise? Happening is abolished, or not yet thought of.

34

ncient light refracts in slices of glass, the springs of a four-poster bed store energy under the weight of two lean boys, the air curls in invisible waves as they exhale, but all because this is the order of things, like day after night after day after night after day, change without difference, sequence without consequence, like the endurance of absent things in memory, like the knowledge that although everyone else in Pendurra is asleep, Iseult and Silvia and burned Guinevere and even the cat, there's "someone waiting downstairs."

Gawain's got to his feet. He's standing by the bed, watching Rory. Over the past couple of years his eyes have taken on that unfathomable look, bequeathed to him by the prophetess along with her two-faced gift.

"Is there," he says. "Shall we go and see?"

"OK," the boy says, and pushes back the covers. He's naked, but neither of them cares and there's no one else to see. The two of them go down barefoot to the room at the bottom of the stairs, with its three windows and almost dormant fire.

Everything's made out of shadow, every solid substance interchangeable with its neighboring space. In the chair (all planes and angles of varying dark) where Iseult sat before, she sits again, shrouded and dissolved, though the winking embers pick out a face from which nearly twenty unspent years have fallen away. She's holding the silver crucifix in her lap.

"Gawain," she whispers. "Gawain."

He goes to sit in the chair opposite her. The other boy stands behind him.

"Is it really you?" the woman says.

"It's me," Gawain answers.

"My boy," she says. "My child."

"Hello, Mum," Gawain says.

"Could I touch you? If you wore the ring? Would that be allowed?"

"Sorry. We can't do that. And Rory has to hold the ring. He's the one who brings it all together. He found your crucifix, and Silvia. The god appeared to him."

"Don't say his name."

"I won't. I don't even know what it is."

"Don't let him come. Don't let him send me away from you now."

"It's all right, Mum."

"I'm so sorry for everything I did. Can you please forgive me, Gawain? Is that why I'm here?"

"There's nothing to forgive."

"There is. Please say it. I need to hear it."

"If you're trying to say sorry for leaving me, of course I forgive you. You couldn't help it."

"Was Lizzie good to you? I didn't know where else to turn."

"Lizzie?—oh, you mean Mum. Iseult. She tried her best."

"And Nigel?"

"Nigel's a prick."

"I'm sorry."

"It's OK. I managed. We all managed."

"It's my fault."

"You're not to blame for Nigel being a prick."

"It all began with me."

"That's not true. I promise it isn't. It's all an old, old story." Gawain looks like he wants to reach across the gap between them, put his hand into the shadows which make up the woman. "It's time for you to forget it all. Let everything go."

"I want to, Gawain. But he won't let me."

"The god won't?"

"Don't say his name."

"It'll be better now, Mum. Now that everything's come together. Auntie Gwen's here too, did you know that? We all found each other. Even Silvia. I think that's what you've been waiting for, isn't it?"

"I've been waiting for you."

"And that."

"Only for you. To hear your voice. I can actually see you. Like you were here with me in the flesh. You look so like Lizzie."

"Everyone always says that."

"I made her promise never to tell you that you weren't hers."

"She never did."

"Can you forgive me for that?"

"Of course I can. You don't need forgiveness."

"I do."

"Well, not from me."

"From everyone. I do. From the whole world."

"It's not like that."

"It is, Gawain. You can't imagine how terrible it is. Since magic came back."

"I've seen it, Mum."

"Terror. Chaos. Such awful things."

"The world's always been full of bad things happening. That was true before."

"No, you don't understand. I've seen even good people do unspeakable things, just to keep themselves alive, or their children. And the hunger is everywhere. Hunger's horrible to watch, it's like being tortured to death. And the grief. Everywhere. I can't stand it."

Gawain waits a while and then says, gently, "I think you'll be better if you said what happened to you."

"I can't."

"I think it's what you need. The last thing. Tell me how I began."

"I'm frightened to."

"Don't be. Nothing can go wrong here. I'm with you."

"I don't want to say his name."

"You don't have to say any names."

"I don't want him to come. I don't want him to speak to me. Or to you. Anything but that."

"Mum, listen. He's my father, isn't he?"

The shadow-woman doesn't answer, but her silence answers for her.

"I'm not a child," Gawain says. "I changed. I can't really explain how, but I'm not afraid anymore. Of anything. You can tell me."

"You should be afraid," the woman whispers.

"Tell us what happened. It's all right."

"He can make me suffer like this even though I died. I'm here, I can see you, I want to touch you, I want to talk to you forever, I want to be your mother. He won't let me escape all this wanting."

"Silvia says you traveled with her to that place in Greece."

"Silvia. Poor little Silvia."

"She's all right now. Everything's turned out all right. She told us most of your story. You stayed with her until she went to sleep, is that it? You were going to walk to a temple."

"Don't, Gawain."

"It's OK, Mum. I'm here. You went to the temple, didn't you? That night."

"Don't. It'll burn me."

"It won't."

"The words will come out and they'll burn everything. He is the Plague. He made ruin."

"Mum, I spent too much of my life pretending things hadn't happened. Honestly, there's no alternative to the truth. That's what's happening out there. That's all it is; it's just truth. The Plague, magic, all of it. Tell me. You found the temple. What happened, did you pray? Iseult told me you always wanted so much to believe in miracles."

"Don't."

"You'd been all that way with Silvia. You must have known she had a gift. Did you want to say thank you? Is that it?"

"It was terrible."

"Someone told me once that truth hurts. But this'll be the last time. I promise."

"I lay down." A deep tremor has come into her voice. "It was so warm. The night was so wide. Incredibly soft. The temple's covered in scaffolding, I was crushed when I saw it. It wasn't much better than a building site. But just near it there was a stand of oaks. Old trees. So beautiful in the starlight. I thought, That's the real temple. You could tell as soon as you went under them it was a magic place. And little Silvia, her name was *acorn*. It felt so right. It's all stony and dry up there but just in that one place, just among those trees there was a little grass, where the water ran underground. Dry grass, but soft. It was all so blissful I had to lie down. The journey with Silvia had been such a struggle but I'd done all the hard parts, it was almost over. I'd never thought I'd want children but she'd become like my own daughter. There were acorns in the grass. I kept picking them up, touching them, thinking about her, how she'd grow, what she'd become. How she might change the world. Thinking about what grows from something small. Touching them . . . I hadn't been with a man for half a year. I was tingling with joy, Gawain, buzzing with it. You have to imagine what it was like. So far from everywhere, so wonderful. I took all my clothes off. I couldn't help it. The air was just perfect. I lay there and there were all the acorns under me and in my fingers, and I couldn't help it, I started . . . I started . . ."

"It's all right," Gawain says again.

"I just wanted to say thank you. It felt like the right way of doing it. I did say it. I cried it aloud. I kept saying it afterwards, Thank you, thank you, like that, in the grass." There's no bliss at all in her voice. She's whispering with swallowed horror. "You could feel . . . I knew the trees were listening to me. It was like praying. Like praying's supposed to be."

"And then," Gawain says.

"I didn't sleep. I know I didn't."

"No."

"I wouldn't have. Not with Silvia back in the village by herself. I'd never have done that."

"It's OK."

"I didn't. I made myself all dreamy but I know I didn't let myself go to sleep."

"Right."

"But . . ."

"The sun came."

"Don't say it!"

"Tell me, then. Say the words yourself. I've done it, see. It's all right."

"The sun came. Oh, God. It was still night, I swear it was. It was like fire under the trees. It was my fault. I'd been lying there, all blissed out. I knew I was in a temple. I said it aloud, I said, Whatever god lives here, whatever god led me to Silvia and her gift, I want to . . . I want . . ."

The shadow shudders into silence.

"You wanted the god to show himself."

"Don't," she whispers.

"So he did."

"Oh, God. The light."

"And you were scared."

"It was terror. He was terror."

"You called him, and then when he came you said no."

"No!" The woman almost screams. "No!"

"Just like Cassandra did, once. At the beginning."

"I ran. Like running through lava. I could feel it at my back. Burning. I ran down the mountain. God help me, I ran away. I left Silvia. A little girl. That fire was all over my skin. Trying to get inside me. You can't escape it. I don't want to say any more. Let me go now, Gawain, please. Close the door."

"Nearly. You're nearly finished, Mum. Nothing can hurt you. Not where we are now."

"No. You can't hide."

"You tried, didn't you? Iseult told me. She said you came back to England, joined those Christians. She said you wouldn't go outside in daylight."

"You can't." The ghost of Gawain's dead mother is fixed fast on those two words. "You can't."

"But he found you."

"The force of him, Gawain. The fire of a god. He made me like a spark. Tiny, like nothing. Like a speck of dust in a tornado. He burned my tongue so I couldn't say no. Or yes. I didn't matter. I was just a thing; he was fire. He melted me. He split me open. He put you inside me. His gift."

Neither of them speaks for a long time, if *time*'s the right word: things don't start or finish or waste away between the living and the dead.

"Which," Gawain says at last, "is also a curse."

"Undo it," the woman says, with a sudden hopeless urgency, the desiccated fervor of the dead. "Give it back. For my sake."

"Is that why he gave you back your voice? To tell me that?"

"I can't tell you why. Reasons are for people in the world. Not for me. Or him. I just know you can do it. If I'm allowed to tell you my story then I'm giving you a way back to the beginning. I'm showing you where you began. You can undo it."

"I can't undo myself."

"You know who you are now. You can choose not to carry that weight. You're not him, you're my boy too. What else is my story for? If my sin was irreversible I'd be nothing, I'd be finished. You can put it right."

"It wasn't a sin, Mum."

"I called him into the world. I did it."

"He's always been in the world."

"I didn't mean to! I just wanted . . . For that one night, in that place, I so wanted it to be true. It was all so magical. I thought, if ever there was something more wonderful that we know about, this would be the place. Like when I was thirteen and reading books about dragons and so so wishing that world was true."

"It was always the truth," Gawain says. "People just forgot. For a long time."

"Then let them forget again. Give back your gift. You said it yourself; it's a curse. The world can't bear it. I know. No one knows like I do. He hounded me, Gawain. You can't imagine the terror of it. Let it all go quiet again. Hide yourself here, away from the world.

Leave the ring alone. Bury it, let it be forgotten. Please. We're better off without gods."

Gawain answers reluctantly. "I wouldn't know."

"I remember being young. I hated the banality of everything. Ask Lizzie, she'll tell you. I so desperately wanted things to be different, not stupid and empty. I never noticed how hard people work just to make existence bearable. All those things I despised, comfort, money. The things everyone spent all their time thinking about instead of God. They did it because the gods are intolerable. It must have taken centuries of struggle for people to forget magic. So much effort. And I brought it blazing back and threw the world into catastrophe. You can turn it, Gawain, my love. I know you can. Send the gods away. Hide us from them again. Oh. Oh, my mouth is drying up. This is it. This is all I have to say." In the shadows she's harder to see already. "These are all the words allowed me. Gawain?"

"I'm here."

"I love you. I'm sorry."

"You're forgiven. Totally."

"I love you all. You and Lizzie and Gwen and little Silvia. You most of all, though I never knew you."

"All right. I understand."

"Return." The fire's finally gone out altogether. The woman's voice is drifting away like the last thread of smoke."

"Return the ring, you mean."

"Refusal," she says, though the word is barely anywhere at all.

"Refuse the gift."

"Love" is the last thing distinguishable from mere air.

Gawain says nothing.

He waits a long time. The boy stands behind him, the ring on his finger still.

Then Gawain leans forward and at last touches the folded shadows in the opposite chair.

The woman twitches and makes a sleepy noise.

"Mum?" Gawain says.

"Mmm?"

"Mum? The fire's out."

"Gav?" She stretches.

"Let's get you upstairs. Find a proper bed."

Iz pushes her hair away from her face and sighs. "I still can't believe you're back," she says. "Is that Rory?" She squints into the dark corner. "I thought you'd gone to bed ages ago. Do you want some pajamas?" She gets up, holding on to Gawain. "I had a dream about Iggy."

"So did I," Gawain says.

35

The boy roams the house, an enchanted forest of architecture, a secret garden of oak and iron and plaster. Its only season is night. Time, growth, and decay have abdicated. Everything sleeps, or stops rather than sleeps, perfectly hidden behind the impenetrable briar rose. |Even Gawain sleeps, a blessing almost forgotten. The boy can smell his dreams: salt air, wet canvas, the ocean. The house has dreams too, rhythms of motion alternating with emptiness. Smoke and dust. Everything is equally substantial and insubstantial. The boy himself is both body and ghost, thought and ignorance. His own bed dreams of a girl growing up. She smells of the ocean too. He passes in and out of the sleepers' rooms. Everything that has happened is a tapestry, flat, soft, pressed into one plane and one frame. He sees it, but what he sees is not a picture but a hundred thousand twists of colored thread, muted by night, which makes all colors the same color.

It is the nature of cats and owls to roam their houses at night, with no one to know or afterwards say, This is what they did. This is what happened. The boy and the cat meet at the bottom of a secret stair. They ascend to a secret window and come out into the owl's house, slate and stone and moss under their feet and only air above. An owl whickers to a stop on a shallow gable beside the boy and says "'obbits!"

Uccellino, says the boy. Little bird. Threads of the tapestry run through his fingers. Each has two ends: Then and Now. At the far end is a boy, himself, Rory, and another night, when he was surprised in darkness and his story changed. The owl coughs "'obbits!"

The boy holds out his right arm. On his right hand is a magic ring. All the magic in the world, the magic of all the world, all the world made magic. The owl blinks and reminds him again, "'obbits!"

The boy takes off the ring and he's sitting on the roof. He's still naked, but it's not cold, or rather *it* is but *he's* not. Though he is, suddenly, tired. His head's spinning in the aftermath of wearing the ring. Not actually spinning, it just feels like that, whereas the owl's head is, literally, swiveling. There are damp piles of autumn leaves caught among tiles and in gutters.

"Lino!" Rory says. He's glad to see the owl. He'd like to pat it but he doesn't know how you'd do that to a bird. He can hardly see it anyway. The stars are gone, clouded over. There's a grey radiance from somewhere, diffused moonlight perhaps, but it's not much.

The owl screeches softly. Rory looks at the ring in his hand, or rather feels it: it's too dark to make out.

"Probably if I put this on again I could talk to you."

The owl pecks at its feathers.

"Maybe even turn you back into Lino. I don't know. Though he said it doesn't actually do anything, didn't he. This is it, by the way." He holds it out in his palm. "The ring Silvia told you that you were going to find."

The beak clacks fretfully.

"Funny how things turn out," he says.

A yawn ambushes him. It fades into a shiver.

"I should go back to bed," he says. "I'm glad you're here, though. I should have known it was you all along. You really helped me out."

Lino makes a throaty noise. Whatever kind of owl this is, it doesn't hoot.

Rory turns the ring over in his hand. "I'll give it to you if you want it. I don't mind."

The owl watches him. He can't see its face but he remembers the ferocious expressionlessness.

"But actually," Rory says, "I was thinking." He closes his fingers over the ring. "The hobbits? They weren't actually looking for the ring. Actually they were trying to get rid of it. Weren't they? That was the whole point. You're not even supposed to wear it." He feels the small hard circle trapped in his fist. "All those bad things happen whenever he puts it on."

The owl vanishes. A ripple of chilly air disturbs a few dead leaves. It's flown off with barely a sound.

"I wonder if that's why he gave it to me," Rory says aloud. He feels around for the ledge of the window the cat led him out of. His hand brushes fur, and a moment later a grating purr starts up.

"It's pretty weird," Rory says, to no one in particular, "that he turns out to be the son of God."

He wriggles back inside and feels his way down to the corridor at the top of the house. It's completely dark but he remembers the way. He gets himself back to the bedroom Silvia found for him. He remembers that the bed used to be Her bed, which is also pretty weird, but the memory's there (the salt flavor, the sweet-sharp tang). For a moment he's tempted to put the ring on again and taste Her as he lies there.

He'd rather sleep, though. Like everyone else.

He rests. The last point of consciousness in Pendurra fades out.

36

I t's a bit like me," says Gwen. "Burned to bits but all right on top." She taps her head with her good arm.

They're up by the monstrously overgrown gate where Rory lied his way in. It's morning. The air smells of roses. They're all standing together, looking at the half-ruined cottage with the strange statue planted outside.

Rory's come to rather like Gwen. She's surprisingly funny. He doesn't think of her as the burned woman anymore, though even after drinking the water from the well she's horribly scarred all over her face and hands, and one of her arms is withered up to the elbow. She says she's already better on the inside. Iz said she'd be better on the outside too if she went to the pool but Gwen absolutely refuses to go there, for some reason.

"I don't think I'll be moving back in, though," she says. "Did any of my poor books survive?"

"I haven't looked," Iz says.

"And this," Gwen says, limping towards the house, "must be Holly."

"Clever clever," Corbo croaks.

Rory's not startled when the tree statue moves. He ought to have known all along, really. She's the exact burnished green of holly leaves, and her face was always too watchful to be anything but alive. He even heard her humming; he just didn't want to admit to himself where the sound was coming from. Her branch-limbs untwist and she bows to Gwen. When she speaks it's like bells chiming.

"Worse than dead," she says, "and yet by grace recovered. You wear your flesh more wisely than my once-master did, burned though it be."

"Don't let's talk about that," Gwen says.

"As you wish." Holly bows again, this time with her head only. Her skull is crowned with tiny white flowers. "Forgetting is licensed here, and forgiving. For you too, liar." She turns her red gaze on Rory. "And for myself. I have almost forgotten that I was once free."

"Long time," Corbo says.

"This is Rory," Gawain says, resting a hand on his shoulder. "He belongs here as much as any of us."

"I only lied 'cos of Silvia," Rory says. "I was just trying to help her."

"I make no accusation," Holly says. "Was it not I who welcomed you first? Welcome again. The third boy-child to enter under my watch, and the last."

"All finished," Corbo agrees.

"I'd like a look inside," Gwen says. She slurs her words; her lips don't move properly and one side of her face is shriveled, pulling her mouth out of shape.

Holly swings a limb towards the broken door. "This is a homecoming," she says. "Everything returns."

Gawain's still right beside Rory, so no one else hears him say "Almost everything." Surprised by the bitterness in his whisper, Rory glances at him.

Gawain hasn't asked for the ring back. He hasn't said anything about it at all, though he's still wearing the slender silver chain around his neck, inside his shirt like he's pretending he's still got it. The ring's in Rory's trouser pocket.

"Can someone give me a hand?" Gwen says, approaching the jumble of smashed wood which is all that remains of the entrance to the cottage. Iz steps forward, and the sisters pick their way inside together, leaving the rest of them standing by Holly. It's the beginning of a mild autumn day, or at least that's what it feels like: the air and the trees are autumnal, the light's a morning light. How days and seasons actually pass here Rory wouldn't like to say.

Silvia folds her arms and comes close to Gawain. "Something is bothering you," she says.

Gawain acknowledges her with a look but doesn't answer.

Silvia gives him one of her intense stares. "Here there is no trouble, only peace. But not for you."

"Girl trouble," Corbo says.

Gawain sighs. "Don't you miss anyone, Silvia?" He waves at the wall of thorns. "Anyone out there?"

"I learned not to," she says. "After your mother left me. I taught myself, no more love, no more pain. All I wanted is to find her again. No one else. Now that's done . . . No."

"The gypsy is wise, once-boy."

"You know what kind of world it is beyond," Silvia says. "Or maybe you don't, If you were on a boat for a year. But I do. I saw enough of it. I'm ready for grief."

Again Gawain doesn't answer. From inside the cottage comes the sound of the sisters talking, Gwen laughing painfully.

"When I was talking to Rose," Rory says, "she said that's what it used to be like in here."

Gawain and Silvia are suddenly both paying attention to him. Holly too, as far as he can tell.

"At peace, I mean. Everyone was happy. That's what she said. She said it was hidden away, no one knew this was a special place so it was sort of forgotten. She was talking about The Old Days. You know. Before magic and stuff."

Gawain studies Rory.

"Do you remember," he says, "when we spoke to my mother in the night?"

"Yeah."

"The last thing she said before she went. She said we ought to make what you call the old days come back again. Remember that?"

"Is that what she meant?"

Gawain nods. "One of the things she meant."

Silvia looks confused. "Your mother?"

Rory doesn't want to try explaining. "You mean go back to when magic was only here and no one else knew?"

"I think so," Gawain says. "Return the gift. Refuse it. That's what she was talking about."

"You have this power?" Silvia says.

"Yes," says Gawain.

"You can lose your gift? Like me?"

"Hide it away," Gawain says. "Like Rory just said. For hundreds of years magic lived on here when it was nowhere else. Some people must always have known, I suppose, but no one would have believed them anyway. We could do that again. Finish all our stories here. In this enchanted garden, hidden away from the rest of the world."

"And everyone inside happy," Rory says, remembering Rose's words.

Gawain nods towards the cottage. "Like them. They don't want to be anywhere else. They're ready for grief too. God knows they've earned it. You'd all be all right here. You too, Rory. There's no disease here, no one goes hungry, the house'll always be fine. We could let everything go back to how it used to be."

"Except," Corbo says.

"Ah," Holly sighs. "Except. One place sits empty at the home-coming."

"Yes," Gawain says. "Except without Marina."

They're back in the hall that's like a church, sitting around one end of the long table. There's food in big heavy dishes, baked squash with honey, some kind of chewy yellowy bread which is incredibly delicious, pears, blackberries. No one's eating much.

"She didn't belong here, Gav," Iz says. She's gone back to looking like she'll never laugh again. She clasps her hands tightly together. "It's not her place. She couldn't manage it."

Gawain's expression is the most miserable of the lot, which is saying something. Since they started talking about Marina it's like winter has entered the house.

"Couldn't you have brought her home?" he says, so dully it's hardly even a question. He already knows the answer. He's given up.

"I would have. I should have!" Iz reaches for Gawain's hands, hesitates, holds back. "I didn't understand about her until it was too late."

"So what happened to her?"

Iz shakes her head. "I can't say it. I can't. Her mother took her in the end, that's all that matters. She was all right then. Gav, I promise. They held each other like this." Iz wraps her fingers around each other. "She went where she was supposed to be."

For a while now Rory's had the feeling he's got something he needs to tell them, but he doesn't know when or how to say it. The adults are all ignoring him. They're watching Gawain, nervously.

"I always knew," Gwen says. "We all did. It was always going to happen one day. We had this lovely fantasy, Tristram and I, that our lives would go on forever, but we were fooling ourselves. Year by year, the older she got, you could see more of her mother in her. She's better as she is. Honestly, Gav dearest. She must be."

Rory remembers: *Where I used to live there was a room which was wider and higher than your whole house.*

"I'm certain of it," Iz says. "She's safe in the sea. Completely safe."

Rory remembers: *I want you to be safe with me. Where it's always quiet.*

"I watched what happened to her mother," Gwen says. "She loved Tristram more than I've ever known anyone love anyone, but she couldn't stay with him. She had to go back. They're not the same as us."

Them Them Them. I wonder why They hate us so much.

Silvia's angry. She doesn't like the way Iz and Gwen are talking. "You think this boy is finished with his life?" She means Gawain. "Like you, like me? When he's not even a man yet?" She turns to Gawain and speaks more gently. "I see your face when you think about her. You can't just forget. I think what you want is to leave this place, go and look for this girl."

Iz is shaking her head. "She chose the sea, Silvia. She's gone."

"You say this? You? Who sat in that chair in this room, a year, two years, waiting for him?"

"This is Gav's home," Iz says quietly. "Marina went to hers."

"The thing is," Gawain says, interrupting before Silvia can come up with an impatient response, "I made a promise."

Everyone looks at him.

"To her, in fact. The day I left her. The hour. The minute. I was standing on the step outside the front door. I told her, the next time I entered Pendurra again I'd never leave."

"You left her alone?" says Silvia.

"Try to imagine," Gwen says. "This was the only place she'd ever seen. I mean *ever*. For thirteen years she'd never been out the gate. She couldn't. How could anyone think of taking her away from here?"

"A girl of thirteen? And you leave her by herself? In this house? It's like a tomb for a child."

"Believe me," Iz says, though Silvia's shaking her head. "It would have been so much better for her if she'd stayed here."

"How can I break a promise?" Gawain says.

"Does it matter so much?" Silvia's unimpressed with everyone now.

"Yes," he says. "Yes, it does. I can feel it in my mouth. It's the same with everything I say. I can feel how it needs to be true."

Gwen's sitting next to him. Her hands aren't much better than twisted claws, but she pats his arm. "I think you must have known what you were promising," she says. "Even if you didn't realize it at the time. You knew you'd have to let her go."

"It's done, Gav," Iz says. "She won't come back. She tried the world and found out what it's really like out there. She wouldn't even talk to me at the end."

"Marina?" Gwen says. "Wouldn't talk?"

No one smiles. "A horrible thing happened to her," Iz says. "She changed. She was so like her mother when she left me. She didn't care at all. Like the sea."

Rory remembers: *They hurt me inside and out, one after another.*

Gwen's still holding Gawain's arm, gently persuading. "Swanny loved Tristram like, I don't know. Like her own life, you'd have thought. But you saw what she did to him in the end."

"Killed him," Gawain says.

"Took him to the sea." Gwen's not correcting, just finding another way of saying it. "They're not like us, the mermaids. Even their love is merciless. I watched Swanny and Tristram try. Her mother and father. It was so awful. They wanted so much to find a way to be together but it's the sea and the land, isn't it? There's no overlap. We thought Marina might grow up half and half but you can't be half this and half that, not when they're opposites."

Rory remembers: *My father was a man. I never told you that, did I?*

Silvia sits back from the table. "He loves this girl," she says, looking between Gwen and Iz. "I can see it in his face."

"There's nothing he can do," Gwen says, "even if he wanted to. No one could find her in the sea."

Gawain closes his eyes in pained resignation.

"You're here now, Gav love," Iz says, nodding. "It's all finished. You've reached your end and she reached hers. She's all right now. That's the only thing that matters, isn't it? She's where she's supposed to be. Like the rest of us."

There's a long silence.

Rory shifts in his seat. No one else is going to say it for him, so he might as well get it over with.

"Actually." He spins his plate on the table, trying not to notice that they're all suddenly looking his way. "I think I might know where you can find her."

V

Fall

37

If Rory's honest with himself, he hasn't thought that much about the future. You don't, when you're ten. If one of the others had asked him, he'd probably have said, Aren't we all going to live here now? Like this? There's a big house, safe, dry, at peace. There's food, though he hasn't seen exactly where it comes from; it's magic, he supposes. None of these people are his family but he's decided he likes Silvia as much as he's ever liked anyone, and Gwen and her sister are a bit like the Nice women on Home except without getting tired or cross or smelling of fish. Anyway he saved Silvia's life, all by himself, and his family's all dead. So it wouldn't have seemed very unlikely—if he'd let himself think about it—that they'd all just, whatever. Stay. Go on. And nothing else would happen. End of.

It's not going to be like that now.

The really weird thing is that it's his fault. Nobody made him speak up. He could have let them all forget about Her, like Gwen and Iz were saying they ought to. But no. And now everyone's worried, everyone's unhappy.

He wonders whether this is why Holly's started calling him *serpent* as well as *liar*. It's not an insult, as far as he can tell, but it stings a bit all the same. He's not sure he's all that comfortable around Holly. Her eyes are like something out of the horror comics. He's not too sure about Corbo either. Being stared at by Corbo makes him feel like food.

It's one of the reasons he's decided he's going to go with Gawain. Deciding who's going and who isn't is what's causing all the unhappiness. It's like being back in the Abbey. There must be something about the process of making decisions that makes people miserable, Rory thinks. Iz is the worst. She's desperate for Gawain to change his mind and stay, but he's not going to, so she's torn between wanting to go with him and knowing she can't face the outside world again, which given what Rory's seen of it seems fair enough. Silvia's torn as well, wanting to help but dreading the idea of going without her gift, not knowing what she's doing. Only Gwen is certain she doesn't want to leave Pendurra, but even she's tormented with worry about parting from Gawain. It doesn't help that Corbo keeps clacking around muttering the word *unwise*.

Gawain's made up his mind, but he knows he's about to break his promise and he's brooding over it. Rory finds this a bit peculiar, though he's careful not to say so. Does it really matter what Gawain said to someone six hundred and something days ago? People promise things all the time when they don't mean it. Whenever Pink says *I swear*, what she basically means is *Actually I'm not going to do this and we both know it*. In the first months after Dad and Jake and Scarlet sailed away his mother used to tuck him in every night promising they'd all be together again soon. The world's made of lies, big and little, black and white. Perpetual truth would be like that god, too unbearably bright to live with.

Though one of the names Holly greets Gawain with is *oracle*, so maybe he's tried living like that. He's got a look about him like he's got too close to a fire and been burned by it, like Gwen except with all the burning on the inside.

Rory's got to go with him, anyway. Who else can show Gawain the exact cove at the far northern tip of Home where She always appears? And how could he let anyone sail to Home without going with them? Someone's got to explain to Kate and everyone what's been happening.

There's another reason too. It's currently in his trousers. He turns it between his fingers sometimes when he's got his hands in his pockets. If it's really a magic ring—*the* magic ring—then isn't Gawain going to need it?

He's already tried giving it back to Gawain, quietly, when it was just the two of them. The man just looked at him and asked whether he remembered what his mother had said. Flustered, Rory mumbled that he did, yes.

"I think you'll know what to do, then," Gawain said, and that was it.

He won't, of course. He has no idea. He doesn't understand the ring at all. He's beginning to think Hester the Professor and Silvia were both right, and there's actually no such thing, it's just a hoax. Maybe that's what Gawain means. The ring's not for anything, it doesn't do anything, they're just supposed to get rid of it. Like those hobbits.

He keeps it in his pockets anyway, though.

So now they're scrambling down through steep-sloping woods, just the two of them, Gawain barefoot as always. The undergrowth's straggly and twisty and the ground's slick with old leaves. They've said their farewells. Rory kept hoping until the very last minute that Silvia would change her mind and come with them, but she didn't.

"Promise you'll return to me," Iz said to Gawain, more than once. Her face when he couldn't promise was terrible to see. Rory kept thinking of Molly sitting in the brown chair in the corner of the big room in the Abbey after Ol died, not saying a word, looking utterly destroyed.

"So are we coming back here afterwards?" Rory asks, as they pause to get their footing, both holding the same contorted bough for balance.

"I don't know," Gawain says. He sounds distraught. "I promised I'd never leave her, once. That was on the day her father died. Then it turned out I had to, so I promised I'd come back here and stay forever. That's broken too. I don't know what I'm doing anymore."

Rory finds this surprisingly frightening.

"Maybe we should," he begins, after Gawain's been staring at him for a while. He can't finish, but he looks back up the slope.

"No," Gawain says. "I've got to try to find her."

He doesn't sound like an oracle when he says that. He sounds like an unhappy boy, not quite a man yet after all.

* * *

The slope levels out, the ground becomes rock, and there's the river.

Within the enchanted confines of Pendurra, Rory's stopped thinking about the outside world. He's forgotten how bad it was. Here's the truth of it, stretching upstream and down as far as the eye can see. The river's a graveyard.

He'd imagined the thorny rose encircling Pendurra like a castle wall. Now he sees there's no need for it on this side. No one's ever going to cross this moat. Plenty of people have tried, by the looks of it. Tried and died. The wrecks lie so thickly in the dull dark water you could almost use them as stepping-stones.

To the right, downstream, the river widens, and there, where it meets the cursed sea, the smashed and sunken boats are at their most colossal, tankers and container vessels, some no more than looming peaks of rust, others still almost whole but overrun by the waves, smothered in kelp. To his left the wooded banks press closer together and the ruins are small boats, launches, yachts, gigs, dinghies. The yachts' masts stick up at all angles, some of them trailing fouled canvas like collapsed tent poles. Mostly they're crowded near the wilderness of purpling bramble on the opposite shore.

There's just one boat riding upright and sound. It's at anchor near the rocks where Rory and Gawain have come down to the shore. It's a single-masted sailing boat, scratched and battered. It was probably once mostly white but it's turned the same grey as the river. The stern's facing them. The name, painted in black capitals, is LOOKFAR.

"Gwen's idea," Gawain says. "Marina loved that book. Mum says she had it with her when they met."

"What book?"

"Never mind."

"You and Gwen really came all the way here in that?"

"And Corbo."

"From America?"

"Canada. Yes. Halfway round the world. It felt like the whole way round."

"It should only take us a day to Scilly." Rory looks at the sky.

"What time is it? Is it still morning?" There are layers of low cloud, passing in slow motion. "Where's the wind coming from?"

"It's always followed me before," Gawain says. "Let's hope it does today."

There's a rigid inflatable pulled up in a shingle cove nearby. Rory gets in first and lets the man push them out into the river. As Gawain rows them out to the yacht Rory tries to read the inflatable's name, stenciled on its side in letters faded almost to invisibility: SHENANI-GANS, HARDY, B.C.

"B.C.? Is that how old it is?"

"British Columbia. Part of what used to be Canada."

"What is it now?"

"Something else. Did you grow up in the Isles of Scilly?"

"Yes. Always."

"And is it the same place now?"

"Oh," he says. "I see."

As they're climbing aboard, Rory says, "Are we really going to make everything go back to how it was before?"

Gawain offers Rory a hand over the rail. The boat sways and settles under them. The decking and the cabin are pale wood, scoured completely smooth.

"You can't undo what happened," he says. "Nothing's going to make the lights come back on, just like that."

"But no more magic? Isn't that what your mother said?"

"All I'm trying to do," Gawain says, "is find a friend who never deserved to be abandoned."

"But I thought she told us—"

"That's all I'm trying to do," Gawain says, this time with an emphasis on the *I*. Not for the first time, Rory's left wondering what the man means, and by the time he's got himself moving again Gawain's already busy with something else, unknotting the cover from the boom.

There's no wind at all where they are, though out towards the mouth of the river a stand of tall evergreens is nodding as if in answer to a breeze. Gawain lets the ebbing tide take hold of the boat as he winds up the anchor. The creased and smeared sail hangs limp.

Rory takes the tiller—he feels like someone ought to—but there's no pressure on the rudder at all, he might as well not bother. They're spinning in the current like a bath toy. Gawain isn't concerned. He sits himself forward of the mast and watches as though it doesn't matter at all that the waters ahead are clogged with giant slabs and reefs of wreckage.

"Should I steer?" Rory calls out, in case Gawain's forgotten. You wouldn't put it past him.

"They'll take us out to sea," Gawain answers, over his shoulder.

"Who will?"

"Whoever they are. Marina's people."

"Oh," he says again. "OK."

"At least I hope they will. They brought me in."

"Right." Rory doesn't bother asking what'll happen otherwise. You only have to look around to see the answer. Something's steadying their course already, though. The bow stops drifting.

"After that it'll be up to us to sail," Gawain says. "I hope you know the way."

"Me?" His heart thuds.

"Don't you?"

"To the Isles?"

"More or less straight west from the Lizard, right?"

"Yeah." Isn't it? "Roughly."

Gawain turns. "We'll find them," he says.

At the river's choked mouth the current becomes furious rapids. Rory doesn't notice how angry it is until they're almost caught up in billows of dirty foam, and at that stage he decides it's much better not to look at all. The half-submerged tanker lying slantwise almost from shore to shore breaks the tide into sucking eddying channels between rock and rusting steel. When the boat starts tipping into that channel under the huge shadow of the wreck he throws himself forward into a little hollow by the cabin roof and curls up into a ball, cursing himself for not staying in Pendurra with the others. The boat groans and bucks. A wall of spray slaps over him. He can smell dead metal and weed. The sail flaps and cracks above his head and they heel over. He can't help opening his eyes as he grabs for a handhold. There's Gawain, already at the wheel, an arc of canvas stretched tight behind him. They're out. The wreck's receding and there's open sea ahead. Under a sullen sky a coast stretches away, fading into smudgy obscurity. He can even see buildings in the distance, and, closer, a church tower struggling up between trees. The ruins of England, still there, where he left them.

It's cold. He steadies himself and stuffs his hands in his pockets. There it is, small, hard, smooth: all the magic in the world.

They sail along the coast under an easy steady wind. Rory sits by the rail, dangling his legs over the side, looking down at the water. He's thinking of how it must be full of drowned people. His family. Everyone else's families.

"You know when there wasn't any magic?" he says.

Gawain's staring forward without apparently looking at anything, the way people steering boats always seem to. "Before all this started, you mean?"

"Yeah."

"What about it?"

Rory fingers the ring again. "Where did it go?"

He's worried it's a stupid question, but Gawain appears to be considering it carefully.

"It didn't go anywhere," he says, eventually. "What happened is that people stopped seeing it. They forgot about it. Looked the other way."

"Why?"

"Easier that way, I suppose. You can see how you might prefer living in a world that did what you told it and didn't answer back."

"What about the ring?"

"What about it?"

"If it's . . . If all the magic's in it. Where did it go?"

"It was lost," Gawain says. "Hidden."

"Where? How did you find it?"

"I didn't. It was in the sea. And under a spell."

"A magic spell?"

"Presumably."

"Even though there wasn't any magic?"

"There was," he says. "Always was, always will be. It's just the way things are. You can hide the truth, though, that's the thing. Or ignore it. Work around it. Replace it with something else. People do that all the time. In fact I'm pretty sure that's what makes people people. Different from every other kind of being."

"So, like, Them. The mermaids. They were always there, all along? But no one noticed?"

"It's amazing what you can choose not to know," Gawain says, which is sort of answering the question but also sort of not, leaving Rory stuck again.

He pokes around belowdecks for a while. It's a lot nicer than the boat he sailed in with Silvia and Per and Lino. It's very empty and bare but it doesn't have that stale plastic smell. Gawain's told him where some warmer clothes are stored. They all turn out to be too big but he's used to that from the Stash on Home. He finds a thick fleece sweater with a big collar. It goes down almost to his knees and up over his neck. There's a picture of a leaping killer whale on the back.

He wonders what they're going to say when they see him sailing into the Gap. It takes a lot to surprise Kate but he's betting she'll be completely speechless for once. He wonders how much he's going to tell them. He might leave out the bits about meeting God. It just makes things more complicated.

He looks out a porthole and sees the tops of the satellite dishes like warts on the line of the horizon. When they make magic go back where it came from, will that stop the Plague? Will those dishes start bouncing messages around the world again, instead of sitting like dead faces turned to the heavens where the bad god lives? He spots a few people down at the shore, on one of the slivers of beach beneath the overgrown cliffs. Women, they must be, or they wouldn't come close to the water. Digging clams, maybe. They all straighten and watch the boat sail past. He wonders if they'll go back and tell everyone else that it's a sign. There are boats on the sea. The curse is breaking. He wonders where

Ellie and Soph are, if they're anywhere. The beast didn't kill him, so maybe it didn't kill them either. At least he managed to cut them free.

He comes back on deck just as the sea roughens. The swell's rising. The coast beside them is coming to a blunt stop, and beyond it the waves are hills and valleys. Gawain swings the boat around a steepling block of land surmounted by a lighthouse, turning to put the wind behind them.

"Looks like we're being blown west, more or less," Gawain says, peering at a compass mounted beside the wheel. "Seems about right."

Their course begins leaving the land behind. The coast withdraws to starboard, becoming a long thin colorless line bracketing the view north. Gulls come out to investigate their passage. Rory discovers he feels a bit less sick if he stays on deck. The swell's strong but even. There's a sort of rhythm to it which he could almost get used to. He shades his eyes despite the clouds and studies the receding land. There are the satellite dishes again, the only interruption to its low profile, until . . .

He peers, clinging to the cabin hatch with his free hand.

"Is that the Mount?"

"Saint Michael's Mount? Looks like it. Yes."

It must be twenty miles off, right at the limit of the huge bay that's opened out to starboard, but the shape stands out even so. He thinks he can even see hints of the buildings that crown it. He tries to picture himself sitting on the beach beyond it, in the shelter of a looted container, waiting to meet Silvia again, with no idea that she's abandoned him. No idea of anything, really.

He *can* see the buildings on the Mount, miles distant though it is. The shine of a wet gable, the dewdrop sparkle of glass. They must be catching a shaft of sunlight from a distant break in the clouds. It's beautiful, the only speck of color in a world of greys. It's almost like a lighthouse, but warm and soft like flame, not with the hard brilliance of electric light.

"Look."

Gawain looks. There's an abrupt lurch in the wind. The boom slackens and yanks.

There's something about Gawain's expression Rory doesn't like. "What?" he says.

Gawain looks up at the sails, frowning. As if on cue, the wind hesitates again. The jib folds and flaps uncertainly.

The gleam on the Mount is intensifying. It looks as if it's caught in its own private sunset, picked out by a ruddy spotlight. Or—

"Is that fire?"

Gawain lets go of the wheel. Completely lets go of it. Rory never sailed as much as Dad and Jake but he's pretty sure you're not supposed to do that. The whole boat's turned limp and useless. The swell's picking them up and dropping them still, but its rhythm has gone. It feels like they're driftwood. The boom thunks from side to side, following the rocking of the waves. Quite suddenly, there's no wind at all.

"What's happening?"

Gawain comes forward, ducking, and crouches at the base of the mast. "Let's take down the sails," he says. He sounds weary. "Though I don't think it'll make any difference."

"To what? What are you doing that for?" He's already started, though, loosening knots and pulling in an armful of canvas. The boat's wallowing horribly.

"We've lost the wind," he says. "Look over there."

The far-off light around the Mount's become an aura. It's too deep and rich for any sunlight and too intense for fire. It's a reddening of air. It's also growing, fanning out slowly, like blood in water. No, Rory realizes, not spreading. It only looks that way because it's coming closer.

He's about to repeat his stupid question, *What's that?* but doesn't, first because his throat's gone tight, and second because he knows what it is. He recognizes it.

What was it Gawain just said? *It's amazing what you can choose not to know.* Did Rory simply choose to forget Per in the night, his face burnished with the weird light from his magic staff, and a hideous alien voice coming from his mouth saying, *It is mine?* When did he decide not to think about the man-shaped phantom of flame that came into the room where he slept with Sandra and Soph and begged him to be its master, and then mocked him when he refused? It told him it was going to find someone else. And it also warned him they'd meet again.

There's nothing to do except hang on and watch. Gawain's winding in the mainsail, unhurriedly but busily. The red-gold glow is blazing towards them. It's beginning to fill the sky to the north. Fiery ghosts, arrowing over the sea, coming for some kind of reckoning.

The jib bellies suddenly. The boat tugs forward, slapping the side of a wave, tipping hard. Rory feels a warm wind on his face. It's changed direction entirely. The bow's been pushed around to face north, towards the unholy light. He clutches at a stay and reaches for the wheel.

"Don't," Gawain says.

"But it's forcing us—"

"It won't help."

He's very calm. He doesn't look the slightest bit frightened, though Rory's own heart is trying to push itself up his throat and out his mouth.

"What is that?"

"An old acquaintance."

"Is it all right, then?"

"No. Definitely not all right."

This isn't at all what Rory hoped he'd say. The weird warm breeze is gathering strength, pushing them hard now across the chop, northwards towards the distant shore and the burning light. It's becoming noisy, whistling in a way that isn't quite right for wind.

"What if we get the jib down?"

"We might as well leave it. There's still time."

"Time? For what?"

Gawain looks at him. "For you to make your decision."

Rory's so astonished he forgets he's supposed to be frightened. He tries to say *Me?* but can only mime it, so all that happens is his mouth drops open.

The problem with the sound of the wind is that it has voices in it, sinister hollow whispers. The red stain to the north is gathering.

It's bright enough now to make a reflection, capping the swell with crests of molten metal.

"I gave the ring to you to look after," Gawain says. "Someone gave it to me once, and I didn't know what I was doing either when I accepted it. Not even slightly. Don't worry. It's that sort of gift."

Rory bumps down onto the deck and clutches at his pocket.

"The problem is," Gawain goes on, rather absently, as if this were all happening somewhere else, or in a book, "that there are people who want it. Badly. I don't need to tell you that, you've met some of them. Silvia's friends. You've seen what they'll put up with to try and get hold of it."

"Here," Rory says. He's trying to get his hand in the pocket. The oversized sweater's getting in the way and his fingers are stiff in the sea chill. "You take it. OK?"

"That's one thing you could do," Gawain says. He sounds absurdly thoughtful, as if he doesn't mind at all about the fact that some demon thing is streaking over the sea towards them.

"I don't know what's going on. I don't know anything about it. I don't want it." He can't find the stupid pocket. He's sitting too scrunched up. He tries to kneel but the boat's tipping violently now, driven by the evil wind. "It's nothing to do with me."

"Hardly."

"It's not. I'm nobody."

"You brought Silvia and her companions here. You found the crucifix that belonged to my mother. You walked into the Valley. No one else has ever done that and lived. You walked into Pendurra. No one can do that either, it's forbidden. You know Marina. You've seen a god. Silvia ran into you thousands of miles from here, on the day my mother vanished. That was before you were born, Rory, and you know as well as I do Silvia's not lying. Everywhere any of us turns, there you are."

There are occasional moments when Gawain seems like he might not be completely serious. This definitely isn't one of them. He means it.

"But," Rory says, "none of that's because of me. I didn't do anything. It just turned out like that."

"How else does anything happen?"

"But you know all about magic and that. I'm just . . . I'm not special."

"And I'm the son of the god Apollo," Gawain says. "I go barefoot because a prophetess who I loved more than I've ever loved anyone told me to. I don't suffer hunger or cold or pain. The spirits of earth and air and sea recognize me and let me pass unharmed. I went halfway around the world to fetch that ring because it was given to me. It's my inheritance. But do you know what, Rory? I don't want to be the son of a god. I don't want to be an oracle. I don't want my inheritance. I want to be an orphan. I want my old mum to pretend to be my mother like she did before. And I want Marina to be her father's child. I want her to be just a girl, like she used to be. I don't want to know anything about magic at all. No, that's not right. I want to keep remembering one thing about it, which is that I can't bear it. No one can. It's unbearable. They want it, Rory." He points towards the bow and the approaching fire. "You know they do. You traveled with them, they spoke to you. You know where this wind is going to take us. You've got a little longer. Not much. And then they'll be here."

Rory gapes. "What am I supposed to do?"

Gawain answers without urgency. He's not shouting, he's not cajoling. More than anything else he sounds like he's giving up.

"Whatever you want," he says. "Even if you don't really know what you're doing."

Rory's finally managed to get his hand into his pocket. It closes around the ring. He draws it out. They both look at it, amid the swaying and jerking and bumping around.

"No," he says. "I don't get it. You'd better have it back."

He's being stupid, he can tell. He forces himself to look at Gawain, expecting to see disappointment. Instead he encounters an expression very familiar to him from the women of Home: a sort of hopeless, worn-out patience and resignation. Gawain holds out his hand.

Rory's about to give it back to him when he remembers: *'Obbits!*

"Hang on," he says. "Wait a sec."

The onrushing light no longer appears as a single distant glow. It flickers, dances, shoots out twists and arabesques of short-lived flame. Rory knows now what he'll see when it reaches them. He remembers the phantoms whirling around Per's staff. He remembers their wheedling, hissing voices. *We are friendless as yourself.* He remembers their hunger, the pressure of their desire.

He's remembering what the hobbits were supposed to do with the magic ring.

He drops to his stomach and worms across the pitching deck to the stern. Spray fizzes up and spatters his face and hands. He holds the ring out, thinks about stopping to think, doesn't. He drops it into the sea. There's an infinitesimal puncture in the crisscrossing veins of windblown froth, and it's gone.

He twists around to see if he's done the right thing. Gawain looks back, no smile, no frown. Rory holds up his empty hand to show what he's done, hoping for at least a nod. Nothing.

"I dropped it in," he says, crawling back.

"OK."

"Was that right?"

"It was lost for a long time," Gawain says. "Maybe now it'll be lost for good." He holds out a hand for Rory to shake. Rory takes it, feeling shy and rather silly. Gawain doesn't let go.

38

They're still crouched together like that, free hands clasped, when the air becomes a blaze around them and they're wrapped in swarming ribbons of fire. Among the ribbons seethe faces with lidless pupil-less eyes, appearing and vanishing swift as spray. Their voices are whispers but together it's a roar. They seem to lift the boat and send it skimming, or perhaps that's just the effect of the forest fire wind. Rory and Gav huddle together, closing their eyes against the frenzy of motion. There's a smell fouling the ocean air. It gets stronger and stronger as their violent passage goes on: the smell of burning. The deck bruises them. Despite it all, Rory has a strangely reassuring feeling that he's done the right thing. He keeps thinking of what the women used to say, muttering to each other in the big room in the Abbey: *If only everything would go back to how it was before.*

Gav's nudging him: *Look!* He opens his eyes and kneels beside the man to peer forwards over the cabin, through the whirling corona and towards the land.

The Mount is on fire.

It's like a giant's torch thrust up from the water of the bay. The waist of the cone of rock is a complete circle of flame. A huge plume of smoke pours up from it, swallowing the castle at the top except when something flares through the black billows as it catches and burns. They can almost feel the heat of it now as well as smelling it.

Now Rory's frightened. They're being driven straight towards the maw of fire. Could he throw himself overboard? They could try. But

Gav's still holding Rory's hand, and he's not looking for any kind of escape. As far as Rory can tell he's just waiting.

It won't be a long wait. Already Rory can make out the huge wrecks stranded along the rim of the beach. He can see individual buildings in Penzance, the decaying seafront shopping centers and car parks Silvia led him past, not so long ago though it feels like ages. A blur of small movement catches his eye despite the raging phantoms and the tossing of the boat; it looked for a moment as if there were people among the low hills behind the Mount. People on horseback. But it's hard to look at anything other than the gigantic fire. It's so bright now it makes the bottom of the clouds look like they're burning too, except where the column of smoke is obliterating all light. The smoke's like a living thing, a weeping black tree growing from the ruin of the Mount, bending wispy twigs towards the ground. The noise is like the earth being torn and crumpled up, brittle in a giant fist. Just as the whole scene is about to loom fatally huge, their headlong motion slows.

Rory can see two figures standing on the causeway.

They're near its landward end, hardly more than specks above the debris of the beach, but Rory knows them both straightaway. The man is Per. He's found his staff again. He's holding it high, exactly as he did before. Even as a distant speck he's too big, larger than life. The same goes for the dog prowling around his legs, which is how Rory knows it's not really a dog at all but the beast whose savagery slaughtered the Black Pack, the beast the thin-faced foreign man turned into when he put the mask on and the god appeared and pointed at him.

Both man and dog are watching as the boat's propelled towards them.

"That's—" Rory yells to Gav.

"I know," Gav says.

With a chorusing hiss like hot metal in water, the fiery phantoms all sweep upwards, spiraling around the mast and then arching into the sky. The dry wind fades. The boat drifts on towards the beach, then scrapes, stalls, tips. The keel's run aground. Rory grabs at the cabin roof as the tipping becomes listing, leaning, toppling. His fingers aren't strong enough. He slips and the deck pitches him down, crashing him into a rail. Shallow water seethes beneath him, lit by the fire. Terrified that the boat's going to capsize on top of him, he looks around and sees that Gav's already slid into the sea and is half wading half swimming ashore. "Wait!" Rory croaks. What's the idiot doing? Why isn't he trying to get away while he can? Gav won't wait, though. He doesn't even look back. Rory holds his breath and drops himself between the rails into the sea. It's brutally cold. The oversized fleece becomes quickly waterlogged. He kicks and splashes and splutters after Gav. A wave picks him up and breaks over him; when he rights himself, coughing, wiping salt from his eyes, his feet can touch. He stumbles up the beach. "Wait!"

Gav still won't wait. He's just walking on, the wrong way, towards the causeway, towards Per and the beast. In the marshy mud-colored sand of low tide each of his footprints fills straightaway with water and becomes a miniature pool reflecting the blaze on the Mount, so it looks like he's leaving a trail of wet fire behind him, like he's burning the land as he goes. He must be insane. Rory's seen what that dog can do. Even thinking about it for an unwanted heartbeat—the screams, the men running and falling and not getting back up, the indescribably horrible snapping and tearing—is enough to make sick rise in his throat. "Stop!"

Gav doesn't stop.

So Rory goes running after him, as best he can. There are other people heading towards the causeway too, he can see them appearing and disappearing through gaps between the abandoned buildings of the town behind the beach. Smoke drifts around, stinging his eyes. His sodden clothes slap heavily against him. It's hard enough trying to run on wet sand without their weight as well. Gav seems like he's almost gliding across the beach, not hurrying or running but always staying ahead no matter how much Rory shouts. "Wait! Wait for me!" The fire's a constant thrum and crackle, like the massed feet and hooves of an approaching army.

By the time he finally catches up with Gav they're almost to the tumble of barnacled black stones flanking the raised causeway.

There's Per. He's supposed to be dead. He looks dead. His crazy hair's limp and damp all over his face. He's acquired a long overcoat which flaps like seaweed. He hulks under it, heavy and cold. His eyes are burning. Actually burning. Not reflecting the fire, but fire themselves, shimmering circles. They're the only part of him that looks alive.

The dog faces Gav and Rory. It bristles, then howls.

Rory's out of breath and can barely open his mouth for terror anyway, but he clutches Gav's arm and tries to say something about turning around, now, before it's too late. To his complete astonishment Gav puts an arm around his shoulders, gives him a small hug, and guides them up onto the rocks.

Three or four mounted people appear above the sea wall. They're struggling to control their horses, and Rory can't see anything well enough to recognize them for sure, but they're definitely Riders. Their homemade armor glints like it's been dipped in blood. For a moment he thinks one of them might have pointed in his direction.

Rory's main thought as he scrambles up among the chunks of mussel-sharp rocks, Gav still guiding and steadying him, is that he needn't have been here at all. He could have stayed in that big and endlessly quiet old house, eternally comfortable and safe and at rest. But he's not. It seems to be his own special favorite mistake, this thing of forgetting to stay put when he can and voluntarily exposing himself instead to the most ridiculous danger. He's pretty sure he's not going to get the chance to make it again.

"Third time's the charm," says a voice in Per's dead mouth, as Gav and Rory climb at last onto the cracked causeway stones.

His fist around the staff is the sickly color of the polluted froth left by the retreating tide. The staff itself is writhing with light, a kind of red smoke slithering up and down and around it. It's impossible to tell what the flaming circles in Per's eye sockets are looking at, but if he sees Rory he doesn't know him anymore, or doesn't care.

The blaze at the other end of the causeway feels like hot breath on the back of Rory's neck. It's so huge it casts shadows, multiple dusty shadows, melting into each other and into the dark slabs they're standing on. It's roaring like a wave about to break.

"Have you at last brought me what is mine," the voice says. It's an old voice, throaty and dry, like fire talking. It makes the question sound not at all like a question.

"No," Gav answers.

The monstrous dog snarls. Its head is as high as Rory's chest.

Far behind Per and the dog, by the sea wall, a woman's voice shouts, "Rory? That's Rory!"

"Why, then, are you here," says the thing Per's turned into. "What do you have to bring me, except the gift you wrongly took."

"I'm here to tell you," Gav says, "that the world's finished with you. And with me. Time's up. For both of us."

Per steps forward. Four shambling steps, like an automaton. He raises a hand towards Gav's neck. Rory can't help himself; he squirms out of Gav's grip and backs away.

Gav's only reaction is to take hold of the hem of his navy blue sweater and pull it over his head. He doesn't have a shirt on underneath. His back is a mess of nasty scars, but Rory barely notices them, because Per grabs at the thin silver chain around Gav's neck.

The massive dog crouches, bares its teeth, and whines.

"It's gone," Gav says. How he can stand there, let alone speak, with that thing looming in his face, actually touching him, Rory can't imagine; but he does. "Lost again. Forgotten."

Per tears the chain off Gav's neck, making Gav wince and stagger, though only for a moment. Per steps back. The slender silver chain dangles from his corpse fingers, glittering like a stream of tiny sparks.

A horse whinnies in panic.

"You let it go," the old voice says. "The door to all the knowledge that runs in the veins of the earth and blows around the stars, and you let it go. You. A boy."

"We don't need to know everything," Gav says. "I have a feeling it's better if we don't, actually."

"You are a child." With a clumsy swing of his huge arm Per tosses the chain away. "You think knowledge is the first of sins, like all the other children. You would rather live and die with your eyes sewn shut."

"Maybe I would," Gav says. "Maybe you would too. You knew the prophetess when you were a man. She didn't want her gift. All she wanted was to sleep."

A horrible grimace disfigures Per's slackened face. "I gave her that wish. I'll do the same for you. Boy."

Gav shrugs. "You might as well not bother threatening. It's not like I can stop you this time."

"Who do you imagine will save you? The harridans on their horses. The spirits I command will madden their steeds until they run headlong into that fire."

"I told you," Gav says. "I don't imagine anyone saving me. I've made my end. I don't belong in this world either."

Despite the fact that his blood's pounding in his ears so violently he can scarcely make out what anyone's saying, let alone attend to it, Rory finds himself staring openmouthed at Gav's back. Does he actually mean that? Is he trying to commit suicide?

"You don't deserve life. Boy. You are the rankest of cowards. Afraid to keep what you were entrusted with. The prophetess had lost her wits when she chose you."

"I wouldn't call what you have *life*, exactly," Gav says mildly.

"You dare taunt me. Don't presume to mock me because I did not fear to become immortal."

"I wasn't taunting."

"This flesh welcomed me. These spirits sustain and obey me. I am not hindered by the frailties of man. I will find the ring."

"No," Gav says. "You won't."

"But first," the voice says, as if Gav hadn't spoken, "you must die, to cancel the prophetess's choice."

Beyond the end of the causeway, in the gap where the ramp breaks through the sea wall, Rory can now see the Riders gathering. Their horses are twisting and shying but they're trying to force them into a line. He thinks—perhaps it's just desperation—he can spot Soph among them, that bit taller and straighter in the saddle. Can he wave to them? Can he get them to charge? Is there even time? The monstrous dog's up out of its crouch. It's lowering its head and growling, a horrible rumble almost like a tremor in the stones.

Gav turns around. "I'm really sorry," he says. "If you see Marina, tell her—"

Then he stops.

Everything stops. It's the weirdest thing. Nothing's actually changed but all at once the mad terrified thudding of Rory's heart goes calm, the fury of malice around him drains away. Even the cacophony of the fire suddenly sounds like music.

Gav's looking at a point somewhere over Rory's right shoulder. He's so utterly still Rory's wondering if the Per thing has killed him, just like that, without anyone noticing.

A clear voice behind Rory says, "Hello, Gawain."

In a whisper hoarse with longing, Per's mouth says, "The ring."

Rory turns around.

Even when he's looking the right way he's never been able to see how she does it. She's appeared without a sound. Behind her the Mount is a pyramid of fire and smoke. Its upper gardens are burning now, and the walls and windows overlooking them have begun to pop, coughing out balloons of flame. She's shining all over with that terrible light.

"And hello, Rory," she says.

The plain brown ring is on the fourth finger of her left hand, where it fits perfectly.

"I didn't think I'd see either of you ever again," she says.

"Fetch it," groans the dead man's voice. "Slay it."

The beast moves so fast Rory doesn't even have time to be frightened. It bounds past him in a silent blur and leaps up. Someone far away shouts a useless warning: "Rory!" He's flinching as it reaches him.

"Stop," She says quietly.

The beast twitches and curls up in midair. It drops onto the causeway stones like a sack. It presses itself flat. All this has happened in less time than it takes Gav to finish his one step towards her.

There's a rising commotion behind, back where the Riders are. Hoofbeats are scraping on the ramp, and more than one voice is shouting now. "It's Rory! It's that kid!"

Marina squats down beside the prone and quivering dog and touches it, almost curiously.

"Careful—" begins Gav, but something's happened again, too fast or blurry for Rory to follow. He thought it was the dog lying there, stretched out like it had been skinned and turned into a rug, but it isn't anymore, it's a man draped in filthy black furs, flattened and gasping at Marina's feet as if she's just floored him with a punch. What a moment ago was the huge animal's head is now just the dead eyes and ears and muzzle of a dog's hide over his shoulders. A blunt black mask is lying face-up on the stone beside him. He's pale and sweating. His hands claw weakly at the causeway.

"It's all right," Marina says to Gav. "It was just a man, you see. Men do what we want them to. Get up."

The man hauls himself weakly to his feet. It's the leader of the Pack, the same man Rory saw with the mask before, when the bad god turned him into the beast; the sharp-faced one with the foreign accent. He sways as he stands up. He looks ill.

"You," he says, staring at Marina. His face fills with something that could be dread or could be guilt. He stumbles, turns, and runs towards the beach, dodging past Gav and Per.

Per roars and raises his staff. The aura wreathing around it surges brighter, like embers when you blow on them. He grasps it in both hands and swings it to point at Marina, a gesture of unmistakable malevolence. Rory looks at Gav in panic: *Do something!* Someone's got to do something. Should he do it himself? Rush forward and knock the staff out of Per's leprous fists?

Gav's smiling. Properly smiling. Rory's never seen him do anything like it before.

Per begins to growl a strange word.

"No," Marina says. "Quiet."

The word chokes in the dead man's throat.

"Let them go," she says. "Actually, no. I'll do it."

The staff drops with a startling clatter onto the causeway. Per stands there with his arms out. Suddenly he looks as if the fires have consumed him inside. He's wasted, hollow.

"He was a man too, you see," Marina says. She comes forward to pick up the staff. "All of them were. Except poor Gwen, but she's not part of this anymore."

Gav finds his voice at last. "Marina," he says. "You've grown."

The clamor among the Riders becomes whoops and yells. A group of them are pushing down the ramp onto the beach. They're hurrying. He can definitely see Soph now, taller than the rest, wearing her patchwork armor. She survived; she's alive. She's near the front but horses are slipping and squeezing past each other. The man running along the causeway sees his way blocked by the tide of mounted women and skids to a stop, but it's already too late for him. There's Ellie at the front now, alive too. She couldn't look more alive, in fact, lifting herself out of the saddle as she drives her horse into a gallop, outpacing the others. She's not bothering with the whooping and shouting, she's all business. Even Marina stops to watch for a moment as Ellie brings her horse up onto the causeway and rides the man down. He crumples under the charge. Rory can hear the air go out of him and the crunch of his bones. Ellie reins the horse in and turns it with amazing speed. It rears up, front hooves pawing, and drops on the man again, and then the mass of Riders catch up with her and they're all on him, screaming, stamping, stabbing.

Ignoring the carnage now, Marina picks up the staff. Per's arms drop. His whole body shivers and goes slack. He falls to his knees. The voice in his mouth emits a kind of strangled sigh.

"You," Gav says, and he's grinning from ear to ear now, "are amazing."

"Do you remember that time in the woods?" Marina says. "The day Daddy drowned? You made these spirits leave the mask. I understand what you did now. This ring makes everything open, doesn't it? Come out." She addresses the last words to no one Rory can see. She might even be talking to the staff. "Come out and be seen."

Light flares. Horses whinny. Rory has to shield his eyes. When he rubs them clear a moment later, Per's fallen face-first on the stone, dead as the rusting ships on the beach. A man-shaped ghost of flame is hovering in the air in front of Marina. It's twice her size. It shimmers and burns with silent glory, flickering, restless, consuming and re-forming itself. Its head is the image of an old tired man.

"We would not have our freedom," it whispers. The Riders have fallen quiet, transfixed by the phantom's appearance, watching from the end of the causeway, so Rory can hear the whisper quite clearly, though it's as dry as the cackle of the blaze behind.

"You wanted to stay a man," Marina says. She's completely unafraid. She's exactly as Rory's always known her, implacable and beautiful as the sea. "You still want that, don't you? Even now."

"We know the secrets of heaven and the lightless places," it says. It's the hiss of a broom across a slate floor. "We will serve you without question. Only let us have life still."

"And because you're still trying to be a man," Marina says, "I rule you." She folds her naked arms as if suddenly uncomfortable.

"We would be ruled. We are obedient."

She shakes her head, brief and awkward, almost pained. "That's just wanting to be master, but upside down. I know what men do." She points at the phantom with her left hand, the one wearing the ring. "You're free," she says. "Die."

She puts the staff down and steps on it. Just lightly, not stamping or anything like that, but the staff cracks like glass and snaps in half. The phantom frays into a thousand tongues of flame, its old man's face surviving only long enough to close its old man's eyes before it's not any kind of shape at all, just windblown leaves of transparent fire, then sparks splintering from the leaves, then nothing at all. One piece of the broken staff rolls slowly across the causeway and drops off the edge, bouncing down to join the plastic and polystyrene and flotsam snagged on mats of kelp.

Marina looks different. She's not glowing as brightly. Rory looks over his shoulder and sees that the volcanic inferno on the Mount has faded to embers. A massive pall of smoke stretches away over the sea.

Gav and Marina are looking at each other. Neither's moved for a bit. Rory's suddenly embarrassed to be right there with them. He looks away shorewards. More Riders are milling around by the sea wall, some steering their horses carefully onto the beach. Soph sees him looking and waves. He's too shy to wave back.

"Is it all right for me to touch you?" Gav says.

Marina's arms are still tightly crossed over her chest. She doesn't answer, so Gav steps towards her, carefully, the way you'd approach a wild animal. He's a lot taller than her. He opens his arms and wraps her up in them, resting his chin on top of her head. He closes his eyes, as if he's thinking, *That's it. Finished.* A moment or two later and she closes her eyes as well.

Rory's mounting discomfort at having to witness this scene is relieved by an unexpected voice.

"Gavin?"

Among the horses now approaching along the causeway is an extremely incongruous pony, shaggy and stumpy and almost as wide as it is tall. On its oversized saddle is a person thickly swathed in coat and cape and scarf and a woolly hat. This is the person who's just called out, judging by the way she's urging the pony forward.

"Gawain," Marina corrects under her breath, without opening her eyes. Her cheek is smushed against Gav's chest.

"You're not going to drown me, then?" Gav says, almost as quietly.

"No," she says. "Never."

"Gavin!"

Rory recognizes the Rider on the pony now, which is quite an achievement given the way she's bundled up. Something about her voice, perhaps. It's Hester, the Professor, transplanted from wheelchair to horseback. A few of the others are approaching with her. Rory's very pleased to see Ellie and Soph among them.

"Gavin!"

Either Gav's unwilling to move his head from where it's resting, or he just can't. He hasn't answered.

"Gawain," Marina corrects again, slightly irritably. "Things should have their right names."

"I'll tell her," he says. "But maybe not now."

The Riders come clopping up. They rein in at a respectful distance. Hester pushes back the hood of her waterproof cape and pulls off her hat. Rory thinks he's never seen quite such a load of mingled astonishment and joy on any face, ever.

"Hey, kid," Soph says, and winks at him.

"Hi," he says. No one else is talking. It's getting rather awkward. "Who are your friends?"

"Oh. Um." Gav and Marina are still folded together, white flesh and wet clothes, as if the rest of the world has stopped happening. "This is . . ." It feels funny to call her by a girl's name, but things should have their right names now, apparently. "Marina. And—"

"Gawain," Gawain says, without turning his head. "Hello, Hester Lightfoot. Good to see you again."

Ellie cocks an eyebrow, looks at Hester, and says, " 'Again'?"

Gawain detaches himself from Marina at last. All the Riders are looking at her. "We've got something that belongs to you."

"Marina," Hester says. There's a kind of big handle at the front of her saddle. She holds it and pulls herself forward. "The Marina you once told me about? Marina Uren?"

"Yes." Gawain picks up the blunt-snouted dog mask from where it's lying near Rory's feet.

"Pleased to meet you, Miss Uren," Hester says, solemnly polite. "I'm not quite certain what we owe you, but our thanks will do for a start."

Marina looks almost surprised. She faces the Riders. If she were an ordinary person she'd still be a child, not quite a woman yet, and she's naked and pale and surrounded by horseflesh and clothes and armor and sweat, but in a way Rory can't put his finger on she's bigger than all of them put together.

"Too right," Soph says, and eases herself off her horse. One of her feet is wrapped in thick padding instead of a boot, but she dismounts, though awkwardly and with a wince of pain. It's a gesture of respect. One by one all the other Riders follow suit, except Hester, who can't. Gawain hands her the mask.

"I left this in your house before," he says. "But I guess you never got it."

"Gav," she says, and takes him instead of the mask, pulling him by the arm and almost falling off the pony as she topples into a clumsy hug.

"No one wants that." This is Sal, wearing her red headscarf. She's stepped forward to help keep Hester upright. "I vote we take it to the Mount right now and burn it."

"No," Marina says. Everyone's instantly listening. It's that sound in her voice, water humming. "There's nothing wrong with it. He was the bad one, not the mask. It's only ever people who do evil."

"Can't argue with that," says Ellie. Her face is lined everywhere with fading scars.

"How many of our men have you killed, then?" says a woman farther back. It's Jody. Rory wouldn't have recognized her until she spoke. She's picked up a bad wound across her cheek and eye. Some of the women around her glare at her. Hester lets go of Gawain.

"There's suffering," Marina says. "And injustice. I know about them. They're different from evil."

"We've just killed a man ourselves," Hester says, meaning the words for Jody though she doesn't face her. She takes the mask from Gawain. "Thank you. It's so very good see you again."

"Perhaps," Marina says, looking at the ring on her finger, "it'll get easier to understand the difference. Now that the truth's out." She exchanges a quick look with Gawain. "Part of getting the names right."

"We're not letting it go again, then?" Gawain asks her. He means the ring. "We're not going back to the way things were?"

"No," she says. She curls her left hand into a fist. "No more forgetting." She holds her other hand out towards Gawain, palm up, like she's inviting him to dance. "I was happy when I was little but I didn't know who I was. And I've been happy in the sea, but I couldn't forget who I used to be. We're not going back to that."

Gawain hesitates, as if he's trying to make up his mind about something. Everyone's watching very quietly now. He puts his hand in hers.

"So you're not going back to the sea either?" he says.

"No," she says. "I want to go with you."

"Good," he says.

"Always."

"All right."

"This is supposed to be your gift," she says, reaching out her other hand, the one wearing the ring. He takes hold of that one too, so now it looks like he's about to swing her around like she's a delighted child. "But it'll be better if I keep it. We're the same anyway. Born across a divide."

"OK," he says. "Thank you."

There's a long silence. He doesn't swing her around. They don't start dancing. They just look at each other, like a pair of mirrors, reflecting each other over and over and over.

"I feel like someone ought to kiss someone," Soph says.

Ellie's closest to her. She aims a kick. "They're children!"

Soph shrugs. "I'd had my first kiss by the time I was that age. Hey, Rory. C'mere."

He blushes with happy embarrassment. "C'mere," she says again, waving him to her. "Lifesaver." A moment later he's wrapped in a rank hug, his face squashed against the scales of her tunic. She smells of sweat, fish, and horse, but he's in no hurry at all to pull away. A moment later and Ellie's hugging him too, and then it's like a spell's been broken and all the Riders are talking, laughing, pushing past each other and their stamping mounts to come and pat him or each other on the back.

Hester clears her throat. "Miss Uren?"

Gawain and Marina still haven't moved.

"And Gavin?" Hester adds. The happy commotion around Rory settles again to listen. "Perhaps you'd honor us with your company at Dolphin House?"

At least a couple of the Riders stiffen.

"I, for one," Hester says, in that measured way of hers, as though she's working out a problem in her head, "have already spent more than enough of my life being frightened of what I didn't understand. I suspect we'd all do better if we welcomed it instead. Will you join us, Marina? At least for a day?"

Gawain leans close to Marina and whispers something Rory can't hear. Whatever it is, it makes her smile.

"All right," she says, and then, for all the world like a nicely brought-up girl remembering her manners, "Thank you."

"And you, Rory, of course," Hester says. "You'll come with us too, I hope. We've all got some catching up to do."

"Of course Rory's coming," Ellie says. "Or I'll kill him."

"Can we at least get that girl some clothes?" Soph says. "If she shows up at Dolphin like that the boys'll go fucking ape."

39

"There you are."

Even on land he can't see her coming, then. He'd thought he was all by himself. He's been feeling a bit left out, to be honest, or perhaps it's just that he's not used to so many people all crowding round the fire, talking and singing and falling over each other, or perhaps it's just that they're all old friends and he hardly knows anyone. For whatever reason, he's slipped away from the party and taken himself off to sit in the shadows behind an old barn, to look at moonlit clouds through the silhouettes of the trees and think about all the people he's lost.

"You're sad," she says, sitting down beside him. They've given her a grown-up-sized coat with a wide hood. Her legs stick out of it below the knees. They catch a little moonlight, like boughs of silver birch. She has the hood up even though it's dry and long after dark.

"I'm fine."

"I didn't say you weren't."

"I was just thinking about my mum and dad. And brother and sister."

"Do you want to go home after this?"

"Dunno."

"You can if you want. The sea isn't angry anymore. It'll never be kind to people, but things won't be like they have been. My mother can see I'm all right now."

"You're going to stop killing everyone?"

"I wish you weren't angry with me."

"I'm not."

"I've been looking for you all evening. I'd like to have sat down and talked to you but you were avoiding me."

"Just been busy."

"Rory?"

"What."

"Why did you come and talk to me all those times? Before? On Tresco?"

He doesn't say anything.

"All the others hated us. Why didn't you?"

He doesn't answer.

"Even here. With these people. Lots of them look at me and you can tell they're looking at something different from them. You know what I mean. I'm something they'd rather not be seeing, or they don't want to think about. You never looked at me like that. Not even after your friend drowned. You just liked talking."

He has an obscure sensation of being told off.

"And listening," she adds.

He shrugs. "It was nice."

She waits awhile, and then changes tack. She pushes her left hand out of the coat's oversized sleeve. "You know," she says, "it was actually you who gave me this, when you think about it."

"The ring?" He can hardly see it in the shadows. It only stands out because her hand's so white.

"Yes. It went from your hand to mine."

"I didn't know. I had no idea you were there."

"You just threw it away, then." This time she presses him when he doesn't answer. "Didn't you."

"I suppose."

"There are people in the world who'd do the worst things you can think of to get their hands on this ring. Lots of people. Why did you throw it in the sea, Rory?"

Because Gawain told me to. But he didn't. He almost did, but he didn't. Rory's not actually sure if he had a reason. If he was thinking of anything at the time, it was Lino with his funny accent saying *'Obbits!*

"'Cause I thought no one should have it. We were supposed to get rid of it. We're better off without."

"Without magic?"

"Yeah. I suppose."

"Is that what you really think?"

"Dunno."

"But you're not afraid of magic, Rory. Most people are. Almost everyone, I think. But not you. You were never afraid of me."

"I'm not," he says. "But it's not just me. What about everyone else? When we spoke to Gawain's mum she said everyone's better off in a world without gods and that."

"And you think that's right?"

He doesn't know. He's too little to think about what's best for the whole world. He's only ten, for goodness's sake.

"Without this," Marina says, turning the ring in the moonlight, "I'm not my mother's child as well as my father's. Without it I'm one or the other, like I was before. I was a girl, and then a horrible thing happened and I found out I wasn't just a girl, so I became my mother's daughter."

"Oh," he says.

Fiery ghosts, arrowing over the sea, coming for some kind of reckoning.

"But now I'm going to be both. Now and always. And the world can be both too."

The fire's big enough now to carry sparks right over the barn roof. The two of them watch a handful of short-lived stars flow up among the trees.

"So mostly what I wanted to say was thank you," she says. "Since you gave me this. Even if you didn't mean to."

"That's all right."

"Everyone here wants to thank you, don't they. I've been noticing. Those women say you were incredibly brave. When you tried to rescue them from the dog men. You're a bit of a hero."

He's actually delighted by this, but snorts aloud as if he thinks it's ridiculous.

"And you're not afraid of the world's magic." Marina stands up. "There are quite a few children running around here," she says. "Lots of them must be young enough they've forgotten what it was like before. I wonder if they'll grow up to be like you."

"Marina?"

She was walking away, but she stops. It's still funny that she has a name, a normal name, like a normal girl.

"Yes?"

Rory watches a single spark go up, up, and then out. "When that god spoke to me?"

She waits a moment and then repeats, "Yes?"

"He told me what gods were. He said it was things like death and love and whatever, stuff like that. Stuff you can't do anything about."

"Yes?" She can tell he's trying to finish a thought.

"So really, how can you not have gods? If that's right? How could you have a world without them? I mean, that's all ordinary stuff. The sun. He said the sun was a god. What's the point of thinking we're better off without that? What's the point of hoping to live without the sun?"

She plops back down on the crumbling step by the barn door, pushes back her hood, and kisses him on the cheek. It's the single best thing that's ever happened to him.

40

Rory wakes up the next morning possessed of the certain knowledge that it's time to go home.

A lot of decisions have been made in the night. Maybe it was in the air. Gawain and Marina are gone already. Hester's gone with them. Word gets around so quickly that they're all talking about it in the camp by the time Rory struggles awake. Hester at least has left a message, though apparently all it says is that she wishes them well. Rory knows where they're all headed, of course, but he doesn't say anything. If they've chosen to go quietly, he thinks, let them go. He wonders whether the well water can fix Hester's legs so she'll be able to walk again.

He's not upset they didn't wake him up to ask if he wanted to go with them, because he knows he's going in the other direction, west instead of east. Still, he's pleased to find a scrap of paper in the pocket of his trousers as he's pulling them on. It's been a long time since he's seen small writing and for a second or two all he's looking at is pointy loops and lines, like runes, as if someone's planted a spell on him. Then as if by magic it swims into order and becomes a message.

You know where to find me again. See you there one day. Love,
Marina.

He rolls the scrap carefully and tucks it in the inside pocket of his coat.

There's an awful lot of talking going on outside. It's the way they do things at Dolphin House. Hester wasn't in charge—no one was, not really—but at least the rest of them tended to stop and listen when she had something to say. Without her all the conversations are happening simultaneously. He manages to get someone to give him something to eat, and he gets a turn with the warm water shower they've rigged up in an old greenhouse, but it's a while before he can find someone he knows properly and tell them what he wants to do.

"Christ on a bike." Rog is in one of the stables, filling a wheelbarrow with stinking wet straw and horse poo. "You know what, Rory, old son. I'd rather shovel shit all day long than listen to that lot trying to make a decision."

"I need someone to help me get back home," Rory says.

Rog stops shoveling poo to lean on his pitchfork. "Do you, now."

"I've got to go and tell them what's happened. Kate and everyone."

"You mean over on the Scillies."

"The boat we came in's probably still there. Past Penzance. If someone can sail it for me it won't take very long. Marina said it's safe now."

"You're a determined little bugger, aren't you?"

"I don't know who to ask. There must be someone. It's not very far. Just a day."

"Yeah," Rog says slowly. "I'm pretty sure there'll be someone."

A little later Soph finds him kicking a football around a patch of wet grass with some of the smaller kids, who turn out to be pleasingly awestruck by his presence. He's famous.

"Hey. Tiger."

The two of them walk down the long avenue towards the road. She asks a lot of questions about Home, how they do things there, what kind of houses they live in, what they eat. It takes him longer than it ought to have to work out that she's not just asking out of curiosity. When he finally understands he can't stop the question leaping out through his mouth from his heart.

"Do you want to come with me?"

She grins at him with her terrible teeth. "Me and Ellie, we reckon we've had enough of the excitement here. A bit of island living sounds good."

He's too unexpectedly happy to speak.

"Not too many people, water all around. Sounds balmy. No adventures. You'd have to promise no adventures."

"OK," he says.

"Besides." She squats down in front of him. "Ellie and I reckon we owe you a couple. You lost your mum and dad, didn't you?"

He nods.

"I know it's not the same, but how'd you like a foul-mouthed Kiwi auntie?"

"A lot," he mumbles, ashamed he can't say it better than that.

"Rog'll go wherever Ellie goes, of course, so he's coming too. Not that he's complaining. Island full of women, I reckon he's pretty excited."

They walk down to the gate. Soph climbs up the rungs and picks her way on top of the adjacent hedge, looking up into the crowd of bedraggled objects dangling by ribbons and strings from the branches of the overhanging trees. "There." She's tall enough to grab a low-hanging token, a knitting needle. She uses it to pull the bough down. Among the hanging things is a small rectangle of soggy cardboard wrapped in plastic. She gets hold of it and tugs it free.

"That's my one." She shows it to Rory. "Fag packet. You take down whichever one's yours when you leave." She taps it against her fingernails and smiles at him. "Magic."

It all happens quite quickly after that. There are good-byes to be said, but since everyone's talking at once they're a bit random and chaotic. No one lingers over them, or cries. They've all seen far too much proper loss to waste grief on a happy occasion. Sal wants to give Rory something to take with him. In the end they settle on a horseshoe. "As a reminder," she says. "And for luck." She shows him which way up to hang it so the good magic stays in. It's heavier than he expects but he puts it in a pocket.

Then he's up in the saddle with Ellie again and riding out into the autumn woods. A whole group of them go out together, the others coming so they can bring the horses back, or perhaps just for the company. Apparently the boat's still where Lino and Per tied it up, the patrols have seen it. The Riders are cheerful and chatty at first, but by the time they're skirting the hills above the ruin of Penzance everyone's gone quiet. The Mount's a blackened heap to the left as they ride west. It's still smoking faintly. People see them coming and emerge from farmhouses and side roads to talk. Everyone wants to know about the fire, and if it's really true that the Black Pack destroyed itself. Some of them have heard a story that one of the man-eaters came ashore and put the fire out. Ellie nudges Rory in the back and winks at him, but keeps quiet.

They're riding slowly. There's no hurry. Why hurry? Tomorrow's as good as today. Winter's on the way but for now it's October, the free wind's stirring the world all around them and a low sun's turning all its base metal into gold. By the time they come to the end of the land the clouds have unwound themselves into wisps and feathers and half the ocean's blazing under western light. They ride down into the abandoned town. The corpse has gone from the beach but the boat's still there as promised, the boat Rory's mother went to fetch so she could take him away from his fate. Rog and Soph are quickly aboard. They know about boats. *Of course I can sail a fucking boat, I'm a Kiwi.* Ellie takes longer. She's going to miss the horse, Rory can tell.

"You don't have to come if you really don't want to," Rory says. "Or you could go straight back afterwards. Some of the women are going to want to see the Mainland."

"Oh, no," Ellie says. "I know what I'm doing."

"Ellie's ready for a bit of settling down," says one of the other Riders, an older woman with a spectacularly weathered face and an accent that's never left Cornwall. She prods Ellie above the waist. "Be a new islander coming along before next summer, eh?"

Ellie smiles away the teasing, but when no one except Rory is in earshot she leans close to him and says, "I'm having a boy. The mermaid told me. She said she'll come when it's time, and bless the birth."

It's too late in the day to set out now. They'll sleep aboard, the four of them, and make the passage the next day, or the day after, whenever the weather suits. There's no hurry. As the shadows lengthen Soph takes Rory by the arm.

"C'mon, Tiger," she says. "Let's go for a walk. Up the cliffs and watch the sunset."

"But—"

She nods in the direction of the forward cabin, where Ellie and Rog have disappeared. "Half an hour should do it."

"Half an hour?" comes Rog's shout, indignant. There's giggling.

"Maybe we can spin it out a bit longer." Soph nudges Rory. "Let's go."

"Oh." He thinks he gets it. "OK."

The road ascends steeply through a jungle of bramble, still thick with berries. Soph can reach the top ones; Rory digs around underneath. At the top of the cliffs the wind has scoured away everything but gorse and grass. They find one of the tracks beaten clear by the Riders and follow it out to the coast. To the south the sea's turned a deep glassy blue. Westward it's too radiant to look at, a glittering sheet of unbearable light. Rory shields his eyes and squints as best he can nevertheless, out past the near rocks with their expired lighthouse and impaled ships.

"Can you see the islands from here?" Soph says.

"You could see the Mainland from there," he says. "If it was really clear. So it should work the other way round."

"Can't get much clearer than this," she says. "Look at that sun. Looks like it's right on top of us."

Maybe there's a few specks on the molten horizon, or maybe the light's just making spots in his eyes. He'll be there soon anyway. He tries to imagine them sailing into the Channel, under Briar Hill, the seagulls going mad with excitement. Everyone will see a boat coming. The first arrival since The Old Days, bringing the news that they can finally stop wishing those days would come back. They'll all be down on the quay at the Harbor, waiting to see who it is. They'll see it's him, and they'll think, Someone's come back. At last, after all this time, someone who left has come back. It'll be like a tide turned, sorrow to joy.

But that's tomorrow, or another day. He sits beside Soph on warm stone and they watch in silence together while the sun descends, until there's that moment when its rim meets the horizon and it looks as if it's come all the way down to touch this blissfully, bitterly enchanted earth.

IF YOU ENJOYED ARCADIA, PLEASE READ THE PREVIOUS BOOKS IN JAMES TREADWELL'S ACCLAIMED SERIES!